She was unquestion ... wice the size of any wolf I'd ever seen. Her muzzle was on a level with my chest. Her eyes were emerald green, and they glowed with an impossible light. I knew she was only a dream.

Then her paws smashed into my chest and I tumbled down into the gutter.

I tried to get up, but she straddled me, silver and sparkling against the night. I smelled the musk of her fur, pungent and sweet. Her muzzle curled back. I saw wet, glistening white teeth big as daggers. And then her muzzle dipped toward my throat. Her breath steamed against my face in panting clouds, tinged with an alien spice; her eyes never left mine. I made a hopeless attempt to turn my face away.

She blinked; her eyes glowed through the membranous lids. Her fangs like daggers sunk through my flesh. Slowly, I felt her warm, rough tongue lapping my welling blood. She growled softly, musically, from deep inside her; a growl of very great pleasure.

THE WEREWOLF'S TALE

Richard Jaccoma

FAWCETT GOLD MEDAL • NEW YORK

This is for E., and for L.

A Fawcett Gold Medal Book
Published by Ballantine Books
Copyright © 1988 by Richard Jaccoma

All rights reserved under International and Pan-American Copyright Conventions. Published in the United States by Ballantine Books, a division of Random House, Inc., New York, and simultaneously in Canada by Random House of Canada Limited, Toronto.

Library of Congress Catalog Card Number: 88-91161

ISBN 0-449-13290-0

Manufactured in the United States of America

First Edition: December 1988

Prologue

The Eternal Female groan'd! it was heard all over the
    Earth . . .
Shadows of Prophesy shiver along by the lakes and
    rivers, and mutter across the ocean.

                         —William Blake

Picture this, if you will . . .

1939.

Night and fog on the outskirts of Prague . . . In the ancient Jewish cemetery at the end of Ostrava Street, there are screams and prayers in Yiddish, snarls and curses in German.

Troop carriers roar, vomiting smoke into the icy mist. Children are wailing, women sob. A searchlight slashes over a line of waxy white faces, eyes glistening wide, frozen with fear.

Shovels chink into dank graveyard dirt as the last careful touches are applied to the edges of the yawning slit trench.

Dogs bark, soldiers shout and kick, the first twenty prisoners are chased to the lip of the trench.

Brrrrrrrpp brrrrrrpp and they flop in like snipped puppets. Two heroes at the ends of the trench dig in their boot heels and squeeze off a short, final spray to make sure the dead stay down, as the next naked batch is hustled up to the lip. . . .

An armored Daimler limousine idles at the edge of the madness, its headlights slicing the fog. Two black-uniformed Tottenkopf SS orderlies stand guard at the limo's rear door.

They stiffen as their lieutenant runs up, step away as he throws the limo door open.

"We have found it, sir!" the man puffs.

"About time, damn you!" the limo's occupant snarls. He clambers out, a tiny little Oriental man. His face is golden yellow, his eyes heavily lidded and of the true cat green. His voluminous greatcoat is black leather, standard Gestapo officer issue, but his green leather gloves match only his eyes.

A woman's wail rises over the general clamor. The stitch of a machine-gun cuts it short. The dwarf crooks his head, seems to hear and taste and smell the death all at once.

"Perfect." He grins carnivorously. "Now hurry!"

He and his escort rush through the cemetery, away from the noisy business of extermination. The men practically carry him in their haste.

"There is no possibility of error?" the dwarf puffs.

"None, Excellency. The grave keeper led us right to it . . . an old grave, or at least precisely old enough. And Neurath reads Hebrew. He says the inscription is unquestionable. The name, the exact date, the . . ."

"Have you disposed of the grave keeper yet?" he interrupts impatiently.

"Why, no, I thought you would . . ."

"You will do so at once."

"Certainly, Excellency. We'll find him a nice spot at the head of the line." The lieutenant sounds quite pleased with his joke.

"Idiot! You'll do it yourself. Do you think you can handle the task?"

"Certainly, sir," he mutters, stung by the insult to his professional ability.

Their electric torches stab through weeds and mud, ricochet off pale marble slabs. But the path is easy to follow—kicked-over stones mark the way to a tree-rimmed rise and the single tombstone on its crown. Three SS men struggle with shovels. They haven't even reached as far down as their boot tops yet. The ancient grave keeper hunches a few paces away, trembling, fragile as a bird in his tattered black suit, weaving and praying in his horror at the sacrilege. The dwarf shrugs off his helpers, strides to the diggers.

"Neurath!" he snarls. "What in hell are you doing?"

One digger pushes himself upright, the others just freeze. "We're . . . that is . . . this is definitely the one, Excellency," he puffs. "Look here . . . 'May, 1887 to March, 1906.' Precisely the dates. And the name . . ."

"What you're doing is totally unnecessary." The dwarf smiles, and suddenly his green eyes begin to glow. "I have gone through quite enough trouble to come this far. As for these last few meters . . . my pet is perfectly capable of coming to me quite unassisted now."

His gloved hand slashes contemptuously. "Stand away, damn you. They are quite ravenous at first, you know."

The men's eyes widen in fear and they clamber out of the shallow charnel pit. The dwarf glances mildly at the lieutenant, then at the old grave keeper who still trembles a few paces away. The lieutenant nods briskly.

"You! Yankel!" he snaps and begins to unholster his pistol.

The lieutenant recoils involuntarily as the dwarf catches his arm.

"Not like that please, Lieutenant," he chides gently, as if giving an instruction in manners to a thoughtless child. "Do it over here. And if you don't mind? The shovel."

The lieutenant barks orders. The old man is dragged to the edge of the pit. Two men stretch his arms out. The lieutenant himself kicks the backs of the old man's legs so he buckles and drops to his knees.

He hefts the shovel, judges the distance. The shovel arcs up in his stiffened arms, freezes for an instant at apogee, then hisses down edge first and crushes through the top of the old man's head like an egg, splitting his skull open to the bridge of his nose. Shards of bone, morsels of flesh splatter up, and as the shovel edge is wrenched from the wound, dark blood wells out and runs down his face. His final crimson tears. The men release his arms and he pitches facedown, his frail body twitching.

The lieutenant is panting like a dog; he looks silently to the dwarf for approval.

But the dwarf just murmurs, "More blood, please," and watches impassively as the shovel rises and falls, rises and falls. Rises. And falls.

At last his green glove signals a halt. The men back away without a word being spoken, step back far enough so they cannot see the dwarf's gestures over the grave, or hear the words he chants softly in a lost, ancient tongue.

The blood-soaked clay of the grave begins to crumble and heave. A mound of earth swells upward and suddenly two rotted, skeletal hands burst from the muck like nightmarish tendrils. The blind, grasping hands waver, trembling for the briefest of moments, then clutch the grave keeper's mutilated corpse by the shoulders. Hideous strength . . . the bloody offering is hauled slowly, inexorably toward the swelling mound.

The mound splits apart and a leathery, sightless skull pushes through. Lipless jaws gape wide, glistening fangs clamp down on the pulpy remains of the grave keeper's ruined face. The thing begins to suck and drink in loud, thirsty gulps.

And now it is nothing but the paradox of fear that keeps the men rooted to their spots—fear of this hideous creature plucked from its unquiet grave, and their even greater fear of the tiny monstrosity who has caused this all to occur.

As it drinks, the creature writhes and wriggles, working free of the pit. And so, long before the meal is done, it is already crouching beside the gaping grave. When it has slaked the worst of its thirst, the creature pauses, twists fleshless fingers into the old man's matted hair, jerks his head to the side, and plunges its fangs into his throat. It begins to suck and drink again, but more slowly, wheezing with dreamy pleasure.

The dwarf gazes down with a gentle bemused smile. A rotted bit of linen drops away from the monster's breast, and the dwarf stoops to pick it up. Delicate needlework is obscured, the pure white soiled with grave slime. He touches the fabric to his lips.

"Lovely," he whispers as he hovers over the monster. "In fact . . . you will be the jewel of my collection." He reaches out his hands. "Come to me now."

The creature's head lolls dumbly as it peers about. It arches its back, tries to rise. Parchment flesh peels away, its gore-choked mouth opens and a groan of torment fills the night.

"Poor little pet," the dwarf clucks. "Rebirth is very nearly as exhausting as birth, isn't it? Come now . . . we will go and rest." He nods to two of the men. "Well?" he says quietly. "What are you waiting for? Help us to the auto, please."

Another monument to their fear: They step forward immediately, grasp the crouching monster's arms, lift it gently, and begin walking slowly with it toward the limousine. But Neurath cannot stop himself from turning his head away and retching once over the desecrated earth.

The creature is tumbled into the backseat of the Daimler, the dwarf climbs in after it, and the limo roars off.

Into the west.

BOOK ONE

The Rough Beast

Things fall apart; the centre cannot hold;
Mere anarchy is loosed upon the world,
The blood-dimmed tide is loosed, and everywhere the
    ceremony of innocence is drowned;
the best lack all conviction, while the worst
Are full of passionate intensity. . . .
And what rough beast, its hour come round at last,
Slouches towards Bethlehem to be born?

—William Butler Yeats

1939.

Things were tough all over that year. Back in New York City, for example, within months of the events just described, I would find myself turned into a werewolf. And at the actual moment those events occurred, I was already suffering, shall we say, from a temporary loss of faith in the essential goodness of man.

Blame it on current events: too many of my best friends had recently died in Spain.

Worse yet, I'd watched them die. And as for those of us the Grim Reaper had as yet neglected to reap . . . I might as well admit that when I first got back to New York from slugging it out with the fascist hordes of Generalissimo Francisco Franco in the Spanish Civil War, I did not have a whole lot of patience with most of the people still left scurrying over this earth, at least not the ones I tended to meet during the course of an average day.

Then again, in those days I was dwelling on the island of Manhattan and I was working as a private detective—hardly a combination that regularly exposes one to humanity at its very best.

The daily papers didn't help matters, either. Day in and day out I thumbed through the headlines on my way to the racing results—the racing obituaries, as I came to think of them; day in and day out I could not but notice the constant reaffirmation of a truth I had already experienced firsthand in Spain: The whole world was going to hell in a hand basket and nobody gave a good goddamn about it.

If anything, most people seemed genuinely pleased with the prospect.

Want a for instance? Allow me . . .

The time is three months after the events described above.

A Manhattan springtime night it was, rainy, black, and bone-chilling. Loveless. Yet I was of good cheer, relatively speaking, because I'd just had an unusually good day with the bookies. Let me put that another way: my day with the bookies had been unusual in that it had been good.

But while thumbing through the newspaper to the glad tidings, an accidental glance at the headlines had informed me that far over the waves, a certain tiresome little man in a brown shirt had just ordered his goons to load up and get ready . . . to pound the living bejesus out of Poland.

It all deserved a celebration, and a hasty one, too. I would toast my good fortune before it flip-flopped again. And I would toast the Polish Army for however many Nazi bastards they might manage to kill before the inevitable became the actual and the Panzers of the New Order ground them into kielbasa stuffing.

I checked my mental index file and decided Charlie's Bar on Third Avenue and 79th would be the perfect spot for my party. Charlie served the best pilsner in Germantown. Brewed it himself. I phoned Blaire and told her to lock up—which she was already doing anyway—that I'd be at Charlie's, and that she didn't know where I was.

"So you gets yourself some good strong lampposts on a well-traveled street," Charlie was saying. "Then you rig up some pee-ano wire and some kick stools, and you starts goin' down your list. Serve beer to the crowd. Let'em bring sandwiches and stay the day. I don't mind telling you, Jimmy . . . got me a list a mile long.''

Charlie stopped talking long enough to knock back the shot of bourbon he had just poured me, then chase it with my beer.

"Know how to make a gasoline bomb, Jimmy? You see you takes your five-gallon drum and your bottle of Javelle water. Then you gets . . .''

Bartending is one of those professions that gives a man more time to think than is normally healthy, but Charlie had husbanded his time wisely and developed some pretty unique theories about exactly what the major and minor governments of the world should go do with themselves—or better yet, as far as Charlie was concerned, have done to them. Hopefully by Charlie.

Pretty chilling stuff, some of Charlie's modest proposals. Charlie had been a Wobbly for a while. But on a rainy night in Manhattan, while the dogs were getting ready to make the same kind of meal out of Warsaw that they'd already made out of Madrid and Prague, I couldn't really think of any place I'd rather be than elbows up on the mahogany down at the dark, quiet end of Charlie's bar, guzzling brew in the shadows and getting a nice, healthy earful of bitterness from Charlie.

Dreams of sweet revenge.

The bar door burst open. A sorry blast of the wet chill came billowing in—and worse things, too.

"Hey Charlie! C'mere and set 'em up! It's time to celebrate!''

All that in an eardrum-rattling bellow from a big, barrel-chested porker so wide and fat he filled the door. Porker stomped up to the bar, and the half-dozen ugly mugs who'd been hidden behind his bulk came stumbling after him.

Charlie just frowned and started studiously scrubbing invisible stains on the bar top with his slop rag. But Porker was not about to be ignored.

"Charlie, set 'em up, goddamn it!'' He honked. "Or maybe you want we should do it ourselves, jah?''

Charlie threw down his rag without looking at me, and,

muttering under his breath, went to serve this flock of characters whom, I had already deduced, he did not number
among his favorite customers in the world.

"What'll it be?" he grumbled.

"Hah! Pilsner, *naturlich*." Porker chuckled. "What better to celebrate with, eh?"

Charlie pulled seven steins of brew, and when they were
all set up, Porker sloshed his aloft and crooned, "To the
glorious reich! And their crushing defeat of the Polack Jew
bastards!"

So that was his game. His pals bellowed their approval
and drank. Porker chugged his suds quicker than the others,
belched, and with a foam mustache slobbering off his lip,
smiled unpleasantly at Charlie.

"So hey, Charlie, how come you don't join our toast, hah?
How come you don't cheer for our reich?"

" 'Cause your reich eats the bird, is why," Charlie grumbled. "You can go fuck your humpin' Nazi reich."

As usual, Charlie's political analysis was lacking in sub-
tlety. But I found I agreed with the substance of his position.
Porker leaned over the bar and held his stein up at face height.

"Oh jah? Well you should be nicer to your customers,
Charlie. Maybe I shove this glass up your Commie ass. How's
about that?"

Quick as corn through a goose, Charlie slid a greasy, lead-
tipped shillelagh out from under the bar and slapped it into
his palm.

"Otto, drink up and shut up."

"You think you scare me?" Otto snarled. "We burn down
your whole frigging place with you in it, Charlie." Suddenly
he smiled. "Ah, but not tonight, because if we do it tonight
. . . we have no place to drink!"

All his buddies laughed.

"Otto, you are a regular rip."

"Jah, Charlie. And you are a Commie fuck. So how's
about another round?"

Charlie shook his head and started pulling the brews.

I decided to finish up and take a hike, before I got drawn

into the debate and did something that would overtax the night staff at the nearest hospital.

When the Bund crew was slobbering happily over their second steins, Charlie slunk back over to me with a hangdog look and started scrubbing that same imaginary spot on the bar top.

"You gotta know how to talk to these cheeses," he muttered.

"You've got it down to a science, Charlie," I said.

"No, really," he said too quickly. "These guys ain't half-bad underneath all their horseshit. Just a bunch of working stiffs who got their political consciences screwed on backward is all. Not half-bad underneath."

"It's a point of view," I said.

"No, really, Jimmy . . ."

Charlie was scrubbing real hard on the bar top.

"Turn off the music, Charlie. Do I look like the type to criticize a guy for not getting his bar burned down?" I dropped a sawbuck on the bar.

"You can't buy booze in here," Charlie said, and pushed my money back.

I would have debated the point, but just then the door flew open again, letting in a gust of cold night air and a flash of black, rain-slickened street.

She was a lady of the night.

I've never seen a woman who fit the phrase better. A pretty face, but so pale; her skin was as white and smooth as ivory, her lips full and red. Her eyes were dark. Her long, ebony hair was damp with the rain. Her raincoat was open and she was wearing a clingy, black satin dress that displayed as much of her body as it covered. I could see what I was supposed to see: her breasts were large and firm, her legs lean and shapely. She was young, younger than she should have been, out that late, dressed like that.

At the moment, though, she seemed more like a hunted animal than a courtesan. The look in her eyes was pure, unadulterated fear, only barely controlled. She stepped to the center of the floor, as skittish as a colt, and scanned the tavern faces nervously—I think she missed me in the shadows at the end of the bar.

She got nothing for her troubles but a few vulgarities from Otto and brethren—halfhearted ones, since Otto's type is generally more interested in Brownshirt butt-buddies than romancing the ladies.

Charlie strolled down the bar to her, and she ordered a drink, then took it to a table and sat perched at the edge of a chair.

Waiting.

I found myself wishing she was waiting for me. Doxies aren't usually my dish of tea, but this one was different. She looked beautiful and she looked like a world of trouble. My kind of gal.

The front door blew open again. Busy night old Charlie was having. From the way she cringed back in her chair, I half thought the Dark Angel had come a-calling. But it was just a big, unpleasant-looking geek with rimless glasses, a leather trench coat, and a black slouch hat.

He saw her at once, even though she was trying to make herself part of the furniture, favored her with a gold-filled smile, and tipped his hat. His head was shaved up the sides, Prussian-style. In fact, he reminded me of more than one Nazi personage I'd had occasion to kill in Spain.

She sat with her head bowed, too frightened to look at him directly, too fear-paralyzed to run for her life. Needless to say, her admirer had no such effect on me, and, as I studied him directly, I saw a dead smile playing at the corners of his mouth. Clearly he was enjoying the effect he was having on the lady. I try never to begrudge a person having fun, but somehow his attitude rubbed me all the wrong way.

And then he did something that absolutely clinched it. He turned to the bar and greeted Otto. Wouldn't you know the two of them were old friends?

"Hah! Neurath!" Otto boomed. "Great news, jah? So when we go in and fix those Polacks? Two weeks? Three weeks?"

He started yammering in German, but Neurath stopped

him and began to whisper. I couldn't hear the words, but something told me he didn't have anything pleasant to say. Otto chuckled and nodded. The two buddies strolled over to the lady.

Otto just stood over her smiling, with his hands behind his back, rocking on his heels. Neurath reached out his mitt and showed her something he was cupping in his palm. Whatever it was, it had quite an effect on her. She winced in pain and twisted away, her eyes rolling with fear.

That was Otto's cue. He reached his fat paw into her dress top and squeezed real hard. Otto might prefer boys in brown shirts, but the leer on his yap told me he got a real charge out of hurting girls for fun. He grabbed her arm and lifted her out of her seat like a child.

"C'mon, sweets," he rumbled. "We go to a party. Everybody's waiting for you."

"No! No, I don't want to," she managed to whimper.

"Of course you do," Neurath snarled, and showed her what he had in his palm again. Otto shook her once, viciously, then started walking her towards the door.

Neurath fell in beside her, and out they went. The door slammed shut behind them with the finality of a coffin lid. Charlie was scrubbing so hard I swore he was going to scrub a hole to China. The jokers down at the other end were just chuckling nervously among themselves.

Ah, well. That, as they say, was that. Admittedly, Charlie's Bar was a much quieter and nicer place now that it no longer contained Otto. But relief hadn't arrived soon enough for me. My evening was ruined, my sunny disposition thoroughly tarnished. Time to call it a night.

I pushed the sawbuck back at Charlie and rolled off my stool, but his hand snaked out and clamped on my wrist.

"Leave it alone, Jimmy," he hissed. "Trust me, I know these guys. Please?"

He turned my stomach.

"Too many people leaving too much alone these days, Charlie," I said, and pulled my arm away. "Besides, it's past my beddy-bye time."

* * *

Outside, the cold midnight rain was trying its best to wash away Third Avenue's sins. But it would take more than rain to do that.

The empty chill of it all must have broken something loose in her, because there in the streetlamp and neon brightness she was sobbing like a lost baby and writhing helplessly as the two apes dragged her toward a black Bentley idling at the curb. When they were still a few paces away, the Bentley's rear door opened for her like a hungry mouth.

Maybe knowing what was waiting for her in the Bentley made her stronger than she was for an instant. She wriggled out of their grasp, and she would have run if Otto hadn't punched her right in the face. He grabbed her hair in his huge ham fist and wrenched her head back so hard I thought he'd snap her spine.

"Get in there, bitch," Otto snarled. "Get in or I break your fucking neck for you . . . I hurt you good!"

She was still fighting, and Otto raised his hand because he wanted to hit her again. Like hell he was going to. I grabbed his arm and spun him partway around.

"Not nice to hit a lady, pal," I said mildly.

Oh, I know it was not a particularly eloquent line, but it was all I could do to say anything at that moment, because I was seeing red flashes around the edges of my vision and I was hearing a roar in my ears and I was full, yes, brimming full of what I was going to do.

Otto and Neurath looked at me like I was a cockroach who had just crawled out in the middle of a dinner party. Otto lifted her off the ground in one fist and tossed her against the side of the Bentley so hard that she made a sickening crunch. I thought he'd broken her like a matchstick, but then I saw she was just stunned, and needed Neurath to hold her up in place.

"Take a walk, *sheis hundt*," Otto growled. "This is none of your goddamn business." He brushed my hand away and turned to face me fully, planting himself between me and the Bentley like a wall of muscle.

"Oh yes it is, fat man," I said almost in a whisper. "It is my business. Now leave the girl alone."

"Go fuck yourself, Mack," Otto suggested. I peeked around him. Neurath was already cramming his catch into the auto. But I never stopped observing Otto's right hand—an easy task, big as it was. Suddenly the hand began to get bigger and bigger, knuckles first and most rapidly.

I sidestepped Otto's shot, grabbed his lapels, and let his momentum help to drive his scrotum flat against my rising knee. Otto huffed and his pig eyes went gaga with disbelief. I took a long step back and kicked him in the nuts just as hard as I could. The point of my wing tip connected so perfectly that Otto's feet left the ground for a moment.

Then he was curled up on the rain-soaked pavement, clutching at himself and sobbing and puking. I started to step over him, but I couldn't resist slamming the toe of my shoe right into his yap. Twice.

Neurath panicked. He'd already crawled into the backseat of the Bentley, and he was dragging her in after him by the hair. Now that I looked, I noticed there was someone else in the auto.

A little Oriental gentleman.

I mean little—as in, just the tall side of a midget. Even in the poor light I could see his skin was an eerie, golden yellow, his eyes slitted and of the true cat green. He wore a long camel-hair greatcoat. And leather gloves as green as his eyes. One strange bird.

Our eyes met. He smiled blandly. But he was doing nothing to help Neurath who, I suddenly realized, was still trying to haul the struggling girl in by her hair.

Easy enough to stop that.

I reached into my jacket, jerked my .45 out of its shoulder rig, and pulled off one shot. The muzzle spit flames, the explosion ripped through the soiled fabric of the night.

Neurath's hand was still squirming in the girl's hair. But he had pulled back his arm, and he was staring in disbelief at the gouts of hot blood pumping from his severed wrist. I kicked the car door closed, leaned on it, and heard the satisfying crunch of hard steel grinding the remains of his wristbone to pulp.

His screams were muffled by the Bentley's roar as it lurched away from the curb. Its squealing tires only missed chewing the girl into minute steak because I reached down and yanked her out of the way.

The hand dropped out of her hair. And something dropped part way out of the hand. I put my heel down on the stump to pry the fingers completely open, picked up what Neurath had been holding, and put it in my pocket.

Then she was leaning against me, clutching and sobbing. I helped her up, walked her to the corner, and hailed a taxi-cab.

"Where to?" I asked as the yellow door slid up to us.

"You are Jimmy Underhill," she said. "I have been look-ing for you, Mr. Underhill. Take me someplace where we can talk. Please." Her accent was soft and Central Euro-pean.

As I looked into her beautiful, grateful face, I recall thank-ing my unlucky stars that Jimmy Underhill was indeed my name. I practically carried her over the taxi's threshold, and told the hack my address. She nestled in my arms, lifted her face to mine. Her eyes were large and sparkling, her hair deliciously fragrant. Her lips breathed a maddening spice as she whispered, "My name is Rachel."

We stood at my terrace door and looked out over Central Park. The rain had ended, and setting low in the sky, a full, cloud-streaked moon was bleaching the spring-soaked trees with pale light. I was sipping a bourbon over ice. Just a glass of mineral water for Rachel, thanks. She had put herself back together quite thoroughly, with just a grown-up toss of her hair.

"Mind if we start with the obvious ones?" I asked. "Like your last name?"

"Bukhovna . . . my name is Rachel Bukhovna," she said distractedly.

"Next. You said you were looking for me. How did you happen to find me at Charlie's?"

"Why, your secretary told me you'd be there."

Thanks, Blaire.

"Next. To what do I owe the honor?"

"Jimmy . . . I may call you Jimmy, yes? Your reputation precedes you," she said with an ironic smile. "You're supposed to be the best."

"Am I? How flattering," I said. I just love it when a client tries to snow me.

"It is also well known that you have, how shall I say, an active dislike for men such as those you . . . saw tonight."

"Nazis." I grumbled. "Don't worry, I don't mind dirty words."

"Lo Fang is a Nazi," she said.

"Lo Fang. Your little friend in the back of the Bentley?"

"He is not my friend!" she snapped. "But yes. Lo Fang is a Tibetan. He has lived in Germany for years, though. His friends are the most powerful men in the reich. He helped them to become so. And they are the ones who sent him to New York."

Rachel had placed her water glass on the coffee table beside the chair on which she now sat. She hadn't touched a drop. She reached towards it, touched the cool glass with the manicured tips of her long, delicate fingers. Red, red nails. Her lips were red, too, moist and inviting. Her fingers slid gently down the slippery shaft, circled the base.

Rachel saw me looking. Quite annoyingly, the smile that played ever so briefly on her lips told me that she saw me thinking, too. She fixed me with a wide-eyed, penetrating stare, completely innocent. And completely the opposite.

"By the way, Rachel, how old are you?" I asked, more as a warning to myself than because I expected a straight answer.

"What is the difference?" she said too quickly.

"In New York State? About five to ten."

"I am fifty-two." She smirked.

"That's very amusing," I said, and waited for her.

"I was eighteen on my last birthday," she finally said. "But I didn't seek you out to discuss my age."

"I'll bet you didn't. Which leads us back to a previous question. To what do I owe the honor?"

"Let me ask *you* a question," she said after a moment. "Tell me, Jimmy, do you believe in the supernatural?"

"What specific aspect? Witches? Warlocks? Ghosts?"

"Oh, all of those," she said, without a trace of irony.

"I've known a few of each." I shrugged.

"I have heard that about you, too—you don't share the normal American disbelief in the occult."

What a nice way to put it. Rachel paced to the open terrace window, and stared out for a moment into the Manhattan night. She shivered and turned back to me.

"Lo Fang is an occultist," she said grimly. "One of the best, if that is the right word. The most famous in all of Germany. And you can believe me when I tell you . . . Lo Fang doesn't just study satanism. He worships evil. Lo Fang is a black magician."

"Charming. The next question's obvious. What inspired you to pick him for a friend?"

Rachel stamped her foot.

"I told you Lo Fang is not my friend!" she snapped.

"Really? Just your pimp?"

She recoiled, but then regained her poise almost instantaneously. Quite the lady, actually. I hate being rude to a lady, and I felt like a proper heel. But time was flying.

"Is . . . my profession that obvious, Jimmy?" she asked softly.

"You look like you're very good at what you do," I said, and because even I realized how condescending that sounded, I moved along quickly. "So. How'd you get hooked up with Lo Fang?"

"He . . . took over the establishment where I worked. I didn't have much choice in the matter." She frowned. "He likes having me close to him. I think he . . . it pleases him to have someone who watches everything he does, who is revolted by the things she sees . . . but who cannot escape. Not ever.''

I didn't waste time quoting the Bill of Rights, or asking her how she could be held a slave in the middle of New York City. All of us have chains. I do; you do. Besides, I already had a suspicion. I was pretty sure that I knew what Rachel Bukhovna's chains were made of.

"Why are you here, Rachel?"

"Because this time he's gone too far!" she hissed. "What he's planning is just too horrible! I can't let him win! Not this time. You must help me stop him!"

"What's he planning?" I asked, calmly enough for her to take a deep breath and get on with what she needed to tell me.

"I know you aren't an Egyptologist, Jimmy. But have you ever heard of the priest Entimemseph?"

As it happened, I had—due to my daily newspaper addiction. The Metropolitan Museum of Art had just received a birthday gift from a certain Mrs. G. Rogers-Gracey, one of America's richest women—and one of Adolf Hitler's best American friends. The trinket she had donated was an installation called Entimemseph's Tomb, a stone-by-stone reconstruction, straight from Thirteenth Dynasty Egypt, of the tomb, the mummy case, even the high priest's linen-wrapped mummy itself. According to legend, Entimemseph had been Egypt's most powerful priest at the time of the Exodus—and an insane magician totally devoted to evil.

He had lived for six hundred years.

Now that Rachel brought it up, I remembered wondering, when first I'd read about G. Rogers-Gracey's gift, why she was spending her money on something for the New York masses to gape at. She was known for tossing her loose change in the direction of less egalitarian causes: noble crusaders like the America Firsters, the Ku Kluxers, and Father Coughlin. And the German-American Bund.

I nodded to Rachel that I had heard of Entimemseph.

"And you know his legend?" she asked.

"Just what I read in the papers." I smiled.

"Well, there is a side to his story never mentioned in the daily newspapers," Rachel said. "A thing called Entimemseph's Key. It was a sacred tablet. Supposedly it held the secret of Entimemseph's long life. When the Key was stolen, all his supernatural powers failed. He died at once. Or at least . . . he fell into a deep sleep. One that has lasted for centuries."

"Sounds like whoever took the tablet did the ancient world a favor," I said. "Does the fable identify the thief?"

"The 'fable' comes from the Kabbalah, Jimmy . . . the most profound book in my religion. And the most complex mystical book in the Western world. It tells how the Key was taken by the prophet Moses himself, when he led the Jews out of slavery. Moses was a great magician, too. But he knew, if he didn't take the Key, Entimemseph would have used its evil powers to help Pharaoh stop the Exodus. Instead Moses used its power to part the Red Sea!"

"I always wondered how he did that. And after the Exodus, the Key of Entimemseph dropped out of sight, right? For three thousand years nobody has seen hide nor hair of it, until . . ." I don't suppose I was successfully keeping every hint of sarcasm from my voice.

"Not at all." Rachel frowned. "For three thousand years the Key has been kept safe. It is guarded by the wisest, bravest Kabbalist scholars of each generation. It's a symbol . . . a symbol of human freedom. It is also incredibly powerful, and that is why its existence has been a secret. The world hardly needs another excuse for attacking Jews. In the wrong hands . . ."

"Hands like Lo Fang's?"

"Exactly!" Rachel stepped up to me and put her hands on my chest. "He had Entimemseph's mummy brought to New York. Now he's located the Key. He thinks that if he can bring the two together . . ."

"He can use the Key to control the mummy's power," I finished.

"Yes!"

Rachel grabbed her raincoat from the chair where she'd

draped it. She plunged her hand into a pocket, extracted a thick envelope, and thrust it at me. As I took it, she grasped my hand.

"Don't open it yet, Jimmy," she said. "It's everything you need to know about the man who guards the Key. He's a great scholar. A leader of his community. But he's old. He needs all the help he can get to protect himself, to keep the Key away from Lo Fang. Lo Fang isn't just going to take the Key away from him. Lo Fang is going to kill him! You have to help, Jimmy. Warn him. Go to him and . . ."

"Hold on for a second," I snapped. "Before I go anywhere or do anything, there's just one thing you should know."

She nodded eagerly.

"Everything you've told me is completely insane. There isn't a reason in the world I should believe it. In fact, I don't. I don't believe you at all."

"Yes, you do, Jimmy," she said quietly. "Or at least you want to."

"Yeah, well let's pretend I'm sane for a minute," I grumbled.

She put her hands on my chest again, and looked up at me with those wide eyes of hers.

"Would it help to pretend I'm insane?" she asked.

"Sure," I muttered.

But she wasn't. She was just as sane as I was. That didn't exactly make her blue ribbon material, but it didn't qualify her for upholstered walls, either.

"Fine, Jimmy. Even if what I'm telling you is insane, you have already seen . . . the kind of people who believe me. Or at least . . . the kind of people who don't want me walking around. Insane or not . . . if you help me, you will hurt them. I guarantee it. And besides . . . in that envelope I just gave you? Along with some pertinent information, you will find two weeks worth of your fee. Plus an advance toward expenses. Or is business going so well lately that you can afford to turn away work . . . even work from a mad woman?"

Well, of course everything's relative. I believe I began my account of this evening by saying I had just been rewarded by my friends the bookies for some unusually wise choices I had just made.

The significant word there is *unusually*.

I happened to have a full wallet at the moment. But rent collectors, bar tabs, even certain employees' ridiculously inflated salaries . . . I regarded the sealed envelope with greatly enhanced interest.

"Open it when I leave," Rachel said. "It contains as much as you need to know for now . . . and as much as I can give you. I'll be back before that runs out. I promise . . ."

"Back?" I scowled. "Where are you going?"

Suddenly, she looked paler, weaker, more frightened than she had the moment before. I followed her gaze toward my open terrace door. Outside, the moon had already set. Dawn was still long hours away. But it was deep into that heart-stopping time of night they call the hour of the wolf.

"You know, Jimmy. You know where I have to go."

"Lo Fang."

Her silence answered me. Helpless silence.

"It was hard getting away from him for this long," I said. She nodded. "Why did you come to me? Why didn't you run right to the source?" I held up the envelope. "Why didn't you warn the Key Keeper yourself?"

Her eyes widened. For an instant, she was close to panic.

"No, Jimmy! I can't. And you can't let him know who sent you. He mustn't find out what . . . what has happened to me. What I have become. Already he suspects, I'm sure of it. But if he knew for certain . . . if he saw me, it would kill him!"

"What . . ."

"Oh God, don't you understand? The man you have to help is my father!"

She stopped herself from crying.

Then she reached up, put her arms around my neck, and pulled me down toward her lips. Her mouth was cool and delicious against mine. An enchanted kiss, and I really mean that; I had never had one that was sweeter.

She pulled away.

"Please, Jimmy, she whispered. "You will make sure he is safe? Make sure the Key is safe?"

Rachel pressed herself against me. Then she stepped back at arm's length and looked at me.

"Do this for me, Jimmy. Do this so I can die in peace!"

She slipped out of my arms, and she was gone.

I opened the envelope, counted the money, and was pleased to note that Rachel had quite the inflated view of what two weeks worth of my time cost.

A fine beginning.

I studied the photographs of Dr. Avrom Bukhovna—two clippings torn from a newspaper, actually. One was a portrait, the other was a shot of him addressing some kind of meeting. The portrait showed a small-seeming man in his late seventies; he wore a long gray beard and sidelocks, a traditional black suit and hat. He looked weary. Somehow, the expression on his face said he was tired from all the things of this world that he'd seen—and understood. His eyes were full of a sort of bemused, saddened compassion.

A handwritten note in the margin indicated the photos had been cut from a Jewish language daily called the *Morning Freiheit*, of February 2. The surrounding article had been torn through. But the very fact of Bukhovna's picture being there presented an interesting puzzle.

I was familiar with the *Freiheit*—although not to read. Language difficulties aside, it did not publish the daily racing results. In fact, the *Freiheit* undoubtedly considered horseracing to be a capitalist plot, a vile, bourgeois scheme aimed at separating poor working people from their gelt.

Now there was an ideological position I could heartily endorse. But the point is, the *Freiheit* was an unabashedly leftist journal, secular, even atheistic in its outlook. Why was a seemingly complimentary story of a religious scholar gracing its pages? I studied the photo of Bukhovna at the meeting for clues. He was shown standing at a podium, declaiming. Banners hung behind him. One said, "Fourth Annual Symposium . . . Hegelian Discussion League." Aha. That might explain it. Hegel's a tortuously complex philosopher. Maybe you've had better luck with him than I have: I've always found him harder to fathom than a Brooklyn road map. Karl Marx used to swear by old Hegel, though—based lots of his theories on Hegel's work. In fact there's an old saying: "Marx turned Hegel upside down—and stood him on his feet."

That was why lefty eggheads might see fit to start a Hegel fan club. And as for why they'd invite Bukhovna to address them . . . Hegel might be impenetrable for dodos such as yours truly, but I could see him being meat and potatoes for an old Kabbalist scholar.

Rachel's file included Bukhovna's address and telephone number. But he lived all the way on East Broadway, on the Lower East Side, and since I didn't know much about the old duffer, I had no reason to assume he'd appreciate a three A.M. call from an imperfect stranger. I knew that, if the situation were reversed, I personally might not, even though I am among the most tolerant of souls.

I decided to take a risk and assume that the good Dr. Avrom Bukhovna and whatever in hell he was guarding would keep until the clear light of day.

I issued myself several stiff belts, a long, steamy shower, and a short dive in the sack. I knew there was no danger of oversleeping: Blaire took great delight in waking me each morning to the evil thereof, even on Saturdays.

Even on this particular Saturday.

I dreamed I was a fish, and a gaffing hook jangled deafeningly as it speared me under my ear, whipped me about, hauled me back up from the sweet land of dreaming, and flopped me gasping for air on the cruel, rolling deck of my mattress.

With a telephone in my hand, and an ache as big as all outdoors cleaving my head. Good old Blaire.

I believed she was smiling as she read me my missives. She always sounded as though she was smiling. And I believed, too, that her smile derived from the mental picture she held, of my swollen eyes creaking wider and wider with each blow her call delivered to my peace of mind.

I pretended to be diligently writing down every message by grunting during each of Blaire's pauses, and meanwhile planned my day. First a pot of java. Next, an Underhill Three-S Special (concluding with the Shower and Shave).

And afterward, a call to Dr. Avrom Bukhovna would most definitely be in order.

Blaire seemed to have reached the end of her list of unpleasantries—my list, to be strictly fair about it. But then she gave me one last oh-by-the-way-almost-forgot message. My old pal Gina had just sailed back from Palm Beach, was just calling to check in. I caught a tone in Blaire's voice that I might easily have mistaken for jealousy. It pleased me to no end.

It pleased me to hear Gina was back in town, too, because Gina was someone who could be very helpful when she was of a mind to be. Very helpful indeed.

But first the cup of joe, the ablutions, the second and third cups over the newspapers fished from outside my door.

This day's headlines were reassuring only in the sense that they demonstrated the earth had not been knocked out of orbit overnight: the Wermacht was still doing the Mexican hat dance on its neighbors to the east, Russia was still suggesting that the nations who had signed the Treaty of Versailles should order a halt to fascist aggressions, the Treaty nations were still pretending they had bananas in their ears.

Closer to home and pocketbook, I noted without surprise that my predictive abilities had returned to normal.

I threw the papers in the garbage where they belonged— my daily version of killing the messenger who bears ill tidings—and dialed the number Rachel had given me.

I had already let the phone ring six times when I realized I was wasting my semiprecious time. This was Saturday, the Jewish Sabbath, the day the Lord rested from a job poorly done. The Orthodox took the day more seriously than He obviously had. Saturday was a day for prayer, reflection, rest.

No work was to be done, not even anything that could be construed as work, like making telephone calls. Or answering them. Avrom Bukhovna's phone would ring until sundown before anyone would pick it up.

That left Gina as the only dialing worth doing.

Gina was an actress, which is something lots of girls say in Manhattan. But Gina was a wild success at it. She was recently and happily married, too, to a Greek shipping magnate richer than Croesus and crazy—or smart—enough in love with her to let her do anything she wanted to do any time she wanted to do it.

The chips hadn't always fallen like that for Gina, though. A few years back I'd had occasion to remove her face from a particularly nasty frame. If I hadn't, she'd have been dimming the lights at Sing Sing around now, instead of lighting up the night sky on Broadway.

Maybe I'd have been a happier man if I made it a habit to call in all the markers from people who were grateful to me for jobs I'd done for them. Most likely I wouldn't be. But I wasn't beyond asking a favor every once in a while, especially from places where I knew I wasn't overly likely to be turned away.

"Jimmy!" she chirped when her maid told her who was on the line. "Will wonders never cease? That tramp secretary of yours actually gives you my message *and* you call me back. Let me guess . . . you need money."

"Always and forever. But no cigar."

"A place to hide?"

"Not yet."

"Don't tell me you're horny, honey. It's not nice to get a girl's hopes up."

"Since when have you known me to trifle with a married lady? Especially one whose hubby could order my liver fried for supper?"

"Oh, I'd *never* accuse you of trifling, doll," she murmured. "I'd never accuse you of that. And as for Ari . . . you know he's not the jealous type. He likes you too much. Guess what Ari says?"

"I'll bite. What does Ari say?" I was pretty sure I'd be sorry I asked.

"Ari says, 'Jimmy can take what he want. Just so long he give it back when he finish.' " Gina did a good impression of a Greek accent. No surprise, she being a professional actress. She shifted back into her sultry sex-kitten voice—a voice I much preferred—and breathed, "You'd do that, wouldn't you, baby? You'd give me back when you were finished with me, wouldn't you? Hmm?"

The girl was getting herself all worked up, and it wasn't even lunchtime yet. Or was she? Gina wasn't getting to pick and choose her Broadway roles because she was gorgeous and blond and built from here to tomorrow. Or at least not just because of all that. She was a good actress, Stanislavski method, very convincing. Then again, a truly convincing actress needs to convince herself first, or so I'd been told. So one way or another, she was probably getting herself just as steamed as she sounded.

I wondered if her maid was still in the room. And I wondered what Gina was wearing, whether she had on those frilly little knickers and whether she was fiddling with . . . But that was a fruitless line of speculation, a line which would most definitely not lead to the accomplishment of my professional goals for the day.

I cleared my throat and growled, "Cut the crap, Gina. Or I'll come over there and smack your bottom."

"Ooh, honey! You know *just* what a naughty girl needs!" she squealed, in what I believe was her impression of Betty Boop on Spanish fly.

"I'm serious, Gina. Can it."

"James Underhill, you are no fun. You are becoming practically middle-aged."

That was quite the ominous accusation from a twenty-six-year-old, but at least it was the real Gina talking.

"I was born middle-aged, doll. I thought it was part of my charm."

"Who ever said you were charming?"

"Only you."

"Never believe what a girl says when she's lying on her back."

"You weren't. You were lying on your belly with a pillow under you, and you were biting on the corner of the blanket because you were afraid you were going to yell too loud and wake up the maid."

"And then what?" she asked dreamily.

"And then you yelled too loud anyway. And *then* you most definitely said words to the effect that all a guy has to do is ask. That he can have anything he wants. I believe your exact words were . . ."

"No fair, Jimmy."

"Why no fair?" I chuckled.

"First because now who's trying to get who worked up? And also no fair because when a girl says you can ask her for anything, you're still supposed to know what she wants you to ask for."

"Don't I? Am I not always the gentleman?"

"That's not the same thing."

"It'll have to do for now, doll. I'm on a job."

"Oh, okay, Jimmy." She sighed. "Let's have it. What do you need?"

"Just a telephone number. And an introduction."

"To whom, may one inquire?"

"To Mrs. Glenda Rogers-Gracey."

"That bitch? Since when did you develop an interest in nauseating causes? You know me and politics, Jimmy. But even I stay away from her. The things she wants you to give money for . . ."

"Gina?" I cut her off gently. "Just do it."

"I will, I will. But I actually do need to see you, you know."

"I'd love it, ma'am. But as I said, I'm on a job now. No time for the higher pleasures."

"As it happens, I'm talking professionally. I believe I need your services again."

"Uh-oh. Nothing sticky as last time, I hope."

"So do I."

"Let's hear it," I grumbled.

"Nope. It'll wait. I'm pretty sure it'll wait. Go see your darling Mrs. Rogers-Gracey first. But Jimmy? Do try not to catch anything."

"Your concern for me is truly touching."

"For you? Believe me, I'm just thinking of myself."

It's amazing what a shipping magnate husband and a few Broadway hits will do for a girl's social influence. Within fifteen minutes Gina called me back with Glenda Rogers-Gracey's private telephone number, and the okay to use it.

Unfortunately, the number was for Mrs. Rogers-Gracey's South Hampton address. And when I called, she told me that, yes indeed, she was out there for the entire weekend, "opening the summer cottage." Oh, but certainly, I was *more* than welcome to drive out and see her for the day. Spend the night in the guest house if I wished. Gina had told her *so* much about me.

Praise be to Gina; the old bat couldn't have been more cordial. But I never was the nice-drive-in-the-country type. So I thanked her gushingly and said that, while what I needed to see her about was indeed quite important, it would certainly wait until tomorrow afternoon, when she returned to town.

It now being the crack of noon, I ushered forth from my dwelling. The weather had turned balmy, and even though the sun was a wee bit too bright and cheery for my taste, there was in the air that certain heartbreakingly sweet smell, that nostril-flaring, delirious springtime scent of eternal return from which not even New York can escape.

I decided to walk to my office, on the way checking in with my contacts amongst the Times Square street nobility. Just to see if there was any gutter talk about, shall we say, personages exhibiting an excessive interest in such cultural institutions as, for example, the Metropolitan Museum of Art. Any talk about a field trip to the joint? After regular hours? Maybe to the Egyptian Wing?

Unfortunately, my Times Square contacts were about as informative as the paper on the bottom of a bird cage.

Not that I really expected any red-hot information; I merely wanted the world to know that Jimmy Underhill, of all people, had developed a burning interest in Egyptian cultural news. Around the Square, news on just about any subject has a way of coming to those who formally announce their interest.

News or a knife in the back.

As the sun expired in the Jersey marshes, I rang up the good Dr. Bukhovna and got through to him almost at once. In deference to his daughter's request, I told him a story that was vague but tantalizing . . . certain information I had gathered during the course of another investigation . . . certain persons who had designs on a rare object which he might possess.

At least I thought the story was tantalizing. Bukhovna, on the other hand, seemed otherwise preoccupied. He agreed to see me, but not until Monday evening. I assured him the matter was rather urgent, and he assured me he understood, but any sooner was quite out of the question.

I considered begging him to *please* let me save his life and his holy artifact. Believe it or not, I decided against doing so, though. To hell with him.

Not that his attitude left me with a whole lot of options. In fact my major remaining choices were either to wait or to wait. And my sub-choices were either to spend the evening hours pacing my cage, or to do what any normal, unencumbered male might do on a Saturday night, namely, go out and hunt up a good time. Needless to say my instinctive choice was to pace my cage. So I went out just for spite.

And found myself unable to avoid thinking about a beautiful, black-haired woman with eyes so deep you could drown in them. At least I could. And I thought about how her kiss had tasted. And about how afraid she was. And about how the sharks circling around her were the same sharks circling the city, the same sharks circling Europe, the same sharks that had been circling the world ever since the Old Man in the White Beard booted the bad angel out of the nest and made him grow horns.

And I wondered just how big a bite those sharks had already taken out of Rachel, and whether I was going to be able to help her. Or see her again.

I suddenly realized she might be trying to reach me. So I called Blaire from a telephone booth somewhere between my third and fourth dive of the night.

Blaire informed me of exactly what the hell time it was, more loudly than was really necessary, and that no, no one loved me anymore, and why the hell didn't I do myself a favor and try to find my way home.

Easier said than done.

But eventually I did find myself standing beside my very own bed and yanking my shirt off without having first removed my tie.

The phone jangled. It was Blaire, and she sounded so p.o.'d that for a second I thought I'd just called her again. But as it happened, somebody else had—an old pal who needed to see me immediately if not sooner.

No particular problem there.

If I tried to sleep I'd probably just have nightmares anyway. Bright lights . . . a rowdy crowd . . . I needed noise . . . a taste of after-hours nightlife, and my old pal's summons might be just what the doctor ordered.

I gave Blaire a nighty-night peck—and got a nighty-night obscenity in return. Then I crawled into a clean shirt, called downstairs for Ernst the night doorman to hail me a cab, and headed uptown.

At three A.M. on a Saturday night, Velma DuPree's Crystal Lounge and Buffet Flat was just starting to jump—with everybody who was anybody in Harlem. I plowed through the crowd to the bar. I suppose I could have felt uncomfortable, since there was not exactly an overabundance of ofays in the joint. But Velma's felt too much like home for that. Besides, Velma served the best late-night menu in Manhattan. In more ways than one.

I nodded at Jackie the bartender, and a moment later an empty spot magically appeared at the bar. He set up a bottle of bourbon and a syphon of soda as I climbed the stool, and I started drinking myself sober. By the time the bottle was three fingers lighter there was a plate of catfish and eggs sitting in front of me. And by the time my cornbread was sopping up the last of the yolks, I heard a rich contralto voice behind me shout, "Jimmy! C'mere, you!"

I managed to swallow as I was spun around on the stool, and my face collided with a delicious, pillowy wall of perfumed breasts. I pulled back and peered up over them into Velma DuPree's smiling face.

Velma was gorgeous. Big as a statue and dark as ebony and hot as a pit barbecue.

"Hi ya, Gate," she chuckled. "Give Mama a kiss."

I regarded those eye-level, sequin-cupped mounds.

"Where d'you want it, Vel?" I grinned.

"Mmm. Up here for starts," Velma murmured.

Her scarlet lips parted and she pushed her thick, sweet tongue into my mouth. When we pulled apart, I was in no condition to stand up. But since I wasn't reciting in Sunday school, I stood up anyway.

Velma was holding a reefer in a long, ivory cigarette holder. The reefer was thick and neatly rolled and half-smoked. No question about it: Velma DuPree was, like they say, a viper.

She glanced down and noticed how inspired I was. She raised her eyebrows in mock surprise, drummed her fingertips over my inspiration appraisingly, and nodded her approval. Then she took a puff, sucked it in deep, and started blowing a thin, bluish cloud toward my face.

I put my finger on her cheek and turned her head away.

"None for me, thanks," I said. "Remember? I'm here on call."

"Course I remember. Ain't I the one who called you? So let's go upstairs, *Mister* Underhill, honey . . . I got something to show you."

"What's up, Velma? Time for the donkey show?"

I was teasing, but I wasn't joking. Just in case the term isn't familiar, Velma's place was not called a "buffet flat" because of her catfish and eggs. Not even because of her smothered ribs and collards. Velma had the finest kitchen in Harlem, and you weren't a big-time jazz act if you didn't show up to jam in her main room after hours. But the really wild show was upstairs.

The buffet.

You know the kind of show I mean, and a different act in every room. Freakish broads who could take on five Joes at a time and still find room for a German shepherd. Somewhere.

A lot of the stars were local talent, but there was more than one room where the featured act was some rich, high-toned downtown Jane. I'm talking genuine, chauffeur-driven, garden party types, who clearly had thought it through carefully and decided, oh what the heck, as long as I'm going to be a nymphomaniac, I might as well be one in Harlem—in front of everybody . . .

That's show business.

Once I saw a monstrosity that drove all the house girls wild: a little Spanish pinhead with no forehead and a solid yard below the belt. The poor palooka knew how to get a boner, but couldn't remember how to lose it . . . until one lucky debutante finally caught a hosing that looked like it was going to last for forty nights and days.

And as for that donkey, don't ask me how Velma got him up the stairs, but he was there every Saturday night, along with Lucille the Freakish Farm-girl . . . the gifted young artiste who so ably assisted him in his performance.

"Lucille's not on tonight," Velma shouted over the jazz-band as she led me across the dance floor. "Gots her monthlies. Girl never works when she's on her monthlies."

The floor was packed, but they moved out of the way for Velma. After all, it was her joint. Mez was up on the bandstand in the middle of a solo.

"Well den you dream about a reefer
Nine feet long
Not too hot! Nice 'n strong!
When your throat git dry
Then you knows you high
If you's a viper!"

Mez saw me and Velma from the stand. He looked at her, winked at me, and waggled his tongue. Didn't make me no never-mind: Mez could think all the naughty thoughts he wanted.

But I suddenly recalled the specifics of the message Blaire had so ungraciously related, and I decided thanks, but I had already had quite enough novelty, quite enough newness, for one evening. And then some. A peek at the program notes was most definitely in order. So, when we reached the bottom of the plush, carpeted stairway to the private rooms, I turned Velma around and made her look right at me.

"Vel? What's up? It's bad, isn't it?" I frowned like the old worrywart I am. And patted her rump. "You didn't call for me to sample the catfish."

She pouted, hooked her finger into the top of my belt, and started walking me up the stairs as she talked.

"Smart boy, Jimmy. Sure it's bad. I've never seen him this bad. Not by half." Then she gave me a little smile and a wink. "When you get so pushy, though? You forgetting how to take your time?"

"Nope. I just hate surprises is all. Surprises mostly stink."

Velma turned around and yanked me up onto the same step as her, real close.

"Oh yeah?" she breathed. "Well, you try this one on for size, Jimmy Underhill."

The look on her face was pure hunger. Reefer always did hit Velma DuPree right between the legs, bless her. Like I said, like Mez said—a real viper. She drove her tongue into my mouth, pushed one big thigh between my legs, started doing the Shave 'Em Dry all up and down me. When she broke for air, I started laughing.

"What you got in mind, Vel? This here's a public hall-way."

"Oh yeah? Well it's my public hallway. Besides . . . this is what you get when you make me wait so goddamn long. This here's all I got time for . . . all *you* got time for . . . gonna do you right up against the wall!"

Before I could protest that I wasn't that kind of guy, Velma had my pants unbuttoned and had taken certain matters into her own hands—matters that demonstrated quite clearly I was precisely that kind of guy.

Oh, what the heck. I let her push me back against the wall at the top of the stairs. She shrugged the straps off her shoulders as she dropped to her knees, and since I needed the lifting exercise, I fished both big, brown globes out of her loosened dress top. Her nipples were thick and black and rubbery. I fiddled with them while she did what it seemed she'd been thinking about doing for some time. I let her have her fill, but after a while I tugged her back up and made her hike her dress.

Good old Velma.

So anxious to see me that she'd forgotten to put on her bloomers. I smacked her bottom and grabbed her cheeks and helped her climb aboard. I don't know how long a ride we took, and I can't say the numerous tricks and trollops who strolled giggling past us absolutely ignored our presence. But Velma sure ignored theirs. After a certain point I got the funny feeling she was ignoring mine, too. Velma was wailing and shaking and absolutely lost in her own World of Delight, like William Blake calls it.

So was I. Right around the time Velma finished up on me, I finished up myself. My eyes rolled back and I saw stars and planets and I think steam snorted out of my nose and ears and I know I hooted louder than is polite in public places.

Afterward, Velma tidied up with my handkerchief, tucked us both back in, and led me down the hallway—to her private chambers. It was a short trip down that hallway, and I was about to tease her with a query as to why she hadn't been able to wait for twenty paces. But Velma paused with her hand on the knob and answered my unasked question.

"Okay, Jimmy." She frowned. "You know how he gets. He is gonna talk trash. But you gotta help him anyway. He been ranting and raving for you half the goddamn night."

An enormous Negro was sprawled out on Velma's divan with an empty hooch bottle in one fist. An ancient, ugly scar as shiny and black as a licorice twist wriggled down from the corner of his right eye to the middle of his cheek. His head was huge and completely shaved; a pearl-handled .45 revolver bulged out of the shoulder rig in his fancy, French-cut suit.

All in all, he did not look like anyone's dream of a kindly old Uncle Remus. He didn't even look nice. And as a matter of fact, he wasn't. He was Joe Jefferson, the meanest cop on Harlem Homicide, and he was stewed to the gills.

On eye slitted open as we walked in, and he started making windmill motions seemingly aimed at pushing himself up-right.

"Velmuh!" he rumbled when he'd almost managed to sit up. "Whut fo you bring this white muthah fuckah in here?" He made a fumbling, hopeless dive into his jacket to whip out his gat.

Velma walked right up to Joe Jefferson and planted her feet wide. She smacked his right hand away from his gun butt. She smacked the hooch bottle out of his left. Then she hauled back and slapped his face so hard his ears flapped.

Velma was a lady, but nobody ever said she didn't have balls. That shot would have knocked a lesser man's head into the outfield. But it actually seemed to wake Joe up. At least he opened both eyes.

"I brought him 'cause you wanted him, fool. You been callin' for Jimmy all night. Till you got too goddamn drunk to know what the fuck you want."

Joe looked up and even managed to focus on me. I watched him as he thumbed through his mental mug-shot file, and I believe I saw the precise moment he realized who I was. Then in the next moment I saw something I hope never to witness again. Joe Jefferson's big, mean face seemed to break apart like shifting lava, and suddenly he was sobbing like a baby with his head in his hands and his doorway-wide shoulders heaving. The sounds Joe was making seemed to be coming from all the way deep inside him. It was very frightening.

Velma looked back at me and said not a word. She didn't need to. She sat down next to Joe and pulled him into her lap and cradled him and rocked him and hummed. I picked up her phone, called the bar, and told Jackie to send up a great big pot of coffee.

Wait. Make that two pots.

It took half an hour, a gallon of java, and a cold shower without benefit of disrobing, before Joe Jefferson was back among the living. But at long last the time came. Sitting barechested and bleary-eyed, Joe drew his hands over his face. When his ugly mug reappeared, he looked at me and smirked.

"So how *you* doing, Underhill?"

"Great. Playing nursemaid to a lushed-up gorilla is my idea of fun on a Saturday night. Want to tell me to what I owe the honor?"

Joe had a severely reduced jocularity threshhold. He frowned and shook his head as if to drive away a vision.

"It's a bad one, Jimmy. Never seen one as bad."

"So I gathered."

"Yeah? Well, gather this. It's right up your alley. I'm calling you in as an expert consult. Five bucks a day and all you can eat."

"Just what I needed. Which particular alley did you have in mind?"

"You know, Jimmy. 'Long-legged beasties and things that go bump . . .' I've seen devil cults before. But this one takes the cake."

"Devil cults . . . Awe, for Christ's sake, Joe. What are you bothering me for? What's the matter with Woolcock?"

That was the Right Reverend Doctor Elijah P. Woolcock, M.D., Ph.D., D.D., West Indian Holy Man and Spiritualist and, truth be known, head of Harlem Homicide's Anti-Hoodoo & Voodoo Division. Eli was a pompous old bastard . . . and damn good at what he did. No one below 125th Street was supposed to know Woolcock's division existed, but if it hadn't . . . I hated to think of what Harlem would have looked like in the middle of a hex war. Things were lousy enough up there without the West Indian warlocks fighting the Haitian voodoons fighting the East African witch doctors fighting the Spanish santarians. . . .

Woolcock managed to keep a lid on the lunacy, and the hexing and hoodooing down to a dull roar. Under his watchful eye, or crystal ball—I didn't want to know what the hell he used—the mojo shops and the gypsy ladies restricted their potions to the relatively nonlethal.

Sound like a lot of mumbo jumbo? That's exactly what it was. And if you don't believe Doc Woolcock was performing a life-or-death service to the people of Harlem, lend me a lock of your hair or some fingernail parings. I'm just an old ofay, but I have seen things uptown that made my skin crawl.

He was the expert, though. As I believe I have indicated, all I had to offer was a nodding acquaintance with the spirit world. Enough to realize it was indeed out there. Not nearly enough to do anything about it.

"Woolcock's been all over this case, Jimmy. And guess who he recommended I should call?" Joe Jefferson smiled, not a pleasant sight under the best of circumstances.

"I still don't get it. Why me?"

" 'Cause what I got here is not your garden variety voodoo church. This one's ten times weirder and a hundred times sicker. Besides . . . there's not that many palefaces even believe hoodoo's real, to say nothing of having a clue as to what to do about it."

"Sure, I know what to do about it. In the words of the immortal Mr. Fetchit, 'Feets do your stuff.' "

"Too late for that, pal. Remember the New York version of Newtonian physics? Crap flows up hill around here. This particular load landed in Harlem. But dollars to doughnuts, it started in your part of town."

"Downtown witch cults? Far be it from me to defend lower Manhattan. But how can you tell?"

"Can't tell you, Jimmy. Got to show you."

"Show me what?"

"Oh, just Harlem's most facinating nightspot. Ready for a treat?" Joe stood up and stretched, and reached for his shoulder rig. "Velma? Git me a clean shirt."

Now there was an invite I could hardly pass up. I knew just what Joe meant, and I hadn't been there in ages.

The Central Harlem Morgue.

Cold air, running water clattering on tiles, bright lights, echoing footsteps, the smell of disinfectant, and, ever so faintly, the stench of you-know-what. The attendant took us down corridor after corridor, past bin after bin.

But finally we reached the right one. Joe grabbed the handle.

"Hope you're not ready for this, Jimmy," he snarled, and hauled the bin out of the wall. "Here. Feast your eyes!"

What I saw was no feast.

I could tell she'd been young and shapely and black. Maybe her face had been pretty. But it was too battered in for me to be sure of anything but that she had died trying to scream, died with a wide-eyed mask of terror plastered onto her face for eternity.

Her throat had been chewed out . . . torn open with insane, methodical care. A series of big precise bites had cut through her larynx and peeled open her major blood tubes.

But her windpipe wasn't blocked. Oh, no. Whoever had done her in had wanted her breathing . . . and pumping blood, until he, she, or it was quite finished. Quite finished with all the brandings and cuttings that had been made on her breasts and her belly and her thighs.

Very high up on her thighs.

Things had been tortured into her flesh, and when I studied those things I realized why old Doc Woolcock had told Joe to call me. I realized more than Joe could possibly suspect.

There were weird symbols I had never seen before. And

there were hieroglyphs I knew I'd see again as soon as I took the trip I was planning to the Metropolitan Museum of Art.

And there were swastikas. Lots of swastikas.

My stomach and I debated whether it should retain possession of my most recent meal. I won, but not by much.

"You got anything?" I rasped. "Any leads?"

"Leads? No, Jimmy. I got no leads. But you know what I do got? I got a matched set. A service for six. That's what I got!"

He grabbed the handle of the bin above her and pulled it out. And the one above that. And the two next to that. And . . . there were six of them in all. All of them could have been pretty; all of them were young. All of them were Negro.

"No clues, Joe? *Nothing?*"

"What you see is what we got . . . at least, the last half dozen."

"Last? How many all told?"

He jerked his head toward the first bin. "That's Miss Sweet Sixteen over there. They been turning up three, four a week for over a month now. Get the picture, Jimmy? Do you *get* it? Every day I go to work and I sit there and wait for the next one. And the next one . . ."

"Sixteen."

Blame it on the late hour, but right then I said something so stupid that, as soon as I heard my own words, I felt like rolling them up and smacking myself on the nose with them.

"How you been keeping it out of the papers?"

The look Joe gave me was just as disgusted as I deserved.

"Guess you let your subscription to the *Amsterdam News* lapse, huh, Jimmy? They been lambasting me twice a week. Could be worse, though, right? Could be *white* frails turning up dead. Then the downtown papers might even think the news was fit to print. Oh. One thing's real interesting though."

"What's that?"

"These janes?" he whispered. "They're an embalmer's dream, Jimmy. Somebody's doing half his work for him."

"Huh?"

"They're empty. You hear me? There's not one drop of blood in any one of them! Sucked dry. So tell me Jimmy, you believe in vampires?"

"Sure, Joe." I shrugged. "This is Manhattan. Anything's possible. Vampires, witches, goblins . . . you name it, I believe in it."

"Yeah, well have any of the above been littering your office lately?" He asked the question as if he wanted a serious answer.

"My office? No."

He squinted at me suspiciously. But all he said after a moment was, "You are going to look into this, Jimmy. And you are going to tell me what you find out. As soon as you find it."

"Sure, Joe. That's what friends are for. I'm going to earn that five bucks a day I didn't ask for."

"Don't want it? Give it to charity."

"That's just what I had in mind."

"I'll bet. Aqueduct? Hialeah?"

"My personal favorites."

"Jimmy?" He frowned. "Don't jive me. This ain't just business. This stopped being business somewhere around number five. I *am* gonna settle the score."

"Don't jive *me*, pal," I grumbled. "We both of us got scores to settle. We live unwholesome lives. Know what I mean?"

He held up one of his big paws.

"Okay, okay, Captain," he said. "I saw the swastikas, too. That's one of the reasons your name came up. So let's say I'm just asking like an old friend of the International Brigades. You find anything out, share the wealth. Fair enough?"

I shook the hand he offered.

"And if you do *better*"—he smiled—"save me a piece. A nice big piece."

"You people." I grinned. "Give you an inch . . ."

But the truth was, I was already pretty sure that sooner or

later I'd be able to give Joe Jefferson a piece big enough to choke a horse.

More likely sooner than later.

Gentleman Joe called a squad car to ferry me home. But when we reached Columbus and 75th, I told the driver to pull over and let me out. Dawn had not yet touched the sky, but I calculated that, if I walked the rest of the way, I'd be just in time to greet it from my terrace door. Maybe the combination of the walk and the view would wash off some of the night.

I suppose it would be fair to call that decision my first major mistake of the case.

I was in the middle of 75th Street between Columbus and Central Park West, strolling past an alleyway crammed full of trash cans and stacks of empty wooden crates.

Suddenly, a shadowy mass of silent motion smashed into my side—so blindingly quickly that I still don't know whether it had been hiding between two parked autos or just dropped down on me out of the sky.

Pain.

The air *whoosh*ed from my lungs and I was cartwheeling through space. I bowled into the pile of crates and lay stunned and breathless in a noisome jumble of garbage and splintered slats. My face was pressed against an Andy Boy Broccoli box end, and I recall marveling anew at just how neatly the young lad's hair was parted. But only for the briefest of moments, because I was not too dazed to haul out my roscoe, clamber into a crouch, and look for something to shoot.

Ten paces away, a huge silhouette paused at the mouth of the alley, blocking the light. It began stalking toward me. Black hat, some kind of black cape, face totally obscured in shadow. I was in no mood for formal introductions, though. I raised my cannon chest-high and squeezed off two blasts. The deafening double roars careened off the alley walls; the muzzle spit flames.

The thing staggered ever so slightly . . . and kept coming toward me!

Sweet creeping Jesus. For an instant I'd seen its face in the muzzle flash. Pale, white skin as cracked and dry as parchment stretched tight across its skull; insane, bulging, red, beady eyes; an open, lipless mouth glistening with drool, unable to close over wet, dagger-point fangs.

It looked thirsty. My gun dropped from my numbed fingers. But I didn't bother trying to retrieve it. Guns are worthless when you're trying to kill the undead.

The vampire . . . yes, that's right, vampire, stepped up and loomed over me, hoisted me like a garbage sack, and threw me back into the heap of shattered crates. Its cape whirled, and it dropped down over me, smothering me beneath its tent of blackness.

Such strange and hideous strength.

The creature felt light . . . no more substantial than air. And yet its whole weight was crushing me flat. The inexorable force of undeath. Bony, steel-hard fingers twisted into my hair. It ripped my head to the side with so much force my spine creaked, exposing my pulsing throat. Its hungry maw dipped toward my neck.

The stench.

Its open mouth reeked of rotten blood and dank graveyard clay. I writhed beneath its crushing grip, and I might as well have been trying to walk through the alleyway wall. A sick wave of paralyzing fear washed over me. I could not move the monster an inch. Nothing. I was helpless.

Helpless.

And that, of course, is precisely how all the horrors of this world defeat us: by filling us full of the sick illusion of deathly inevitability . . . *their* inevitability. Even in the midst of my fear, I knew what it was doing.

And I hated it.

In fact, quite suddenly, I hated it a good deal more than I feared it.

I hated Lo Fang, too, the miserable monkey, because I knew good and goddamned well he was the one who had sicced Mr. Nosferatu on me.

Too bad for both of them, I suddenly remembered a thing or two I knew about vampires.

I could not hold back those fangs dipping closer and closer to my throat. But I pushed my right hand out to the side, made it wriggle and grope until it found what I needed. A broken wooden slat.

I latched onto the slat, flipped it up against a space between two of the monster's ribs. Then I prayed the wood had been broken off jagged enough, and *rammed* it home hard and fast.

Trust me, I don't take the credit for what happened next. It was perilously close to the dawn, and I believe that the coming rise of the blessed, invisible sun was already draining the monster's power. Another form of inevitability. The vampire . . . or its master . . . must have been very desperate indeed to have attacked me just there and then, so very close to the day.

The blood-slimed jaws glistening in my face suddenly parted wide, and the creature howled with rage and pain. It kept on shrieking, too, and tried to wriggle itself off of the wooden slat I was twisting into its maggoty heart.

But I just held on and twisted and jiggled the stake until I was sure I had slashed its rotten innards to shreds.

When I threw it off of me, its power had already left it, and its husk was as light as a scarecrow. I staggered dizzily to my feet and for a moment gazed up at the milky blue slab of brightening sky visible way up above the top of the alleyway's well. I turned and looked down at the vampire's corpse.

Then I spit on it.

And I kicked and kicked and kicked at its moldering carcass until there was nothing left but rags and clumps of leafy filth. When I was done I stumbled out of the alleyway and down the long block home, using building faces for support, squinting in the quickening light of the rosy-fingered dawn.

By the time I reached my apartment, I knew just how the monster had felt. I needed a drink, too.

* * *

As soon as I'd administered the restorative belt, I made a beeline for the bathroom and stripped down to my skivvies. I gave my body a more careful inspection than it had received in years—at least from me. Then I washed—a long hot shower with lots of soap—and looked myself over again.

I found a couple of bruises, including a real winner along my left side that I knew could mean I'd cracked a couple of ribs. I speculated I'd gotten it when Dracula had eight-balled me into the alley. But while I saw, and recalled fondly, a good dozen familiar scars among the bruises, I found no place where my skin had been newly broken. Especially, I was pleased to note, not around my neck.

Vampires are not the strangest denizens of planet Earth I've met up with over the years, although my latest run-in was the closest, the absolute very closest, I ever hoped to come to one. But everything I've read or heard or witnessed about our pointy-toothed pals indicates the same thing— vampirism is a catchy disease. Get bitten but not killed by one, and you might as well start dusting off your cape and coffin.

Me, a vampire. Just what I needed, with all my other character flaws.

Suddenly it occurred to me that Lo Fang would have been quite as well served by having me infected as out-and-out murdered. In fact, he probably would have gotten a boot out of watching me sprout long teeth and bat wings. Either way, dead or undead, he'd have me out of his hair.

On the other hand, that fight had been a matter of life or death, kill or be killed for yours truly.

Those weren't just lousy odds. Those were *very* lousy odds. And having once failed to do me in or otherwise neutralize me, I saw no reason to assume Lo Fang would behold the error of his ways and call it a day. In fact, if the dear departed vampire had been an old family favorite of his or something, I envisioned the possibility of Lo Fang being even more steamed, more determined than ever to do me harm.

Certainly I could balance things up a bit with those two

standard vampire remedies—garlic and crucifixes. No problem there: I love garlic. And anticleric though I am, I actually had a crucifix or two lying around the house. For reasons I'll go into on another occasion.

But with all the defensive precautions in the world, I was still playing in someone else's game. I wouldn't have bet much on my chances against a storefront voodoo doctor; and I had the nagging suspicion that Lo Fang was more accomplished a master of the mystic arts than the friendly neighborhood mojo seller.

I reviewed my options. I could quit the case, return Rachel's money. No good. I'd already spent a hefty bit of it. Besides, something told me that Lo Fang would not be deterred by even the most solemn of vows on my part to cease and desist from interfering with him.

Besides *that*, I didn't want to call it quits. I wanted Lo Fang dead, along with all the rest of his New York Nazi pals. And any other stray pets he had hanging around.

Maybe it was the setting: a Fifth Avenue mansion does wonders for a girl's looks, especially if she happens to own it. But one way or the other, Glenda Rogers-Gracey looked considerably better in the flesh than she did in her *Daily Mirror* "Talk of the Town" photos. Even better than in her *Herald Tribune* "Society Corner" shots. Better than her *Daily Worker* snaps too; but that was easy, since the *Worker* usually published her picture with horns and fangs drawn in.

Glenda was what I believe is called a "handsome" woman—a bit over the hill, but still well worth a roll in the hay. Statuesque she was, with big, firm everythings; an aristocratic, finely chiseled face; thick, golden-red hair, which she wore braided and up in classic Teutonic style. She could have been the pack leader for a swarm of Valkyries—or a squad of female storm troopers.

In fact, Glenda probably had precisely such fantasies about herself.

Have I made it clear as yet that high up on my long list of

active dislikes is the vast majority of the small minority that owns the vast majority of America? Good. But as far as I was concerned, Glenda Rogers-Gracey was numbered among the worst of a bad lot.

From Henry Ford to Joe Kennedy . . . of all Adolf Hitler's rich, outspoken American admirers, Glenda was the richest, and the most outspoken. Oh, Glenda was much too genteel to actually appear in the flesh at Madison Square Garden Bund rallies or Ku Klux Klan cross burnings. The only way she supported those worthy organizations was with her checkbook. But America First parades, Father Coughlin benefit balls . . . you name it, Glenda was out there telling America what a friend we have in Adolf. A real charmer.

Still and all, I had every reason in the world to be a perfect gentleman with Glenda. She had donated Entimemseph's Tomb to the Metropolitan Museum in the first place. She was a big time Hitler-loving whore in the second place. It didn't take an Olympian intellect to conclude that she might know the whereabouts and plans of a certain pint-sized Tibetan. Not that old Glenda was likely to open her heart to me on the subject. But under the circumstances, a short game of cat and mouse couldn't hurt.

I hoped.

She greeted me in a cathedral-sized drawing room, over-looking Central Park at 89th Street. The room was bathed in golden, late-afternoon sunlight. A properly cadaverous but-ler had already brought me a nice big glass of very old bour-bon over spring-water ice cubes.

"Regina has told me so much about you, Mr. Underhill," Glenda burbled, and offered me her hand—a warm, per-fumed hand with perfectly manicured nails and so many rocks that, if I bit off just one of her fingers and pawned it, I wouldn't need to work for a year. I resisted the temptation and kissed her hand instead.

Glenda was wearing a low-cut lounging gown. It molded to every hill and valley of her landscape, and, as she bent forward to sit down, allowed for an inspirational view of the landscape's overflowing bounty. I decided that maybe, just maybe, she wasn't so bad after all. For a Nazi bitch.

"Nice of you to see me." I grinned. "Call me Jimmy, if you don't mind."

"Only if you call me Glenda."

"Agreed. I hope Gina found some things to say about me that weren't too terrible."

"You're too modest, Jimmy," she said. "Gina raves about you. But I'd heard of you long before Gina called. I do read the papers, you know. Quite a few of your cases have made the headlines. Or should I say your *solutions* have made the headlines? I admire a man who can tackle a hard problem ruthlessly . . . and solve it quickly. It's the best kind of valor. Quite out of fashion in Jew York City."

She smiled at her witticism. Even at the risk of being a poor guest, I did not. The Butler of the Living Dead reappeared and served her a tall, fluted-stem glass of sherry. Glenda took the glass, touched it to her mouth, sucked in a small taste of the thick liquid, licked her full, moistened lips delicately. Looking right into my eyes all the while.

"Now, what can I do for you, Jimmy?" she asked softly. There was just a hint of amusement dancing at the corners of her eyes.

"Possibly I can do *you* a service, Glenda." I smiled. "It's come to my attention that certain . . . disreputable people have become interested in something of yours."

"Really. Well as I'm sure you can imagine, that is not unusual. What particular something are these disreputable people interested in?"

"Your recent donation to the Metropolitan Museum."

"No. Entimemseph's Tomb? How perfectly awful!" she gasped. But she was not the best of actresses. Couldn't hold a candle to Gina, for instance. "Of course, as you yourself pointed out, the tomb is not precisely mine anymore. I donated it to the Metropolitan on what is called a permanent loan basis."

"Yes. Everyone was very impressed that you did so. Making world culture available to New York's masses."

"Well, those who are more fortunate must do their very best to enlighten the American masses to the higher realities. Impossible as the task seems."

"Noble sentiments," I said, and took a long swig of bourbon to wash it down.

Glenda acknowledged my praise with a regal nod. Then she molested her sherry glass again, observing my appreciation of her performance with that amused smile of hers. She was actually quite good—with sherry glasses, I mean. I could get her a job at Velma's any time, if she wasn't familiar with the buffet rooms already.

Glenda frowned, as if suddenly realizing that she ought to appear concerned, and said, "So. You think thieves have designs on the Entimemseph collection. Whom do you suspect?"

"I don't want to give you the impression my information is anywhere near that detailed. I don't have a suspect . . . just a suspicion, if you get my meaning. I can't even say for sure that a definite danger exists. The possibility of a danger would be more like it."

Glenda sucked her fingertip thoughtfully, a schoolgirlish gesture, quite possibly meant to look pleasingly perverse. I tried to decide whether the effect was a success, gave it only my very conditional approval. Ah me, if only I didn't see swastikas waving every time I tried to look at Glenda with a roving eye.

"Got it!" she said brightly after a moment. "It's the Jews, isn't it!"

"Huh?"

"The Jews are after Entimemseph's Tomb. The legend does have it that Entimemseph was a sworn enemy of the Israelites. Tried his best to keep them in bondage . . . where they belonged. Not that I believe in kike fairy tales, of course, which is all the Old Testament really is . . . but imagine how much better off the world would be if only the hymies had never escaped from Egypt! Don't you agree, Jimmy?" She was talking quickly, thoroughly enchanted with herself.

"It's a point of view," I said flatly.

"Oh," she caught herself. "Of course. . . . Don't worry, Jimmy. I am perfectly aware your political vision is quite different from my own. I don't hold it against you at all. Honestly I don't."

"How wonderfully tolerant of you."

"Tolerant? That's one thing no one has ever accused me of being, darling." She giggled.

"In any case, I do hate taking up your valuable time," I said. "If we could return to . . ."

"Don't worry about my time, Jimmy. This chat has been quite stimulating. Now, if the Jews *are* behind an attempt on the Entimemseph collection, I'll have Maurice contact the Metropolitan to increase the security at the exhibit. To make sure there's no real danger. And then we'll let the hymies know we're onto their game. I do have a bit of influence in the local papers, you know. Some strategic editorials in the *Journal American* and the *Daily News* should let them know they've outsmarted themselves this time." Her jaw fairly quivered in righteous indignation. "Mockie bastards! They think they can . . ."

"Glenda? I'm afraid you're barking up the wrong tree." I hoped she realized how literally I meant the metaphor. "I have no indication there's any outside plot. In fact, if anything, I'd say an inside person . . . from the museum, even from your own circle of acquaintances . . . has some unpleasant plans."

She pouted so dissapointedly, I actually felt a twinge of guilt for spoiling her fun. But of course I was perfectly aware that she knew we were just gaming with each other. And that she also knew that I knew that she knew. And that I knew that she knew that I knew that she . . . Forget it. I also knew the time to say good-bye was drawing nigh.

"So." I patted my knees. "If you can think of someone who's been acting suspicious in some way . . . showing too much interest in things Egyptian . . . Do give it some thought. *Do* contact me if something comes to mind. Anything at all."

I took a card out of my jacket and handed it to her. She

took it, pretended to study it with a smile, ran her fingertips along its edges.

"Anything, Jimmy?" she murmured. And when I just smiled blandly, she said, "Well, as I said I will have a talk with Maurice. He's sure to be interested . . ."

"Maurice?"

"Oh sorry, my personal curator. Maurice Chen. The name is familiar?"

"It rings a bell."

"The restaurateur. Maurice advises as a personal favor to me. He is a brilliant art historian, you know."

Right. I knew a few other things about Mr. Maurice Chen, too. Those gossip columns again. Chen was the richest restaurant owner in Gotham; quite the tabloid's darling, since his New York watering spots provided them with so much grist, *and* his own past was so romantically lurid.

Chen's father was a French military man. His mother, the major's mistress, was impoverished Szechuan nobility. That much I knew from reading the daily bird-cage liners. And from my unhealthy fascination with modern geopolitics, I happened to know that in his salad days, Maurice had been head chef for a particularly brutal, mandarin warlord assassinated by the Young China Movement.

General Chiang had been poisoned.

I'd actually had the unpleasant privilege of meeting General Chiang during my own stay in China. ("Your stay in China?" Yes, I must remember to describe *that* tea party sometime.) I'd never run into Chen, though.

Chiang was the vilest of the vile; the person or persons who spiced his chicken with a little something extra one night deserved a medal, as far as I was concerned. More likely, they'd merely been rewarded with the right to take up where Chiang had left off.

Around the time Chiang was summoned unto whoever in hell his Maker might be, Maurice had departed from China— with a fortune derived, as the best fortunes so often are, from unspecified sources. He'd opened up a high-tone hash house in Paris, made a raging success of it; come to Gotham and done the same here in spades. Le Bistro d'Or was the place to be seen, if you were anyone worth seeing.

I had never been there myself.

No offense, but I'd heard glowing reports of exactly how and for how long the poison had worked on Chiang. Most satisfactory for his enemies, but hardly the best possible rec- ommendation for a chef. I hadn't even dined at Maurice's Mandarin Palace, the most celebrated gourmet restaurant in Chinatown.

End of file on Maurice Chen.

Oh. With one exception. Somewhere along the way Chen had picked up a fine-arts education. Certainly he had the checkbook to back up any claim to expertise he might care to make. He was reputed to have one of the best private collections in the city, and the prices he paid were high enough for his shopping sprees to make the papers. His spe- cial interest areas: French Expressionist paintings and Tang Dynasty jades. Neither of which quite explained how he fit into Entimemseph's Tomb.

Believe it or not, I decided not to ask. I'd done quite enough fishing for the day, listened to quite enough racial theory, asked quite enough questions, received quite enough horse- shit answers. Besides, my drink was finished. I parked my empty on a marble coffee table.

"Well," I said, with as much cheer as I felt like muster- ing, "I've taken up too much of your time. But if you begin to suspect anything . . . please don't hesitate to call. The number on that card works at any hour."

Blaire loved when I told people that.

Glenda popped up happily and stepped toward me, ex- tending both her hands for me to take.

"Thank you for your interest, Jimmy. I will call the very moment I suspect something. And I will thank Gina for mak- ing it possible for me to meet the dashing Mr. Underhill."

Sure, lady. Her pose made it clear I was expected to peck her cheek, and I leaned forward to do so. Her perfume was delicious.

But at the very last moment, naughty Mrs. Glenda Rogers-Gracey turned her face to mine, and our lips touched. And pressed. Our mouths opened and then our tongues were dancing back and forth. Glenda's body felt strong and firm against mine. My hands seared over hot, satin-covered flesh. Very nice.

Sorry. I was disappointed with myself too. But then in the next instant, I was sorrier still. Because Glenda sucked my lower lip between her teeth and *bit*.

I jerked back, and I do believe that if my lip hadn't been moist enough to slip out from between her teeth, Glenda would have gone on chewing. I could already feel with my tongue tip that my lip was puffing slightly. It had just missed being cut.

I looked down at her impish, self-satisfied smile. There was an ever so slightly loony glint in her eyes, and she tilted her head up toward me, lips parted for another nibble.

I held her arms—it felt as if I were holding her at bay—and shook her slightly. She seemed to like that, too. Hmm.

I hooked my thumbs in the top of her dressing gown, and briefly admired its opulent material between my fingers.

Then I ripped her gown open to the waist. I smiled with satisfaction at the sound of its pearl buttons clattering away over the marble floor. When I let go of the fabric, her gown slithered down over her flesh and lay around her feet in a soft pink puddle.

Glenda's only remaining items of attire were the thick strand of pearls at her throat and the backless, high-heeled mules on her feet; and those two articles conspired to make her appear naked rather than nude. Glenda didn't seem to mind.

She had a confused, faraway look on her face, her eyes wide, her lips parted. I held her arms again, traced with my thumbnails along the creases beneath her full, pendulous breasts, then drew my fingertips up to her pink, puckering nipples and pinched them—not too hard, but not too gently, either.

Glenda's brillowy nest was as carrot-red as the hair on her head. I nudged her legs slightly apart, and cupped her fully in my palm to hold her steady. She was very warm, and quite wet.

Then with my free hand, and with every bit of my strength, I *smacked* her freckled rump, a sizzling, openhanded slap high up on her bountiful flank.

The clap echoed resoundingly through the cavernous room. My palm stung, but I had managed to convert Glenda's expression instantaneously from dreamy and self-satisfied to breathlessly shocked. Her jaw dropped, her eyes snapped wide and started to water involuntarily, her chest heaved in a frozen gasp.

But then her hindquarters trembled, her eyes rolled up, and she moaned and half swooned against me. Glenda clutched my lapels and seemed to be trying to embrace me with her entire body.

Some people.

I pushed her back at arm's length and steadied her upright. As soon as I was sure she wouldn't topple over, I took her chin between my thumb and index finger and shook her head gently.

"Not nice to bite," I murmured.

She winced as I patted her rump where it was welting up rather satisfyingly.

I turned and left. When last I saw Glenda, she was standing a bit pigeon-toed, looking suddenly awkward in her mules and the ruins of her gown.

As I reached the door, something hissed past my ear and smashed into glitter dust against the gilt frame of what I assume was an original Vermeer. Luckily there was no sherry left in the glass to ruin the varnish. Or stain my suit.

Night.

I was all decked out for an evening on the town, in what I currently deemed the very pinnacle of fashion . . . all things considered: nice dark suit, newly blocked hat, crucifix in my pocket, clump of garlic around my neck.

I hoped Lo Fang didn't own any atheistic vampires, or ones who liked spicy food.

I had toyed with the idea of motoring over to Dr. Bukhovna's neighborhood, but decided my Packard's hubcaps were entirely too new to risk it. So I had Ernst hail me a taxi instead, and told the hack to drop me on Houston in front of Katz's delicatessen. I knew I'd make it down the side streets faster on foot; more enjoyably too, with a pastrami sandwich firmly in hand.

It was a balmy late Monday, and although there was not a green thing growing in sight, springtime had undeniably dug its spurs into the neighborhood.

People swarmed along the streets.

Old men in beards and hats and ancient black suits yammered as they ambled, bickering over fine points of Talmudic logic or the wholesale price of yard goods. Brats squalled in the crooks of their mother's arms; grime-caked urchins wrestled over filched apples, oblivious to the curses of pushcart merchants. Big-chested matrons leaned out of windows, their elbows resting on pillows, their pillowy breasts pressed against their forearms as they screeched and chattered from their perches at the passing parade of minor vice and tarnished virtue.

A young slut on a street corner, her face painted with an innocent earnestness, recited her entire menu of services for me in an accent that could have been learned in any of a dozen crowded corners of Central Europe.

She stopped her list in mid-act, as a leering gutter brat two or three years her junior groped her ample buttocks through her cotton dress so deeply that half his bony hand disappeared. She batted her purse at his head; he ducked and scuttled off down the street; she scampered after him, cursing and lurching precariously on borrowed high heels.

Bukhovna lived in the grimy, cluttered heart of it all, in a decaying brownstone on East Broadway, nestled between a settlement house and a Talmudic school building.

I threaded through a crowd of wiseguys, grade-A electric-chair material, gathered near his stoop. They were taking the greatest of pleasure in tossing a red-faced yeshiva boy's skullcap back and forth, back and forth just out of his reach.

As I started up the steps, one of the smart asses stopped the game long enough to begin a comment aimed in my direction . . . and then to take a painful-sounding jab in the ribs from a buddy who recognized me, if not by name then at least by category, as a type of trouble worth avoiding.

The good doctor's front door was locked. I pressed the buzzer, faintly heard its ring echoing deep in the building's recesses. The character who finally answered the door gave me the once-over with the chain bolt still in place. I flipped out a card and held it up at eyeball height.

"Underhill," I said. "I have an . . ."

The door slammed shut. I felt an instinctive urge to kick it in, but then I heard the chain bolt being clattered out of its hasp, and the door was thrown wide.

Big he was, with ice-blue hawk eyes and a fiery red beard that began high up on his cheekbones and descended to midchest. The beard only partially hid the scar slicing across his left cheek from below his eye. Even beneath his shabby black suit, I could see the ripple of muscle as he stepped aside to let me in. "My name is Ruvon," he offered. "Dr. Bukhovna is expecting you."

His accent was Oxfordian English, but his tone was as warm and friendly as a junkyard dog's. I browsed through my memory of the recent past and wondered what I had done to merit such a display of cordiality. No matter, I didn't like him either.

Ruvon closed the door behind me. We were standing at the head of a narrow hallway. The runner on the floor was threadbare, the painted walls bleached by age. But everything in sight was perfectly ordered and spotlessly clean; and all the faint smells in the air . . . old books, meat roasted in garlic, rose petal sachets . . . had an almost narcotizingly comforting effect.

I felt ridiculously as if I were home.

But I wasn't. And now I watched as Ruvon frisked me

visually. I knew he'd caught the .45 bulge under my left armpit, and I pinned the roscoe his armpit was warming, too. Ruvon held out his hand, palm up, glanced at my hidden shoulder rig, and smiled unpleasantly.

"Pardon me, Mr. Underhill. I do hope you won't mind, but . . . certain necessary precautions . . ." There was not even a hint of apology in his tone.

"Sorry," I said politely. "It's against my religion to give up my gat."

The air between us bristled, in a way I have often felt air bristle just before someone dies.

I heard a voice call from the landing just above us. "Ruvon! It's all right. Just bring him up."

Ruvon frowned and shrugged, disappointed at not being allowed to try his chances. I was disappointed too, in a way. But he did as he was told, led me up a short flight of stairs. Warm honey-colored light poured from an open doorway.

Dr. Avrom Bukhovna's cavernous study was brightly lit, and yet filled with shadows. Books were everywhere, a dusty, chaotic universe of books: stacked on ceiling-high shelves along all four walls; tottering in precarious piles that sprang up in unlikely spots all over the floor like toadstools after a rain; seated in armchairs and perched on a leather couch's back and cushions, like a flock of silent guests; flapped open on the ancient Persian rug in the center of the room.

The doctor was sitting at—almost buried behind—a huge oak rolltop desk in a far corner. He rose, wasn't much taller standing up, strode across the study to greet me, and gave me an alarmingly strong, sinewy hand to shake.

"Hello, Mr. Underhill," he said mildly. "How kind of you to come all this way just to warn me of the death and destruction about to rain down on my house."

He glanced at Ruvon and, when Ruvon did not respond, raised his eyebrows in mild annoyance. Ruvon gave me a final glance utterly devoid of charity, and grudgingly withdrew from the room.

"I see you've made a friend." Bukhovna chuckled.

"The admiration is mutual. But 'death and destruction' are rather strong terms. I believe I only said . . ."

"I know what you said," he interrupted. "And I know what was behind your words too. My old friend Lo Fang has arrived in town, and he has asked you to deliver a message. He has the arrogance to warn me of what he means to do. He is a very arrogant man, Mr. Underhill. I pray that one day his arrogance will be his undoing . . ."

"Wait," I snapped. "You really believe Lo Fang sent me here?"

"I know he has, Mr. Underhill."

"In a pig's ass he has, *Mister* Bukhovna. I do lots of things to put bread on the table, but being a Nazi errand boy isn't one of them. Not for him, not for anybody. I called you to warn you because . . ."

But unfortunately for the good doctor, just then I noticed his eyes widen ever so slightly. So despite his commendable manipulative skill, the deft craftsmanship with which he'd managed to ignite a blaze below my hindquarters, I saw through his game. And I caught myself in time.

"Some unpleasant characters may have some unpleasant designs on something you possess," I concluded blandly. "Just as I told you on the telephone."

He threw up his hands in a gesture of surrender that I didn't believe in the slightest.

"Very good, Mr. Underhill. The truth is I know you are not a hireling of Lo Fang. I fear that, if you had been one, Ruvon would not have been able to contain his desire to . . . dispose of you. He is a bit overly enthusiastic in his protectiveness."

"He should work on that," I grumbled. "It could land him in trouble some day."

"Few of us are strangers to trouble these days, Mr. Underhill. But I do owe you an apology. You have earned quite a reputation as an enemy of . . . many things Lo Fang stands for. I know you would not wittingly become a messenger for him, and perhaps I did overstate the case. Never the less, I fear he has managed to impose upon you."

"If you want to believe that, feel free." I shrugged. "But I'll tell you again, my information didn't come from Lo Fang. And as for him imposing on me . . . I'm happy to say I managed to return the favor last night."

"Meaning?"

"Meaning, I had occasion to put one of his pets to sleep. I killed a vampire." I saw no reason not to say it. In fact I was curious to see how Bukhovna would react.

He took it right in stride. As if he heard it every day.

"The Kabbalah calls them 'the undead children of Lilith,' " he mused. "I congratulate you on your escape. Lo Fang commands many such spirits. I had suspected he would bring a small army of them with him to New York."

"He's doing quite a job of keeping his army fed," I muttered.

"What do you mean?" He frowned.

"I mean I spent an evening at the Harlem morgue recently, Doctor. I counted quite a few corpses."

A look of pain crossed the old man's face.

"Of course," he said sadly. "Of course he would feed them on the poorest, the most vulnerable . . . the ones whose deaths would attract the least notice."

"I wish you could have seen what they looked like, Doctor. The corpses, I mean. He's doing more than feeding his vampires. He's letting them play with their food."

Bukhovna frowned and shook his head.

"I believe I know what you mean," he said grimly. "Unfortunately the explanation is not so simple. The children of Lilith are not the only members of Lo Fang's legions who require . . . living food."

"Really." I frowned. "Just what else does Lo Fang have in his menagerie?"

"I cannot honestly say I know. But if you can think of an unclean creature of legend . . . I would say it is not outside the realm of possibility that Lo Fang owns one. Or would like to."

"Really. Werewolves?"

"Certainly. And shape-shifters of other kinds too."

"Zombies? Goblins? Succubi?"

He peered at me suspiciously for a moment.

"Are you being flippant, Mr. Underhill? I wouldn't be saying these things to you, if you had not already encountered Lo Fang's supernatural minions yourself. Or if you hadn't broached the subject."

"Flippant? Not at all, Doctor. I just want to know the full range of Lo Fang's occult arsenal. So to speak."

"I see. Regrettably many of the demons who serve him defy categorization. As do many of the demons he serves. In fact, if one can find a common bond of all such creatures, it is simply this: they are not truly alive themselves, and they need to feed off the living in order to retain even the semblance of life. Undeath, you know, is just a pathetic attempt to keep death itself at bay. They must feed . . ."

"How's about mummies, Doctor? Does Lo Fang have any mummies up and around?"

There, I'd said it. And I was pleased to note it had precisely the hoped-for effect on Bukhovna. He studied me for a moment, then held up his hands in the surrender gesture again. This time I came closer to believing him.

"Ah. So you *do* know a great deal, Mr. Underhill. Very well, we will stop playing games. But I must request one thing."

"Yes?"

"I would like to know your sources. Where did you find out about Entimemseph?"

"As I've already indicated, not from your enemies."

"Would you care to be a bit more specific?"

"Sorry." I grinned unpleasantly. "I learned it during an investigation. Privileged information . . ."

"Very principled of you." He smirked. "Now then. How do you think I can help you?"

"There are lots of ways. For instance, you could begin by telling me exactly why Lo Fang is so interested in the Key of Entimemseph."

He studied me suspiciously at my mention of the Key,

seemed to consider a possibility, then to reject it. Finally, he said, "You really do know a great deal, Mr. Underhill. I am almost tempted to question you more deeply on the subject. To compel an answer as to your sources."

"Don't even think about it," I grumbled.

Something happened to Bukhovna then, a thing that is difficult to describe adequately. I can say that without any real movement, he suddenly seemed to *grow* . . . not just in stature, but in power, too. His eyes flashed and even in the brightly lit study, he now seemed to radiate an inner light. The light of a terrible strength.

"Don't presume to tell me what options I should or should not consider, Mr. Underhill. Believe me, if I wanted what you know badly enough, I would simply take it. And you wouldn't do a thing about it."

He allowed the light to fade—and the rather alarming crawl at the nape of my neck to disappear. "But I do have more respect for you than that. You have been tested in many fires already. I won't take what you know by force. Even though I probably should. So. Entimemseph's Key? You may already know it was a talisman of the Egyptian high priest's power . . . and the secret of his long life."

"Yes . . . but I don't pretend to know what would happen if Lo Fang got his hands on the Key."

"A great deal would happen. To begin with, he could use the Key to bring the high priest back to life."

"Excuse me?"

"Well, in a sense that is not accurate. Because Entimemseph is not really dead, strictly speaking. He sleeps now in the twilight world Lo Fang loves so dearly. He is undead. As he has been since the prophet took away his power so many years ago.

"Oh, don't stare at me so incredulously, Mr Underhill. What I'm describing to you now has nothing of the mystical about it. 'Undead' can be thought of quite simply as a physical state. Even at this moment, Entimemseph breathes, his heart continues to beat. But slowly . . . very slowly."

"You mean, if I popped over to the Metropolitan Museum with a stethoscope, I could actually . . ."

"What does the Metropolitan have to do with anything?"

"That's where Entimemseph is, of course."

"That's where drek is, of course. A forgery! Lo Fang has brought the mummy to New York. And hidden him safely. That junk in the museum is meant only as a challenge to me, a taunt . . . an advertisement, if you will. As I said before, he is an arrogant man. He flaunts his possessions . . . and his plans. But in any case . . . he would bring the priest to life. Of course he could do so even without the Key. Lo Fang has skill enough to do that much unassisted. But without the Key, Entimemseph would be nothing more than a *golem* . . . a stupid, lumbering monster of clay. And quite uncontrollable. A mad dog. *With* the Key . . . the Key kept firmly in Lo Fang's hands, . . . he will be an immensely powerful destructive tool."

"Do you have any idea of specifically what Lo Fang would do with a well-trained mummy?"

"Specifically? Not really," he said grimly. "But I assure you, Lo Fang would devise all manner of mischief . . . first here, and then back in Europe. He'd undoubtedly be quite creative in that regard. And of course, there's the other side of it, too."

"Namely?"

"Think of the Key as a power source. The *uses* of the power are infinite. Once he awakens Entimemseph, Lo Fang would learn a great deal about the Key from him. So the mummy would be more than a tool. He would be a teacher. Grievously effective."

A shamefully cynical thought suddenly occurred to me. I decided to share it.

"What about you, Doctor? What if, instead of Lo Fang getting your Key, you got his mummy? Think *you* could find some use for a golem? Uh . . . hope I don't sound too suspicious," I added, even though I didn't hope so at all.

"I'd be rather more foolish than I am, to tell you if I had any plans to seize the mummy for my own, wouldn't I?" He shook his head. "But since I do not, I can afford to tell you the truth. I do not want Entimemseph, and Entimemseph has nothing I want. Nothing. The little I have learned in my years has at least taught me this much, Mr. Underhill . . . it is *never* wise to trifle with evil. In the end, a man never profits from doing so. Too bad. I wish it were not the case. But I have seen too many good men destroyed by entertaining that same wish . . . to use evil means for good ends . . . and yielding to the temptation.

"And yet . . . I can see the elegance in it. You know, through the ages, scholars have used the Key . . . to fashion golems for the protection of the community in times of its most dire need. In that sense, Entimemseph, the sworn enemy of my people, is the father of golems, and thus the protector of Jews! The power of his Key is what has allowed the golems to live. A nice irony, eh? A profound beauty. As I said before, such beauty can be seductive."

"Get back to Lo Fang. You must have some more specific idea of his goals."

Bukhovna frowned at my impatience. "He would awaken Entimemseph. With the Key, the mummy would be horribly powerful. Lo Fang would experiment until he felt he could control the full potential of both mummy and Key. Then he'd take this . . . instrument back to Germany and put it at the service of Mr. Adolf Hitler. And Hitler in turn would utilize it in pursuit of his ultimate goal."

"Namely?"

"You know quite well what Hitler wants. He is a plain man, with quite elementary needs. He merely desires the utter dominion of evil on earth. The Kingdom of Satan."

Not exactly the way I'd have put it, but not particularly out of line, either.

"So what are you going to do about it, Doctor?"

"Do?"

"To stop Hitler, to stop Lo Fang."

"Why . . . nothing, Mr. Underhill." He actually seemed surprised I'd asked.

"Nothing."

"That is, I will not voluntarily give up what I possess. I believe I have ways of keeping it safe from him. But I take your question to mean more, and more I cannot do. You would like me to leap up on my horse and go charging at Lo Fang's horde, wouldn't you?"

"You're the one who pointed out that he's invaded New York. Brought a whole army with him."

"Quite certainly." He frowned. "I don't believe you have seen the worst of his . . . soldiers as yet."

"Maybe not. But I've seen what they can do," I snapped. "It's hard for me to believe what I'm hearing. You know what he's planning. And you say you won't do anything to stop him."

"I'll say more, Mr. Underhill. What if I told you that I believe Lo Fang has sent you here to tempt me into attacking him?" He held up his hand to stifle the explosion he knew was coming. "No, no. I'm not back to accusing you of working for him. But don't you see? The most convincing messenger is one who believes his message. You have been tricked. Sent here to tempt me by urging me to do what I would dearly love to do . . . and must not."

"You know, it never ceases to amaze me." I sneered. "The lengths people will go to justify their own cowardice."

"If that's the way you want to put it." He shrugged. "But I believe you saw the rewards of confronting the whirlwind, in Spain."

"I saw no such thing! I saw what happens when smug, complacent people sit back on their fat asses. I saw what happens when the so-called democracies of the world pretend to be neutral while they're actually . . ."

"Spare me the soapbox, Underhill," he snapped. "Your pontifications are wasted on me."

"I wonder how you'd feel if those were Jewish women up there in the morgue instead of Negro ones," I grumbled. "Would you still think there was nothing you could do?"

Ruvon burst in. He whispered something worriedly to the

doctor. Bukhovna nodded grimly. When he turned back to me, he suddenly looked very old, and very tired.

"Yes, that's right, my friend. Not a thing. I'd weep for them, just as I grieve for those poor unfortunate women who are there in fact. And I would still do nothing. Not until something I did could do some good. Do you understand me, Mr. Underhill? Did I say that too quickly for you? No? Good. And now if you don't mind . . . this interview is over."

Boy, was it ever. The old bastard. But there was one last thing . . . one jab I could not refrain from throwing.

"How about if he *really* took one of yours, Bukhovna? How about if he took your daughter for instance?"

That felt much better.

I saw the momentary stab of ancient sorrow . . . and then, a look of fleeting suspicion. But in the next instant his face went hard.

"The Lord in his wisdom has made that impossible," he said bitterly, his anger just barely controlled. "I have no daughter, Mr. Underhill. My daughter is dead. Now get the hell out of here."

Dr. Avrom Bukhovna turned his face away, as if I were already gone.

Back outside, the sidewalk was empty; the hand of night had swept the street near clean. I wandered down the block alone, and pondered the good doctor with quietly amazed disgust.

The old goat.

Since I had no offspring myself, at least none I knew of, I could not with utter certainty swear that nothing a daughter of mine might do would ever make me talk about her as Bukhovna had just talked about Rachel. Could I become so totally enraged at my own flesh and blood that I would cut her off completely; kill her in my own mind; tell myself and the world she was dead?

Of course I wasn't blind. I knew if Rachel were *my* daughter, I'd probably have wanted to knock her around the block.

But I saw Rachel in my mind's eye . . . her fragility, the vulnerability just below the surface . . . And I thought about the guts it had taken to slip away from a monster like Lo Fang . . . How could a father cut himself off from his own flesh and blood for "dishonoring" him . . . or whatever her offense had been?

I wondered what Bukhovna would have said if I'd told him how I'd seen his daughter being treated.

Or how she'd made the money to pay me to save his life.

Oh well. Nobody ever put a gun to my head and decreed I had to like my work. Certainly liking was not numbered among the various reasons my profession and I had chosen each other. So, like it or not, like *him* or not, at that moment I resolved I was going to protect Bukhovna and his goddamn precious Key.

Just for spite. As good a reason as any.

I was already half a block from Bukhovna's town house. But the explosion, when it came, was so powerful, it picked me up and threw me flat in the gutter.

The last thing I heard clearly was a thunderclap that seemed to fill the universe. I scrambled back to my feet almost immediately—and realized the same force that had flattened me had also knocked my eardrums for a loop. I could hear nothing but a high-pitched ringing monotone.

The street in front of Bukhovna's house was littered with shattered brick and rubble. Flames and oily, black smoke were billowing out of his second-story study; bits of charred debris still crumbled from the edges of the blast hole.

I raced toward the house . . . and just missed colliding with two mugs in black leather coats as they barreled out of the alleyway beside it. Surprise, surprise, I recognized the one in the lead: a big, rangy gorilla who had been toasting Adolf in Charlie's bar the other night.

He drew on me, the fool. Not that I'd have let him go anyway.

Dumdum bullets are real time- and trouble-savers, especially in a .45 long barrel. I jerked my rod and cracked off one shot before the gorilla's Luger was halfway out of his pocket.

The slug made a small hole going into his chest, and a big splatter coming out of his back. The mess hit the alleyway wall. It hit his partner too, and in the next instant the gorilla bounced into him, then dropped to the pavement, dead as a smelt. His partner saw me, froze, then honked in fear and made a run for it.

It certainly was Old Home Week, there in the doctor's alleyway. I was quite disappointed to see Otto up and about so quickly, and I made a mental note to work on my drop-kick. But at least I could take some satisfaction in noting that he was limping and waddling as he scuttled past me.

His tiny pig eyes were open round as marbles. I very nearly felt sorry for him. But not quite. So I gave him five yards, then I shot him dead.

Lights were blinking on in tenement windows. The gun blasts had cleared my ears; I heard shouts, the slaps of running feet. Bukhovna's front door was blown out, swinging slowly on one twisted hinge. I dove through, piled up the rubble-strewn steps to his study.

The study! I saw it all in an instant. Shattered glass and splintered wood and fluttering, shredded books. A huge hole gaped where the window had been; outlined against the lesser black of the night, faintly lit by the flames that flickered up from a dozen fires, two dark shapes were locked in silent strife.

The larger figure suddenly lifted the smaller one high above its head and flung it down into the rubble. Avrom Bukhovna cried out in pain as he hit the floor, struggled to rise, flopped back down and lay still. The flames danced up cheerily, and in their sudden light I saw the other figure for what it was.

A vampire, its mad eyes ablaze.

A second monster joined the first at the window, holding up a small bundle in its hands. They both regarded the bundle in silence, then looked up and out of the blasted window.

As if awaiting orders from the night.

"The *Key*!" Ruvon bellowed. "They have the Key!"

He'd been tossed off into a quiet corner of the room, and I had not noticed him. But now he staggered to his feet, reeling as he hauled out his pistol. His face was splashed with blood from a wide gash across his forehead, and with his red beard, lit by the dancing, amber flames, he looked like a gruesome study in scarlet.

"No!" he bellowed, and fired a shot, then three more.

I'd have joined right in with him, if I'd felt like wasting perfectly good bullets.

The vampires glanced at Ruvon contemptuously. Then they leaped out of the window and instead of falling, whirled *up* into the endless night.

We both ran to the opening, stared hopelessly at the blind, black well of the sky. The monsters were already gone. Ruvon turned and staggered over to Bukhovna, dropped down beside him, reached his hand gently, hopelessly to the old man's face.

Bukhovna moaned. He opened his eyes, smiled faintly, and patted his assistant's wrist, as if to reassure him.

The flames leaped higher around us. I felt their warmth on my cheeks.

"Ruvon!" I snapped. "Let's go . . . got to get out of here."

Bukhovna glanced up at me, smiled again, and mumbled, "The fires of Hell, Mr. Underhill . . . as illusory as Satan's pleasures, I assure you." He turned back to Ruvon. "They . . . they took it?" Ruvon nodded fiercely.

Bukhovna grimaced. Then he made an odd, complex gesture about him with his left hand. All the fires in the room went out at once. Hardly even a wisp of smoke remained. On the floor, beside a broken stand, lay a single, tiny table lamp, its porcelain base shattered. Bukhovna gestured toward it feebly.

"My favorite lamp," he grumbled. "Those miserable shits."

The lamp's bulb was broken too. But it sputtered to life, washing the study with its slight, pale light. Ruvon looked at me.

"Just go," he said. There was no hatred, no anger in his voice.

Far away, I heard the thin, helpless wail of sirens approaching, clamoring for an explanation. I still didn't have enough of that particular commodity to go around. So I turned and left again.

I walked out into the middle of the night, not knowing or caring where I went. I needed to think, and think quickly, for a change. It wasn't terribly likely the Great Odds-Maker in the Sky was going to allow me many more blunders.

First, I'd turned myself into vampire bait. That alone would have been end-of-story had it not been for a broken Andy Boy broccoli slat.

Next, I'd made the very worst mistake you can make when dealing with Nazis: I'd underestimated how vicious and sick they were. And how fast. I should have been ready for the attack on Bukhovna. I should have . . .

Forget it. But I wouldn't make any more slipups. Even I knew what three strikes gets you.

Right now, for instance, my first instinct was to do the obvious: charge on up to Glenda Rogers-Gracey's place, boot down the door, and beat the living piss out of her until she told me where to find her Tibetan toad and his stolen merchandise.

But no, I would not fly off the handle. Instead I would hop a cab, go home, and reason things out carefully. The night was still young. If I didn't have a brainstorm in the next hour or so, then I'd go and beat the piss out of Glenda.

When one's life has been as ill-spent as mine, turning off the lights when one leaves home is truly a false economy. I make a point of walking into as few darkened rooms as possible, even if they are my own.

Especially if they are my own.

Ernst the doorman had assured me that there'd been no messages and no visitors. But when I unbolted my door and saw the living room lights had been turned out, I knew it was just plain good sense to walk in heater first.

She was sitting on the couch facing me, with her back to the open terrace door. The moonlight spilled onto her, and in its bleaching light she seemed to glow and shimmer; her wavy, ebony hair, her pale skin, her bare shoulders, her white dress.

I watched a glistening liquid glitter of moonlight trace a sparkling trail down her cheek.

"I'm sorry, Rachel," I said. "I didn't think they'd hit so fast. I . . ."

A sob caught in her throat and she seemed to glide off the couch toward me. We collided and she crushed against me, molded to me, so soft. The fragrance of her hair, the spice of her lips; we kissed and her mouth against mine was softer and firmer and sweeter than any I'd ever tasted.

Yes, I knew kissing her was wrong. Start with the minor reasons, like her age. Then go on to . . . but no. There was nothing I could do about it. I felt myself whirling away, down into that secret place where I knew Rachel and I would be together, one being, forever. Nothing mattered. Nothing. I didn't care what Rachel was, or what being with her would make me become.

Rachel pulled her lips away from mine. Just in time.

The glistens on her cheek . . . I'd taken them for tears, but now, even in the moonlight I could see they were scarlet. I pushed her back at arm's length, reached for the lamp switch.

"No!" she hissed. "Leave it. Just . . . come here. Sit down beside me."

I did. And I held her. She was light, light as air. I kissed her again and her fragrance was all around me; her lips were sweet and cool, her body soft and strong.

I put my hand against her throat.

Cold. So cold.

And suddenly, for absolutely no real reason I could put to words, I realized Rachel was dying.

I'm almost certain that's the word for it.

I brushed the bloody tears from her cheeks, cradled her in my arms. She sighed, murmured into my chest, "He hurt me, Jimmy. He knows how to make pain so *bad* . . . it . . . it goes on forever and it only gets worse and worse and worse!"

"It's over now," I whispered. "I'm going to find him. I'm going to find him and get it back. I should never have let him take it but . . ."

"It's not your fault, Jimmy. It's mine," she said softly. Her body shook with a tremor of remembrance. "He . . . he hurts so much. He hurt me until I told him!"

She looked up at me, and I saw again her eyes were filled with tears. It was so strange. The tears were blood; the blood was tears. I'd never seen the like. But it was just one more thing that didn't matter.

"He showed me why he's been . . . keeping me. All this time I thought it was just because he hates my father so much. But he's *known* . . . all along he's known what I know. He made me tell him tonight! He made me tell him the secret place my father has always kept the treasure. And then he did something even worse! He . . . he made me tell him the *words*. The words of power Papa uses to keep the treasures safe. Do you understand, Jimmy? That's how he got the Key! *I gave it to him!*"

She burst into tears, tried to bury herself in my chest. But I took her shoulders, held her gently. There was no more time.

"Tell me now, Rachel. Tell me where he's gone with it."

She shook her head. "You don't understand. You think you know how powerful he is, but you don't. You won't be able . . ."

"*You* don't understand, Rachel," I said quietly. "I know just how powerful he is. I'm going to take it away from him. And then I'm going to kill him."

She shook her head. "You can't!" she hissed. "Lo Fang doesn't die!"

There was no more time for horseshit. I grabbed her wrist and pressed her hand against my chest, right over the spot where the garlic and the cross were hidden. I waited a moment before I let her pull away.

"Oh yes he does, Rachel," I snarled. "He dies, I die, you die. We just all of us do it differently, is all. Now tell me where he took it!"

She did.

And when I got up to go, she stopped me and put her arms around my neck and kissed me again and then stepped back and stared at me. She looked so unearthly beautiful in the moonlight.

"I've run away from him for good this time, Jimmy. I'm never going back. You . . . you know what that means?"

I nodded my head.

"I'll wait for you here as long as I can, Jimmy," she whispered. "Will you hurry back?"

I looked at my watch. It was just after midnight. Southampton was no short ride. But from what Rachel had told me, I knew the whole operation wouldn't take long. It couldn't.

"I'll be back before dawn," I said. I didn't bother adding that, if I wasn't, I wouldn't be back at all.

"Good," she said. "You remember what I told you that first night. I . . . I need you to help me, Jimmy. I . . . I don't think I can die alone."

I did a quick change into my work clothes—black pants and shirt, black gum soles. Then I fished a gear bag out of the bottom of my closet, and left.

Ernst smiled when I hit the lobby. He'd seen me leaving for work before, and even if he didn't know the details, he knew it usually meant bad news for people we both disliked.

He'd already hauled my Packard out of the garage and left it idling at the curb. But I don't think he was responsible for placing Joe Jefferson casually against the front fender.

Joe uncrossed his ankles as I reached the car door.

"What's up, Jimmy?" he said. "Going to visit some friends? Mind if I tag along?"

"Yes I am, Joe. And as a matter of fact, I do."

"How come? Ashamed for your high-tone friends to know you run around with colored folk?"

"It's my friends I'm ashamed of," I said. "You don't want in on this one, Joe. You really and truly don't."

"That's what you think." He dug into his pocket, came up with a large wooden crucifix. "See?" He grinned.

"Joe Jefferson gets religion." I laughed. "What a terrifying sight. That'll scare 'em off for sure."

He walked around to the passenger side and opened the door.

"So what's up, deacon? You going to shoot the breeze, or you going to play golf?"

"Just for the record, Jefferson . . . this is a bad one."

"Do tell."

"Yeah. Well, I bet you a fin you don't come back."

"You're on. Now drive the goddamn car."

There was light in the sky that night, entirely too much of it for my taste, a bright, gibbous moon that whitewashed the landscape like a naked bulb in a cheap hotel.

Glenda Rogers-Gracey's Southampton beach mansion stood on ten rolling acres of manicured lawns and formal sculpted gardens. The main house was perched on the crest of a hill above the Shinnecock Inlet. The peaks of its gabled roof were visible even beyond the high stone wall that ringed the estate.

I slid the Packard into a stand of trees a few dozen yards from the wall and cut the engine.

"Right," Jefferson grumbled. "Let's get a move on."

He started to get out, and I grabbed his arm.

"Wait up," I said in a nice, calm voice. "Listen once and listen good, Joe. This here's my party, get it? I cut you in. Now *I* lead, you follow. You stick with me like shit to a blanket. Any problems with that, Joe? I'd love to hear them."

For the briefest of moments a shadow crossed his face. Then he smiled.

"Sho'nuff. Ah hears real good. You de boss, Captain. Is it time to go now?"

"Yeah. It's time to go."

"Then let go of my arm, Jimmy."

I gathered up my supplies from the trunk and we moved out.

We slid along the base of the wall, to the place where it turned a corner and cut down to the water. The wall was high at that corner, but my grapple caught the lip on the first throw.

I froze for a moment on the rim, flattened out so I wouldn't make too easy a target against the moonlit sky. I had a clear view of the Shinnecock. A hundred yards out in the deep channel, a partially surfaced U-boat squatted on the tide like an ebony serpent. I heard and then saw a motor launch putt-putting towards Glenda's dock. A half-dozen men.

Good. There was still time. I rolled off the wall and hit the ground quietly behind a low screen of bushes. I crouched there, surveying the garden while I waited for Jefferson. The night air was sweet with the smell of new-budding honey-suckle.

A guard was stationed on the patio at the far end of the rolling lawn. I saw him by the flare of the cigarette he puffed, smelled the cloying smoke the wind whisked across the lawn.

I hardly heard Joe drop down beside me. A questioning glance told me he'd seen the launch. I used sign language to tell him there was a guard on the patio.

And that he was mine.

I was a shadow sliding over the lawn. A dream of death. I waited until the guard's ember flared; then I flew over the low railing at the patio rim and punched my knife into his heart. He choked on his cigarette and died standing up.

I signaled to Joe, and we sprinted through the shadows toward the inlet side of the mansion and crawled into the bushes beside a stone path leading up from the water. We peered out, watched the Nazi sailors, all in battle gear, tying off their launch at a quay. I counted four Walther machine pistols, two Schmeisers.

A tall woman in a dark, melodramatic cape stood watching the men. Then she turned and led the way up the path toward us. The leader of the sailors wore a black leather trench coat. He looked more like a Gestapo goon than a navy boy. As they drew near, he carped at the woman, in German.

"You say he's not ready with the demonstration yet? Well, when in hell does he expect us to unload his damn precious supplies?"

"When he is good and ready for his precious supplies to be unloaded," Mrs. G. Rogers-Gracey replied, also in German. "Do you object, my dear captain? I will inform Lo Fang at once."

"I . . . that is . . . this tide won't last forever," the captain sputtered. "And then there's the American Coast Guard to consider. I'm only concerned with the success of his . . ."

"Concern yourself with following orders," she snarled.

"Precisely what I am doing," he clipped. "But if I am to observe his progress *and* deliver his cargo, he absolutely must . . ."

"Pig! Don't you *dare* to say what he must do! You will regret angering *anyone* here tonight. Clear?"

"Clear, Madame. I simply thought . . ." But then he thought better of it, shook his head, and lapsed into silence.

They passed through a low, arched doorway, started down a steep flight of steps. We saw torchlight, stone walls. Then the guards they left behind closed the heavy, wooden door. Two guards.

I wrapped a length of piano wire around my gloves while I waited for Joe to circle to the other side of the path.

I was behind the guard, my arms crossed on my chest, the wire loop between my lips to keep it from fouling. I flipped the wire over his head and jerked it hard as I jammed him back against my raised knee.

I couldn't see Joe in the darkness across the path, but I heard the horrible, satisfying crunch of heavy steel against the other guard's skull. He stiffened and dropped onto the path. I tightened the wire on mine just a bit more than I needed to, and didn't let up until I heard his blood splattering on the stones.

Joe stepped from the bushes, knelt, and lifted in both hands the head of the guard he'd sapped. He rotated it carefully, quickly, until the neck *crick*ed. When he let go, the man's head thumped on the stones like a melon.

Then we were through the door and down the marble steps into a cavernous, damp smelling, faintly lit basement. We slipped from brick piling to piling, toward a faraway glow. We stopped when we were close enough to listen.

And watch.

Glenda and the Gestapo captain stood a few paces from a large steel table. At its head was Lo Fang; behind him four of his long-toothed pets stood with arms folded, soaking up the darkness, their ember red eyes half-shut, dreaming sick dreams of the devil knew what.

Somebody must have gotten Lo Fang a big stack of telephone books to stand on, because I could see him quite clearly over the thing that was lying on the table.

It was gigantic, too big for a man, although it was unmistakably man-shaped, over seven feet long, wrapped tightly from its head to its feet in thick swaths of linen mottled white and brown.

Entimemseph himself.

Lo Fang wore heavy saffron-colored robes. He held a clay tablet in one green-gloved hand; in the other, an enormous cut-crystal chalice filled with crimson liquid.

If I'd felt at liberty to whisper, I'd have made Joe Jefferson a side bet the liquid wasn't wine.

"Please, Herr Doktor," the captain was saying petulantly. "Whatever you do *must* be done quickly! The tide . . ."

"Silence, you cretin!" Lo Fang hissed. "Do you think we are baking a cake? Everything must proceed at exactly the right moment. In just the right way. And that reminds me. You have brought all the required tanks of fresh blood with you?"

"Certainly. I am instructed to assure you that the . . . sources were all healthy juvenile specimens, and that the quantity is precisely as ordered."

"I hope so for your sake," Lo Fang said. "Because when our friend here wakes up, this sip of refreshment will not keep him satisfied for long. My other pets are thirsty, too.

I've been forced to send them out hunting more often than I'd like. . . . I can hardly afford to attract undue attention at this delicate juncture. But I will *not* run short again. When we finish, I will inspect the shipment. If I judge it insufficient, you and these men will be volunteering to do your patriotic duty.''

"We will do no such . . ." the captain began.

"You will do as you are told!" Lo Fang shrieked. "What in hell have they sent me here!" he asked the darkness.

"I am perfectly aware of my orders, Herr Doctor," the Gestapo captain snarled back. "And they do not include ordering these men fed to some . . ."

"*Ordering?* Who's talking about ordering?" Lo Fang said. "I'm simply talking about obeying! Obeying Entimemseph's will . . . and mine, you worthless creature! But since you seem to doubt me, I will show you what I mean! Come *here*, dear Captain."

Lo Fang placed the clay tablet gently on Entimemseph's chest. Then with his freed hand he gestured at the captain, a mild-seeming wave of his spidery fingers. The captain stiffened. His whole body arched painfully, he spasmed up on his toes like a puppet, his face contorted with pain and helpless fear. He lurched toward Lo Fang, whimpering as he staggered on, totally against his will.

When he was near the dwarf, Lo Fang held up the blood-filled chalice toward him—and then dashed its contents into the captain's face.

"My, my," he said, as the captain gasped and choked. "Look what you've made me do. I've spilt it all. I'm afraid *you* must refill it."

The captain screamed. His body arched impossibly backward, a bow bent by an invisible hand; arched until, all against his will, his trembling fingers were reaching down for the sea dagger lashed to his boot top.

He grasped the dagger's black handle, unsheathed it, crossed it to his other wrist, and pressed the razor-sharp blade into his flesh. He gashed himself deeply, dragging the blade completely through the wound. Hot, black blood spurted out the moment the blade left his wrist.

He thrust his arm toward Lo Fang's empty chalice. Blood pumped into the crystal, filled it to the brim in moments. And only when blood was welling over the cup's lip did Lo Fang clutch the captain's wrist and hold it tightly for a few seconds, grinning delightly at his little joke.

He pushed the wrist away from him as if it and its owner were so much trash; chuckled when the captain, suddenly released and staggering limply, stared in disbelief at his wrist.

The bleeding had stopped. In fact, from my position, I could no longer see any wound at all.

"Now move away, please, Captain," Lo Fang said to the sobbing man.

Lo Fang gazed down fondly at Entimemseph. I looked too, though less fondly, and what I saw was far from encouraging. The tablet Lo Fang had placed on the mummy's chest was gently rising and falling, rising and falling, with each slow, dreamy breath the monster took.

Quietly, oh so quietly, I knelt, opened my gear bag, and began wiring the mechanism of the toy I had brought along. There was still time to contribute my fair share to the general merriment: the mummy was still wrapped in the Sleep of Ages; he and Lo Fang and the tablet were no more than twenty yards away. And I had enough dynamite in my gear bag to blast the whole sick shooting match into all the dusty corners of hell.

Hats off to Ruvon.

He was even quieter and faster and stronger than I imagined he'd be. I didn't have a clue he was there, until his hand clamped over my mouth like a vise and his blade was pressed against my throat.

I managed to peer to my right, and barely to see that behind the next pillar, someone I didn't recognize was doing a similar service for Joe Jefferson.

"*No!* Don't move!" Ruvon hissed. "Not yet, damn you. You'll ruin everything."

I moved my hands from the bomb. Ruvon took his from my mouth and throat.

"Just watch," he whispered. "Do nothing till I tell you."

Ruvon got to his knees beside me, sheathed his knife, unshouldered his other weapon, and took aim with it. A crossbow.

We waited.

There was a scuffle at the far end of the cellar and two leather-jacketed guards came in, dragging between them a little man who kicked and fought ineffectually.

Dr. Avrom Bukhovna.

"We found him skulking around outside," one of the guards grumbled. "Goddamn Jews, they're . . ."

"You!" Lo Fang screeched. His tone was half-triumphant, half-suspicious fear. "Pathetic! You think you can stop me now that I have *this*? !"

He grasped the tablet from Entimemseph's chest— oblivious as the sleeping mummy gasped and froze in midbreath. He waved the tablet aloft. "Watch now, you kike dog! Watch and be damned. When he finishes this goblet . . . he'll drink *you*! Hold him right there!" he snapped to the two guards.

Lo Fang began to sway and mutter as he waved the crystal chalice and the tablet over Entimemseph's head and chest, tracing arcane patterns in the air.

The syllables he uttered were in no language I have ever heard, but I caught the words "Cthulhu," and "Yog-Sothoth," and "Nyarlathotep." All of those are names of the Elder Gods—names right out of the worst pages of the *Necronomicon*.

And if you have never heard any of those names before, I will not trouble your dreams by saying any more about them here.

For a few moments, nothing happened; I neither saw nor heard anything . . . I was about to say, anything unusual. But *something* began to gather and to grow, a strange, disquieting force, a sickening pulsation, a hum I could feel with my body more than hear with my ears. The hair at the back of my neck rose, I felt a slight wave of nausea, and the lights of all the candles and torches in the cellar seemed encircled with ghostly coronas.

Lo Fang tipped the chalice and let a few viscous drops splatter onto Entimemseph's forehead.

The mummy began to tremble, slightly at first, then more and more as if in a monstrous fit. The heavy steel table shook, its feet *skreek*ing against the stones. I heard a muffled growl of pain and rage.

And hunger.

Rotten linen swaddling began to stretch, to fray, and then to snap apart in tiny explosions of decayed fabric and dust. Suddenly massive, gray-wrapped arms burst out, ripped the bands away from a barrel chest, columnar neck, bulging torso. A filthy stench of inconceivably ancient decay filled the basement, a vile, sour reek from beyond the grave. Only Lo Fang and the dormant vampires standing behind him seemed unaffected.

Lo Fang began to weave and mutter and wave the tablet even more frenetically. The mummy tore the covering away from its face. Entimemseph's horrid visage was leathery and gray, a universe of desiccated folds and wrinkles; his eyes were shut tight, his deep-gouged features still frozen in a millenia-old grimace of hate—and a thirst for vengeance.

His lips split open in a snarl, peeled back from yellowed fangs embedded in leather. He kicked away the last tatters of swaddling, pushed himself up, and swung his enormous legs over the edge of the table. He reached out and jerked the proffered goblet from Lo Fang's hands, gulped down the thick liquid in three thirsty swigs, then tossed the crystal away to shatter in the darkness.

Lo Fang keened again in the same arcane tongue . . . and gestured toward Bukhovna, who stood trembling just a few paces away, his thin arms stretched wide by his two guards.

The mummy loomed up to his full height, tottered forward with his arms outstretched. His long, ochre nails were as thick as shells and as sharp as scythes. At the last moment, the terrified guards stepped away from their tiny prisoner.

The mummy reached out for his meal.

But suddenly his arms snaked aside with blinding speed and snatched up both of the guards by their throats. He lifted them wriggling like eels and *squeezed* till their heads bobbled crazily . . . and dropped off of their shoulders!

Huge gouts of blood hosed up from their headless torsos. Entimemseph picked one guard up and began to drink from him like a goatskin, kneading his trunk to make the blood spout faster.

Beside me, Ruvon shouted, "Now!"

His crossbow twanged. So did a half-dozen others. The vampires all shrieked in torment as thin wooden bolts plunged into their hearts. They clawed impotently at the buried shafts for a few moments—and then began crumbling away into rotted rags and dust.

The U-boat men raised their machine pistols. But Dr. Avrom Bukhovna reached into his frock coat and jerked out the sawed-off shotgun strapped to the lining. His first blast cut the Gestapo captain in half; his second bagged two sailors at once. Another sailor hit the wall with a crossbow bolt in his forehead, and Joe Jefferson and I nailed one each with our .45s.

Then I took careful aim—right between Glenda Rogers-Gracey's eyes. But just before I squeezed off the shot, Glenda's head wobbled, her eyes rolled back in her head, and she pitched forward into the pile of rags on the steel table. I looked around for another target. What the hell, it's not polite too shoot a woman who's fainted.

Lo Fang held up the tablet again and howled at Entimemseph. The mummy tossed aside his empty guard and turned back toward Bukhovna, even took a faltering step in the old man's direction.

But in that instant Bukhovna seemed suddenly to *grow*—just as he'd done in his study. He raised his arms apart and shouted to Lo Fang in Yiddish.

"Host of the Darkness! Lord of the Empty Places! Father of Shadows! Go! Your master calls you. There is nothing for you here. Go! Or die the death . . ."

The mummy growled with rage and made a lunge for Bukhovna. One step was all he took, then he shrieked in pain and stumbled back. Lo Fang snarled at Bukhovna and raised the tablet high, but the old man made a quick stiff-armed gesture toward the Key. It began to glow brightly; first yellow, then cherry-red, then blue, then white. Suddenly it leaped out of Lo Fang's paws, seemed to tumble slowly through space, smashed against the corner of a heavy brick column . . . and shattered into a dozen jagged pieces. Lo Fang wailed in despair. He scrabbled over to the pillar and began scooping up the fragments.

"You kike! You Jew! You dirty sheenie fuck!" he squealed shrilly as he grabbed at the precious shards.

"Be gone, Children of the Night!" Bukhovna bellowed. His voice was inhumanly loud, more an explosion than a shout. The stones around us shook with it, and gritty mortar sifted down from the ceiling onto my face. "Back to Gehenna! Back to the Dark Mother's womb!"

The dwarf and the giant both tumbled away before that voice's power. But they clambered to their feet almost instantly and ran. The mummy was a blur of speed, but Lo Fang was faster. He disappeared into the gloom, still hunched and clutching his ruined treasure. The mummy pounded after him.

We leaped from our hiding places, all the relatively good guys: Joe, Ruvon, his men, and me. We tumbled past Bukhovna, into the darkness.

"Wait!" Bukhovna shouted.

When we stopped and looked back, he was just an old man surrounded by shadows, weighed down by the darkness, old and frail and bone-weary from all he'd done.

"*Lozim gayen,*" he muttered, and then in English, "Let them both go. Enough for tonight. There's nothing more we can do now."

Outside, from the manicured crest of the lawn I could see the U-boat in the channel. It had already come about and was steaming away. Joe Jefferson and I walked beside Bukhovna and Ruvon as we made our way to the car.

"We lost," I said. "After all that, we lost. But I suppose it could be worse. Tell me I'm right."

"How so, Mr. Underhill?" asked Bukhovna.

I nodded at the channel. "There goes Lo Fang with the mummy, alive and kicking. But the Key . . . you were able to break its power. You broke it, too."

"As for the tablet, a tube of crockery glue will mend it quite nicely. The Key could be pounded into a million pieces without affecting its strength in the slightest."

"You beat Lo Fang, Key or no Key."

"Only for the present." He frowned. "Only because he doesn't fully know how to use the Key's power. Yet. But he has acquired the perfect tutor."

"Entimemseph."

"Of course. I'm sure Lo Fang will be a quick study. Regrettably quick. And there is one aspect of the Key's power that he will discover very quickly."

"Should I ask?"

"The more the Key is used . . . the more powerful it becomes."

We walked in silence for a moment, while I digested that unpleasant morsel.

"Will Lo Fang head for the reich now?" I finally asked.

Bukhovna glanced back toward the channel.

"It certainly seems logical, doesn't it?" he mused. But then he shook his head. "Somehow . . . I doubt it. No. Not yet. I think his plans are still centered on this part of the world. He hopes to cause a great deal of harm here."

"Any idea what his plans might be?"

"Not really. At least . . . nothing worth discussing."

His tone told me not to waste my time asking again.

"Your candor with me is certainly gratifying," I drawled.

"I see no need to burden you with idle speculation. And as far as that goes, you can hardly claim you've been totally candid with me."

"For instance?"

"For instance how did you and your colleague happen to be here tonight? Who told you where Lo Fang had gone?"

"Your daughter told me," I said.

"Don't toy with me," he snapped bitterly.

"I'm not."

"I told you I have no daughter, Mr. Underhill. My daughter has been dead for thirty-three years. Rachel . . . I buried her in Prague. She was so beautiful, so . . ."

And then he understood.

He gasped and stumbled against me, clutching me for support. I held his arm.

"I . . . I should have known. He found her grave; he raised her. He made her one of his . . . his . . . Where is she, Mr. Underhill? Where is my baby? Where *is* she, goddamn you!"

He grabbed both my arms and shook me. Weakly.

"Tell me," he sobbed softly. "I just want . . . just let me see her once more."

But he knew it wasn't possible.

"No," I said. "She's free now. She's going back . . . where she belongs."

It hadn't taken much time at all.

Manhattan was still dark, and as near to asleep as it ever gets, when we rolled off the Triborough Bridge onto 125th Street. I pulled up in front of Velma's to let Joe out. He hadn't said a word during the entire trip.

"They aren't finished yet," he muttered to the windshield as I eased the Packard into neutral.

"Hmm?"

"The bodies in the morgue. I got more on the way."

"Maybe, maybe not. We thinned out the bloodsucker population pretty well back there. Things might just quiet down for a while."

"You believe that?"

"Nope."

"You owe me a fin, Underhill."

"Huh?"

"The bet. You owe me a fin."

"Take it out of my first consultation check."

"Got a better idea. How's about double or nothing the next time you go to a party?"

I let my hand disappear in the paw he offered.

Joe got out and I headed for home.

She was still sitting on the couch, with her back to the open terrace door. The moon had set and she was encircled only by morning stars, but I could see her quite plainly.

"Is it over?" she whispered.

"Over," I said. "Everything's fine."

"Entimemseph?"

"Lo Fang still has him. But he can't do any harm. Your father broke Lo Fang's power. And he destroyed the Key."

Some of that was possibly true.

"Lo Fang?"

"Gone. Gone for good," I said, even though I knew it was a lie.

"Kiss me, Jimmy."

I did. I sat beside her and kissed her until I was spinning dizzily through a black space I wished would go on forever. But it needed to end. I tried to pull away from her and couldn't, had to wait until she pulled away from me. As I trusted she would.

"How long have you known . . . what I am?" she asked.

"I suspected right after the fight outside the bar. When I pulled the crucifix out of that hand. But I didn't know for sure until tonight. Until your father told me about you."

She stiffened in my arms. "He knows?"

"No. He doesn't know anything, really. He only told me you were dead."

Lies. Too many lies. Why do we always tell lies to the dying?

"Why aren't you afraid of me, Jimmy?" she asked gently.

"I don't think I have any reason to be, Rachel. I think you want more from me than blood."

Of course there was still the crucifix and garlic around my neck.

"Do you want to see what I . . . what I look like?"

"If you need to show me," I shrugged.

"I do. *Look!*" she said, in a voice suddenly deep and chilling, and even farther away than the grave.

Her eyes flashed, as red as the blood she craved, as red as the cold flame of undeath. She opened her mouth and her teeth were daggers, savage, glistening, cruel. Ravenous.

"Am I as horrid as the other ones, Jimmy?" she said in the same deathless tone.

"No, Rachel," I said calmly. "You're different. You were always different from the rest of his slaves. That's why you're here now."

That was true, too. Her face changed, and Rachel was back with me again. A single crimson tear welled at the corner of her eye. It felt good to have said something true to her, and to have her be soothed by it. So much better than soothing her with lies.

"There's something else I want from you first," she said.

She reached up and loosened whatever had been holding her gown on her shoulders. It slid away, and she was white and perfect in the starlight.

"It's all right, Jimmy," she said. "Really it is. I couldn't do anything to hurt you."

I was pretty sure I believed her. But if I was wrong, I didn't care. And if you've ever wanted anyone as much as I wanted her at that moment, you know what I mean. I leaned over and kissed her lips, her neck, her firm, perfect breasts. As soft as flesh, as cold as stone. So delicious. And strange.

"Quick, Jimmy! *Quick!*" she whispered. "I can feel it now. It'll be here too soon!"

The dawn.

"No, not too soon," I said.

I kissed her then, long and deeply.

"The cross . . . the rest of it . . . You have to take them off, darling," she whispered. "Don't worry, I won't . . ."

But I was already unfastening them.

We kissed again and she took me inside her. We rolled together, and it was so good.

Better than ever.

And when we were through I kissed her again and held her tightly, so tightly and in a way she would not be able to escape, no matter what.

We watched the dawn begin together.

"Oh my God, Jimmy!" she gasped. "It hurts! Oh God, it hurts so much."

She moaned with the pain and tried to wriggle free; and in the end, I needed the garlic, power of the earth, and the cross, cruel symbol of a tortured god. But I did what she wanted, and she could not get away.

The dawn's red fingers clawed into the room; the deadly sun slashed over her face. Smooth, pale flesh peeled away, cracked, shattered.

Brown, dried leaves; twigs, brittle, dead.

Rachel screamed again, a lost, horrible scream, very long. But it seemed to cut off in the middle, in the center of her pain.

By the time the sunlight covered me fully, I was alone, surrounded by a pile of dust.

Outside in the heartless morning brightness, the world was busy dying. And for a while I sat and cried.

BOOK TWO

The Traveler's Dream

Tho thou art Worship'd by the Names Divine
Of Jesus & Jehovah, thou art still
The Son of Morn in weary Night's decline,
The lost Traveler's Dream under the Hill.

—William Blake

After that morning with Rachel I decided to take a short rest cure, a change of scenery; not to put too fine a point on it, a vacation in a bottle. It didn't work. I tried my level best to think happy thoughts, to manufacture them, in fact. But I kept on replaying everything that had happened instead, over and over and . . . Enough.

To tell this tale in order, we're going to have to backtrack a bit. And we might as well take this opportunity, while Underhill staggers off in search of the elusive stupor, to observe an unpleasant drama unfolding far from the highways and byways and alleyways of Gotham; in the Tellenburgh railway station, Geneva, Switzerland, about six months before all we've seen so far.

Picture this, if you will . . .

Conductors bellow over steamy blasts of air brakes; loud-speakers echo in languages no one understands; a whistle of departure wails, then one of arrival, and finally a third, fluttering grimy pigeons from their roost in the bare girders high above.

The Tellenburgh is mobbed, and there are few contented faces in the purposefully milling crowd, no smiles except of sadness, no laughter except of pain.

Families from the north and the east stand stunned in the shafts of sooty light filtering through opaque windows beyond the black iron rafters, surrounded by their bundled lives, the few pathetic possessions they have been allowed to carry away.

There are hundreds of them in the billowing swirls, swaddled in the reeks of steam and disinfectant and fear, Czechs and Slovakians and Austrians and Jews, not yet daring to believe what their presence here proves: that for the time being at least, they have wriggled through the nets of death, that on this particular day and in this particular place, they are not to be cursed or beaten or killed.

They detrain clumsily, count baggage and children, search train windows for familiar faces, bicker in tense whispers, a fugitive herd, dressed in travel-soiled browns and grays, trailing the tatters of yesterday's terror.

One couple stands out.

The man is old, tall and frail and gray, aristocratic, handsome, heartbroken. The woman is years younger, just past girlhood, and just over the threshhold from pretty into beautiful. Her hair is black, her eyes are large and piercing blue, her cheekbones high and prominent, like his.

The old man is calm—sadly, curiously at peace amid the thronging chaos. He lifts his head, seems to gaze far beyond the choked railway station.

At last he shakes himself, looks down at the woman, speaks in a musical Austrian dialect, in a low, gentle voice only she can hear.

"It . . . will either happen today, or on May 4, 1974. In . . . in Tampa Bay, Florida, of all places."

He considers his own words with mildly amused surprise. But the woman's eyes widen in fear and she digs her nails into his arms, clutches at him and buries her face in his chest. He pats her hair soothingly, then pushes her back and smiles.

"Can you tend to the baggage, darling? They *will* lose the trunk with the workbooks if they are given even the slightest encouragement."

The old man's smile freezes as he sees what is coming,

reflected in the woman's staring eyes. He whirls around to meet it, she screams piercingly, still clutching at him. An engine whistle just beside them shrieks; a stubby shotgun barrel is jammed up under his chin, in the crook between his jaw and throat.

The grinning man in the slouch hat and leather trench coat snarls a soundless, "Heil Hitler!"

And squeezes the trigger.

The explosion is deafening even though it is muffled by the old man's flesh. His whole body is lifted up and back, into the screaming woman. His face rips aside from the jaw-line, revealing a hideous mask of red meat and bone that totters for just a moment atop his shoulders, then topples away in a spout of blood.

The woman is still screaming long after the train whistle stops, long after she and he have tumbled onto the filthy, blackened concrete. His headless corpse slumps away and she lays there wailing beside him.

And no one in the circling crowd dares to touch her, because her face and chest are completely painted with gore and her screaming mouth is filled with blood, and they have no way of knowing that all the blood is her father's.

I missed large portions of the spring, summer, and fall that year. A pity really, because I hear they were very beautiful. Then again, I also managed to be unavailable for comment on the day der Fuehrer dropped the other boot and actually invaded Poland. Ditto for the day France and England woke up, smelled the coffee, and declared war on the reich. Too little, too late. The trickle was already a torrent, and soon the whole damned world would be awash in red.

Ah, me.

If I'd had the courage of my convictions I could have cleaned up at the books, betting on just how lousy France and England's chances were against the Wermacht. Couldn't do it, though. Betting on people's stupidity is about as sporting as shooting large fish in a small barrel.

With a sawed-off shotgun.

But let us now take up the strands of this narrative, on a grim, gray Manhattan afternoon smack dab in the middle of winter. Meet me at my office, 49th Street just off Broadway; and dress warmly, the boiler's broken.

It was Christmas week.

Blaire had just left. After a solid afternoon of listening to her shivering and bitching, bitching and shivering, I had sent her home early. To be more accurate, I had threatened her with mayhem if she didn't vacate the premises.

I stood in the new and blessed silence, peering out of my window between the *s* and the *U* in "James Underhill, Investigations, Inc." The dear girl would be having a bit of inconvenience on her walk from the elevated to her home in Sunnyside, I noted without excessive concern. A wet, sloppy snow had just started to fall on the Square, covering its crowds and cars and buses and trollies, its billboards and marquees, all its pathetic attempts at Yuletide Good Cheer with a sticky, sugary glaze of white and gray.

Big fat flakes and falling fast.

Directly across from my seventh-floor office, the crowds were thicker, and they appeared to be moving more purposefully than elsewhere. I heard a drumbeat, then an incoherent chant, all muffled by the snow. I squinted and saw the flash of an illegible placard on a stick.

The explanation came to me all too quickly. Madison Square Garden was just down the block. What I was looking at was a group of stragglers from the German-American Nazi Bund rally in progress, I now recalled, at the Garden this very moment. And filling the joint to the rafters.

Merry Christmas, dirty Nazi bastards, soiling the gutters of my beloved Times Square.

I reflected for the thousandth time on how few encouragements to sobriety the world seemed to provide these days, slid my fingers into my jacket and let the tips caress the butt of my .45 Webley in its shoulder rig. I strongly considered the possibility of taking it out for an airing.

Perhaps it was the tension induced by thoughts of what I would have dearly loved to do at that moment; perhaps it was the unvoiced memory of similar desires I had indeed acted upon in other times and places. I'm not usually the skittish sort—at least not to the point of whipping out my gat just because someone opens my office door without knocking first.

But that's what I did just then. And found myself standing in the two-hand fire position with my roscoe aimed right between Gina's big blue eyes.

"Compliments, compliments," Gina drawled. "And how are *you* today, Mr. Underhill? Long time no see."

"Fine, thanks. And yourself?" I grumbled, while stowing the gat as casually as possible.

"Could be better, since you ask," she said. "The weather's revolting, I'm going to be hopelessly late for my Sardi's meeting with Busby, which I *cannot* afford to be, thank you, and coming over here the streets were absolutely *choked* with horrible people. Those disgusting mobs at the Garden!"

She made a comically disgusted face, managing—a typical Gina trick—to continue to look ravishingly beautiful while she did so. Then for a change of pace she tossed a long, golden lock out of her eyes and flashed me her very best Glamour Queen angle.

And without dropping a beat, she threw the door shut, tossed her purse in the general direction of my hatrack, trotted over to the window where I stood, and lifted her face to be kissed.

What a performance; what a gal.

Gina was wearing very high-heeled pumps, but she was still quite a bit shorter, it always tickled me to note, than she appeared to be on the silver screen. She looked just as pretty, prettier actually, in full color; but real-life Gina was not the long, tall, slinky vamp she often played.

Despite her petite size, a whole army of minks had undoubtedly marched on to glory for the sake of the thick coat that swathed her from her alabaster neck to her slender ankles. Good minks, too, the shiny, pricey-looking kind.

Her blond hair glowed like gold against the fur.

Gina smelled very delicious and very expensive. I leaned

around, to kiss her on the cheek in deference to Aristotle—
her husband, not the philosopher, although anyone who
stayed married to Gina had to be something of a philosopher—but Gina grabbed my chin between two fingers and
made a moue of displeasure.

"Don't be such a weisenheimer, Underhill," she grumbled.

She kissed me on the mouth and her lips were soft and
firm and sweet as ever. I was trying to keep it short, but Gina
gave a whimper like an annoyed puppy, grabbed my hair,
and made it long and hard. The kiss, that is. She was still
swaddled in her mink, and when I ran my hands over her,
the fur was cool and slick and damp with the snow.

Oh, what the hey, Aristotle *was* a philosopher.

Besides, as I believe I mentioned near the start of this
narrative, Gina and I went back a ways. If I hadn't gotten
lucky and managed to remove her pretty mug from a certain
frame some few years prior, she and that shipping magnate
hubby of hers would never have met, or fallen in love, or
married.

With our lips still locked, I reached up to undo the top
stay of her mink, and winked one eye open to scout a good
landing spot. The couch had a spring poking through, but
Gina would look fine against the green leather. Besides, we
could put the fur on the . . .

Gina wiggled out of my arms, grinning like an imp.

"Well, well, James!" she chirped. "Nice to see things
aren't quite as bad as I heard. The way Blaire talked, I was
afraid you were totally gone."

"Very goddamn funny, Gina."

"Now, now, honey. Don't take life so seriously. Blaire
said that, too. That you're just not the same fun-loving Jimmy
anymore. You remember him . . . the one who used to return
my phone calls every now and then? So. Let's get down to
business."

"Fine, Gina. Terrific idea. Park your mink and stay awhile.
Just toss it anywhere."

I gestured around the office and smiled nastily, because if
Gina could find a tidy spot she'd be doing worlds better than

me. Cleaning is not Blaire's strong suit.

Gina snuggled deeper into her fur.

"Thanks anyway, but it's colder in here than a polar bear's hindquarters. What's the matter? Forget to pay your heating bill?"

"It's included in the rent. Which I'm also forgetting to pay until the rat landlord fixes the boiler. And speaking of forgetting . . . I've already deduced why you're *not* here. Do you happen to recall why you did drop by?"

"Well, as it happens, I have a job for you."

"Sorry, Gina. Dance card's full."

"No it's not, sweets. Blaire and I had a nice long chat. By the way, she says to remind you payday was last week."

"And I thought she came to work for love."

"We all come here for love, Jimmy. But you of all people . . . you should know how unreasonable those landlords can be."

"Okay, Gina. What's up?"

"Such enthusiasm. Don't worry, Jimmy. You're going to love this one. It's so far up your alley it's in your kitchen. Does the name Rolf Steiner ring a bell?"

"*Doctor* Rolf Steiner. Only you could ask that. Remember? I read the papers."

Steiner was an Austrian scientist and philosopher. World famous and brilliant—known as much for his writings on occultism and psychic phenomena as he was for his sculpture, his poetry, his architecture. Oh, and his developments in theoretical physics. Albert Einstein said of Steiner, "He is the only man in this world who understands relativity more deeply than he who wrote the theory."

Not anymore, though.

"What did you read?" Gina asked.

"Tellenburgh Station. Eleven months ago. Some jokers walked up to Steiner and gave him a facelift with a sawed-off shotgun."

But you already knew that.

Gina winced, and I saw her eyes get very damp, very quickly. I brilliantly deduced it was time to watch my mouth.

"Do you know who killed him?" she asked. Her voice was strained, like she was wrestling hard to keep a sob down where it belonged.

I nodded my head.

"Well, so do I, Jimmy, even if I don't read the papers. Rolf Steiner used to call Hitler 'Satan's corporal.' He called the Nazis lots worse too. Uncle Rolf knew all about them, Jimmy. *Secret* things. And he told the world what he knew. That's why they . . . they did what they did to him."

"Back up, Gina," I said gently. "What's this 'uncle' business? Your press agent says you're a nice corn-fed gal from Wisconsin."

"Who used to spend her summers at Mama's sister's farm in the Austrian Alps. Where Dr. Rolf Steiner was an honored guest. He was so . . . so special. Uncle Rolf loved it there, Jimmy. And everybody loved him."

"Yeah, well, almost everybody," I said. "So what's the rest of it? You don't want me to find Steiner's killers. They're already found. And you don't want me to take care of them. They're not take-care-of-able. At least not yet, they're not. What's the story?"

"The story is Clara Steiner. Rolf's daughter. She came here right after Uncle Rolf died. To live with us. I insisted on it. Ari insisted, actually; he's such a darling. . . . We both knew Europe just wasn't safe for her anymore."

"And?"

"And now I don't think New York's safe for her, either."

"Got some dirty details?"

"Nothing yet." Gina frowned. "If I did, I'd have woken you up weeks ago. But you know me, Jimmy. I'm not the hysterical type. You can believe what I'm saying. Clara's being followed. We go out to a gallery, a shop, a matinee . . . I never actually *see* anybody. But there's one thing I'll tell you. I haven't gotten to the ripe old age of twenty-six by not knowing when I'm being tailed."

I held up my hand.

"Embarrassing question . . . possible *you're* the one being tailed? Maybe hubby's keeping tabs. I hear Greeks are jealous.''

''Aristotle? No soap. First off, you know damn well he's no Othello. Believe me, we shook hands on it way before we tied the knot. Second, my thumbs only itch when I'm with Clara. I . . . *we* are being followed, Jimmy.''

''Okay then, next question. Have you considered telling hubby about all this? I'll bet he has . . . ways and means for dealing with unwanted admirers.''

''Of course I've told him, Jimmy. And we both agreed we should get the best man for the job.''

She smiled sweetly and blew me a kiss.

''Why do I not feel complimented?'' I grumbled.

''Why? Because the new, improved Jimmy Underhill is mainly a lazy booze hound who'd rather suck on a bottle than do a dishonest day's work. That's why, hon. Simple as that.''

''Nothing's simple as that,'' I muttered, even though it was. ''So what's Clara Steiner's line on all this?''

''Uh-uh.'' She frowned. ''Clara hasn't noticed a thing, and I haven't said a peep. It's a ground rule. We say as little as possible to Clara.''

''Why?''

''Why? Because when they found Clara Steiner she was lying on the floor of a train station and holding her father and screaming and she had his blood and his brains all over her face. D-do you *hear* me, Jimmy? Do you . . . do you hear what those dirty fucking bastards did to my . . . my . . . ?''

She burst out crying.

So I put my arms around her and held her and kissed her pretty head and sort of rocked her standing up. After a while she stopped and blotted her face on my jacket.

It wasn't what she said next, but the way she said it, that made me feel like tiny spiders with icy feet were doing the Cakewalk up and down my spine. Gina spoke very, very quietly.

''All I want from you is information, Jimmy. Find out

who's on her tail, and find out if they're the same ones who hurt Uncle Rolf. That's all. I'll take it from there.''

"Is that what Aristotle says?''

"That's what *I* say.''

"One last one for now. Do you happen to remember when it started . . . the first time you got the willies about this?''

"A girl always remembers her first time. Three . . . no, four weeks ago. Ari was in Caracas and we were on our way home from a private Happy Holidays bash at Le Bistro d'Or. You know, Maurice Chen's joint?''

Sure, I knew Maurice Chen: the poisoner. You remember him, too. If you don't, thumb to my interview with Glenda Rogers-Gracey.

Back yet?

"I know Chen. At least I know of him. I also know a good buddy of his.''

"Glenda? Small world, isn't it? Remember? What'd I tell you about her? And isn't it funny how Maurice Chen's been calling Clara up a lot lately? Practically courting her. They've only been out in large crowds so far, so I haven't really been able to warn her yet. There's nothing really to *say* about him. At least not without upsetting her. Clara's smart. Sharp as nails. But in a lot of ways she's just a babe in the woods. So pretty, too. The guys really go for her.''

"Oh, do they?''

"Jimmy, *you* keep you damn hands off her!'' she snapped. "We're not playing shares-ies with this one. Clara is not for you. Get it?''

Hmm. I believe I did. I raised my eyebrows. But while I could think of lots of replies, I couldn't think of any that weren't better left unsaid. So I shifted to more relevant, less volatile matters.

"Maurice and Glenda. I wonder if they have the same taste in clothes and accessories. You know, brown shirts, twisted crosses . . .''

Gina kissed her fingertip and pressed it to my lips.

"Darling?'' she cooed sweetly. "Can't we please stop

talking about this now? Like I said, just find out what's going on.''

It was as though her crying—and her outburst of jealousy, had never happened. I kissed her fingertip away.

''In other words, I've agreed to take the case.''

''Of course. I even brought your down payment. . . . God, it's gotten stuffy in here . . .''

Gina undid the top clasp of her mink. And the rest of them too. Then she peeled back the curtains and let me see what she was wearing besides her fur and her very high heeled pumps.

You guessed it. Not a blessed stitch.

Gina's breasts, or breasts exactly like Gina's, were once described by Solomon in song as being ''like two young does which feed among the lilies,'' by which I think the old gent meant to say: large, firm, warm, delicious.

I wonder if the set of does he was using as reference were also milky white and perfumed and sweet and tipped with pretty pink thimbles. . . .

Gina's belly was just ever so slightly rounded; her tuft as golden as her tresses.

But I couldn't help being concerned for the dear girl.

''Uh, Gina? Aren't you just a wee bit underdressed for Sardi's?''

I realized I was worrying needlessly, though. Gina's limo was undoubtedly idling downstairs. If I recalled correctly, it had venetian blinds on the windows. An old trouper like Gina would have to be tops at quick-change.

''Uh, Jimmy? Why don't you just count your blessings and keep your mouth shut?''

She reached up and twined her fingers in my hair. ''Hmmm. On second thought . . . keep it open.''

And she pushed me and she pulled me till she had me right where she wanted. It was chilly on the floor, even lying on the fur. But Gina's thighs made the softest, the silkiest, the warmest earmuffs a guy could ever hope for.

Afterward, when Gina was rewrapped in her mink and

prepared for departure, she handed me a small, embossed envelope. Small, but thick.

"This part of your down payment's from Ari," she said. She kissed me on the mouth, sniffed and grinned.

"Mmm. I taste good," she giggled.

Then she kissed me again, and whispered, "Jimmy? You take care of this for me, like I said. But . . . be careful, Jimmy, huh? We . . . we want you around for a while. Don't want to lose you. Know what I mean?"

I reached up my hand, touched her hair and her smooth cheek. She trembled ever so slightly, and closed her eyes. Then she grabbed my head and crushed her cheek against mine and pulled my hair and kissed me *hard*, almost angrily. As if she was trying not to say something. Then she pushed away and got the hell out.

Gina.

Christmas is just a matter of opinion on Times Square; and for the local heroes it was business as normal, that grim, gray holiday evening. I made some rounds, paid some respects, let it be known I was in the market for information concerning a certain Mr. Maurice Chen, he whose fancy, frog chop-shop was a mere hop, skip and a heave from forty-deuce, up on 55th and Eighth.

No dice; or at least almost none. But I did discover that while Le Bistro d'Or was Chen's cash cow, his base of operations was in his other eatery, the Mandarin Palace, down on the fringes of Chinatown, far and away from the all-seeing eyes, the all-hearing ears, the all-sniffing muzzles of the Times Square information industry.

The information industry, by the way, is very egalitarian. The fact of my asking questions about Maurice Chen would, naturally, become a commodity in itself. It would be sold to the highest bidder, if bidders existed; or, a customer might be solicited, if only the keepers of the knowledge could figure out who might find it valuable. In other words, by announcing my curiosity I was baiting my traps . . . with pure haunch of Underhill.

Yes, I know I could have arranged an introduction and interview with Mr. Chen easy as pie, through Gina. But doing so would not have satisfied my present goal, which was to speak with Chen and yet not have him sure of who had hired me or what I wanted to discover. I like simplicity; it suits my intelligence quotient. But asking Gina to introduce us would have been a tad too simple and direct. As clumsy, say, as calling up Chen's bosom buddy, Glenda Rogers-Gracey, and asking her to introduce us.

Hmm. On second thought . . . but no.

Although I'd had no contact with Glenda since I'd crashed her party those many months ago, I suspected I was not high up on her list of favorite persons. At least I hadn't found any presents from her under my tree. It just shows how ungrateful people can be. I'd done quite a lot for Glenda: administered a sorely needed corrective spanking, refrained from shooting her in the head, murdered only a few of her henchmen. . . .

I baited the traps and called it a night.

The next day I visited the Square again, to check those traps. And got nothing for my troubles. Not a single hapless morsel of knowledge had wandered into the snare, which meant it was time for some direct action, a visit to a certain downtown acquaintance of mine.

A winter's night in Chinatown.

The air was hot and cold, sweet and sour. Kitchen fans blasted the dying ecstasies of roasting pigs and soy-steamed carp out onto the frozen streets. Exotic garbage ripened in cans at the curb, fueled by an inner heat despite the chilly air. Neon flashed; garlic sizzled; street urchins yammered; smoked ducks danced and dangled in greasy windows, dripping onto trays of nameless entrails.

It took me all of five minutes to realize I was being followed.

I stopped in front of a dingy Canton herbalist on Mott and Bayard to window-shop, and examined my new admirers' reflection in the grimy glass. A pair of very unpleasant-looking Oriental characters they were, both over six feet tall, enormous for Asiatics. Their faces were obscured under wide-brimmed hats. Their muscles bulged and twitched impatiently beneath nondescript longshore outfits. Nice doggies.

They looked as if they'd been raised with plenty of big, juicy meat chunks in their fried rice. Raw chunks. I received the strong impression they were eagerly anticipating the use of my legs for a wishbone.

I started walking again; stopped at a shop with a counter open to the street, and studied its *bao* steamer. I ordered a plump, pale white bun, sprinkled soy and pepper sauces on it, and took a bite. Delicious. Thick, soft, dumplinglike dough, and in the bun's center . . . mmmm, yes, shredded barbecued pork.

The counterman put my change of a quarter down on the glass. When I took it, I managed to drop a nickel. I stooped to pick it up, used the opportunity to glance back at my fans.

One was lounging against an auto with his foot up on the running board; the other was standing beside him, rocking on his heels; both gazing casually about, as if they were just a pair of average Chinese Joes who had decided to stop in the middle of a cold, crowded street to admire the pleasant view. Very funny.

I started strolling again as I polished off my *bao*, and realized within moments that I had been dead wrong about being followed: "followed" is when you aren't supposed to know you have a tail. These characters were a positive escort.

No. Wrong again. They were shepherds. They said nothing, but every so often one would walk on ahead of me, stand at the corner of a street he had decided I shouldn't enter, blocking all sidewalk traffic just by his hulking presence, making sure I headed down some other, more congenial byway.

On such occasions I noticed something else about them; or rather, about the other people on the street. The passersby seemed to know my admirers. And how. This was Chinatown, and unseemly displays of emotion were unlikely. But if I had to find an adverb to describe the way the crowds cringed out of my admirers' path, "fearfully" would do quite nicely.

They were herding me out east, toward the darkness at the edge of Chinatown, the dead zone of warehouses and blind alleys and rotting tenements that separates Chinatown from the Lower East Side. As we crossed Chatham Square, I glanced to the right. Two blocks down—or an entire world away—I saw the object of my curiosity: Maurice Chen's Mandarin Palace Restaurant.

I wondered if Maurice was up on the observation deck, watching our parade through field glasses.

Then we entered the dead zone, and Chinatown disappeared from view. The goons had been giving me about forty yards of lead space. Now they closed it up to thirty. And they kept coming.

It was dark in the side streets after Chatham Square's whorey brightness. Yet I feared no evil. In fact, if you think I had been following my shepherds' unvoiced commands up to this point because I was afraid of them, you are mistaken. They were sure they had me cowed. But I could not wait to get the sons of bitches alone.

It was even worse than that: I was seeing those bloodred flashes at the edges of my vision, and I was hearing the roaring in my ears, and I kept needing to take long, deep restorative breaths of rotten garbage to remain calm. Yes. I was more than slightly annoyed.

It's the Falstaff in me. You know: "Upon compulsion? Not one iota." I just can't stand bosses, of any size, shape, class, race, or gender. Except Blaire of course, but she doesn't count. I also hate when people go changing the rules around without notifying me.

New rule: a private detective must not express interest in fashionable Oriental poisoners. If he does express such an interest, and worse yet, goes directly to Chinatown to satisfy it, why then a baboon platoon will be dispatched to permanently rearrange his skeletal structure.

Sure. Right.

Henry Street off of East Broadway was sad and empty, not the least bit touched by Christmas, or by Hanukkah either, for that matter. I ducked onto it while my pals were still twenty yards behind me, sprinted a few paces, then pivoted into an alleyway, flattened against the wall, and ripped my .45 out of its rig.

I heard no shouts, no pounding of leather on the frozen concrete, only the thump of naked, thickly callused feet. That should have been my first real clue, but it didn't register at the moment because, poor excuse, I was too busy choreographing my next move.

The fingertips of my left hand gripped the lip of the alleyway wall. And when the sounds of running feet were just close enough I spun my body out onto the sidewalk. My right arm was cocked, and I lashed it out as I spun, gun pommel first. Fan Number One never had a chance—he was running too fast.

The sharp-edged, steel gun butt cracked right into his big, ugly yap. The impact of the blow jolted painfully up my arm and rattled my brain, even though the shock was cushioned by his lips and teeth and jawbone all splitting, splintering, caving in. He staggered like a poleaxed pig, then wobbled toward the pavement gurgling and choking on the pulpy ruins of his face.

Just for good measure, I snap-kicked my heel into his right kneecap, and he dropped the rest of the way home like a wet sack of road apples.

I heard the vicious *vvvzzzzz!* Ever so fortunately, my back brain recognized the sound and took charge of my body, jerking my head to the left. A five-inch steel disk, a deadly star of scalpel-sharp teeth, came buzzing through the airspace my face had just vacated, slitting through my overcoat, my jacket's shoulder pad, and a quarter inch of my precious flesh as if they were just so much runny cheese.

Needless to say I didn't see the devil, but I heard it clattering in the alleyway behind me, and I recognized it at once. *Lin dai*, or "death flower," is one of its names.

It was my second clue, and it shouted so loudly and clearly, even I heard it. Suddenly, finally, I knew my two fans for what they were. *Dacoits*—trained assassins of the South Asian ritual murder society, the only killers who regularly use the death flower, who love to go barefoot when they close for the kill. In all kinds of weather.

Ask any British colonial officer, and he'll tell you dacoitry was wiped out decades ago. Which shows you how much British colonial officers know. I'd run into dacoits—literally, I'm afraid—much more recently. Still, my last encounter with the cult had been years ago and half a world away. Now I saw all the rumors of the cult's demise had not stopped it from migrating to America, the Land of Opportunity. It restored one's patriotic faith, in a way, but only a limited way.

I glommed a quick view of the world beyond the alley, got another flower for my troubles.

It grew quiet.

Then too quiet; even Fan Number One had finished choking on the pavement in front of me. I glanced down at him . . . and finally found the time to be very frightened.

I think it would have been fair to say he was clinically dead. Perhaps the smack in the chops had broken his neck, perhaps he had aspirated his own gore. Maybe both. He was writhing slowly, horribly, not like a living thing but as if in a speeded-up rigor mortis . . . a grotesque puppet on a string . . . a broken death machine. His hat was gone, and now I could see his face clearly for the first time.

No, not his face. His muzzle.

The dark fur began just above his black, beady eyes, bristled back over his sloping forehead. His ears were flat against his head, large and fleshy and pointed. His mouth . . . my gun butt had done less damage in the left corner of his mouth. His upper lip was curled away and as I looked at the unmangled section of his swollen, purple gums I saw the white tip of a dagger-sharp fang poke through, slither out of the gum flesh to its full, hideous two-inch length, then slide back in like a stiletto blade. His fur was doing it too; shimmering out across his muzzle, wriggling back through the pores to expose his pale, jaundiced flesh again.

In and out, with each spasm of his corpse.

My kidneys felt as if they had been dunked in ice water and all my body's major exits begged to be cleared for flight immediately. This was a new one on me. Oh, I knew what I was looking at, in general terms; I'd heard the rumors about the lower depths of dacoitry, and I'd heard them from so many separate sources I even suspected they were based on truth. The greatest dacoit masters, so say the rumors, can *change* the most willing and able of their adepts, can give them the ability to shape-shift into obscene creatures of legend—werewolves, of course, and other beasts, too.

I studied my friend on the floor, and wondered what in hell he was supposed to be. He didn't look like a wolf. Maybe a werebadger, or a werebaboon. Perhaps he'd just improvised, cobbled himself together, striving for a certain look he couldn't describe in words. . . .

My hysteria-fueled speculations were terminated by a seemingly insignificant, and yet extremely fortuitous occurrence: a humble wooden fence in the rear of the alleyway—*my* alleyway, as I'd come to think of it—was weathered enough to creak as a certain someone vaulted from it. Had it not creaked, that someone would probably have broken my back in his first leap, because he was very strong and very fast.

Fan Number Two.

But it did creak, and my back brain took over again, dropping me to the deck with such speed, Number Two went sailing completely over me. He hit the ground, bowled into his dead buddy, and with a great scrabbling of claws, bustled up into an attack crouch on his hands and naked feet.

He had torn away his shirt, and once again I found myself wondering what kind of a were he was. Not a wolf. Real wolves are much cleaner limbed and more handsome than the distorted halfling hunched snarling before me.

Clumped, mottled fur, barrel chest, thick apish arms . . . he looked as if he'd been forced to shape-shift too quickly, and hadn't done a careful job of it. Perhaps that was indeed the case, and it was uncharitable of me to criticize his appearance when he hadn't had the time to look his very best.

But I hadn't asked him to leave home without checking to see if his seams were straight, and I wasn't feeling particularly charitable at the moment. I wasn't feeling very sporting either, and I didn't give a good goddamn if I woke up the neighbors.

I leveled my cannon just as he jumped at me, and pulled off a blast. The explosion clogged my ears; the dumdum slug caught him in midair and spun him around, punched through his chest and ripped up his lungs like a diesel-powered eggbeater.

That's what I like about dumdums.

I gave him two more in the trunk; then I watched as he wriggled around on the filthy pavement, snarling at me and snapping at his own intestines noodling out of the two enormous, ragged exit holes in his side and striving with all his twisted being to get to me and kill me, even though he, like his pal, was already clinically dead.

I suppose the same hideous strength, the black, berserk frenzy that gives such hateful creatures their power to shapeshift, also makes it difficult for them to lay down and die. I decided to see if I could be of service. I stepped up to him and blew the top of his skull off.

It did calm him down, so I gave his buddy the same treatment, for good luck. Then I stowed my gat and slapped a handkerchief onto my nicked shoulder under the jacket, so the blood wouldn't soak through. It wasn't my best suit, but it wasn't cheesecloth, either. Maybe I could get a tailor to reweave the material. For the moment, I was content just to amble back to Chinatown. I was pretty sure I'd earned the right to ask some questions in peace. Even if they were about Mr. Maurice Chen.

I dusted myself off, stepped over the bodies, and headed up the street.

At first I thought, she's their mother, and when she sees what I've done to her boys she's going to be miffed. She was standing at the edge of the street's single pool of lamplight, watching me with regal calm—and with every fiber of her being.

Then, terrified though I was, so terrified I was weary with fear . . . I still recall holding the thought, ''But she's too beautiful to have given birth to them.''

An enormous, silver timber wolf, unquestionably a female, twice the size of any wolf I'd ever seen. Her muzzle was on a level with my chest. Her eyes were emerald green, and they glowed with an impossible light. I prayed the glow was only a reflection of the streetlamp. But I knew it wasn't.

Something in those eyes. My knees wobbled, and I knew it was time to take out my gun and shoot her, but I could hardly lift my arms at all, to say nothing of drawing and firing.

She left the circle of light, came flying to me down the street as quickly as a murderous thought, more quickly than things of this world can really move. And I knew she was only a dream.

But her paws smashed into my chest and I tumbled down into the gutter, near the two changelings I'd just dispatched. It was all a dance, so slow and graceful, the night spinning away, her impossible eyes paralyzing me . . . she stepped over the corpses, kicked them away with a backward shuffle of her hind paws to show her contempt.

I tried to get up, but it wasn't a possibility. She straddled me, loomed over me, silver and sparkling against the night. I smelled the musk of her fur, pungent and sweet. Wild. Her muzzle curled back. I saw wet, glistening white teeth big as daggers. And then her muzzle dipped toward my throat. Her breath steamed against my face in panting clouds, tinged with an alien spice; her eyes never left mine. I made a last, hopeless attempt to turn my face away.

"Hold still, damn you! Don't you dare move!"

Her vicious thoughts roared in my mind. Words of the beast—soundless, undeniable. She stared through me as her fangs locked onto the flesh of my throat. Gently, gently her daggers held me, as though holding a child.

She blinked; her eyes glowed through the membranous lids. Her daggers sunk through my flesh. Slowly. I felt her warm, rough tongue lapping my blood. She growled softly, musically, from deep inside her, a growl of very great pleasure. Surprised pleasure.

"Delicious. You are delicious, my darling! So good!"

And then she *ripped* my throat open! For one horrible moment I saw my own blood gleaming on her fangs. She lifted her head and howled with joy.

And bounded off into the night.

The chains were gone. I rolled over in the filthy gutter, clutching at my throat to hold back the blood, and managed to push up onto my knees and free hand. I stared down at the cobblestones beneath me, observed the thin, black stream of liquid washing them. The stream began between my fingers, at my throat.

I recall thinking, I'd always suspected I'd end up something like this. Bleeding to death in a gutter: not a particularly glamorous way to go, but nothing I had any particular right to be surprised about, either.

The stream from my neck became a trickle; a drip. And stopped.

A wave of nausea took me, a hideous chill. A shiver racked my whole body. If this was dying, it was too damned uncomfortable. I decided I might as well get up and walk around until I dropped. At least I'd be warmer. I pushed up into a crouch, straightened my back, pushed up further, and stood. The night reeled around me: buildings, streetlamp, sky, street, corpses, buildings, streetlamp, sky. . . . I shook my head and things steadied a bit. I started walking. At first I walked aimlessly, but when peregrination for its own sake became tedious, I decided to set myself a goal.

The Beekman Hospital Emergency Ward seemed as good a first stop as any.

I looked quite the mess by the time I got to Beekman, all bedecked in blood and grime. But two crisp twenty-dollar bills convinced the sleepy intern on duty to shut up and sew me up and not ask too many stupid questions, which is to say, questions a man with bite marks on his throat, tears in his suit, and a .45 in his armpit would be unlikely to answer the second time you asked, if he hadn't already answered the first time.

Those twenties inspired so much generosity of spirit in the intern, he even called a taxicab for me and made sure I got into it, after he'd finished his tailoring job on my throat.

It was long past midnight when the taxi pulled up in front of my building. Ernst the night doorman was on duty, and he came out to open the door for me. He knew I didn't appreciate such ceremonies, but he also knew that when I took more than a certain amount of time to exit from a taxi—especially in the evening—there was a better than even chance I was taking a snooze in the backseat. A fellow could get rolled.

Although I had tidied my clothes as much as possible and pulled my collar up around my neck, Ernst immediately noticed the soiled state of the former, the bandaged state of the latter. And the woozy state of yours truly: The intern had given me my money's worth of painkillers.

"You are having a difficult night, Käpitan Unterhill?" he asked mildly. I never could get him to stop calling me captain, and at the moment I was too looped to try.

"Just a bit, Lieutenant, just a bit," I answered in slurred German. "But I am very happy to finally be home."

"I imagine so." He chuckled.

Ernst had been a lieutenant in Spain. His story was part of the bigger story everyone was so busily trying to forget in those days. So I'll tell you about Ernst, the doorman, while he helps me to the elevator.

Ernst came to Spain like all of us, with the International Brigades; in his case it was the Thaelmann Battalion. That's what the antifascist Germans called themselves, after the German labor leader whom the Nazis had recently thrown into their arrest-torture-murder mill. Ernst and his comrades were the first of the International Brigades to charge into the Battle of Madrid.

They were something to see. Ernst had been an alpinist in his student days. During the fighting around the University City complex on the outskirts of Madrid, I watched him lead his men in a human fly number: They climbed straight up the walls of the Instituto del Rubio with their rifles on their backs and their *armas blancas*—their bayonets—in their teeth. They fought their way down from the roof, beat back the fascist Moroccan Tabors floor by floor, and kicked them the hell out of the building. Quite a piece of work Ernst did.

And he did another piece of work a few years later, after most all the Thaelmann Battalion had been wiped out, after the International Volunteers had been sent home, after the death of the Republic. When he was one of the few of us left alive in Spain.

In the bull ring near the Casa de Campo, the fascists had been killing prisoners so quickly that by the end of the first day the blood was pooling six inches deep in the gutters. But not so quickly that hundreds weren't left in the stands for hours, waiting their turn to die. Ernst decided not to wait. Night fell, and he slipped up to the last rows at the top of the ring—and over the top and down the sheer wall and out of Spain and over the great waters—to a new line of work in the City of New York.

Now Ernst has gotten me to the elevator.

"I said Miss Regina called," is what he was saying. It roused me from the short, almost vertical nap I'd been taking. I shook my head, demanded it make ready to accept information, and asked him to start again at the beginning.

"You will find she has been trying to reach you through Miss Blaire for the last hour or so," he said. And won't Blaire be pleased about that, I thought. "When she could not, Gina called Rosaria at our home, and Rosaria came here to tell me. You must telephone her at once. Rosaria says she was quite distraught."

"Distraught," I said while navigating into the elevator.

Ernst pushed my floor, but he didn't let go of the elevator.

"James? If there is any way for us to help, we will be pleased to do so."

"Just closing the door will do for now."

I tried to wink, but found that was asking too much.

The phone was ringing when I walked in, and it wouldn't stop until I picked it up.

"Jimmy! Where the hell have you been?"

"Central Park Zoo, if you must know."

"In the middle of the freaking night?"

It had to be something serious for Gina to have lost her ear for irony.

"Hey. You think buying some of my time means I clear every move with you? Since when?"

"Okay, okay. I'm sorry. But cripes, Jimmy, you won't believe what I just saw. I don't believe it."

"Tell me anyway."

"It . . . I went to the opera tonight, with Ari and Clara. *The Magic Flute*. Afterward Ari wanted us to go to some private casino in Riverdale, but Clara was tired. So he dropped us back at the house and Clara went right to her room. I had a bath and went to bed, too.

"I had dreams, Jimmy. God. You know those dreams . . . do you ever have those dreams that are *really* sexy and *really* scary at the same time?"

"I can't say that I do."

"Well, you're not a girl. Anyway, I had this dream that started off good and ended up bad. Bad enough to wake me up."

"Was anybody I know in it?"

"As a matter of fact, yes."

"Really? Who?"

"Never mind. So . . . it was just after midnight. Figured I'd go downstairs and fix a drink. I got up and popped on a robe without turning on my light. But when I walked by my bedroom window I saw something move outside. In the garden. There were . . . Jimmy, they were two . . . two *things* . . . I could see them just standing there in the light from a garden lamp. They were standing up on their hind legs, but they were sort of hunched over, like . . . like apes except with these long snouts, and pelts . . . thick fur like wolves. They . . . wait. You think I'm batty, right?''.

"No, Gina. You're not batty. Now tell me what they did."

"They were looking up at a balcony on the other wing of the house. Looking at a third one! It was standing on the rail of the balcony, Jimmy, staring back down at them. Except . . . Jimmy? This one wasn't like the other two. This one was a *wolf*! The biggest freaking wolf I've ever seen and its eyes . . . all the way across the garden its eyes were glowing like big green lanterns! I've never . . . it was *horrible*! And then all of a sudden I realized whose balcony the wolf was standing on. It was Clara's balcony, Jimmy, and her door was wide open!''

"What did you do?"

"I'll tell you what I did. I yanked that little Colt Ari gave me last Christmas out of the night table, and I picked up an ashtray and used it to open the goddamn window the easy way, and I started blasting. I was afraid to aim for the wolf because Clara could have been right behind the balcony door. So I aimed for her pets in the garden."

"Her?"

"Huh?"

"You said, 'her' pets."

"Did I? Well, I think so. No, I'm sure of it. Yes. That wolf was female. Something about her . . . the eyes . . . something. It had to be a female. Not only that. She was . . . this is going to sound sick, but she was *beautiful*, Jimmy! Sexy, even. A big, beautiful, sexy, monster wolf!"

"So how did you do?"

"Hmm?"

"With the Colt."

"Oh. Ever try to hit anything smaller than a barn with a snub-nose .25, honey? All I did was scatter them. The ones in the garden bolted for the back wall, and the wolf went flying off the balcony after them. Then I started screaming to beat the band and I woke up the house and did the twenty-yard dash to Clara's room."

"And?"

"She was fine. Hadn't even woken up till I started slingin' lead." Gina giggled nervously, but she didn't sound so very far away from tears.

"What did you tell her?"

"Just that I saw some prowlers in the garden and I opened up on them. . . . So what do you think, Jimmy? Am I nuts, or what?"

"Nuttier than a fruitcake, ma'am."

"You . . . you really don't believe me?"

"When did you say this all happened?"

"Around midnight."

Right after the wolf had finished with me—and after I had finished her pals. Which meant she had more pets than two. Very encouraging.

"Gina, my love, not only do I believe you, I wish I'd had you along with me this evening." I touched the bandage at my throat. "You're having better luck at animal training than I am."

"Meaning what?"

"Is Ari home yet?"

"Just got in."

"By the way, you didn't do anything silly like call the police, did you?"

"No. We don't believe in policemen in this household— except when we're in the market for tickets to the ball. Ari has such a European attitude about police. Thinks they're more trouble than they're worth."

"What a quaint notion. So have Ari post some guards, and tuck that Colt under your pillow and go to sleep. On second thought, tuck it under Clara's pillow and sleep with her."

"You mean you're not coming over?" She actually sounded shocked.

"To sleep with you and Clara? I thought you said she was private preserve."

"Not funny."

"Well, precisely what would you have me do at one . . . no, one-thirty in the morning?"

"I don't know!" she snapped. "Do what a private detective does. Look for clues, or something."

"Paw prints in the garden? Hmm. Wonder if giant female wolves with glowing green eyes leave paw prints. Remind me to check into that as soon as there's enough light."

"Jimmy Underhill, what *are* you going to do about this?"

"I'll tell you tomorrow, Gina. Really I will."

I believe I heard a stream of singularly unladylike language issuing from the phone as I kissed it good night and set it on its cradle.

I cannot be accused of *never* fighting with my head: I had the plain good sense to lift the telephone from its cradle before retiring for the evening. And so, unmolested by Gina, or Blaire, or anyone else, I slept the sweet, dreamless sleep of the drugged that night; nor did I arise until high-mounted Phoebus had run nearly half his course in the sky. I mightn't have arisen even then, but for a thing that pierced the woolly mantle of Morpheus.

Itch.

In my sleep-sodden state, a slight tickle at my throat goaded me. Not so slight, actually. With my eyes still shut tight, I let my fingers brush against the rough fabric of the bandage. Its coarseness roused me further from my rest.

Itch itch.

The touch reminded me I must not actually disturb the wound, even through the dressing. The intern had spent the better part of an hour sewing me shut, had put in over two dozen sutures, exclaiming all the while about how ridiculously lucky I was: the bite had just missed this major blood vessel over here by the thinnest and reddest of hairs . . . and that one over there, too . . . and this nerve bundle . . . and . . .

Itch itch itch.

I rubbed my fingers around the edges of the thick tape, chafing the flesh. Not enough. The tickle was turning into a crawl.

Itch itch itch itch.

Good God. Must do something. My eyes snapped open. Carefully, carefully I probed with my fingers over the thickly padded wound, rubbing gently at first, but then quite vigorously indeed.

Itch itch itch itch itch!

Rubbing made it worse! My flesh was alive beneath the pad. Insects, snakes, burrowing beasts with tiny razor claws were tunneling under my skin, flaying me alive. I kicked away the covers, swung my legs down, lurched aloft and staggered into the bathroom.

Itch itch itch itch itch itch!

I clutched the cold rim of the sink, stared at my throat in the mirror. There was nothing to see. The heavy, white bandage was right there in place. Oh, a brownish circle of long-dried blood had seeped through the gauze near the pad's center, but nothing visible betrayed the crawling chaos below.

Phantom tendrils inched out from the spot; my inner ear, the root of my tongue, my eyes behind the lids, the very pit of my throat were tingling, too.

Itchitchitchitchitchitchitch!

Gah! Christ on a crutch! . . . Alcohol, witch hazel, some damn thing . . . No. Nothing for it! I tore the cabinet door open, then slammed it shut; peeled up the corner of the adhesive tape, started tugging it away. I did it slowly for a moment, but when my skin just pulled up along with the sticky tape, I simply got a firmer purchase on the dressing and *ripped.*

The itching stopped in the instant.

But now, all at once, I recalled what had happened last night, every horrifying bit, or bite, of it. I stared at the horror on my throat. Here's what I saw: a white-and-pink square on my skin where the tape had so recently been—white from the stickum still adhering to my flesh, pink from the vigor with which I'd ripped the tape away. In the center of the square . . . nearly nothing, a few slightly pink, slightly raised welts, as if from a wound healed long ago. Sutures? Not a one.

Wrong. Precisely one. I leaned forward to peer more closely at the mirror. Near the edge of one of the welts I saw a black circlet of thread, half in, half out of the flesh. I felt a tingle just at the spot. And as I looked, the circle inched forward as if pushed from underneath, then simply *popped* out of my skin and dropped into the sink.

I rubbed my neck. Smooth, cool. Not a bit of pain. Nothing there.

I frowned, shook my head, did a quick sanity review. I did fight those shape-shifters last night. I did kill them, I did have a run-in with a giant wolf, did have my throat slashed, did need to have it stitched up. I did not imagine any of those things. And even if I had, I certainly did not imagine all the blood. There had been enough of it to seep through to the outside of the pad. . . .

I stared down at the pad in my hand. My stomach lurched, my heart thumped in my chest, my knees wobbled foolishly, and I needed to clutch the sink rim just to keep myself upright.

The inside of the gauze was indeed crusted with freshly dried gore. But sitting in the pad were two dozen tiny black circlets—all the rest of the sutures the intern had so painstakingly sewn in a scant few hours before. My wounded flesh, my flesh with its no longer visible wound, had spit the stitches out as if they were just so many watermelon seeds!

A good stiff belt.

That's what I needed more than anything at the moment. I pushed back from the sink and reeled out of the bathroom. My living room was a galleon, tossed upon stormy seas, but I fought against its pitch and roll, navigated all the way across to the bar with only a minor assist from the furniture, and decanted a healthy tumbler of bourbon.

Old habits are truly a comfort. I knocked back the shot with a deftness born of skill and honed by practice; and so the firewater was roaring down my gullet, long launched on its inexorable course, before I realized what I had done to myself.

I had just swallowed a glass of poison. Firewater, indeed.

My throat spasmed shut, my eyes welled up with a torrent of tears, flames seared my tongue, blistered my palate, burned through the back of my nose. Hellfire raged in my gut. The vile reek of the stuff! My head was choked with its ghastly fumes. It was fortunate that so few things in this world are irreversible. Fortunate for me, but not for the antique Persian rug gracing my living room floor.

I retched with my whole upper body as I lurched back toward the bathroom. The poison tasted even worse on the way up. The first wave hit the rug; then I hit the bathroom—literally—and finally found myself down on my bony knees by the bowl, hooting and harping up, and steering the porcelain bus for all I was worth.

Between waves, I scooped handfuls of water into my mouth—from the *sink*, thank you. Sweet, cleansing water washed my face, my mouth, my raw throat free of the poison's bitter sting.

The water worked wonders. I felt surprisingly well, surprisingly quickly. In fact, I was soon even feeling magnanimous enough to wish whomever had spiked my hooch better luck next time.

The moment it was possible for me to do so, I went back into the living room. I skirted the mess on the rug, noting with relief and some surprise that it had not burned a hole through to the apartment below, and inspected the offending bourbon decanter.

I lifted it to my nostrils. And what I sniffed was this: twelve-year-old, oak-aged bourbon's sweet, sharp, *disgusting* smell. Which is to say, I was keenly aware I was smelling pure, unadulterated bourbon with nothing added or subtracted. But I was also aware of my body's reaction to the smell: pure, unadulterated disgust.

I decided to try an experiment, unplugged my Scotch decanter, and sniffed. Same reaction: pure Scotch, pure revulsion.

I ducked below the bar, pulled out an unopened bottle of delicious old Chivas from the middle of an unopened case. I inspected its seal carefully to make sure it wasn't broken, then opened and sniffed.

Blecchh.

Next experiment. I padded into the kitchen, hauled a chilled bottle of Rheingold out of the Kelvinator, cracked it open, and poured it into a pilsner glass. I snuffled the foamy head: yeasty, flowery . . . in fact, a more complex smell than I recalled humble Rheingold ever having.

I lapped a tiny bit onto my tongue. It tingled and burned, a mere shadow of the agony the bourbon had caused, rather pleasantly bitter. But thanks be, I had not suddenly developed an aversion to all forms of booze. Just the hard varieties. I did not crave another sip of beer, though. In fact, I found I had no desire at all for a liquid breakfast. For the first time in some time.

Possibly all I was now experiencing was merely a reaction to the large quantities of dope the intern had poured into me. Possibly, but not likely.

Look at the facts: A supernaturally powerful she-wolf deals me a death blow—a magical wound, which disappears overnight. And suddenly I find hooch makes me puke. Was I merely experiencing the first in a series of symptoms? Would I soon find myself baying at the moon, growing a five o'clock shadow all over my body, and scratching behind my ear with my foot?

I could not help recalling an incident some few months back when a certain Tibetan Nazi midget had tried his level best to turn me into a vampire.

Lo Fang: That night crawler would have gotten quite the charge out of watching me try to sleep hanging upside down from the ceiling; I was sure he'd get just as big a jolt out of watching me lift my leg at a fireplug. Nor did I think it was an accident that I'd been attacked by a wolf while asking questions about a friend of his friend.

But Lo Fang or no Lo Fang, I knew one thing for pretty damn sure: it was high time to consult an expert. I made a beeline for my telephone and rang up the Right Reverend Doctor Elijah P. Woolcock, M.D., Ph.D., D.D., West Indian Holy Man and Spiritualist, and, truth be known, head of Harlem Homicide's Anti–Hoodoo & Voodoo Division.

It was something I should have done ages ago—and would have too, if Eli weren't such an obnoxious old bastard.

Eli lived at the top of Hamilton Place—the highest hill in Harlem, in an elegant brownstone mansion his mother's side of the family had owned for generations. Elisha Mae Cartwright-Woolcock's people were runaway slaves who had prospered on the isle of Manhattan, in the wagon-making trade they'd learned as chattel on a South Carolina plantation.

But years back, when Elijah was but an unruly lad, his parents shipped him down to his father's folks in Jamaica. There, the New York boy had received the full benefit of a West Indian Black British colonial upbringing: in his Auntie Jessica's extended family where he learned the Jamaican language and Baptist hymns; in private boarding schools where he became fluent in Latin, Greek, French, and British; and in the back streets of Kingston Town, where he became first an impossibly young virtuoso of the ancient mysteries of Voodoon, then an adept of the Black Church of Santaria, and finally a master of certain West African witch sects whose names are best not written here. Or anywhere else, for that matter.

Back in the white world, Eli had also managed to pick up a few assorted sheepskins from Oxford; and a doctor of divinity degree at Trinity. Oh, and a medical degree from the Sorbonne. He thought he was pretty damn smart. But maybe he was too smart for his own good; he was definitely too smart for his own peace of mind. In fact over the years, Elijah P. Woolcock had developed a certain dourness of spirit, a soul-deep impatience with his fellowman, an over-concern for modern New Yorkers' collective soul, which hardly allowed him a moment's rest. Eli had declared himself the spiritual lifeguard of Harlem . . . an entirely self-appointed position. And one that needed to be its own reward since aside from the pitiful stipend Harlem Homicide paid him under the table, Eli received not a red cent for his efforts.

Plenty of barter, though. They lined up outside the mansion to see him in his street-level office, a cross section of the Harlem community, from cleaning ladies and bootblacks to debutantes and college professors. They did so because, whatever else you might say of him, Eli delivered on his promise—the promise of the ongoing advertisement he ran in the *Amsterdam News*. That ad, its every meticulously misspelled word chosen with excruciating care, declared in part: "HE offer AIDE to those as has been CROSSED, have SPELLS, CAN'T HOLD money, WAnt Luck, WANT THEY LOVE ONES BACK or to BE GONE, WANTS to stop man-nature or woman-nature PROBLEMS or WANT TO GET RID of STRANGE SICKNESS. ARE you suffering from ILLNESS DISEASE OR SICKNESS HEXING FIXING OR HOODOO you cannot CURE? see this man of GOD today. HE TELLS YOU BEFORE YOU UTTER A WORD."

He did, too. Often more than you wanted to know. Admittedly my own attitudes about life are less than fun-loving. But Eli was too crotchety even for my tastes.

"Okay, Underhill. What you want this time?" Woolcock grumbled. His accent was a perfect blend of West Indian and Harlemite.

He clamped a hooked, golden calabash pipe between alarmingly strong-looking white teeth, and began puttering his long, thick fingers through the many, many pockets of his rumpled tweed suit.

"Mind if I smoke? Good. Didn't think so."

I hadn't said a word.

Woolcock's skin matched the mahogany of his study to perfection. His forehead was high, and what hair he had left was as long and thick and white as wool. His eyes bulged slightly, and they stared off in two directions, each independently of the other, so one needed always to decide which of the two he was using before one knew exactly where he was looking.

His potbelly bulged, too, even though he wasn't fat; his

feet, large and flat and misshapen as yams, splayed out in separate directions that seemed to recapitulate the cast of his eyes.

As often as I thought about Woolcock, the term 'Marsh Wiggle' went through my mind. I don't know precisely what a Marsh Wiggle is, but I imagine the creature crouched beneath a toadstool, writing notes to itself with a quill pen. Elijah P. Woolcock was a cantankerous, unlikable old coot. But he was undoubtedly the most interesting-*looking* old coot I have ever known.

He stopped his quest for fire long enough to decant and hand me a snifter of very old brandy I—obviously—had not requested.

"Here, Underhill." He chuckled. "Much too damn bloody good for the likes of you, rest assured."

His long, thick fingers resumed, and then decided to abandon, their seemingly self-directed search of his numerous pockets without discovering a match. He set his calabash down in a cut crystal ashtray.

Thankfully unlit: Even cold, the sweet, cloying stench of the tobacco-stuffed pipe bowl had been tickling my nostrils. I was not sure I could have abided it smouldering and smoking. Nor was Eli the sort to put out his pipe simply because it was asphyxiating a guest. One more of his endearing charms.

Tobacco. Christ, had I uncovered yet another new aversion? I was pleased not to have the opportunity to find out, just at the moment.

And speaking of aversions . . . the smell of the brandy he'd given me had been unpleasant from the first. Now with the snifter glass warmed in my hand, it was nigh to unbearable. I scouted around the book-lined study for a spot to park it, finally settled on a mahogany pedestal with a bronze statue, three feet tall, of Diana, goddess of the hunt, portrayed as a nude Negress, spear raised high to strike. Her back was turned, her head tossed over her shoulder toward me with a wild abandon that seemed to say she didn't need to look to cast her spear true to the mark.

After all, she was a goddess.

Her long and gracefully muscled legs, her shapely waist, her high, bountiful buttocks . . . this Diana looked familiar, especially those buttocks.

I set the snifter down at her sandaled feet.

"What's that, Underhill? Votive offering to the deity?" Woolcock smirked. "Diana liked the fruit of the grape in all its forms. Not too partial to white boys, though, Diana wasn't. The original sporting woman . . . liked her lovers more, uh, long-winded than the average ofay."

"She tell you so herself, Eli?"

"You bet she did. There's lot of things about Diana they don't teach in your Caucasian mythology books. Like that she was black. You know what that there Ovid says. *Negra sum sed pulcra.*"

" 'Black I am, and beautiful.' Didn't know he said it about the goddess of the hunt."

"Maybe he did, maybe he didn't. 'Black I am, *but* beautiful.' Ovid liked to patronize his dark meat. How's about you, Underhill?"

"Hmm?"

"You like to patronize dark meat?"

"Don't know what you're talking about, Eli. I don't have a preference one way or the other. Can't see all that well with the lights out."

"Yeah. That's what Velma DuPree says," he snapped. "A little south of here they calls it 'nighttime integration.' Familiar with the term?"

I suddenly realized who the sculpture reminded me of.

"What else does Velma tell you?"

"She says she likes the music, but the tune's too short."

"Where'd you get the sculpture, Eli?"

"Had it commissioned awhile back. You come here for an art lesson?"

"I didn't come up for your splendid companionship."

"Well, it's pretty damn good, this sculpture. Accurate in every detail. Take a look at m'lady's chest. Watch out, don't get your eye poked out."

I peered around to the back of the statue—the figure's front, and realized Woolcock did not mean his warning to apply to her high-raised spear. Black Diana was the bitch goddess, and the sculptor had depicted her with not two, but eight perfectly formed breasts, eight of them, in two rows down her naked chest to her middle.

The effect was, uh, disquieting. But it was far from grotesque: the sculptor had been too skilled to allow it to be so. Rather, I had the feeling I was viewing the essence of woman, vibrant, vital, supernaturally fecund, in all her eternal power. Essence of Velma, too: the face, the legs, even those beauteous breasts . . . minus six of them, everything was modeled on Velma Dupree . . . oh, a younger Velma, perhaps a few pounds shy of the exceedingly ample woman of today. But Velma none the less.

"So when did she pose for the sculpture?" I asked. He knew damn well who I meant.

"A few years back, Underhill," he grumbled. "Few years back. But as long as we're putting our cards on the table, I guess I can make it clear . . . the fact of you poking Velma does not exactly endear you to my heart. Understand?"

"Well, Elijah, old skate, Velma never gave me a report on your performance. But personally, I never thought of Velma as the kind of woman who could be poked. More likely she'd do the poking, or the tossing around of one sort or another. Like the last time I saw her, she . . ."

"Spare me the gory details, Underhill!" he sputtered. I squinted, and even in the underlit study I was able to note, with the greatest of pleasure, that Eli was positively blushing. He glared at me with both eyes at once, something he did only when he was really steamed.

The Marsh Wiggle.

"You ever going to get around to telling me what you want from me?" he asked.

"I need an assortment of advice, Eli," I said grimly. "Some medical, some witch lore."

"Those are not unconnected topics. Let's hear it."

"I was attacked by a pack of dacoits last night." I

shrugged. "I killed two of them, then their leader got me down and slashed my throat."

"You mean, if I try to touch you right now, my hand'll pass through you?" He smirked. "I always knew you'd come back to haunt me."

He turned his head aside and spit through his fingers over his shoulder.

"I will, too. But I survived the attack. I think."

"It doesn't look too serious from here," he said, examining my neck with his left eye. "Or were you cut below the collar line?"

"Uh-uh. I got it right here." I pointed to where the wound should have been. "And Eli? I wasn't cut. I was bitten. They were shape-shifter dacoits. And their leader was a full-blown wolf. Female."

Elijah P. Woolcock looked at me with both eyes at once. He didn't ask me how I knew the wolf was female, and he didn't ask why my throat didn't have a mark on it. He just reached out his long, thick sausage fingers and rested the tips gently on my neck right where the scars weren't.

His eyes rolled back in their sockets, his head tipped back, his mouth slackened, and Eli went off somewhere, to a far distant place, maybe beneath the Marsh Wiggle's toadstool, maybe to a place much stranger still. I felt a warmth, a tingling at my throat. It spread out, over my face, deep into my chest.

The warmth faded.

And Eli came back. His face had paled beneath his color. As if what he'd just done had leeched away a great deal of his energy.

"Jesus Christ, Jimmy," he said softly. "You got a world of troubles this time. Did she . . . the werewolf . . . did she *say* anything?"

"Not exactly. She just . . ."

His eyes stared off, and he said in a dreamy singsong, "Hold still, damn you. Don't you dare move. Her vicious thoughts roared in my mind. Her eyes were emerald green and they glowed with an impossible light. . . . She growled a growl of very great pleasure . . . and she lifted her head high above and howled with joy. . . .'' He shook his head, spoke more quickly. ''Just thought maybe I missed something.''

''So what's going to happen, Eli?'' I asked grimly. ''You know the characters I . . . Jefferson and I . . . have been dealing with. They tried to make me into a vampire a few months back. Have they made me into a werewolf?''

''Jefferson and you and *me* have been dealing with them, Jimmy.'' He frowned, shook his head. ''Wish I did know what it all means. Wish I knew more about who they really are. Then again, I wish I never knew nothing about them. Their *presence*, man! I have never felt such a gathering of evil, of death wish. Not here, not down in the islands . . . It's been all over New York this last year . . . getting stronger. Getting stronger all over the world. I . . .'' His shoulders shook as if with a sudden chill. ''You want to know if the bite's going to make you one of theirs? I don't know. I truly don't. . . . Have you had any . . . symptoms? Feel different any way?''

''Booze makes me sick.''

He cast an eye toward my snifter glass.

''So I noticed. It's about time.''

''Funny.''

''Anything else?''

''Not really.''

''Not really?'' He glanced at his pipe and smiled unpleasantly. ''Hmm. Forget what you said when I asked you before . . . Mind if I smoke?''

''Mind if I lift my leg and put it out?''

''Right. Elevation of the senses. Not so great. But those are still normal symptoms, if you'll pardon the expression. The jury's still out, Jimmy. It's gonna stay out a while, too.''

''For how long, Eli?''

He shook his head. ''A week, a month, a year . . . maybe forever. Really. Maybe forever. I have seen that happen, too.''

''Doesn't sound like you've seen that happen very often.''

''What you have is not exactly a common complaint, Mr.

Underhill," he drawled. "But it is true. I have seen people torn half to pieces by shape-shifters, and . . . nothing. No lasting effects once they heal up. Listen. If you'd come right to me last night instead of going to the hospital . . . bah. I won't jive you. Even then, it would have been shaky. Now the wound's had a chance to set overnight. But you're tough, Jimmy . . . *inside* tough, which is the kind that counts. You want the whole picture, man?"

He ticked off the choices on those fingers of his. "There is a chance you'll be just fine. No effect. There's a chance you'll turn into a halfling, like the ones you knocked off. And there's a chance you'll turn into . . . into something nobody expects. Shape-shifter bites. They go lots of ways. Real helpful, huh?"

"Yeah, Doctor. Real helpful."

"I'm sorry, Jimmy. I truly am sorry."

"Nothing for it? No potions you can give me to swallow? No witch bundles to hang around my neck? No anti-werewolf injections?"

Eli raised his enormous hands, palms out. I felt a ghost of the warmth I'd felt when he had put his fingertips on my throat.

"Jimmy? When I laid hands on you just before? I did everything I know how to do for you, right then. Gave you both barrels. Maybe it'll be enough. But I never promise more than I can deliver, and I can't deliver more than it says in the *Amsterdam News*." His left eye sparkled. "Now if you man nature was troublin' you . . . if you woman was fixin' you wif a black cat bone, if yo' mojo wasn't workin' . . ." He shook his head. "But there's nothing more I can do now, Jimmy. And that's the truth."

Real great. I looked around for my hat, and when I found it, I said, "So thanks, anyway, Eli. But there is one thing you can do for me."

"Should I ask what that might be?"

"If I really go off the deep end? Call the dogcatcher."

"I happen to have the dogcatcher's home telephone number. Know how to reach him day or night."

Eli smiled. But the next thing he said, he said very seriously indeed. "I will be watching, Jimmy. And if you really start to go . . . to go bad, I will stop you. I will stop you before you hurt anyone you shouldn't hurt. I will put you down, Jimmy."

"Thanks, Eli."

I believe I wanted to hear that.

"Oh, and Jimmy?"

"Mmm?"

"Marsh Wiggles are Jamaican trolls. They live reeeal deep in the rain forests, and they make their homes under amanita mushrooms. They're very damn bloody smart. Smarter than you, Underhill. So watch your step."

"You mean, like no poking black girls?"

"Well, I allow as to how if the girls being poked are beyond the age of consent . . ."

"Good-bye, Eli."

" 'Afternoon, Jimmy. I will keep an eye out for you. Maybe even two."

It was a bit of a trek to my next stop of the day, so I had ample time for a small indulgence in panic and self-pity. More than ample time. I allowed myself to luxuriate in a few moments of abject terror, in fact reined in my fear's mindless gallop just a few paces short of the land of soiled linen. Then I moved on to a systematic examination of the facts.

Fact: I had been wounded and undoubtedly infected by a werewolf bite. Observation: My symptoms to date were weird, but they were by no means destructive or even debilitating. Conclusion: I had naught to gripe about—yet.

As to my very first symptom, I had never actually heard of anyone complaining about an injury disappearing too quickly. If healing overnight were a problem, it was one problem I wished I'd had in Spain.

It was likewise a stretch trying to sustain any really deep worry concerning symptom number two. Truth be known, even I had realized it was high time to give booze a rest.

I'd miss Dame Rum dearly, and in her absence, undoubtedly find Reality's questionable joys considerably harder to stomach. But my forced departure from drink's glad company hardly qualified for a day of national mourning.

Next: As Eli had indicated, the jury was still out on just how sick the bite was going to make me. If I started keeping the neighbors up by howling at the moon, if I began to harass the postman by nipping at his heels, or motorists by snapping at their tires . . . if things got too bad, I just knew I could count on one or another of my dear, dear friends to put me out of my misery. I only hoped no one got hurt in the mad rush to see who'd do the honors.

And in the unlikely event of no one being available to dispatch me, I could always tidy things up myself. I already knew the nice effect of a bullet in the brain on even the most insistent of shape-shifters.

So much for planning out my retirement, my golden years, my endgame. Here and now, I had chores to get done: places to go, people to see, enemies to injure. What if my days *were* numbered?

Yours are, too.

I rang the bell; the butler let me in, told me he'd been instructed to bring me right up to Miz Regina's bedchamber. Sounded like Gina was in a no-nonsense mood, a refreshing change of pace.

Halfway up the wide marble stairs, the butler and I ran into Aristotle barreling down. The sun had not yet set, but he was already bustling off wearing a tux and trailing a string of toadies . . . uh, assistants, preoccupied as ever.

Aristotle. Silver hair; dark, well-weathered face; amused, appraising eyes; a smile broad and welcoming, gold-edged and openly carnivorous; a lean, well-muscled form beneath the monkey suit.

Aristotle had not become the Lord of the Shipping Lanes by allowing himself an overabundance of trust in the benevolence of his fellowman: his grip seemed to entrap rather than merely shake my hand, a throwback to ancient tribal times when the greeting clasp had the utilitarian purpose of insuring that the person you were meeting could not brain you with his cudgel. Unless he was a lefty.

I don't suppose there remain any lingering doubts concerning my personal opinion of Aristotle's entire socioeconomic class, the whole damn flock of them. I have never met a rich person whose riches did not in the last analysis ultimately derive from squashed human guts. But there was no way around it: I actually liked Aristotle. In a way.

Aristotle. He was too honestly Aristotle, too right-there about who and what he was, not to deserve admiration, admiration of the type reserved for really superior, streamlined predators—the kind you'd like to scratch behind the ears, and would too, if you weren't planning to have some future use for your hand. A tiger, for instance. Or a wolf.

And he cared about Gina, a person I also happened to care about, with a love that went far beyond the merely material, important though the material is. Aristotle loved Gina with a generosity of spirit, an openhandedness, a bemused, tolerant affection that was really something to see.

Of course, if you didn't love Gina that way, she could drive you nuts. And such a love implied a certain emotional distance, a lack of fire—not to say a coldness—that might have explained a propensity of Gina's: her occasional tendency, which we have already observed, to wander away beyond the marriage bonds in search of, well, a bit of warmth. Oh, what the hell, they always have some excuse. My hat was still off to Aristotle.

Aristotle arched one bushy eyebrow, skewered me with his most penetrating Leader of Men gaze, and intoned in a Hellenic accent so thick you could cut it with a Turkish scimitar, "Jimmy! You take care this business, yeh? This shit is no joke. You fix good, right? Names? Addresses? The whole damn thing. Yeh? Good."

I nodded and smiled, not that any response was called for. The question marks were just for decoration when Aristotle gave an order. He examined me briefly, as if checking to make sure he'd selected the correct utensil for the task. Then he nodded curtly, and whisked on down the stairs with all his entourage.

"Nice of you to finally show up," Gina snapped, without even waiting for the butler to leave. The hair on my neck bristled.

She took a big gulp from a thick water glass half-full of booze and melting rocks, then smacked the glass down too hard onto a marble dressing table. She was already half-looped. At least I had instant proof-positive nothing had nibbled on *her* neck last night.

She was wearing a peach-colored gossamer silk robe with only a minority of its buttons in use. She started pacing like a caged thing, and as she did, the robe unfolded almost to her tummy, revealing that once again, Gina was wearing her very favorite kind of underwear: none.

"Bastard," she hissed. "To think I paid you good money . . ."

"Gina? How'd you like a smack right in the ass?" I snarled. "Do I have to tell you again? You do not have your brand on me."

I really felt like belting her, too. Lord knew somebody ought to do her the favor. But the next look she gave me made me feel like the king of the puppy killers. Her eyes welled up, her luscious, bee-stung lips quavered. She stumbled against me and buried her face in my chest.

"I'm sorry, Jimmy, I'm sorry," she sobbed. "I'm . . . I'm so damn *scared*! I . . . there's something out there. Something trying to get us! Never felt anything this strong . . . this strong and *evil*. Nothing!"

She smelled like perfume and fear and a distillery. Curiously, I didn't find the combination unpleasant on her. She blotted her face, on my lapel for a change.

"Damn it, why am I always telling you I'm sorry?" she sniffed.

"And using my suit for a handkerchief? Just natural good manners . . . bred in the bone," I teased gently. "Hey.

You're the broad who smashes in windows and blasts away at the monsters. Remember? Tough as nails.''

She pushed back and looked up at me, her fingernails digging into my biceps. Her big blue eyes were blurred with tears and fright, her red lips were swollen. I don't recall her ever looking more beautiful.

"Jimmy?" she whispered. "Jimmy? Please just hold me tight. Oh, just a little minute, honey . . . Make me forget a minute."

Alone in the icy garden sometime later, I discovered the she-wolf had left her spoor behind.

Gina was in her room, under strict orders to drink an entire pot of java and then, and only then, to have me summoned for an introductory spot of tea with her and Clara Steiner. But she'd pointed out precisely where in the garden exactly what occurred, and I'd gone into the chilled, refreshing air to take a look.

Quite the stately Xanadu Aristotle had decreed.

The frosty winter's afternoon was fading swiftly, and the sky above was a pale and deepening blue. Thin, frozen sunlight still filled the garden, reflecting down from the white marble of its eastern wall, spattering gold over formal groves and arbors, hedgerows and flowerbeds in this season occupied only by evergreens and small banks of forced winter flowers.

In a marble pool, naked bronze nymphs danced and splashed in snow foam, fleeing eternally from grinning satyrs who dripped icicles from their loins and spouted frozen streams onto the ladies from the ledges above.

The garden's architectural style was oddly satisfying: an English Renaissance vision of Hellenic temple grounds, rough-hewn granite walls and steps mantled with dry, black-green ivy, Ionic columns of polished marble and porphyry, carved stone benches ringing votive shrines, a deserted gazebo in the garden's center.

An opulent fantasy of timeless ease and grace, the garden

was. And it all stood in the middle of Manhattan; someone else's Manhattan, not yours or mine.

Aristotle's town house was nearly a quarter block wide, and its wings enclosed the garden on three sides. Beyond a high stone wall at the far end, I noted an empty space—probably the neighbors' less ambitious gardens, and then the rear facades of several smaller town houses. The wolf patrol had most likely entered over the wall, having made its way through the alleys on the next block, and had undoubtedly exited there when Gina opened up on them.

I started my examination at the wall, discovered as I followed the foot and paw prints in the snow and dirt and sand and gravel that they silently affirmed the story Gina had already told.

More or less.

I saw stealthy entry, pauses to watch and wait, the chaos of a frenzied flight. There were several chips in the white marble of the garden's east wall—Gina's slugs, all below a second-story balcony of stone and black wrought iron, its doors tightly shut.

I smelled the smell just below the balcony, smelled it despite the chill: a sweet and musky stink, strong and warm and utterly animal, complex, compelling, exciting—in fact, very nearly enraging. Because it was her smell, the she-wolf's. I had smelled it on her fur when she'd ripped out my throat; now it was here in Gina's garden!

My whole body tensed; I curled into a half crouch with my hand on my gun butt. Was she lurking in the bushes, still hiding? I squinted around for a moment. But when I saw nothing, I let my nose lead me, and found it almost at once, in a small, snowy bank just below the balcony: on a crusty, oldish snow patch, a blot of pale yellow, with several smaller splatters trailing off from it. I dropped to my hands and knees, tossed my hat away, and crawled forward toward that blot.

God's teeth. The *smell*! It drew me, filled my nostrils with its sweet, infuriating essence, filled my mind with a kaleidoscope of images and feelings . . . her fangs above me glistening with blood; her silver fur flecked with black. Fear and rage and . . . something else.

My knees and my hands sank through the snow rind; my face drew closer and closer to that maddening, fragrant reek. Its cold, its heat radiated onto my face, filled my nostrils, burned my eyes and made them water. My mouth was watering too and bless me, I believe I was about to lick the spoor, to taste it.

All in the name of scientific investigation, of course.

And that is how she saw me for the first time. That is what I was doing on the magical moment when first we met. Jimmy Underhill was down on his hands and knees, no, no, not licking a werewolf's spoor in the snow. But yes, yes, very damn close to doing so.

I was saved by a giggle.

I looked up and saw her standing on the balcony almost directly above me, got up and backed onto the path to get a better look. She was wearing a plain, black skirt and a thick, white turtleneck sweater, which neither hid nor made much of the delightful facts of her form: ample breasts, slender waist, wide hips, long legs. Her black hair glistened against the white wool. She had red lips, high cheekbones, penetrating, blue eyes.

The wind puffed at her skirt and she pushed it down into place, but not before I noted a white flash of shapely thigh. She stepped back slightly, affording me less view of her legs, a move I was grateful for, because I wished to be able to compose some few words to her, to utter something other than gibberish.

It is an easy thing, a ridiculous thing to say what I am going to say now, but I will say it anyway, because it is absolutely the truth and because it has never happened to me before or since in all my life: From that very first moment I saw her, I was utterly, idiotically, longingly, mindlessly, childishly, protectively, selflessly, selfishly, despairingly, lustfully, purely, greedily, hopelessly in love with Clara Steiner, only daughter of the late Rolf Steiner. I wanted her for my very own forever and ever.

And I knew we were going to become lovers.

And I knew it was going to end badly.

"May one inquire as to what you were doing there on your hands and knees, sir?" she asked. Her accent was soft and musical, her voice warm and quite amused.

"Clues." I grinned like an idiot. "Looking for clues."

"Really? It looked like you were eating snow," she blurted.

But then she giggled as if surprised at herself, colored very nicely, and hid her giggle behind a long and graceful hand. I cleared my throat.

"Not to change the subject, but . . . I am correct in assuming you are Clara Steiner?"

That took a great leap of intuition, right? But she gasped as if I'd just guessed the Riddle of the Sphinx, and plunging into the middle of the game, said, "Why, yes! How did you know?"

"Elementary. You're standing on her balcony and you aren't dressed like a chambermaid."

"Bravo! But I can't guess who you might be."

I took a moment to brush off my knees, retrieved my hat from the path beside me where I'd tossed it, and swept it along in a mock bow.

"James Underhill. At your service."

"You are James Underhill! Regina has told me so much about you! She worships you, you know, talks about you constantly. She . . . oh . . . but, am I telling tales out of school . . . ?"

"Yes. But I won't hold it against her."

"How gentlemanly." She smiled. "I feel like a beast for having betrayed Regina's deepest secrets. So . . . you really are looking for clues down there, aren't you, Mr. Underhill? Have you uncovered anything?"

The wolf spoor suddenly tickled my nostrils again. I found its insistence even more infuriating than before, an utterly enraging diversion of my attention. Because I wanted to concentrate only on Clara. I snorted the stink away, rubbed my nose.

"This and that. Nothing worth talking about."

"Can't say I'm surprised. I imagine the trail's a bit cold by now. Especially in this weather." She hugged herself for warmth, trembled brightly.

"Sometimes it's better that way," I pontificated. "There's nothing worse than an overly warm clue. The best clues are the ones that've had some time to mature."

"I see. Develop a bouquet?"

"Lose it, actually."

"Well, it's all too complicated for me. I'll leave such matters to experts like yourself, James. Oh . . . I may call you James?"

I was about to correct her and ask her to call me Jimmy. But I decided I liked the way James sounded, coming from her.

Lord. It really *was* going to end badly. . . . I nodded dumbly.

"And how do you estimate your chances of catching the night prowlers?" she continued.

Her eyes were still laughing, and I didn't even mind that the laughter was at my expense. I was pleased actually, because right beyond all our silly joking, just past the veil, I saw the scars of sorrow in Clara Steiner's eyes, the marks of great and recent pain, everything the Nazis had done to her father, and so to her.

"Excellent. Or at least, we can make sure they don't come back."

"Really!" Her face clouded momentarily. "Seriously, James. It is not particularly comforting to think that thieves can just comes waltzing into Regina's garden at their leisure. It reminds me of . . ." she shook her head, waved away the thought, " . . . another place. I hoped things were different here."

"Just the point. Things *are* different here. Once we know exactly how they came in and what they did, we'll know just how to patch up the hole. And then they really won't be back."

The party line, the supposed reason I'd dropped by; Regina had gone over it with me very carefully.

"Is that so, James?" Clara said flatly. Her tone told me that she had an ear for horseshit. "In that case, I'll let you do your work in peace."

She pushed back from the balcony railing.

"Oh, no. Not at all necessary. I can . . ."

"Oh, but it is. Besides"—she grinned—"it's getting chilly up here. And besides *that*, Gina is going to formally introduce us in . . ." she glanced at a small gold locket watch on her breast, "half of an hour. If we get to know each other too well now, I'm sure having tea with me will bore you senseless."

"Not in the . . ."

But Clara was already gone. I was only addressing the empty, darkening garden by the time I said, " . . . slightest."

The scent called to me again; but now it's reek suddenly pierced me with a pang of loss. Terrifying   emptiness so deep, I felt it in my gut and my chest—a dull, thick, throbbing pain.

Alone. All alone. The agonizing emptiness of lust.

It was very horrible.

I strode into the snowbank and kicked the werewolf's spoor apart, scattering snow and ice crystals and moist, frozen clods of dirt.

Smart thinking, Underhill. Now, of course, I had her smell all over my shoes. It took me quite a while to clean them off.

I was still scrubbing the wing tips with snow when the butler cleared his throat behind me and announced that Miz Regina requested my presence in the drawing room for tea.

Night had filled the sky by the time I came in from the cold.

I found the two of them huddled together on a chaise lounge in the cheerfully lit drawing room, whispering and giggling like schoolgirls. They'd been playing dress-up, too. Gina wore an Oriental silk robe, high-collared, long-hemmed, ornately brocaded, a real costume. It did not look silly, but that was only because Gina was the one wearing it. Gina, as anyone who has seen her on stage or screen will agree, would have looked just fine in anything or in nothing at all.

The majority of the effort had been invested in Clara Steiner, however.

Gina had poured Clara into a creamy white silk dress, fashioned with white floral embroideries from heel to throat. The silk undulated over her sweetly voluptuous body; the embroidery underlined each and every one of her many points of interest. Here, flowering sprays twined along belly and hips; there, a bower of blossoms cupped her breasts; and back over here again, trumpeting vines writhed down her shapely thighs. Or up them.

The two witches: No question about it, they were trying to cloud my mind.

"Ah, James! How *nice* of you to join us!" Gina burbled in a dowager-countess voice. "Allow me to present Clara Steiner. Clara, James Underhill, private investigator. A man," she continued with mock bitterness, "who comes and goes as he pleases. Or is it goes and comes . . . ? In any case, he takes his sweet time doing both. James, Clara."

I took Clara's hand as she rose to greet me. She seemed slightly awkward in the dress, tugged it into place as she rose, and wobbled ever so slightly on Gina's backless mules. But the girlishness with which she carried off her get-up was much more appealing than if she'd worn such an overly sophisticated frock with a lounge lizard's ease. Lounge lizards are cheaper by the dozen in the Forty Second Latitude. And though I blush to admit it, in those days innocence radiated the thrill of the unknown for me.

Gina had put lipstick on her too. On her lovely, full lips.

"She's already been presented," I said.

"No she hasn't, Prince Charming," Gina corrected. "You ran into each other in the garden. You have not been formally introduced. Now kiss the lady's hand and tell her you're en-*chant*ed. Then let go of it."

"Hmm?"

"Her hand. I think she wants it back."

The two of them burst into giggles. I realized that perhaps I had been holding Clara's hand for a slightly longer time than necessary. But I also realized it was quite the Girls' Club I was dealing with here. Clearly, the two of them got along like the proverbial house on fire. Good, I supposed.

"Enchanted, Miss Steiner."

I kissed her hand and set it free.

Her hand. It was warm and strong and innocent and fragrant. And, bitchy schoolgirl-jokes or no, it had squeezed mine back very slightly and meaningfully, just before I released it.

We all sat again, they on the chaise lounge, and I, overcoming a mild urge to drop down on the rug and put my chin in Clara's lap, in a nearby Breuer chair.

"So," Clara declared, patting at her dress, "your investigations in the gardens have undoubtedly given you the solution to the case?"

"Depends how you look at it." I smiled. "In real life, most criminal cases don't have neat solutions. One simply manages to discover what happened in a given time and place . . . in more or less detail. No ultimates . . . blacks and whites, rights and wrongs."

"No ultimate truths? Sounds nihilistic, James. If I may say so."

"Just realistic, madame."

"But isn't that the classic defense of the nihilist? That he or she is simply describing reality?"

"It's the classic defense of everyone, regardless of philosophic tastes." I shrugged. "Most people value their own opinions above all others. Don't you?"

Her face clouded.

"No. I don't, particularly. When I was younger, I used to be very sure of things, arrogantly sure. But I'm not young any more."

"Hey, if you're an old lady, then what am I?" Gina teased. "Clara? Remember how we used to play big sister–little sister in Birchenstrasse?"

She reached over and patted Clara's knee.

"And the time I got so angry at you." Clara smiled. " 'A big sister must give more *rules*!' And my father . . . my father overheard me and said, 'If you love a sister, you don't need rules.' So then I was furious at my father for taking your side . . .''

Gina stroked Clara's arm affectionately. Maybe more than affectionately. And Clara caressed the back of Gina's hand.

Strange. It will come as no shock when I say that, for as long as I've known her, Gina had been an any-port-in-a-storm type in terms of bed partner gender. But I'd never seen her so taken with a girl. Of course Clara was a great choice if any girl was. I wondered if anything had actually, uh, transpired between them, though. Nothing had, if I read things right. Clara didn't even seem fully aware of the effect she was having on her hostess. Yet. Still, I wondered if she shared Gina's . . . oh, Jesus, Underhill . . . give it a rest. Jealous already.

"In any case, you're hardly ancient," I said.

"That's what I love about Americans," Clara said to me. "Your directness. You say you don't believe in blacks and whites, in ultimates. But you see things so simply. I don't mean it as an insult. I really do admire it. Everything here is so clear and clean and straightforward. But sometimes things are *not* so simple. For instance, my birth certificate says I am twenty-three. But I am really much older than that. Recent . . . recent events have made me feel very old. Very old indeed. And getting back to my original point, they have taught me just how little I know."

"Your father," I said gently. "I'm sorry about what happened to him."

The mention of Rolf Steiner got me a daggers look from Gina. But Clara had steered us in his direction first. And sooner or later we would have to talk about him.

"Thank you. My father . . . yes. But actually, I was thinking about what I have learned from the Nazis. The Nazis . . . just when you think you are safe, when you think you have escaped . . ." she shook her head. "But I suppose you have had a chance to learn a great deal from them, too. Gina tells me you fought against the fascists in Spain.''

"Sure," I said dryly. "Spain was quite the learning experience. Very instructive.''

"I'm sorry,'' she said. "I didn't mean it that way.''

"Oh, but I do,'' I said. "I learned a whole raft of things. Rules to live by.''

"Such as?''

"For openers? I learned how destructive mercy can be. The deadly power of pity . . . I saw what happened just because the republic neglected to kill a few insurgent generals.''

"Franco's friends?'' Gina chimed in.

"Thought you didn't read the papers.'' I smiled. "They exiled the bastards. And they came back leading armies. I saw the children dead from starvation in the blockades. And the ones blown apart by the Luftwaffe dive-bombers. The Nazi volunteers. Oh, I saw lots of instructive things in Spain. . . .''

"And I thought we were going to have a nice spot of tea,'' Gina drawled.

But she didn't mean it, which was fortunate. Because I had suddenly realized it was high time to stop the games. Clara had just said how much she liked our quaint American directness. I hoped she meant it, for her sake.

"Never touch the stuff, Gina. So let's get down to business, shall we? Clara? Gina thinks the intruders last night may have been after you. And I think she may be right.''

We were both studying Clara. But I for one was not ready for her reaction. She got up and walked to the drawing room's huge bay window. She stared past the reflecting glass, into the cold, black shadows of the night. After a few moments she closed the heavy curtains, shutting out the darkness. Then she came back and sat beside Gina again.

"So I can finally talk about it,'' Clara said grimly. "I thought so too. I thought last night they came to . . . to seek me out. To take me.''

"Why, Clara?'' I asked. "Why'd you think that?''

"Because they have been following me for weeks."

"You knew!" Gina gasped. "Why the hell didn't you *say* something?!"

"Oh, don't you understand? How could I? You and Ari have been so wonderful to me. How could I drag you down into my fight? I thought perhaps . . . most likely they were just watching me. I thought they would leave it at that. They have never considered me a threat before. It was always my father they feared."

"I know this is an ugly question, Clara," I said. "But why did they treat your father the way they did? Usually they chase out who they want to chase out, kill the ones they want to kill. In your father's case they deported him, *then* assassinated him."

"Let's say they realized too late how much of a threat my father was. Almost too late. Do you know what my father did a moment before they shot him? He turned to me and said he would either die on that day, in that place, or in 1974. On May Fourth, 1974. In Tampa Bay, Florida, to be exact."

"Excuse me? I don't understand."

"I am telling you my father predicted his own death. He was a very spiritual man. Very powerful spiritually. His parapsychological gifts were as great as his poetic gifts, his artistic gifts, his scientific gifts." She smiled fondly. "You have heard what Uncle Albert said about my father?"

"Uncle Albert Einstein?" I smiled. "Yes. He said your father understood relativity theory better than Uncle Albert himself."

"Well, you must understand that my father's paranormal talents were every bit as strong as his scientific abilities. And that he used them to the fullest extent."

"He didn't use them to save his own life," I said bitterly.

"Of course he didn't. My father only used white magic. So he could not summon magical aid for his personal gain. That is at the bedrock of the Law. Not for gold . . . and certainly not to save his life, which was so much more valuable than gold."

"What a waste," Gina murmured.

"Not at all," Clara said. "He used his abilities for so many things of great importance. He spied on the Nazis. Observed them at their most intimate moments. He learned their darkest secrets. And he told the world what he knew. He told *everything*."

I remembered Steiner's public statements, and the monographs he'd written about the occult roots of Nazi power. He went into intimate detail, and I'd always believed what he said had the smell of truth about it; the stench of truth, rather.

"Your father had amazingly detailed information on the Nazis," I said. "But he always refused to reveal his sources."

"The truth was there for the world to see," Clara said. "My father *was* a great occultist. James? What would you say if I told you my father was able to spy on the Nazis by means of astral projection? That he had mastered the ancient art . . . could leave his body and send his spirit to observe Hitler . . . and all the Nazis, at their most secret moments."

"I'd say I believed you. But I see your point."

"Few enough believed him." She nodded. "If he had said *how* he'd learned what he knew, they would have laughed him into oblivion. Just another foolish old man."

"And you think the Nazis decided to kill him because they realized he was spying on them while they committed murders, secret arrests, tortures?"

"He saw them do worse things, too, James. Far worse."

"What about you, Clara? Have you continued your father's . . . research?"

"I am an Agarthi adept, if that is what you mean." She shrugged.

"Excuse me?"

"I said I am an Agarthi adept. A student of white magic."

She studied my face, as if trying to see whether I'd understood what she'd just told me.

"White magic? I see." I frowned. "Do the Nazis consider you a threat, too?"

"Unfortunately, I am sure they do not." Clara smiled bitterly. "My father was the master. I am only a student. If they . . . want me, it is only to satisfy their lust for vengeance on my father. My father always said, the desire for vengeance is a fire. It grows stronger the more it is fed. Do you find it so, James? Do you see revenge that way?''

''Very possibly.'' I shrugged. ''But I still prefer the Italian definition of revenge.''

''What is that?''

''A meal best eaten cold.''

And then I thought to myself: but what happens when the taste for revenge gets all tangled up with other emotions? People are so sloppy; they never feel just one emotion purely, for a very long time. What happens when vengeance hunger mixes with fear and regret and anger and perhaps even (perish the thought) with love?

What happens is, everything gets very sad and complicated and messy. But that was my business. There was no need to trouble Clara Steiner with another sad, complicated, messy question.

At least, not yet there wasn't.

I remember my dreams.

I mention this fact merely to clarify the significance of the following statement: After leaving Clara and Gina that evening, when at the end of still another long night's travail, I finally found myself adrift upon the sweet sea of slumber, I experienced what was without a doubt the strangest and most vivid dream of my life.

I dreamed I stood at the edge of a fragrant nighttime woods and peered out from behind the last of its black-barked trees. An empty field of moist, late-summer grass rolled away before me. Beyond the field was a stand of white birch. Beyond the trees there were ebony hills, and beyond the hills a mountain loomed, its tip glowing ghostly pale against the sky.

It was deep night, the hour of the wolf. The moon had set long ago, and the stars were dimmed by a high mist, but I saw quite clearly through the pellucid dark, farther by far than human eyes can see. My ears caught lower, higher, fainter, softer sounds; my nostrils scented richer fragrances on the breeze that puffed into the woods from over the short grass of the field.

I waited, listening with mild amusement to the fluttered heartbeat of some tiny animal huddled close at hand, so terrified of me, it could not even flee for its life. A rabbit, perhaps. It smelled like a rabbit.

Then I heard something more: light, hurried footfalls from the far edge of the field. I heard a woman panting, her heart thumping from fear, fear of me . . . and fear she would not be able to find me.

The breeze puffed again, and I could smell her, too—the sharp sweetness of her sweat, the spice of her breath. And her loins, the delicious, urgent heat of her loins: long before I could see her, her smells betrayed exactly what she craved.

She burst onto the path across the field, the path from the farmhouse slumbering beyond the birch stand; the farmhouse where everyone slept ignorant of her hunger, the dark lust that had driven her into the night.

To me.

I saw her clear as day against the birches, her white embroidered blouse, her full peasant skirt. She kicked off her sandals, stepped a few paces into the field on naked feet. She reached up behind her and loosed her hair, shook her head, and let the wavy black mane cascade over her shoulders.

She undid a stay at her waist and her skirt slipped away; unbuttoned her blouse and shrugged it off; brushed away the straps of her gauzy cotton shift, rolled it to her belly; hooked her thumbs in her waist and peeled both her undergarments down together. She trembled slightly in the midsummer late-night chill; pulled her shoulders back defiantly, proudly. She knew I was looking at her nakedness. Or rather, she prayed I was looking. Her body was exquisitely formed, vibrantly young, perfectly virginal. Delicious.

She stood still in the field, scanned the woods where I waited. I could see and hear and smell her fearful hunger, the desperate extremity of her lust. Her terror was sweet, and I relished it for a few moments.

But she had been good, had done just what was required.

And so I shifted slightly and let her see me. For an instant I watched myself from her viewpoint in the field: I saw as she did, the black and beckoning woods in which I stood, and suddenly, within the horrifying darkness . . . my green, glowing, luminous eyes.

Calling to her.

She sobbed with relief, and raced down the field toward me. My eyes feasted on her: on the thick mane lashing her full breasts; on her wide hips, her well-muscled legs, her dark eyes, her ivory skin. On her hunger. Her wonderful hunger.

I opened my arms for her; she leaped at me, sobbing wildly. We collided, fell, tumbled down together onto the pungent forest floor. She was on top of me, kissing, biting, scratching, but I tossed her onto her back, clutched her knees to hold her legs wide apart.

I plunged into her.

There was a rending, a breaking, a tearing through, and she screamed once, long and loud in pleasure and in pain. I clamped my hand over her mouth. She bit into the fleshy edge of my palm. I pulled my hand away and slapped her face, then grabbed her arm roughly and threw her over onto her belly. I hoisted her up onto her hands and knees. She was panting like an animal when I entered her again and this time I slid deep inside with no obstruction at all.

She raised her head. I nuzzled her ear and buried my face in the perfumed mane of her hair. She tossed her head to lay her neck bare, and I licked her sweet, salty throat, and then I clamped my teeth onto her flesh and *bit* her, hard and deep.

She screamed again, but hot blood was coursing over my lips. I clutched her shoulders as she writhed and bucked below me, and I *bit* again, pressed my teeth into the delicious flesh of her neck, held her tight in my jaws.

Glistening, silvery fur shimmered out all over my body. And so while we clipped and rutted, my pelt covered her nakedness, a rough mantle for a savage, ravaged queen.

She moaned and clawed the earth. Her whole body was trembling beneath me and I knew we were riding up on the

same delirious wave. The wave crashed, but it refused to
subside, and still we rode its crest together. We were a single,
wild beast, rising up, falling, mounting, soaring into the
bright, black, starry, moonless sky; and we *howled* our horrifying delight.

Our sharp teeth flashed like daggers, our wild eyes glowed
brighter than any moon, our shimmering, silvery pelts glistened and rippled. I was hunched over her, my jaws still
gripping her neck. She crouched down on her four strong
legs, arched her head up and snarled joyously as she held me
clamped deep inside her. We howled again from low in our
chests while our claws tore at the moist, bleeding earth.

We growled and bit and rutted for an eternity, and only
after an eternity were we finally through. We twitched our
hindquarters and halved apart and lay panting together side
by side. But just for a moment. She rose up and bayed coldly,
terrifying the night with the complaint of a new and different
hunger.

She bounded off to hunt, and I would have risen and followed after her, but I could not. When I tried to rise, a wave
of searing pain coursed all across my body.

I was on my back in my bed, wide awake.

I had kicked away my covers, and so I could see the horror
I had become, quite clearly.

What I must describe next is repugnant, and I fear the
gentle reader will find it so. I would follow modesty's dictates
and pass over these matters entirely, were they not crucial to
an understanding of all I was and would become. Readers of
too delicate a nature are advised to pass over what follows
and proceed to the next chapter. Or, here might be a fitting
place to put down this narrative entirely.

As for the rest of you . . . what I saw, by your leave, was
this.

I peered down at my body. My legs were constricted, the
knees bent and spread, the muscles swollen, hardened,
shortened, the tendons bulging like rope. My feet were
twisted and elongated; shiny, blackened claws jutted from

my toes. My feet and my legs were covered with clumps of pale, maculated fur. As if in some grotesquely speeded-up film, the fur clumps shimmered out of my flesh, drew back in; shimmered and withdrew. . . .

My chest protruded, yet seemed constricted, too. When I tried to gasp in breath, fiery pain radiated from its core. My thumping heart, my lungs, my guts were roiling. They wrenched about inside me, changing their very shape and position.

My sex . . . between my splayed thighs, my organ pronged up hard as a leather bat. It wove about, conducting the air with a mind, or at least a purpose, of its own. Suddenly, a white filigree of spunk danced up, struggled to scale some wild height, then fell back onto my painfully knotted stomach. Another filigree . . . another . . . and now, just below the terrible hurt coursing through my twisted muscles and bones, there welled another feeling. A glittering delight, a bodily thrill rose up like hot lava. I erupted with a pleasure and a pain I had never known before, had never even imagined a human body could bear.

My fur shimmered away and was gone; my muscles smoothed; my legs could stretch again.

From a great distance I heard a hideous, foreign sound. As a merciful darkness finally took me and dragged me away from consciousness, I recognized the sound as sobbing, and I knew the sobs were coming from my own human throat.

It might have all been a dream, right?

Except I knew it wasn't, just as surely as you do. Several things told me so, within minutes after I arose the next morning. Firstly, I was immediately successful in my search for what we in the private investigations profession refer to as pecker tracks: good-as-gold evidence in any divorce court in the land.

Ah, you say, but such evidence merely demonstrates the occurrence of an *emittio nocturnalis*. If one dreams of Venus de Milo or one's grammar school teacher, the presence of dried spunk in the morning would hardly prove either lady had in fact shared one's amorous couch of the night before.

Certainly. The weird liaison I experienced was nothing but a dream. And the hideous transformation I seemed to be experiencing when aroused from slumber *could* have merely been the product of febrile imagining, too.

But if you believe that, tell it to the judge. And while you're at it, explain the hairs I discovered alongside the tracks. No. Not the hairs, the bristles.

I sat on the edge of my bed, held a half dozen of those bristles pinched between my thumbtip and forefinger, peered closely at them in the sad, bright gray, early-morning light. Longish, and straight, and silvery they were; stiff, spear-shaped, and sharp at the tips, not at all like the hairs of a human. In fact upon close scrutiny they were rather like the bristles of some creature such as, oh, I don't know, shall we say possibly . . . a wolf?

Yes. We shall.

And in that instant of recognition, I suddenly found myself in the midst of the dark forest, back in my dream . . . with her, the woman, the beast in the woods. I saw her quite clearly. Not her face precisely, but *her*. In the illogically logical manner of dreams, I recognized her. She was the she-wolf, the bitch in her human form. Very beautiful.

Then, with no clear idea of *how* I knew, I knew how I'd happened to dream the dream. The she-wolf had sent it to me. She had been lurking near as I slept! There was no question about it.

The she-wolf.

I recalled our nightmare lovemaking, hers and mine, re-dreamed it, saw again the moment of her flight. Gone. Alone. Left all alone again. The ugly, empty sadness of spent lust . . . I felt a shiver of painful pleasure, pale shadow of my dream's shameful ecstasy.

I looked down at the bristles between my fingertips, then shifted my gaze to my fingers. My hand. *My hand!*

Tiny silvery hairs were shimmering out over the backs of my fingers and knuckles . . . and hands and wrists and forearms and . . . shimmering out, glistening in the morning light, growing with my remembered lust.

Fight it fight it nonono . . . !

The bristles wriggled back, disappeared.

I was staring at my smooth hand. It was quite awhile before I remembered to resume breathing.

God's rotten teeth . . .

I lurched to my feet. Pulled my hair. Let go at once and wiped my palms on my chest. Stumbled into the bathroom. Splashed cold water into my face. Washed my hands. Scrubbed them. Scrubbed my face too. And only then did I have the guts to look in the mirror.

I don't know what I expected, but I found the actual sight of my face shocking . . . shocking how normal it looked.

Unchanged.

I touched my cheek to verify my eyes' report with a second sense. Then I sucked in a deep, calming breath. And another and another and . . .

It took a while. It took a long while.

That evening I headed downtown, to see if my good old buddy Carlos Moy could help arrange a certain unpleasant but necessary interview I'd already put off too long.

I happened to know he could.

Moy's Uneeda Beer Garden & Canton Specialty Restaurant (Carlos Moy had not served any food there since 1929, which was when he'd bought the joint) was on Fulton Street, three blocks west of the fish market.

Odd thing: It was middle of the evening, on a weekday night, and yet I had to stow the Packard around the corner from the Beer Garden, because the street in front of it was choked with parked and double-parked cars. Fancy ones, too, big Chryslers and Hudsons and DeSotos, a couple of Cadillacs, even a Bentley or three. And there was nothing on the block but bulk laundries, smoked fish warehouses, and Moy's Uneeda Beer Garden.

I stooped under the awning, plowed through the swinging doors, and surveyed the joint.

The room smelled of smoke and sweat and fish and beer and unflushed toilets. As usual. And the usual fun-loving crowd was there—a dozen or so bleary European sailors, an equal contingent of neatly intoxicated Chinese fishermen, a sprinkling of emaciated, brown-toothed opium gobblers, and a light garnish of tubercular dishwashers.

Lin the bartender was there, too, the big lummox, and he served me a watery brew I didn't really want—sloshed it in my direction as soon as I bellied up to the bar, actually, in his typically friendly fashion. I would have queried him concerning the fine collection of cars the local dishwashers had taken to driving. But asking questions of Lin was about as constructive as pissing up a rope.

Never liked Lin. Sneaky.

He must have slipped his boss the news of my arrival, because before I even took a sip of the swill, Carlos stepped through a door at the back of the bar. I heard the clink of poker chips in the room behind him: the solution to many mysteries.

I raised my eyebrows; Carlos smiled sheepishly, shrugged his shoulders. But then he limped over to me with his arms open, grinning from ear to ear.

"Que pasa, Capitan?" he said.

He gave me a hug and a back slap, then sat on the next stool.

"Nada mucho, Carlos," I said, and nodded at his leg. "How's the hopper?"

Carlos had taken a legful of shrapnel in the Battle of Jarama, had to be carried back down the hill to the trenches, from a bayonet charge quite early in the campaign. He was luckier than about half the guys in that charge had been.

"Great. Or at least good enough to keep me out of the next one." He chuckled.

"So you think there'll be a next one, eh?"

"Don't you think there's one coming?"

"No, Carlos. I think the next one's already started."

"Like hell you do, Jimmy. *You* think the last one never ended."

"It's a point of view." I shrugged.

"That why you're here?" he asked.

He had asked the question quietly. And I noticed he'd checked to see where Lin was before he asked. Lin was a few drinkers down, polishing a glass. Glasses didn't usually get polished in the Uneeda Beer Garden.

"See you've added an attraction in the back dining room," I said. "What do you feature? Just poker? Or a craps table too?"

"Poker, craps . . . we're getting a wheel next week. Right, Lin?" Carlos laughed nervously. Lin just put down the glass and walked away. I suddenly wondered whose idea the casino was in the first place. But I decided to give myself a break and tell myself it wasn't my problem.

"Hey, c'mon, Captain. It could be worse."

"Really? How?"

"How? Well, this nabe's real big on gong ringers. I could've set up an opium den back there. Or a reefer pad. Or maybe a crib. You know, start running prosties, like Velma did. Never could understand guys spending hard-earned money on prosties, though. Or reefer. Now craps, at least you got a chance to take your money home with you. Doxies, you come . . . it's gone."

"It's a point of view."

"Christ, will you stop saying that!" he snapped.

"No," I said calmly. "By the way, interesting clientele you're attracting. How'd the uptown crowd discover the Uneeda?"

He started to squirm.

"Well, we started out strictly local. You know how Chinks are, Jimmy. Every waiter and laundryman in Manhattan's praying he can break the bank and buy steamship tickets for his whole fucking family in Canton. More so since the Japs started going ape over there."

"Nice of you to take your people's money, Carlos."

"Yeah, well, I gave them an honest shuffle, which is more

than lots do. Some of them even got to buy those steamship tickets.''

"Sounds like you were running a regular Chinese Benevolent Association.''

"Damn tootin'. Couldn't have put it better myself. So anyway, word got around. And all of a sudden I, uh, I had a partner. But I ain't complaining,'' he went on too quickly. "It's working out great.''

"So you said.''

"Yeah. All them high rollers back there came with the new territory.''

Carlos glanced down the bar. Lin had slithered closer again, possibly at the mention of the word "partner.'' I gave him a look that I hoped would adequately communicate the extent of the renovations I would have enjoyed making on his face. I was apparently successful, and Lin drifted out with the tide.

"By the by, Carlos . . . this great new partner of yours— he have a name?''

He sure did, and I knew what it was, too, thanks to the information industry. But I wanted to hear it from Carlos.

He cleared his throat nervously.

"So anyway . . . I always enjoy these visits, Captain, but, uh . . . want to tell me to what I owe the honor?''

Fine by me if that was how he wanted to play it.

"Sure. I need a letter of introduction.''

"Gee. It sounds so innocent. Okay, I'm holding onto the bar. Let's hear the lucky individual's name.''

"Maurice Chen.''

"Ha ha. Señor will have his leeetle joke,'' Carlos said in his mock Spanish accent. But he didn't sound amused. He sounded frightened.

"No joke, Professor. I need an in. Oh, and some advice on the best way to approach Mr. Chen.''

"Jesus Christ, Jimmy. How's about not at all? Do you know who Chen is?''

"A rich punk with a couple of slop shops.'' I shrugged. "Believe me, I don't want his autograph. But he may have some information I need, and I don't have a whole lot of time to spare waiting for an appointment. A couple of words could get me in to see him lots faster."

"In's not the problem, Jimmy. Out is the problem."

"I'll handle that part." I smiled.

"Like hell you will. Not with that attitude problem of yours."

"Attitude is the very least of my problems."

"The fact that you don't think you have an attitude is the biggest part of your problem. Maurice Chen . . ." He shifted forward on his stool and murmured, "You know, Maurice Chen could twitch a titty, and within twenty-four hours every Chinese restaurant in Manhattan would be serving you in their chop suey. Stuff like that really does happen, Jimmy. All the time."

"Which is why I only order vegetable dishes. But he's already tried it, Carlos. That, or something like it."

"You think I don't know?!" he grumbled. "How many people you think saw you walking around with those mugs the other night? Half of freaking Chinatown!"

I checked his face, trying to read whether he knew the rest, knew they were shape-shifters, or that I'd killed them, or about my run-in with the mommy wolf. I decided he didn't. Carlos Moy just looked frightened. Not terrified.

"Listen, Jimmy. You are the last guy I want to find in my dim sum. And you're the last guy I want on my conscience. Know what I mean, Captain? You carried me back down the hill."

"I needed the exercise. So do me the favor, will you?"

"Uh-uh." He shook his head. "Rich punk with some slop shops, huh? Guess you didn't notice what happened to the opium trade around the time Mr. Chen hit the city."

"It's Mister now, huh? Sure I noticed. It doubled. Which is one more thing I don't admire him for. I also know who's running half the whores in Manhattan these days. *And* I know who runs the gambling joints, too. Get it, Carlito? So now *you* listen. Your concern for my well-being is touching, truly touching. But if you're so worried about your goddamn conscience . . ." I cocked my head at Lin, who wasn't even pretending not to listen anymore. " . . . ask your scumbag buddy here to make the arrangements. He doesn't love me. Besides, he's running your goddamn show now, anyway. Probably sees Chen all the time when he drops off the take."

Carlos Moy's face went as hard as stone.

"Sure thing, Captain Underhill, sir," he drawled bitterly. "Anything you say, sir."

I wasn't really as steamed as I sounded, and I hated insulting Carlos that way. Putting a guy down for doing what he has to do to survive, it's lousy. But as I have made abundantly clear, I didn't have much time. And with each ticking second I realized I liked Maurice Chen less and less. And I wanted to make his acquaintance more and more.

Carlos gave Lin the necessary high sign and disappeared. A few moments later, Lin handed me a telephone across the bar without uttering a word. I decided to bite and said hello to whoever was on the other end.

"Hello, Mr. Underhill." The voice was feathery and warm; light fingers caressing the back of my neck. "I am Mr. Chen's secretary. You will call me Kristara. Understanding you wish speak with Mr. Chen?"

I took her accent to be Mandarin with just a pinch of British colonial, rather than standard-issue Cantonese.

"Yes. That is correct," I said cordially.

"Mr. Chen inclined speak with you too. Regrettably is occupied for the next hour, but most happy to see you after that. Midnight will not be inconvenient time for you arrival at Mandarin Palace Restaurant?"

"Not at all inconvenient."

"How very fortunate. Mr. Chen say you will wait the time in Mr. Moy's casino. Mr. Chen say you may have unlimited credit for next hour."

"Very kind of Mr. Chen. Please send him my thanks, and tell him I eagerly await meeting him."

"Most assuredly. And Mr. Chen wish you luck in casino."

She hung up; I shoved the phone back in Lin's direction. It certainly was generous of Chen, offering me unlimited credit in Carlos's gambling den. But it also made him sound a bit too eager to have me stay put for the hour. I decided a stroll would be more to my liking. So I spun around on the stool to take my leave.

Lin's hand on my wrist stopped my graceful exit. I looked back at his paw, then I looked at his ugly mug. Lin just shook his head.

Really.

In the next instant my free hand was on his throat, compressing nerves and air pipes and arteries in just such a manner as to make his eyes go wide and watery with pain, and his chest to constrict for lack of oxygen. And his hand on my wrist to flop away like a fish, because aside from giving him pain in every fiber of his body, what I was now doing was paralyzing his voluntary motor control from the neck down.

In a few more seconds he would shit and piss his pants. A few moments later, the nerve damage would be irreversible and he'd pass the rest of his days in a basket. And a few moments after that, he wouldn't have any days left to pass. I tried to decide honestly just how much I disliked Lin. I decided my feelings were in the gray area somewhere between not minding at all if he were dead, and actively desiring to place him in said state of nonbeing. I eased up enough to give myself, and him, a little more time.

Meanwhile, I shared some confidences with him.

"So, I'm going to be leaving now, Lin," I said quietly and pleasantly. "But let me tell you what I will do if you inform *anyone* I have left. I will come back here, and first I will rip off your ears and nose, and then I will pull out your eyes, and then I will stuff all of those things right down your throat . . ."

Chinese people get very frightened when you threaten them with mutilation. Come to think of it, so do I.

" . . . and then I will do *this* to you until you die."

I squeezed a tiny bit harder, to show him what I meant by "this." When I let go, Lin dropped away so clumsily that he knocked over a number of bottles of rotgut and got himself all messy, and laid there in the mess he'd made, gasping and crying. Good for him, corrupter of Carlos Moy, or at least enforcer of the corruption.

Chatham Square had been swept clean by the hour—bare save for the stray puffy-eyed waiter stumbling home for a few hours of sleep, and me, up too late for a change, on affairs that were none of my damn business. I stowed the Packard on Division Street, walked across the Square, and parked myself in the greasy window seat of an all-night java joint I knew from evenings past. I admired the scenery over a cup of pretty good Chinese coffee. My view of Mr. Chen's Mandarin Palace across the Square could not have been any clearer; and I wouldn't have wanted it any closer.

The Mandarin Palace Restaurant was not precisely in Chinatown. It sat on the far side of the Square, peering contemptuously down on its benighted brethren, the tenements of Chinatown proper, huddled together as if in bowed obeisance.

It was a looming, five-story affair all gussied up in the ornately carved and lacquered wood style of a South China Buddhist temple, despite its name. It was nightmare-gaudy by Western standards, but impressive indeed as the Chinese see things. A small, no, a large fortune had been spent on red and gold enamel paint alone.

I was halfway through my second cup of joe when I beheld a most troublesome sight.

A limousine slithered up to the Palace, a shiny black Bentley I was certain I recognized from other times and places. The Palace was closed up tight, but just as the limo stopped, the heavy front gates of the restaurant opened slowly. A tall, willowy woman stepped out and to the side, bowed while holding the gates open.

Fortunately, the gates were high atop a wide flight of steps. Had they not been so elevated, I would not have been able to observe the gentleman who minced out next. He was a tiny chap, no higher than the willowy woman's belly button, even in his black fedora. His greatcoat was black, too. But his gloves were green, such a nice bright green, I could see them all the way across the Square.

Lo Fang, the rotten goblin.

Murdered anti-Nazis, rich poisoners, Chinese werewolf gunsels . . . it was hardly a surprise to find Lo Fang wallowing smack in the middle of it all, with his little green monkey paws elbows-deep in the pie. In fact as I believe I have indicated, I was fairly sure I'd been smelling him for days.

But none of that made the sight of him any more welcome. And what I saw next was even less so. He scurried down the steps; the curbside door of the limo popped open, and a smallish figure in a hooded rain cape stepped out.

She held the door for the master; ducked back into the auto as soon as he'd entered. The Bentley leaped forward with a great squealing of tires, lurched away from the curb weaving drunkenly, accelerated, then straightened out and came tooling up the Square directly toward my seat in the java shop.

It roared to curbside before the window and screeched almost to a stop. The driver let it cruise past me in a slow roll. In the back seat, Lo Fang leaned forward and tipped his hat, leering like a slack-jawed hyena.

The woman beside him glared at me and jerked the rope of the venetian blinds. They crashed clattering down in the instant. The driver hunched forward. The horn blared, the engine roared, the Bentley's huge tires shrieked in agony, and the limousine vaulted forward like a cruelly spurred horse. Next moment, it was gone.

I'd recognized the driver.

His enormous bulk had filled the roomy front cab very nearly past capacity, his gray, leathery face was clearly visible even beneath the black chauffeur's cap crammed down around his ears.

Entimemseph the Mummy.

He'd been grinning wildly, displaying his whole mouthful

of yellow, tusklike teeth; clearly enchanted with his newly learned skill.

I'd recognized the woman beside Lo Fang, too, her flashing eyes, her raven black hair, her pale, pale skin so perfect and so cold.

It was Rachel Bukhovna, come back from the dead.

Again.

My heart sank, the java cup I'd been clutching slipped from my fingers and shattered on the tiles beside me.

Sweet creeping Jesus . . . was it possible? But I'd held her in my arms all that night and horrid dawn. I'd felt her agony, listened to her cries, clutched her close and held her fast. And when the light of the murderous dawn had touched her, she had died her death in my arms and fallen away to earth and leaves and scattered dust. . . .

Dust. Could Lo Fang raise the dead . . . or rather, reraise the undead?

Forget I asked. It was no matter, none at all. At least not right now it wasn't. I'd sort out all the hows, whys, and wherefores later.

Just at the moment I had an appointment to keep.

I paid for my coffee and coffee cup, strolled briskly across the Square, walked up the steps to the Mandarin Palace, and rapped on the heavy glass of the wide front door. It was opened by the willowy woman I'd just observed from afar, and opened so quickly that I knew she'd been peeking.

"Good evening Mr. Underhill, I am Kristara," she breathed while favoring me with a welcoming bow.

Up close, Kristara was somewhere between very pretty and beautiful, more than fulfilling the promise of her voice on the telephone. She was tall and lean and firm, and her racially ambiguous features were as delicate and yet slightly "off" as a factory-rejected Oriental porcelain doll.

She wore a brocaded, high-collared, sea green shift of embroidered silk; quite demure. But dear Kristara had neglected to fasten several of the shift's top stays, and so while she bowed me in, I was treated to a most inspirational view of her warm, honey brown breast, full, succulent and, I could just discern, tipped by a ring of darker brown.

"Please to follow, Mr. Underhill," she said softly, seemingly apologetic for the necessity of interrupting the display. "Master Chen await most anxiously."

In consolation, Kristara turned slowly, allowing me time to observe that high, wooden servant sandals displayed the rear portion of her carriage to excellent advantage, too.

We walked down the Palace's main hallway, Kristara in the lead. But I hadn't followed for more than a dozen paces before I noticed it.

The smell.

So strange, like nothing I'd ever smelled before. No. Wrong, very wrong. I knew that odor quite well. Just never so strong. Never so . . . compelling. It seemed to be coming from behind a padlocked door on the left side of the hallway. As we passed the door, I felt a thrill of delight shivering through my whole body.

A dangerous thrill, a feeling that could grow. Like the feeling in my dreams, like the feeling when I awoke from dreaming, the feeling that could grow and overpower and make me . . . change.

No. No no no!

Kristara kept walking, seemingly quite oblivious to my discomfort. I concentrated on her bottom, undulating ahead of me in the gloom. The smell faded, and with it, the dark desire.

Good. Very good.

There was work to be done.

I followed Kristara through the darkened restaurant, across shadowy ballrooms, down deeply carpeted corridors. Only the lowest two of the Mandarin Palace's five floors were devoted to dining. All the others comprised the palatial private quarters of Mr. Maurice Chen—quite the luxurious variant on the immigrant custom of living over the shop.

Strange night music wailed behind a closed door, rose and

then faded as we passed it. Incense and whispers in the darkness, the sound of bells. A small dog barking savagely, a peal of laughter, far from friendly, smells of sex and pain . . . I paced the entire length of Chen's private domain. And my journey behind Kristara did not end until we had reached a richly carved teak and mahogany door on what I counted as the building's top landing.

Kristara paused with her hand on the knob. "Master Chen . . . his private study," she murmured, and stepped aside to bow me in.

A snake in a tuxedo. That was my impression of Maurice Chen in the very first instant of our interview. He was standing with his back to the door, staring at a jade statue of a snarling demon, possibly praying to it. I felt a twinge of guilt for interrupting him at his religious devotions.

I peered into the study's shadows.

It was a dimly lit, cavernous space, jam-packed for as far as I could see with jade sculptures and gold panels and ivory screens and inlaid mahogany furniture—all manner of the precious collectibles for which Chen had gained so enviable a reputation of expertise.

But I wondered whether the study's shadows also held any unpleasant surprises, especially surprises of the sort that might have their cross hairs fixed on yours truly's vitals. Something—perhaps a new sixth sense, maybe just a recent improvement on one of my plain old five—told me that was indeed the case.

Chen turned to face me—first his head, then his neck and shoulders, then his torso, then what was left of him, all fluidity and effortless ease. He was tall and gaunt and sinuously muscular. His heavily lidded eyes were, yes, serpentine, and he regarded me like a cobra dreaming of its next meal. I believe Chen's snake stare was designed to inspire fear, or at the very least discomfort.

I'm sorry to report the effort was wasted on me, though. I'd shot the heads off of too many snakes to be mightily impressed by one more. But while Chen mused about me, I mused about how cleanly a .45 dumdum placed between and just slightly above his eyes would remove the entire top of his skull, nicely and neatly, like the tip of a soft-boiled egg. Nicely and neatly.

"I hear you have been asking a great many questions about me, Mr. Underhill," he murmured at last. "I cannot honestly say I am flattered by your interest."

His voice was slow and treacly, his eyes glistened moistly. And the tiny black dots in the center of his irises, the glowing, glassy sheen of his lifeless pupils, told me the rest of his story in an instant.

Mister Maurice Chen was a hophead, a gong ringer, an opium eater. And just at the moment, he was flying higher than a Chinese kite.

"Not a great many questions, Mr. Chen. Just a few." I nodded at the jade demon. "Lovely piece of carving."

"I'm so glad you approve. Know something about Chinese jade, do you?"

He was trying his best to sound contemptuous, was doing credibly well at it, too. But the effect was somewhat marred by the opium slur in his voice.

"Not really. But I know what I like. And I like Chinese sculpture. At least some of it."

"Some of it. How refreshing. Well, this is an early Q'uang Tung Period piece . . . North China, First Dynasty. The eleventh century B.C. Over three thousand years old. Sculptures from that period are impossibly rare. This one is literally priceless."

Just what I wanted: an art lesson from a doped-up asshole.

"Do you really think so?" I asked in Mandarin. "I would have said *late* Q'uang Tung. And in fact I would have said a Chang forgery from the nineteenth century A.D. Doesn't it look like a First Dynasty copy piece from Master Chang's workshop to you? Observe the gesture of the right foreleg . . . I understand Master Chang ran quite the production line in First Dynasty forgeries. Beautiful in its own right though. And over one hundred years old. I hope you didn't overpay for it."

Chen's eyes had grown positively round.

"Nonsense!" he finally sputtered in English. "This is an original!"

"I'm sure you are correct." I smiled and bowed slightly.

"In any case, I didn't agree to see you to discuss art," he muttered.

He picked up an ivory pipe stem and fumbled with it a bit clumsily. Our art history chat seemed to have rattled him. "I said you have been asking too many questions about me. Too many . . ."

"And *I* said not too many. Just a few," I replied in English. "A certain client of mine . . . this client's safety seems somewhat compromised at the moment. I'm sure you'll understand I have to investigate everyone in . . . this client's . . . circle of acquaintances."

"I can't say I do," he continued more calmly. "And who might this client of yours be?"

"Clara Steiner."

That's right. After all the effort I'd expended to meet Chen in a relatively neutral way, in a way that wouldn't reveal my motives in advance, Lo Fang's presence outside had demonstrated quite clearly I'd simply been wasting my time. There was still lots of room for probing and pussyfooting, still whole volumes of information I wouldn't share with Chen. But there was no longer any particular reason to hide my connection to Clara and Gina.

The mention of Clara's name didn't produce any major outward reaction on Chen's part. Then again, in his present doped-up state, it was hard to predict what *would* produce a major reaction. Art history ticked him off. But he might just yawn if someone started yanking out his teeth with a pair of pliers. Go figure hopheads.

"Clara Steiner. Hmm. Yes, a lovely girl. Charming. Quite charming. I've had her at several parties at Le Bistro d'Or and she's been a sensation. Very cultured, very beautiful. You say her safety is compromised? How distressing. Who would want to harm a sweet young thing like that?"

"Oh, people who disapprove of her politics . . . or her father's."

"Her father? Ah yes, wasn't her father some kind of Communist?"

"No, Mr. Chen. He wasn't. But he didn't like the Nazis."

"Well, that isn't very smart, now is it? I hate all politics. Politics simply bore me senseless. But one is bound to have trouble, if one goes against the wisdom of the majority. And Mr. Hitler is quite popular in Europe these days, isn't he?"

Sounded like he'd been getting his news of the world from his rich Hitler-whore pal, Glenda Rogers-Gracey. He lurched over to a large, ornately carved chair, flopped into it, and draped himself with a casualness that was both fluid and awkward. He didn't offer me a seat, so I just tossed my hat on his desk and found one myself.

"I suppose it depends on who you talk to." I smiled.

"Doesn't it always," he drawled. "But at the risk of sounding impolite, even though this is all fascinating, I fail to see how it concerns me."

"Clara Steiner and her friend . . . I believe you also know Regina . . . have discovered they are being followed. And worse."

"You aren't suggesting that I would have them followed."

"Not necessarily. But I . . ."

" 'Not necessarily'? I really do not like your tone, Mr. Underhill," he said with sudden pique.

"A figure of speech," I said mildly. "But even if you find politics tedious, some of your friends do not. They have convictions that are the opposite of Miss Steiner's. And they are willing to act on their convictions. It could get very unpleasant. Even more unpleasant than it has already been."

"Once again, I don't know what you mean, Mr. Underhill. None of my friends would do anything unpleasant. I do not befriend unpleasant people. I still fail to understand why you are here."

"To find out what you know about the people bothering Miss Steiner." I shrugged. "To suggest that if you do hear of people bothering her, you warn them of just how unhealthy doing so could become."

"Then this interview is over, Mr. Underhill. I can't help you in either regard."

"Somehow I believe you can."

He shook his head with surprising vigor, as if brushing off my comment like a mosquito. Or signaling some hidden servants to get themselves ready.

"I said the interview is over. But I don't mind telling you this before you go . . ." He suddenly uncoiled his limbs from the chair and leaned toward me. "I truly do not appreciate your interest in me," he hissed malevolently. "And I truly suggest your interest should cease. If it does not, *that* could become very unhealthy. Very unhealthy indeed."

Ah. So now we saw the real Chen peeking out. Mr. Maurice Chen: poisoner, drug dealer, pimp, dope addict, darling of high society, and pal of assorted Nazis in and around Manhattan. I was impressed, but not favorably, and not in the way he would have liked.

"I'll take my chances," I said quietly.

"Most unwise. Believe me, Underhill, you won't live long if you continue to take chances like those. Life is full of dangers. This very room is full of dangers. As it is, you wouldn't even be leaving here alive if certain *persons* . . . had not expressed an inexplicable interest in seeing you survive this night. I could easily be tempted to override their wishes, though. Very easily."

It was very sporting of Chen to call my attention to the obvious—to the people and things in the shadows around us who did not have my best interests at heart.

I briefly wondered why Lo Fang had warned him not to kill me, but I hadn't been counting on Lo Fang's benevolence when I went to see Chen. I'd known from the beginning that my best chance of surviving an interview with him lay in drilling it through his thick skull just how unhealthy any attempt to harm me would be. For him.

I let my fingertips inch in the direction of my gun. I could have killed Chen with my hands or my feet or with a number of objects I'd noticed scattered about the room. It takes only an instant to kill a man. Less if you are really dedicated to the task.

I'd already decided I wanted to use the gun on Chen, though. I would give him some wounds that were fatal, yet long enough acting and painful enough for him to feel them quite well, even through his opium haze. I'd been completely aware of every sound and movement in the room around us since the moment I'd entered. And I was fairly confident I could serve Chen his death on a platter before he could signal for mine.

I also saw I had communicated my confidence to him. I watched him relax. The signal for my death—and for his, would not come. It suddenly seemed a good moment for some more candor.

"I'm surprised to hear you wasting time with childish threats." I grinned. "Especially after what happened to your shape-shifters."

"Excuse me, Mr. Underhill?" He seemed genuinely puzzled.

"The shape-shifter dacoits you sent after me the other night? I don't suppose you have an unlimited supply of such pets."

Maurice Chen was hardly the robust, out-of-doors type. But he instantly blanched so sickly pale that even I, who didn't like him, worried for his health. It was entertaining to finally see something worth reading on his face. I watched shock, then puzzlement, then understanding, and then fear, all in brief and rapid succession.

"Sh-shape shifters . . ." he finally managed to blurt out. "So that is why you are not to be touched. . . . I . . . ahem." Now he seemed frightened by what he'd just allowed himself to say. "I, that is, I was naturally aware of your street brawl the other night, Underhill. I, along with the rest of Chinatown. But I was unaware the dacoits were shape-shifters."

"Really? You should have your employees fill out more detailed questionaires."

"Don't be a fool! They weren't mine!" he hissed. "But I

will tell you this. You've made some very unpleasant enemies. You have attracted interest from some very unpleasant
circles indeed.''

"It's the story of my life." I smiled.

My smile did not have a calming effect on him. He looked
like he had a case of the jitters only a bowl of poppy paste
would cure.

"I mean circles you know nothing about. Nothing! Good-
bye, Mr. Underhill. It is not even wise for me to have you
here as a visitor. Please go at once!''

It was clear Maurice Chen's nerves had finally gotten the
better of him, and I saw little to be gained from continuing
to bear witness to such an unpleasant sight. He needed a
long suck on his favorite pipe much more than he needed my
continued company.

So I retrieved my hat and left him to his pathetic, frightened pleasures.

I could not have been more pleased with the results of my
visit to Chen, on several counts.

Firstly, I had obviously managed to scare the pants off of
him, and without any major expenditure of energy. That alone
made the trip worthwhile. Then, too, there was that strange
smell from behind the door. Intriguing, and unquestionably
worth a second sniff. And lastly, I had gleaned more from
Chen than I had any right to expect, professionally speaking;
mountains more than one usually gains from an initial visit
to an uncooperative interviewee.

Namely, I had established that Chen was a treasure trove
of fascinating, relevant information. He knew a great deal
indeed, loads more than he had told me yet. An absolute
gold mine.

Gold mine. That was it exactly. I reflected on just how
much fun it was going to be to find him alone some time
really soon, and dig every bit of information I wanted right
out of his dirty, rotten hide. I could hardly wait. In fact, I
decided not to. I decided to do something naughty instead.

I cranked up the car and motored around for a while—

long enough to verify that I was not being followed, and also long enough to give Maurice a chance to settle in for the night. I was fairly sure he wouldn't be straying far during the next few hours. When we had parted, he'd already looked loaded enough to take a snooze face-first in his egg foo young at any moment, and it was also clear he had every intention of reattaching his head to the nozzle immediately if not sooner.

I doubled back toward Chen's neighborhood after about thirty minutes and parked the auto at some distance from the Palace, in a spot so deserted I knew I would not be observed as I opened the trunk and donned my working clothes: black pants and pullover, gum-soled shoes, even a bit of burnt cork for my hands and face. I took along my tool kit, too. I wanted to revisit Maurice. But I did not wish to disturb him.

My approach to the restaurant, by way of an entire block of adjoining rooftops, was unobserved. And Chen's own roof door was latched but not securely locked, since his main source of protection from the cruel world around was the cruel world's abject fear of him. So gaining access to his inner sanctum was no major task, either.

I padded down the hallway I had so recently crossed with Kristara, paused before the door to the master's study, and listened.

In just a matter of moments, I heard a most curious sound; a long, high, shuddering moan. A woman had made it, and a bleak, exhausted sound it was, as if far from the first of many, as if there were many more to come.

Sure enough . . . I heard another.

And if I had to choose just one from those two great polar principles of human existence, I would have been willing to bet heavily that the moans I heard were not born of pleasure.

Ah, but now I heard a grunt, and a mirthless chuckle. Not a drop of pain in either of those.

They had issued from a man. I was fairly certain I knew the man's identity, but I dropped to my knees at the keyhole just to make sure. I'd already broken and entered the den of one of the richest thugs in a town justifiably world-famous for its rich thugs. I hardly had much to lose by adding a pinch of Peeping Tomism to the list of Chen's possible reasons for disliking me.

I couldn't see piss-all. The keyhole wasn't blocked, but all it afforded was a view of an absolutely stunning lacquered breakfront—I made it to be late Fifth Century Ch'ung Dynasty. Now *that* was an original—and in mint condition, too. I'd have been thrilled to be examining it, if I'd been in the market to dress up my digs with a priceless antique or two; under the circumstances I was ever so slightly disappointed, though.

I heard a clink, as of a chain being jerked. And the woman moaned again.

"All the way in, you damned monkey bitch!" the man slurred thickly. "Spill one drop, I break your miserable neck! You whore! You dirty sow! You broken night-soil pot!"

Oh, it was Chen all right. He kept on yammering at the woman in Mandarin, cursing her up and down the block. Then he started in with a gravelly, grunting sound, a sort of "rehh . . . rrehhh . . . rrrehhhh," like an old car with a weak starter. With every grunt there came a clink of the chain, and with every clink, a muffled, gagging groan from the woman.

There was quite the nasty synergy at work, from the sound of it. The more he clinked, the more she groaned; the more she groaned, the more he grunted. Clink, groan, grunt, clink groan grunt, clinkgroangrunt . . . Ah, the gentle joys of the love couch, a regular coupling of the gods. I am no stranger to the primal act, nor am I unfamiliar with the very imaginative performances mounted by the esteemed Madame Velma. But just at the moment, I was thankful all I could see was the furniture.

I have heard many a professional woman complain that hopheads make the worst customers. Gong ringing fills their heads with wild notions but removes much of their flesh's ability to carry out orders. So they get nasty—blame the hammer for bending the nail, start to play all manner of ugly games with the ladies.

At last Master Chen concluded his elegant pleasures. He let out a long, rumbling wallow of joy. Then for several minutes I heard nothing but his deep, increasingly regular breathing and along with it, the quiet sobbing of the lucky girl who had just served as his receptacle. I thought perhaps Maurice had drowsed off to sleep for the night. But no such luck.

"Get my bowl, miserable cow!" he grumbled, still in Mandarin. "Go do it good and fast, damn you!"

A clink, a whimper, the sound of wooden sandals scuttling across the floor, and a naked woman staggered into view.

It was Kristara. Her long hair was tangled and she looked quite the worse for wear.

She dragged open a compartment of the breakfront and fussed nervously with golden bowls, ebony boxes, ivory pipe stems . . . an assorted jumble of fancy dope-pad paraphernalia.

For a moment she let her fear or her despair get the better of her. She hunched her shoulders, buried her face in her hands, and burst into tears. A pipe dropped from her fingers.

I heard the clink again, and her entire body went rigid with pain, as if she were being jerked toward the couch she'd just scurried from.

"Damn you whore, I said *hurry*! And watch what you're doing!" Chen raved on. "Dirty bitch dog, you do nothing right! *Nothing*! I permit you to breed, and what do you offer me? A female. *Female*, damn you!"

"But . . . but . . . perhaps he is mistaken?" she sobbed. "Could he not be wrong just this once? Perhaps I will give you . . ."

"Silence, you sow!" he shrieked.

Kristara stiffened again; her teeth clenched, her tormented eyes flashed round and white.

And then I saw it: the light, quite sturdy looking golden chain. It led back toward the couch, but its near end was buried between Kristara's legs, in the dark notch just below her perfectly rounded buttocks.

I didn't know exactly how the chain was attached, and I didn't want to know. I didn't need to know: I was already revolted enough with Chen to do everything I'd have to do to him and more, when the time came.

She gathered up his gear in a panic and scurried back, sobbing hysterically. But when she reached him I heard the clatter of her putting it all down clumsily, and a thump as she dropped to her knees before him. From her muffled tone, I'd have said she buried her face in his lap as she wailed.

"Oh please, Master! Please! I try so hard to serve you! I beg you by my parents. If you hate me so much, *destroy* me! Destroy us both! Don't let me go on dishonoring you! Just kill me. Put me to death. If you cannot be bothered, at least give me permission to end my own life along with . . . what grows inside me. I will die blessing your name. I and my unborn will sing your praises for all eternity in the Hell of Slaves. Please, oh . . ."

Good grief. In Mandarin, Kristara's Anti-Emancipation Proclamation sounded both formal and highly impassioned. But I still wondered what Mental Health League Chen had fished her from.

"Now now, little frog." He chuckled. Suddenly his tone was surprisingly amused and gentle. "You are mine, and what grows inside you is mine. You must not ask me to destroy my property, even if it is worthless."

"I . . . I'm sorry, Master. I . . ."

"Shhh! Besides, even if you are worthless for breeding . . . you are becoming better at serving me each day. You learn more about my needs. . . . You aren't completely impossible to instruct. Would you have me waste all of the effort I have devoted to training you? What a selfish frog!"

"Oh, no, Master. It is just . . . . I seem to give you so much displeasure. I . . ."

"Enough! Tell me, do you love me more than you love anything in this world or the next?"

"Of course! I love you more than my life, which is worth-less. More than my parents' lives, which are . . ."

"I see. And would you do anything I requested of you?"

"My Master must know I would do anything . . ."

"Good. Then open that lamp and pour the oil on your face and light it. I want you to be so ugly that only I, who know how devoted you are, will find you beautiful."

Jesus. I heard the lamp being opened as soon as he gave the order, before he even explained his romantic reasoning behind it. I smelled the reek of lamp oil, heard her fumbling with a box of matches. I wondered what would happen if I kicked in the door and stopped the action. Would they be annoyed at me for interrupting their lovemaking? But then Chen burst out in a fit of laughter.

"Wait, frog. Do you really think I'd let you do that here? Why, you might burn my rugs, or my couch. Perhaps some time soon I'll let you die. But not now. Not here. Fix my bowl. Then go clean yourself."

"Yes, Master. Anything you say, Master."

Lucky Kristara. Saved by Chen's love of furniture. My Mandarin was a tiny bit rusty, but to my ears she sounded genuinely disappointed.

I'd have liked to stay longer, in the hope of hearing new and even greater wonders. But in another few moments Chen would be in poor condition for interrogation, and Kristara would be popping out for a wash. Might as well move on, before the hallway got too crowded.

That strange smell from behind the padlocked door . . . No time like the present to see if my new nose's reports were to be trusted.

Quickly, quietly, I slipped through the sleeping corridors of the Mandarin Palace, deeper and deeper into the entrails of the slumbering dragon. I reached the first floor, found the door I wanted, and inspected it carefully. It wasn't just pad-locked; it was triple-locked, with more serious hardware than any I'd found so far in the building. But my tool kit had me through in seconds.

Just beyond the door, a steep flight of stairs dropped down into shadows. I padded down the wooden steps, found myself in a musty-smelling basement—damp, cement floor, crumbling stone and plaster walls. There were several heavy doors to storage pantries and vegetable coolers and meat lockers standing off the central space.

My nose told me which to choose, third door, left hand wall.

As I stepped toward it I suddenly felt another horrid thrill, much stronger than the one I'd felt walking behind Kristara. A delicious spasm shivered through my whole body, a wave of dark delight. I doubled over, forced myself to straighten up at once, smothered the ugly urgency I felt.

But I knew bristles of fur were shimmering out through my skin, then wriggling away, out and back, out and back.

I could not be bothered to stop the fur, but I managed to hold down the rest of the urge.

It was the damned smell, of course. I opened my tool kit again and went to work on the door locks. My control was good, and my hands stayed completely human—even if they were covered with grayish fuzz—so I got through the tumblers quickly.

I hauled the door open, too hastily as it turned out. The smell billowing from the cold storage was so strong I lost control again for a moment, doubled forward in an exquisite spasm of shameful joy.

Gasping, snarling, I slammed to the ground on gnarled and thickened paws. I was all tangled in my ill-fitting clothes, drooling and slavering like the ravenous beast I'd suddenly become. I sucked in a breath, *forced* my lungs to expand, to take in air. And forced the worst of the change away.

I lay panting on the dank floor for a moment, then rolled over on my side and wiped the slaver from my chops with my sleeve. I could feel that the front of my trousers was soiled with spunk.

That would give the dry cleaner an item for gossip, but there was nothing I could do about it at the moment. No matter. The important thing was that when I crawled back onto my hands and knees and pushed myself erect, I was a man again. A bit hairier than usual, but human.

I could see perfectly well in the gloom of the meat locker, but I yanked on the naked overhead bulb from force of habit. And so I set the horror before me awash in radiance, cruci- fied it in a luminance more bright to my sensitive eyes than the clearest light of day.

They were hanging upside down from a steel butcher's rack, gaffed on big meat hooks: half a dozen human bodies, headless, handless, footless, gutted and dressed like cows or pigs. They smelled freshly slaughtered. Very delicious.

All I could tell of them by sight was that five were Negroes and one was white—a working man from the musculature of his carcass. The Negroes appeared to be female, but they'd been butchered so completely that it was difficult to say for sure.

I put my nose to work and discovered a bit more. Yes. All the Negroes were female. And all were adolescents, in their early to middle teens. They had all been healthy when they died.

And none of them had died particularly quickly.

Well, well, well. It isn't nice to say, but I felt as if I'd just discovered gold. The only question was how I'd spend it.

I could do the most enjoyable thing—namely go back up- stairs, drag Maurice Chen out of his bed by the scruff of his neck, haul him down to the locker, and pull him apart until he told me all I wanted to know upon threat of extinction, and then kill him anyway, even more slowly than the poor creatures hanging around me.

Or I could to the professional thing, the thing a private detective concerned with holding onto his license is required to do the moment he discovers a felony has been commit- ted—namely drop a coin to the men in blue. It wasn't as ridiculous a notion as it sounds. Remember that Joe Jefferson qualified as a man in blue. And wouldn't he be pleased when he noted the racial balance in Maurice Chen's meat locker.

Or, I could try something totally out of character, and do the smart thing for a change, which is to say, I could close everything up just as tightly as I'd found it, get the hell out, and call it a night.

Sound crazy? It was even crazier to think I could really pick Maurice Chen apart without waking up at least one, and then all, of the bodyguards and other assorted beasties I knew perfectly damn well were lurking in and among the sleeping shadows of the Mandarin Palace.

Maybe I could fight them all off in furred or shorthaired form, for a while. But the odds against long-term survival—long-term defined as living to see the next sunrise, a not so distant event—were too lousy for even a dedicated collector of lost causes and worthless racing stubs such as myself to want to wager upon.

As for calling in the Law . . . thanks, but no thanks. Having Chen arrested would have been easy enough. Having a charge—any charge—stick, was about as possible as slapping the cuffs on all of Fifth Avenue and Park Avenue and City Hall and Wall Street and . . .

Chen was Mr. Manhattan. All the high-tone fat cats loved his uptown joint. They loved *him*. Which was more by a mile than could be said for yours truly. Maurice would be in and out of the slammer faster than hay through a heifer. And I'd be lucky if all I got for my troubles was a breaking-and-entering charge in the bargain. Probably be accused of planting the stiffs. Talk about losing my private dick card.

No. When the time came for settling up with Chen, the reckoning would have to come far from the eagle eyes of blind Justice, well out of reach of the long, palsied arm of the Law. Chen was going to get every single thing he had coming to him. Nicely and neatly.

But not tonight. First, he would lead me to the much bigger fish I really wanted to fry. No dying allowed until then. Frustrating though it was, the wisest choice for the moment was clearly to pack up and get the hell out, add the wonders I'd found in the Mandarin Palace to the file, and wait for further developments. . . .

I suddenly realized that all the while I'd been musing, my

hand had been stroking the smooth, cold flank of one of the poor unfortunates.

Very smooth and very cold, and I am sorry to say, very delicious feeling that flank was. As I stroked it and pondered, my body had been bowing ever farther forward. By the time I regarded my hand and understood what it was doing, it had become a hideously gnarled, beastly paw.

The rest of me wasn't about to win any beauty contests, either. This time I had shifted slowly, so my pullover and loose pants had roughly adjusted to my new shape. But I looked like hell: a hideous, hunched-over halfling, no better than the two foul monsters I'd killed in the gutter.

On the other hand, I had just shape-shifted without noticing it, which is to say, without any pain and without the inconveniently pleasurable sensation, an encouraging first. I felt strong. I was fairly sure I had this . . . thing under control at the moment, could allow it or stifle it as I saw fit.

I studied my hand, then *made* its silvery hair slither away. My shoulders straightened; my vision dimmed. Good. Very good.

But I let my pelt shimmer out again immediately. There was no reason to force the beast back in its cage. In fact, there was work for it. I had a notion—a nasty idea born of my beastliness, and of my human frustration. And my desire to give confusion to the enemy. I wanted to taunt Chen, to let him know one of his most preciously guarded secrets was uncovered.

Throw it right in his goddamned face.

And so it was that Jimmy Underhill, the halfling beast, grasped the haunch of cold human flesh hanging beside him and *bit*! I tore an enormous chunk out of the carcass with a single slash of my razor-sharp teeth.

I felt no shame for what I did.

The beast was stronger in me than it had ever been before; the flesh was perfectly good, and this poor thing I ravaged had not even been my kill.

I felt no passion either.

The huge gobbet of flesh clenched in my jaws was cold and tasteless.

I didn't even eat a morsel. I had other plans for it. I held it carefully in my teeth. With infinite care I reclosed all the cellar locks I'd picked, and made my way back up to the door of Chen's top floor study.

The door was locked. Briefly.

He was sprawled out across his wide bed in a stupor. Kristara, freshly scrubbed and perfumed, and wrapped in a robe, lay on the floor at his feet, sleeping as fitfully as a beaten puppy.

I padded up to the bedside and loomed over him for a moment, delighting in the knowledge of how easily and in how brief an instant I could crush his wretched life away.

Then instead, I spit the chunk of savaged flesh onto the pillow beside Maurice Chen's ashy, dope-soaked face, and turned from him, and was gone.

I went home, stowed the Packard, and washed the burnt cork off my hands and face in the garage sink. I didn't bother changing out of my work clothes, though, since Ernst, the soul of discretion, was manning the lobby.

"You have had numerous messages and visitors, James," Ernst said. "And you don't look very well at all. You should get more sleep."

"Top of the evening to you too, Ernesto," I grumbled. "What are the messages?"

"Two are from Blaire. She asked me to tell you that Miss Velma called. Also Miss Regina. By the way, Blaire did not sound to be in a very good humor. For instance she did not actually call Miss Regina, *Miss* Regina."

"And what did she call her, pray tell?"

" 'That rich slut,' I believe. Of course it is true Regina has had quite a run of luck lately. But I would not have thought she qualified for such a description. If I knew no better, I would say Blaire is afflicted with jealousy. Could this be the case?"

"The world is full of wonders, my friend," I drawled.

"Anything's possible. So what do you think? Is Blaire an ill-mannered fishwife, or what? I should fire her, shouldn't I?"

"I have known some fishwives to be much more even-tempered than Blaire. You should fire her, if you like. But I wasn't aware you had that option. I thought you owed her . . ."

"Nobody likes a realist, Ernesto," I warned. "Not really. People say they do, but they don't."

"Excuse me." He laughed. "In that case, yes. Dismiss her, by all means."

"Excellent idea. Who were my visitors?"

"An unusual-looking little man was one."

I didn't like the sound of that. There were two possibilities, and neither was pleasant. I decided to opt for the least palatable first.

"Was this little man wearing green gloves? Was he Asiatic?"

"Why, no. No green gloves. He was Jewish, in point of fact. Dr. Avrom Bukhovna. He wanted to wait, but I assured him there was no telling when or if you would arrive. And I promised to make you call him at once. He seemed very upset. Angry. You know, I have heard Bukhovna lecture many times. Remarkably gifted Hegelian scholar. I was tempted to invite him to stay just so we could talk Hegel. Fascinating man. I am impressed with the quality of your guests of late, James."

"So glad you approve. Who were the other visitors?"

"Ah, but you didn't let me finish with your calls. Regina telephoned directly about half an hour ago. That is, she telephoned Rosaria, and Rosaria came to tell me . . . Regina's message was that Clara Steiner had disappeared."

My heart dropped; I grasped Ernst's shoulder angrily.

"What?! Damn it, why in hell didn't you say so first thing?! What's the . . . ?"

He picked my hand off his shoulder and frowned.

"Firstly, because I am quite annoyed with you, James. Why didn't you tell me Rolf Steiner's daughter was in New York?"

"Frankly, it didn't occur to me that you would care."

Ernst's frown deepened; he winced as if to banish a painful memory.

"Rolf Steiner was a dear friend of mine. His death wounded me, James. It wounded us all. The whole damned world has been pushed closer to the flames because he is dead. Naturally, the people who killed him know that."

I shook my head with annoyance.

"Still, you should have given me the message at once. You of all people . . . do I have to mention the obvious and say there's still a war going on?"

"Hardly. But I also didn't tell you at once because there is no longer any great urgency. A few minutes after Regina called last, Clara Steiner was found."

"What?"

"She arrived here, looking very cold and bedraggled." He held up his set of my house keys. "Since you seem to know her, I didn't think you'd mind. I took the liberty of bringing her up to your flat and offering her some hot tea. Don't worry, Rosaria is sitting with her. And I have called Regina to tell her how things stand . . ."

I was already sprinting for the elevator, but Ernst snared my arm with those alpinist reflexes of his, turned me around, and grasped my shoulders.

"You goddamn wait, Käpitan Unterheel, damn it!" He barked. Ernst always lost a little syntax when he got riled. "Before you go upstairs, you will listen. A long time past you should have told me about all this; a long time past. Now I tell *you* about Rolf and Clara Steiner. I tell you what the Nazis did to them. I will talk and you will listen. I tell you things you don't know yet. . . ."

Flames danced cheerfully in the living room fireplace. But Clara, nestled deep in a big chair before the hearth, still looked bedraggled despite the comforting glow.

Very bedraggled and terribly beautiful.

Rosaria was sitting and knitting beside her in a wooden ladderback chair, a credible picture of the proper Spanish duenna minus only about thirty years, forty pounds, and a mustache. She got up to go without saying a word. I suppose she could see how I was looking at Clara—how I could hardly help looking at Clara. Her parting expression spoke volumes, all on the general theme of "here you go again, Jimmy."

Just before she closed the door I made a face at her.

"Why didn't you tell me everything yesterday?" Clara asked as soon as we were alone. She looked small and frightened in the big chair.

"Everything? I don't know everything, Clara. Never claimed to. What particular part of everything would you especially like to discuss?"

"I think you know quite well what I mean. How in hell you have the audacity to treat me like some kind of damned child is beyond me. Worse. You have treated me like . . . like . . . I don't know what. But I thought I was your friend."

"I'm working, Clara," I said wearily. "And when I work I don't have friends. Just clients and potential felons. Everyone I can place outside those categories is irrelevant."

"I wonder how good a worker you can be with no friends. My father used to say . . ."

"Actually, I'm very good at what I do," I interrupted, because I didn't want to hear any more from her about Rolf Steiner at the moment. "People who have acted badly are afraid of me. With reason."

"And you are truly proud of that"—she shook her head—"of people fearing you, of yourself being able to divide up the whole world into clients, felons, and irrelevants?"

"Fear has its uses, Clara, don't you think?" I shrugged. "And I didn't say 'felons.' I said 'potential felons.' That's a bigger category."

Of course even as I made all those fine pronouncements about what a hard ass I was, I was wishing I really believed them myself. It would have made my life and my work ever so much simpler. Because the truth was that all I really wanted to do at the moment was to put my arms around Clara and hold her and, oh, I don't know, take it from there.

Take *her* from there.

I wanted to run away with Clara, just bag everything. The train that was hauling the whole damn world straight to hell would surely continue doing so whether I went along for the ride or not. I wanted to get off, beat it, take it on the lam. Forget about everything, and I do mean everything. Including the beast growing inside me, the beast I was becoming, the beast that was becoming me. And the she-wolf. And Lo Fang and all his many friends. And the job I'd signed on to do for Gina. And . . .

Fat chance.

It all filled me with rage, the enormous distance between what I wanted and the way I knew things were going to be. You see, I had already figured out a great deal about what was going on. Maybe not the fine print, but the big picture. And a very ugly big picture it was, too. You are soon to understand exactly what I mean. For now, simply remember how bloody *angry* I said I was that night.

Back to Clara. She looked properly put off by my display of biliousness.

"Very nice, James. Well, since I am not directly your client, may I at least choose the lesser of two evils and assume you merely find me irrelevant?"

"You can do anything you damn well please. It's very late and I've had a long, hard evening. On the other hand, I hear you've been spending your time frightening your supposed friend by pulling a disappearing act on her. Maybe you think that endears you to me. It doesn't."

"Disappearing! Don't you *dare* go on the offensive with me, James. Your lack of candor has almost cost me my life!"

"What?"

"The so-called prowlers who broke in to . . . to take me the other night? Exactly what kind of creatures were they?"

"The truth?"

"For a change, yes."

"Two of them were apparently what are called shape-shifter dacoits. Those are Asian cult assassins who are able to . . ."

"I know perfectly well what they are," she snapped. "And the other one?"

"I'm just not sure, Clara. Some kind of shape-shifter too, but much stronger. She . . . I'm positive it's a she . . . can change completely into an enormous wolf. She's very powerful, whatever, whoever she is. So. Now you know as much about the prowlers as I do."

That was nearly true.

"Thank you, James."

"Feel better, do you?" I asked dryly.

"Actually, I do. At least I don't feel like I'm being lied to."

"Most sane people would have exactly the opposite reaction to being told that supernatural creatures are after them."

"I don't recall ever making any major claims to sanity." She smiled. "After what I told you about my father's spiritualist abilities and battles . . . you should have known you could tell me this from the first. You *should* have told me, in fact. At least it would have given me the chance to take part in my own defense."

"Maybe, maybe not. I had no way of knowing how you'd react. I decided it was safer to say nothing, and make sure Aristotle turned his house into an armed camp."

"Gina posted guards in the garden as soon as you left," Clara said. "That's how I learned the prowlers were shape-shifters. I overheard two of the men gossiping. And that's how I knew I had to leave Gina's house."

"What do you mean?"

"You never asked what we were doing at the Geneva railway station when my father was killed, James. But I don't suppose you know, since our plans were quite secret. We were leaving Switzerland for a hiding place . . . somewhere in England. Shape-shifters. They had been haunting the grounds of my father's institute in Switzerland. We . . . my father and his colleagues had been aware of them, had managed to keep them at bay for several weeks. But then, something new happened. My father said he sensed the presence of an entirely new entity; something hideously powerful.

Shape-shifters are strange creatures, but at least they are flesh and blood. They can die. This new thing, though . . . it was too strong for even my father to fight against. He had to yield before it. And so we were fleeing. Right into the barrel of a gun, as it turned out.''

"You said a new entity. What was it?''

Clara frowned, shook her head.

"We were never sure exactly. A force . . . something most strange and strong. And evil. My father would never describe it in detail. He said that to do so would only have added to its power over us.''

Clara shuddered involuntarily. The fire had ebbed in the hearth. She unfolded herself from the chair and stepped closer to the low flames, letting their warmth drive the demons of memory away. But when she turned to face me again, fear was still printed on her face.

"There was something about that force creeping up around us. Even I, who was so much less skilled than my father, even I could feel its gathering power. Have you ever felt the presence of the undead, James? Such beings radiate a horrid energy. Quite unique. It is easy to feel when they are near. Easy for me at least. Too easy. The thing that forced my father to run was undead. And when I overheard those guards tonight, I knew what was at the root of the unease I have been feeling. I knew the undead were stalking me here, as they stalked us in Switzerland.

"And I also knew I had to leave Gina. She and Aristotle have been too good to me. I can't let them be wiped out the way my father was. My being with them puts them in too much danger.''

"You overhear two loose-lipped guards and you decide to pack up and leave a house guarded better than Fort Knox? It doesn't make much sense, Clara.''

"The fact that I was able to slip away should tell you something about how well the house is protected, James. But the guards weren't what decided me. What I overheard just made me realize the truth. What I *saw* convinced me to run.''

She sank back into the chair, folded her arms over her bosom, clutched herself. She shivered, seemed to be trying to drive a nightmare back into its cave. I wanted to take her into my arms and tell her everything was going to be fine. But I knew everything wasn't going to be fine at all. So I sat quietly and waited for her to continue.

"It was about nine this evening and I was in my room, reading on my couch. I still heard the guards out in the garden, stamping their feet to keep warm. I'd been hearing the ones in the hallway outside, too, but for several minutes it had been quiet.

"And then I felt it. My skin started crawling. I suddenly knew there was something *horrible* in the hallway . . . something just outside my door. Waiting. Whatever it was . . . it was calling out to me. Whispering my name, softly, so softly. Oh, not with real words. More like . . . like an idea in my mind . . . a terrible thought that I could not stop thinking. I felt as if I were trapped in the middle of a nightmare and there was no way for me to wake up . . . nothing for me to do but to live it out to the end.

"I got up and walked to the door. God, the handle was so *cold*. Ridiculous the things one remembers. And all the while I knew I was walking out to meet death. Undeath.

"I pulled the door open. There was nothing there. The hallway was empty. But the call . . . I could feel the thing so strongly, it seemed to be breathing on my neck. Undeath was somewhere close by, waiting to take me. I stepped out and looked to my left. Nothing. I turned around. She was standing almost beside me! Oh god, James.

"A woman. A very beautiful woman, not seven paces away. She was naked. Stark naked. Her hair was long and her skin was pale. She was beautiful, James. Very beautiful. But . . . so strange. It was as if I was viewing her in a dream. There was something . . . indistinct about her. I knew she was beautiful. But even now I could not tell you precisely what she looked like.

"And then, suddenly her whole body . . . it seemed to *melt* . . . and shift and grow. I was seeing it and not seeing it. One minute a naked woman was standing there, and the next instant . . . it was a *wolf* . . . an enormous, green-eyed wolf. Bigger than any wolf I have ever seen.

"She had come to take me, James. To kill me. Now she was sliding, flying toward me. She moved faster than a living creature can possibly move. I turned to run away and . . . I was sitting up on my couch. I had bolted up from sleep and I was screaming and shaking.

"Do you understand, James? The she-wolf. She was just a dream. But I will tell you this. She was most definitely not *my* dream. *They* sent her to me! I . . . I suppose I should have been grateful that she had not been real. But I was as terrified as when she had been standing in front of me. Because I knew exactly what she . . . what *they* were doing. The beasts who destroyed my father, the monsters who have been haunting me all these months . . . they were toying with me, James. They wanted me to know that not even my dreams are safe from them. They can take me . . . can destroy me whenever they please. I am theirs. I belong to them.

"So I knew I needed to leave. They are powerful enough to do whatever they want to me. But I won't watch them destroy the people I love. I slipped out, and at first I thought to myself, 'I will wander around until they take me or until I die of the cold.' I walked into Central Park, and I thought maybe I would just find a quiet place in the snow and lie down and go to sleep forever.

"Then I thought about you, James. And I knew I had to come to you. What you were saying before, all that damned coldness and anger of yours . . . I know that it is really just for show. I know how much you feel, right below all that. But I sense something else about you too, James. Something I can't really put into satisfactory words. There is . . . a darkness in you. How shall I say it, a destructive strength. Something that can be very frightening and very cleansing. And the strange thing is, I am not afraid of it. I know that *they* have more to fear from your darkness than I do. And I think that most likely I am one of the doomed. But if anyone can possibly save me, you can.''

She stopped then and sat studying her hands in her lap.

Darkness . . . of course, what she was talking about was the beast in me. She was sensing its presence. She had judged it correctly, too. It would never hurt her; I would never let that part of me hurt her, no matter what. Because I loved her too much.

And at the risk of spoiling some of the suspense I will tell you here and now, the way things worked out, Clara's instinct was correct. Right up until the very end, I never hurt a hair on her head, neither as a man nor as . . . whatever else I would become.

I felt very tired, and very sad, and very empty. And I knew there was one thing more she was going to say, so I decided to help her say it and get it over with.

''Clara? Was that all the reason you came here?'' I asked gently.

She turned to the fireplace, stared past the flames. After a few seconds she shook her head.

''Then why else, Clara? Why else are you here?''

''Do I really need to tell you, James?''

''Yes.''

She kept her eyes cast down, her face turned away, and she addressed the dying fire in a whisper.

''I came here because from the very first minute I saw you . . . from the very first second . . . I knew I loved you. And I knew you loved me, too. I don't think it will end very well between us, James. Because this much love is a fire that burns too hot. But for however much time we have, I am yours. I am meant to be yours and I don't care what you do with me. I love you too much to . . .''

So I turned her from the fire and stopped her talking by covering her lips with mine.

And that night, as the old Tuscan poet says, we did not read any further.

* * *

I had known her all my life. Everything about her was new. The night was endless, and after an endless time we lay in the shadows and whispered over the map of love.

"So smooth here. Like velvet."

"How did you get this?"

"Moroccan bayonet."

"It's still red."

"Not that old. What's this?"

"Where?"

"Here. Such a beautiful beauty mark. Have you always had it?"

"I don't know, James. I do not often look there."

"Really? If it were mine, I would."

"It is yours."

"Do you like when I do this?"

"Oh."

"This?"

"Ohh."

"This?"

"Ohhh . . . Don't stop don't stop don't stop don't . . ."

We slept.

I woke with her lips on mine. So sweet.

I slept.

And gasped up from a dream of falling.

"Clara!"

"Shhh. I'm right here, darling. I was watching you sleep. You fight in your sleep."

Her body's warmth, all its sweet, hot smells and tastes ebbed away.

"Where are you going?"

"Shhh. I'm just going to wash. I'll be right back."

I slept.

"Kill her."

I gasped awake again; listened for a moment. To the quiet night song of water on tiles. I smelled lathering soap, saw the far light of my open bathroom door.

She spoke again.

"Go in and kill the dirty bitch. Rip her throat out. Tear her to pieces and eat her hot flesh. Go!"

The voice echoed behind my ears, flooded into my mind. A dream voice, a whisper, horridly loud and utterly soundless.

"Do it now, damn you. Get up and go into the bathroom and kill her. Easier to clean up the blood in there. Go!"

Yes. The voice spoke only to me. And I knew who spoke. She filled my mind with her urgent whisper. She was not very far away. I heard the click of cold, hard claws on wood, then a thump and a quiet squeak as my bedroom door, directly across from the bathroom, was nudged open.

She looked enormous there in my doorway, impossibly huge. Her eyes burned coldly, her grinning, slickened muzzle was chest-high. It would have been on a level with my chest if I had been standing.

She was stunning, vibrant, more gorgeous than she had any right to be. I saw her as she had been in my nightmare . . . in the nightmare she had given me. And I knew how good it would be to make love to her. Horribly good.

Her cold laughter echoed in my mind.

"You liked the sweet dreams I gave you, didn't you, darling. Oh yes. But tonight I'll give you something sweeter. So sweet." Suddenly her voice went hard. *"Now get up and go in there and rip the stinking whore open. Chew her guts. I want to watch you do it, my darling. Then we'll fuck in her blood. Look look look. See how beautiful you are tonight?"*

She was beautiful. And her unvoiced words compelled me so powerfully, I believe if she had been asking me for any other life, or a dozen other lives, I might have given them to her. But not this one. She could not have this one. I already told you—I would never harm Clara. I would do some of what she asked, though. I would get up.

And then I'd go to the monster who had made me a monster, and destroy her. Tear her to pieces. I rolled over, started to stand.

Pain!

Christ, I hadn't felt such agony since the first time . . .
the first change. A world, a whole universe of pain seared
through my twisted body. But the pain subsided when I
stopped flailing my limbs. And when I tried to move more
slowly, it was easy enough. Just a matter of feeling my way,
not trying to move my body like something it wasn't. Something I wasn't.

I crouched on the mattress. And then stood up on my four
strong legs. The bed creaked, for I was even larger than she
was. I glanced back at myself. My pelt was clumpy and
mottled, not nearly as beautiful as hers. But my long, full
tail lashed the air like a razor-sharp saber. Killing time. I
snarled and, with my enormous jaws wide open, I leaped off
the bed not just at her, oh no, but directly at her throat.

"No no no, you fool!" her mind screamed.

She turned and bolted with blinding speed. I hit the polished floor and tumbled through the jamb. By the time I
righted myself she'd already bounded across the living room
and out the opened front door with such speed that her passing blew it shut behind her.

Kill!

I charged the door, leaped again and smashed completely
through, blasting it out along with half the frame. The hallway was empty, of course, but there was no possibility of
her getting away. My apartment was the only one on the
floor. There was only one way she could have gone. I would
follow her and catch her and kill her.

I flew down the hall to the fire door. It was steel, impossible to batter in, and so I skidded to a stop before it. I
stretched out my paw, forced the change to shudder through
me . . . just enough for my gnarled hand to be able to grasp
the doorknob. I threw it open and made myself the wolf
again.

I poked my head under the banister, peered into the shadowy stairwell. Was that a flash of silvery pelt a half-dozen
floors below? Oh yes, most assuredly. I plummeted down
the stairs faster than sight. The wind of flight streaming past

my muzzle brought me sure knowledge—the smell, the *taste* of her.

Maddening. So good. It was going to be so good to tear her apart and eat her.

I was closing the distance between us. By the time I reached the stairwell bottom and burst out into the basement, she was very near indeed.

And suddenly I heard her voice again, clearer than ever. No. Not her voice; her thoughts, her terror, her mind. I was inside her, just as surely as she'd been inside me. My body froze as I probed her.

Panic, fear of death, rage at me, hurt, confusion; panic, fear, rage, hurt; fearragehurt . . .

Her deeply injured love.

"Damn you damn you damn you! Oh I hate you, you dirty son of a bitch! Damn you go away don't touch me! I'll kill you. Don't touch me. Leave me alone. Oh. Please don't hurt me. Please don't hurt me. Please . . ."

0And then suddenly, she vanished.

A trick! She had sidestepped me like a toreador. Her mind shut off and she was gone. I was out of her, could no longer even scent her presence. Oh no. She wouldn't escape that easily. A door creaked. I barreled towards it, smashed through, and bounded up the servants' entrance out onto Central Park West.

The street was bright and black and empty. I lifted my muzzle and tasted the night. Nothing.

The park: I knew she must be hiding there. I raced across the street toward a low stone wall, set myself to leap over, to the dark winter trees beyond. But in the instant before my paws left the pavement, a small figure detached from the shadows at the wall, a tiny figure.

"Stop!" he shouted. His voice was impossibly large for his body.

I did.

Even on my four legs I stood taller than he, and my eyes, I knew, were glowing a ghastly green. But Dr. Avrom Bukhovna regarded me without fear.

"So this is what you've become," he said quietly. There was no anger or contempt in his tone. He simply stated the obvious.

"Where are you off to, Underhill?" He gestured over his shoulder toward the park. "Dining out tonight?"

"I am chasing the female to kill her," I thought.

"Sounds like an excellent idea," he said. "But she hasn't come this way. I doubt I would have missed her."

Oh, no!

"Clara!" I suddenly thought.

"Very possibly," he snapped. "Quick! Go back up the stairs. I'll take the elevator!"

My penthouse was the building's twenty-first floor; I reached it long before Bukhovna and Ernst. I raced down the hall and skidded to a stop in the rubble of my entrance. I listened and looked and sniffed.

And I knew the truth in an instant. So I shifted back to human form and stepped naked into my living room. I was halfway across when I heard the elevator clatter open and then the sound of Ernst and Bukhovna running down the hall. I was at my bedroom entrance when they reached the door. Without turning back, I signaled them to wait.

My bathroom door was shut, but it wasn't locked. I turned the knob and pushed it open slowly.

Clara was sitting on the white tiled floor in the corner where the tub touched the wall. She had her knees up and she was hugging a towel that could not cover her nakedness. Her black hair was still wet and it hung down in ringlets. I thought to myself her wet hair made her look more vulnerable, more beautiful than ever.

For just a moment I was filled with the overwhelming sadness of loss; my throat ached and my eyes itched.

And I hadn't even lost her yet.

I believe she was feeling something quite similar. She looked up at me sadly, numbly. No fear in her eyes. Calmly. Too calmly.

"It's all right now, Clara," I said.

"Who are you, James? What are you?" she asked quietly.

"I'm a werewolf, Clara."

Her eyes widened; she stared at me.

Then she stood up. The towel dropped away. She walked to me and she put her arms around my waist and pressed her cheek against my chest and hugged me tightly. I put my arms around her.

And we stood like that for a very long time.

"Tell me, Underhill. What did you do with my daughter?"

Clara was dressing; Ernst had gone for some tools to patch the door; I was entertaining Bukhovna alone in just my trousers and an undershirt.

"I helped her to die."

"She was already dead," he snapped. "Exactly what did you do with her?"

"Do you really want to hear this?" I asked, but when he said nothing, I shrugged and went on. "Lo Fang raised her from the dead and made her a vampire. Her only escape from him was to die a vampire's death. She came here and asked me to . . . I held her back, kept her from returning to her coffin that morning. When the daylight struck her, she died."

"How did you keep her back?"

"I just held her down, mostly. She was stronger than I am, of course. But she wanted it to be over. So she didn't fight until the end. At the end I had to use the garlic and the crucifix."

"And what happened then?"

"It worked. She crumbled away into dust with the first light."

"Dust? Literally dust?"

"Dust, leafy flakes. Nothing more really, not even any bones."

"Sounds like quite a mess. And how did you dispose of . . . her remains?"

"I swept them off the floor . . . brushed them off the couch, then I . . . are you really sure you . . . ? I swept everything up and emptied it all into a paper bag and then I dropped the bag into the incinerator.''

"And was the incinerator actually on at the time?''

"Burning? I don't think so. They only burn garbage . . . I mean . . . they only turn it on once a day, evenings usually. I disposed of her remains in the morning.''

"Damn you, Underhill!'' he snapped. "Damn you, you cretin, I thought it was something like that. I should strangle you. Really I should. Do you know what your bungling has done? He's raised her again, of course—Lo Fang. He's stolen back her earthly dust and reanimated it.'' His face contorted with pain, her pain, and with anger at me. "I think of how brave she was, how much hurt she had . . . And all for nothing, thanks to your idiotic bungling. How could you be such a fool . . . ?''

"Bukhovna, shut the hell up,'' I snarled. "Now *you* listen. I did what Rachel asked me to do. No more, no less. She wanted to die, I helped her do it. She didn't say a word about any special funeral arrangements. Nobody did. Nothing. I did all I thought was needed. I'm sorry it worked out badly. Truly sorry. But that's it. Over.''

"Hardly, Underhill,'' he said a bit more calmly. "It's hardly over for Rachel. And if I were she, I'd be quite angry indeed. Angry enough to do something about it.''

"Such as?''

"I'd keep my windows closed at night, if I were you. And invest in some more garlic and crucifixes, too.''

"I'm never without them,'' I drawled.

"James . . . is it all right? May I join you?'' Clara asked from the bedroom door.

"Certainly,'' I grumbled. "That is . . . if my esteemed guest here is finished with his tantrum. Avrom Bukhovna, this is . . .'' I began.

Bukhovna stood to greet her—a surprisingly gracious gesture.

"Yes, yes, of course, Underhill. Miss Steiner, I am delighted to meet you. And . . . so sorry about your father.'' He took her hand, held it gently. "He and I met only a few times, quite a while ago. But we maintained a correspondence over the years. His letters are precious to me . . . all the more so now. I should be happy to show them to you some time.''

"I should love to read them," she said.

Nice to see Clara and Bukhovna hitting it off. But it hardly seemed like the time for polite chitchat; so I decided to steer the conversation back in a more useful direction.

"I saw Rachel tonight," I said grimly. "Her and the rest of them."

I told him about Lo Fang's Chinatown joyride. When I finished, he shook his head.

"I knew he was still in the city," he said. "As I told you months ago, it is unlikely he will leave until he gets the rest of what he wants here. But he's been staying hidden. It isn't a good sign that he feels strong enough to let himself be seen."

"What does it mean?"

"That his plans are coming to fruition, of course. And before you bother to ask . . . no, I don't know what his specific plans are. I am not keeping anything from you. I simply don't know."

"I suppose this is a ridiculous question, all things considered. But do you think it's time for us to actually start working together?"

"Do you have any idea why I came here tonight?"

"To report me to the dogcatcher? Or to lambast me for throwing Rachel's remains away?"

"You *are* a lamebrain, Underhill. But I wouldn't make a special trip just to tell you the obvious. And as for your new wolf nature . . . what did the she-wolf want with you tonight?"

He asked the question as if he already knew the answer.

"She wanted me to kill Clara. She was ordering me to, in fact."

"Interesting. You know, if you'd actually started to destroy Clara, I believe the she-wolf would have stopped you. No doubt Lo Fang's greatest pleasure would be to see you infect

Clara, turn her into a night creature. Evil loves to contaminate.''

"No doubt it does," I interrupted. "But you're wrong about Lo Fang's plan for Clara. He wants her dead. Or at least the she-wolf does."

"And I say *you're* wrong," Bukhovna replied mildly. "But let it pass. . . . Of course, making a werewolf is a tricky business. The results are unpredictable."

"Unpredictable? How?"

"I'll tell you in a minute. Answer me this first . . . Were you tempted to do what the she-wolf asked?"

"Not in the slightest," I snapped.

"Didn't think so, didn't think so," he said placatingly. "But I know her kind. And I guarantee you . . . such hideous strength . . . there are very few who could have resisted the psychic commands of a creature like that. When Elijah told me what happened to you . . ."

Elijah P. Woolcock, that old stool pigeon.

" . . . he also told me what he hoped you would become. I'm happy to say you have lived up to his hopes . . . our hopes. Lo Fang and his minions have succeeded in making you a werewolf. But I believe they have gotten more than they bargained for. You are evolving, James. You are evolving into a being who will be quite beyond the control of evil ones like that."

"That all sounds great, Bukhovna," I said. "But it doesn't answer my question. I asked you if you wanted to work with me for a change. Fight Lo Fang and his pals together."

"I heard your question, James," he said calmly. "And I am answering it. All around the world, there are millions of people who are struggling on the material level against Lo Fang and everything he represents. Their struggle is the most important, the most horrific one of all, and it has hardly even begun. Soon the mountains of dead will be piled higher than you can possibly imagine. . . .

"But on another level . . . on the spirit plane . . . almost nothing is yet being done. The plane of the spirit is an unguarded flank . . . a bared neck in the battle against Darkness. It is very lonely fighting on the spirit plane, James; and you are going to find it lonely, too. When you fall, few will even know you have fallen. Because that is the nature of things. But I will be honored to have a being such as you . . . such as you are becoming . . . I will be honored to have you fighting beside me. And I really mean that.''

He did mean it, too.

All of it.

In the morning, while a crew of workmen replaced my front door with one that I hoped would be more difficult to huff and puff down, I took Clara back to Gina's. The mansion was not exactly an island of safety, but neither was my domicile. And in an imperfect world I believed I had some ideas for improved security that might make Gina's more nearly a Lo Fang–proof fortress than anything else Manhattan had to offer.

Gina greeted us in the drawing room. But "us" is not exactly the word for it.

The moment we walked in, Gina tossed aside a lit cigarette, rushed across the room with her arms flung wide and a look of near hysterical relief on her face.

"Thank God, oh, you had me so damn scared, honey . . ." she gasped.

And threw her arms around Clara.

And kissed her on the mouth, long and deep.

Clara stiffened at first, but then she kissed Gina back. And put her arms around Gina and slid her hands down her back.

Meanwhile, Gina stroked her face and kissed her lips as though Gina was dying of thirst and Clara's lips were the fountain. They clasped and embraced like long-parted lovers united at last.

Which, I saw with blinding clarity, was exactly what they were.

Well. Great going, Underhill. There I'd been . . . speculating, wondering, worrying: How far have Gina's feelings for Clara gone? How much does Clara suspect about Gina's feelings? Does Clara share those feelings . . . You know, musing over the subtleties, pondering the great imponderables. And meanwhile there's them, wrist-deep in each other's poodles.

How charming. Oh, but no problem. So what if the woman I loved and the lover I liked were sapphically involved. After all, we were all civilized adults, fully capable of engaging in civilized relationships. Right?

Besides, they made a lovely couple.

Gorgeous, actually.

A blond-haired beauty and a dark-haired angel; why, we might even make a beautiful triad. Each one of us possessed extremely intimate knowledge of both the others. We were already all lovers in every sense but the most strictly synchronous. Why not find a nice warm sack built for three and hop in?

Why not? I'll tell you why not. Because I was too busy deciding which of the decadent tribades I wanted to kick right in the ass first.

I noticed the cigarette Gina had tossed aside was smouldering on the rug. So I removed the flowers from a nearby vase and dumped the water on the embers.

Then I cleared my throat.

When that didn't work either, I coughed. But it seemed I could have had a consumptive fit without causing them any undue discomfort. I was aiming a boot at Gina's arbitrarily chosen bottom when she and Clara happened to break for air and also happened to notice my continued presence.

They both looked ravishing. But Clara's lips were soft and slightly bruised, by our own night of lovemaking, and now, by her other lover's ardor, too. She was the more beautiful, to me. I ached when I looked at her and I felt the now familiar stab of sadness, the sure knowledge of my coming loss of her.

Once again.

"I forget my Emily Post. What's the proper question?" I grumbled. " 'How long has this been going on?' Or, 'Who's better . . . me or her?' "

I was talking to Clara. But she just shrugged and favored me with a sweet smile composed of equal parts apology, embarrassment, and amusement. Oh, and challenge. There was a challenge in her smile, too.

It was Gina who finally answered.

"Come off it, Jimmy. This is me you're talking to. We've been to entirely too many late night parties, you and I. You can't pull a Comstock on me." She snuggled next to Clara. "How long has it been going on? Since before we knew what it was for. That's how long. In fact, Clara was the one who showed me." She turned and nuzzled Clara's ear. "Or did I show you . . . ?"

Gina giggled. They both giggled; but only Clara had the decency to blush at the same time.

I really did not know what to do. So I crammed my hat on my head and turned to storm out.

Damned bull-daggers. Diesel-dykers. Let 'em have a ball.

I hadn't even stormed as far as the drawing room door when I felt a hand on my left arm. And another on my right shoulder. Both were trying to turn me around, but the one on the left won.

Clara locked her arms around my neck. Gina knocked my hat off my head.

Clara put her mouth on mine. So sweet. She made it entirely too hard for me to stay angry.

We were very tired; we were very merry. Clara and I, that is. I had taken her out for a long, long walk in the cold Manhattan sunshine; with Gina's blessings. So generous of her.

It felt good walking through the frozen Manhattan midday with Clara. I was sad, and angry, and happy just to be with her.

We had made our way to the East River Drive, were strolling along the walkway. Chunks of soiled, crusty ice lumbered downstream; the clear wind licked like razors; a few brave gulls flapped and squealed their discomfort. I didn't feel the cold, though, and Clara, bundled in her borrowed fur, was warm enough, too. We had the sun-splashed, icy walkway all to ourselves; there were few other fools abroad in the punishing chill.

After a time Clara stopped me, and turned me to her.

"Perhaps I am being stupid," she said. "But I really don't understand why you are so upset with us."

Her words came in small clouds of fragrant steam.

"Which 'us'? You and me? Or you and Gina?" I asked bitterly.

"Both. All three. Oh . . . you know what I mean."

"Let's say there are some things I don't like sharing."

"Neither do I, James; neither does Gina, I suppose. And of course none of us has much sharing to do. Gina and I love each other like sisters. Or at least . . . the way we do. The way we have done since we were children."

"Sure."

"You know . . . when Gina kissed me like that . . . at first I was terrified. Mortified. God how I wished she hadn't done it. I was so embarrassed having you see us . . . that way. But then I realized . . . I *wanted* you to see. I wanted you to know about us . . . about me. And I wanted you to accept it."

"Sorry I can't oblige," I grumbled.

"Stop it, James! Really do stop it," she snapped. "Now think for a moment. Don't you see how absurd it is for you to compare our love . . . yours and mine . . . to mine and Gina's? Gina and I are a comfort to each other . . . sisters. And you, Mr. Underhill, are the love of my life. Not a comfort at all, I might add. Besides, if there were any jealousy worth feeling, I suppose I could find it in heart to be jealous of you and Gina. *You* two are man and woman, after all."

"That's different," I mumbled.

"Oh. Naturally," she teased. "But that isn't why I don't feel jealous. I don't feel jealous because we don't have the time. Do we?"

She was right, of course, or at least, right enough.

So I did the sensible thing: I lifted her chin and kissed her sweet lips. And I made it a sensible kind of kiss, which is to say, I kissed her as though it were the last kiss we'd ever have. Just in case.

Then I took her back to the mansion, dropped her off, and went to work.

Velma had ordered Jackie the bartender to send me up the minute I reached the Crystal Lounge. She hadn't added he should stall me at the bar if I happened to arrive fifteen minutes early.

Too bad for Velma's prior guest.

While padding down the hallway toward her private suite, I found myself drawing ever closer to the joyous sounds of giggling and grunting, the happy slaps of flesh on flesh. Long before I reached her door I could smell what was going on, and not because of any supernaturally elevated senses, either. They were working up quite a funk in there, and I knew in my heart they did not wish to be disturbed.

So I knocked.

I heard an immediate *shhhh*, an urgent whisper, and then Velma's rather gruff, "*Who*, goddammit?"

"It's me, Vel," I declared to the door, loudly and cheerily. "Hope I'm interrupting something."

"Jimmy? Uh, you early, sugar." More whispering and buttoning. "How's about you fall down to the bar a minute? Reet, Gate? Be with you in two shakes."

"Ah, c'mon, Velma," I declared impatiently. "Just tell him to tuck it in and zip it up. I swear I won't be jealous."

Velma threw the door open. I could see her guest fumbling into his clothes behind her.

"What do you mean, you won't be jealous?" She frowned. "You trying to hurt my feelings?"

Velma Dupree was wearing shiny black high heels. She had pink silk stockings and rosy red garters on those great big legs of hers. But not a stitch on her great big butt. She was twirling a pair of turkey red bloomers, the ones with what she called a rumple seat, over one upraised finger.

I could tell from the bloomers' bouquet that Miz DuPree had vacated them rather recently.

Ah, Velma.

She shrugged into a red silk robe that would have hidden a less heroically proportioned female as completely as a tent.

"You surely know how to pick a bad time to show up early, sugar," she drawled.

"Don't have time to be late," I said.

I stepped all the way into the room, tipped my hat, and smiled delightedly. "And a good evenin' to you there, Reverend Woolcock. Helping Sister Velma with her devotions, I see. So sorry to interrupt you when you were obviously so deep in . . . what's the word? Prayer."

I tossed my hat at the hat rack.

"I get deeper than you'll ever get, boy," Elijah P. Woolcock grumbled. His face darkened, and his left, no, his right eye glared at me. "And that there is a fact. Velma, how's that Leroy Carr song go? 'She say she like the music but the tune's too short'?"

"Ah yes, Velma, the Reverend has quoted that chapter and verse before," I said. "He certainly does love those sacred songs. But Reverend?" I said solicitously. "Before you go greeting the rest of the congregation, you might want to remove your shirttail from your fly. Wouldn't want anyone in the Amen Corner getting the right idea."

"Underhill? Why don't you go out and chase a car? Fetch a stick or something," Eli snapped.

But he did stuff the tail of his shirt back into his trousers.

"Just trying to be of service," I said with a smile.

"Service yourself, goddammit."

"How'd you like me to knock both your knotty heads together and throw both your skinny asses outta here at once?" Velma inquired, arms cocked on hips. "Jimmy? I thought you called this meeting for something important. How's about getting to it?"

"We're waiting for the final guest to arrive," I said.

"He just did," Joe Jefferson rumbled.

Joe was dressed to the nines as usual, and he looked as

pretty as a picture—a picture of a blue-black gorilla with a shaved head, and a licorice-twist scar wriggling down his cheek. And a long-barreled roscoe bulge under the left arm-pit of his three-piece, silver-gray French sharkskin.

"Okay, folks," Joe said as he lumbered in and dropped himself down on the groaning sofa. "Who's gonna testify first?"

He smelled like a brewery.

And now with all assembled, I reflected to myself on what a truly superior band of heroes I had before me, most val-iantly to strive against the Forces of Evil: a lushed-up flat-foot, a horny old bible thumper, and a nymphomaniacal madame.

It warmed my heart. Actually, it gave me heartburn.

"What about you, Joe?" I said. "Why don't you tell the congregation . . . how's business?"

"Anybody wanna guess?" he growled.

"I'll take a stab at it," I answered. "I'd say your busi-ness is medium lousy. I'd say those bloodless bodies have stopped showing up, since we trimmed back the Manhat-tan vampire population a few months ago. But I'd say your Missing Persons division has suddenly started getting very popular. And I'd say the persons missing are mostly young and female for a change. And finally, I'd say that doing some predictive math, you have deduced that based on the number of girls being *reported* missing, the *real* numbers being abducted are higher. Much higher. How am I doing, Joe?"

"Great, Underhill. Right as rain. In fact, any righter and I'd be booking you on suspicion."

I studied Mr. Jefferson as he said those words, to see if perhaps, just perhaps, Eli had been spouting off to Joe any of the gory details he'd clearly given Bukhovna about me.

Joe saw me looking. And he saw me glance at Eli.

"No, Jimmy," he said. "Eli didn't tell me. At least not at first, he didn't. I found out all by myself."

"What did you find out?"

"That some shape-shifters attacked you. That now you have developed some peculiar abilities of your own. Don't worry, your secret, like they say, is safe with me. With us. I'd have put you to sleep ages ago if I thought you were developing any uncontrollable urges for meat on the hoof . . . especially dark meat."

"Are you sure, Joe?" I asked calmly. "Are you sure you'd know how to put me to sleep?"

"I'm sure I could work something out," he said. And just to be a wise guy, he moved his fingers ever so slightly in the direction of his heater.

You have undoubtedly noticed how short-tempered I'd become in those days. Which was undoubtedly why Joe's self-assurance irked me.

I decided a small demonstration might be in order.

And so I went to the place where the beast was always waiting. I let myself shimmer, let the change flash through me in a pale fire of joy. Not all of it, though. Just exactly as much as I wanted.

It happened in no time.

What Joe and the others heard next was an impossibly deep, wall-shaking growl. A rumble from a beast the size of the room. What they might have seen if they were looking carefully was a flash of silver pelt and the lunge of a manlike shape, manlike because I didn't want to rumple my clothes by fully forming the wolf. And I needed to keep my human hands.

In the next instant, the same instant actually, I was standing where I'd been standing. My clothes were neat; my hair was perfect. And I was holding Joe Jefferson's silver-plated Ivor-Johnston .45 out to him—by the barrel, so as not to unduly alarm him.

"I'm not saying you couldn't do it, Joe," I said softly. "But if you ever decide to try . . . make it a good try. Okay? Make it damn good."

Joe's face had gone ashy.

Velma was staring round-eyed and slack-jawed.

Only Eli was smiling. Proudly.

And that made me realize just how much I loved the old bastard.

"I'll keep it in mind," Joe managed to say. He cleared his throat, reclaimed his revolver, and spoke.

"Uh, where was I before I was so rudely interrupted? Oh yeah. All those missing maidens. Now I don't suppose you have any brilliant suggestions about where I might find them, do you, Captain Underhill, sir? I would so dearly love to know where in the fuck they are. Or at least who is disappearing them."

"You mean, before your bosses downtown give you the reward you so richly deserve and toss your ass onto the breadline?"

"Something rather much like that."

"Well yes, Joe. As a matter of fact I do know who is disappearing them. At least in general terms. And I know what you can do about it. I know what we can all do about it. Even Eli here, if he keeps his britches hitched."

So, we got down to business, my band of heroes and I. And we made us some very interesting arrangements.

With all my uptown affairs in order, I decided it was high time I concluded a major piece of unfinished business.

I called Blaire from my apartment and had her do some work for a change. At my request, she verified the present location of a certain individual, caused that location to be observed with extreme care, and stood by to inform me the moment it seemed likely I might visit said individual at said location without other guests being present.

I dressed in my work clothes, and waited.

Sometimes I sat by the telephone. Sometimes I got up and paced slowly. Sometimes I stared at my hands and made the fur wriggle all the way out, and all the way back, and all the way out . . .

I played a game. First change the left hand. Then change the right. Then change the left back. Then right changes back while the left turns into a paw. Left back while right turns. Right back while left turns.

Leftbackwhilerightturnskeepswitchingandaddthefeet . . .

Near to middle evening, Blaire's call finally came: The coast was clear. Glenda Rogers-Gracey was home alone, unattended save by her serving staff, seemingly preparing for an evening out on the town.

I hopped a cab and sped over. My plan was simplicity itself. I would catch Glenda alone, ask her a few pointed questions I'd been meaning to put to her for ages, and when she didn't answer them to my satisfaction, I would beat the living piss out of her.

Glenda.

Ever since the night I'd had her in my cross hairs and elected not to blow her head off, I felt an almost proprietary interest in her. Certainly in a very real way I was responsible for her continued existence. I cannot honestly say Glenda's life was a burden I bore with pride, but at the very least I felt I was entitled to get some mileage out of her. Nor had I the slightest doubt that in addition to all her many sterling attributes, Glenda possessed the fascinating answers to many equally fascinating questions.

Her time of reckoning had come, and I was the reckoner. She could live or she could die. But she would tell me everything I wanted to know.

Blaire had actually been quite helpful for a change; she had filled in my sketchy knowledge concerning the layout of Glenda's Fifth Avenue mansion, had even informed me of the approximate location of the dressing suite where I would most likely find my quarry.

Here's what I did.

I trudged into the servant's entrance of an apartment building around the corner from Glenda. Just another tradesman. I made myself a halfling in the basement and bounded up the firestairs to the roof. I slowly became a man again while I loped across the rooftops, had turned wholly human by the time I was peering over the parapet of the building beside her mansion. I rappelled down to her roof, still a man. But when I found her roof door deadbolted shut, I changed again and peeled it open with a speed and silence that only my wolf-strength made possible.

I was still a halfling when I slipped into her upper hallway, and I intended to stay that way while my nose and ears sought her out.

But I heard her at once.

Glenda Rogers-Gracey was bellowing like a banshee. So I shivered myself back to human form and navigated toward her raging shrieks.

Boy, was she ever steamed. I was quite close before I could even make sense of her howling.

"Bitch! I'll fix you, I swear I will. Out! All the rest of you out of here! Go, goddammit! I want her alone!"

I flattened against the wall as three Negro maids, all in formal French black-and-whites, went scurrying out, puffing their relief at having been passed over. The door to m'lady's chamber stayed open a few inches, so I could hear even better, as if that were necessary; and I could see a bit of the fun, too.

What I saw was a fourth maid, a pretty mulatto probably still in her teens. She stood trembling, her honey-colored face underneath pale with terror.

"Dirty cunt!" Glenda shrieked. "You're a total idiot, aren't you!"

And now I could see Glenda, too. She wore a black evening gown, not yet fully fastened. She stepped up to the quaking girl and towered over her like an avenging Fury. Glenda's thick, red hair roiled down in wavy curls, and as she screamed, it writhed around her shoulders and breasts like serpents.

"Y-yes, madam," the little maid ventured.

"*Yes!* You say yes to me?!"

And she leaned back and slapped her across the face so hard that I heard the poor kid's neck crack. The girl didn't move, though, didn't even raise her hands from her sides. She just stood there quavering, her cheek reddened and swelling and her tears streaming down.

"You do have eyes and ears, don't you? You *have* noticed what happens to girls who get me angry?"

"Y-yes, madam."

"Yes? *Yes* again? Oh really," she said mockingly. "And what does happen to them? Eh?"

"They . . . they die, madam."

"They what?! What do you dare to say?" Glenda screeched into her face.

"They . . . oh, I mean . . . that is, I don't know! Something bad. Nothing. I swear I don't know nothing! I . . . Oh . . . !"

She burst out sobbing, then gasped when Glenda hauled off and hit her full in the face again. Glenda grabbed the girl's hair and yanked her head back so savagely that she bowed down onto her knees.

But it wasn't enough.

Glenda's hand darted to the dressing table beside her and suddenly a pair of long, silver hair scissors were in her fist, clutched like a dagger.

"Why, you dirty nigger slut, you! I'll kill you right here! I'll cut you up! I'll . . . I'll . . ."

And then with her hand poised to plunge, she stopped. And raised her head.

Suddenly, Glenda's wild eyes stared. She cocked her head, and her nostrils flared as if scenting the air. Her face was lit by a weird glow, and she glanced toward the opened door.

Glenda grinned.

It almost seemed she was grinning at me. Even though I knew I was invisible in the hallway's gloom, I drifted deeper into the shadows.

Glenda tossed away the scissors and wrenched the girl's head so hard that a whole clump of hair came away in her fist. Then she kicked her in the breast, an awkward job in high-heels.

"Out!" she snarled. "Out, you dreadful little coon! Out and tell them all . . . I am *not* to be disturbed! Not by anyone, not for anything. Understand? *Do you understand?!*"

"Yes, mistress! Oh, yes!" she wailed.

Glenda pummeled and kicked at the girl's breasts and ribs and buttocks as she crawled away on hands and knees.

Once the maid had been booted as far as the hall, she clambered up and bolted. Glenda, clutching the door frame, threw a grazing kick at her departing rump.

I floated further back and watched Glenda as she leaned panting against the frame.

"Well!" she finally managed to puff. "What . . . a . . . lovely . . . surprise."

She raised her head and stared directly at me again. "Please. *Do* come in, Mr. Underhill."

Oh well, why not?

I strolled out of the shadows toward her, as casually as possible. She regarded me appraisingly from the door frame.

"I love these informal visits." She chuckled. "It's been ages since you've dropped by, Jimmy. I must say you're looking very well. Black suits you. Won't you . . . ?"

My stroll was about to take me through rather than past Glenda, so she backed up before me, into her room. I kicked the door shut, twisted the latch on the handle, and turned to her.

"You have a great deal of information I need, Glenda," I said quietly.

"That is very true." She smiled.

"I'm glad we agree. Now I'm going to ask you some questions, and you are going to answer them."

"Hmm. I see," she said. "Could you give me a hint as to the general topics your questions will cover?"

"Yes. I'm going to want to know the present whereabouts of Lo Fang and several of his associates. I'm going to want to know about his current plans in New York. His plans *for* New York, too."

"I see. Anything else?"

"A number of interesting minor issues. Like what your friend Mr. Chen does with all those butchered bodies he keeps in his basement. And why you all seem so interested in Clara Steiner. And Gina."

"Well, Jimmy. So many questions. And they cover such a lot of ground."

"Really? I would have thought they were quite closely interrelated."

"I suppose they are. But tell me this. What possible reason do I have for answering you?"

A perfectly valid question, and one deserving a carefully considered reply.

All in an instant, I opened the doors of the beast, and gave Glenda a good clear look at the face of the thing that wanted to rip her to bits. My beast's hands grasped her arms and my beast's claws dug into her flesh and my beast's terrible strength bent her back and held her with her spine near to snapping. My glowing eyes pierced her and my growling cough rattled her bones.

I tossed her away and stood up; human again.

"That's why, Glenda," I said. "Because even if you scream your heart out, I will kill you before help comes. And because I'm not just going to kill you. I'm going to tear you to pieces, rip your lungs out. You will wish . . ."

I stopped then, because I saw the effect my terror tactics were having on Glenda. Her eyes went wide. But with something other than fear. She clutched my trouser legs and kissed my shoes. She pulled herself up, rubbed her cheek against my shins, kissed my knees, my thighs. She wrapped her arms around my legs and stared up at me ecstatically.

"My God, you are magnificent!" she gasped. "They told me how strong it was in you, but I had no idea. I've never seen anything like you Jimmy. Nothing . . . *God* what power . . ."

She had slithered almost all the way up me. Her evening gown, already a bit tattered by my handling, had simply fallen away somewhere. Her eyes had a loony glint I seemed to recall from an interview past. A glint and something more.

I smelled her, too. I am sorry to say her smell was not exactly displeasing. Please excuse my bluntness, but Glenda Rogers-Gracey smelled quite literally and precisely like a bitch in heat.

I grabbed her bruised arms and held her away.

"*Talk*, Glenda," I snarled. "You're going to start telling me things."

"Oh yes, Jimmy," she breathed. "I'll tell you anything. Everything. I'll tell you everything you want to know; I swear! Just sex me."

"What?"

"You heard me, Underhill. Fuck me. Hump me, dick me, bang my box. Shove it up in my hole, shoot your peter off inside me . . . oh God, Jimmy! Just *do* me. All these months! I've been lusting for you. Haven't been able to think of anything else. And now to see what you are! Such power. Such awful power. God, I'll do anything for you! Just *give* it to me. Do you hear me? Just do me once . . . !"

Ugh.

Then again, who knows what madness fizzles through the addled brain of a Nazi slut? I should have known if anyone did. Glenda was a real nut case. Grade A, certified, rubber-room material.

If only she hadn't been raking her fingernails over my chest. And grinding her sex against my leg. And there was still that smell of hers to contend with . . .

I'm sorry, I'm sorry. But I did let her grab my hair and kiss me on the lips. And although I knew better than to put my tongue in her mouth, I did let her drive hers into mine.

I closed my eyes and kissed her, because, I blush to report, Glenda tasted and felt very, very good. And I didn't open my eyes again until I felt something I wasn't supposed to feel.

Of course in the higher sense, none of it was anything I was supposed to be feeling. But I am talking about a very specific sensation: the soft, gentle tickle of fur against my face.

My lids snapped open, and I found myself staring, predictably enough, into Glenda Rogers-Gracey's eyes. Her glowing, green, penetrating eyes.

And her fur, the mottled, silvery fur that was wriggling out all over her flat, misshapen face.

Glenda's lips still retained their basic form, but glistening razor fangs had slithered out to fill her mouth. Her body was hunched and gnarled, thick fur clumping up all over it in unkempt patches. She wriggled around and wagged her buttocks at me. They reeked of estrus musk.

In short, Glenda looked like hell. Smelled like it too.

"Rut . . . rut . . . mate . . . me," she thought.

Glenda's words came across faintly, as if from a poorly tuned radio. I shifted easily as far into wolf shape as she, yanked her back facing me, and held her at arm's length to inspect her.

At first I thought what you may be thinking: Bukhovna and Eli and I had all missed the truth—the cruel, fair beast who had menaced Clara and Gina, the seductive, lustful she-wolf who had bitten me and who haunted me still, was none other than Glenda Rogers-Gracey.

I didn't hold the thought for long, though. Glenda's body spasmed once, twice, then stopped. Her change was completed, and she still looked a mess, a pathetic halfling.

That was all she was.

"Please . . . you . . . me . . . sex," she thought.

Because her thought power was weak, she whimpered the same words aloud; a difficult task with her mouth full of fangs. The words were just a drooling garble.

I pushed her away and pulled off my sweater and trousers and shoes. Glenda stood hunched and glaring, devouring me with her eyes. Her mouth opened in a carnivorous grin, her tongue hung out. Hungry slaver dripped from her jaws.

I shimmered completely into wolf form.

Even standing on four legs, I was as tall as Glenda. Her fiery eyes widened and glowed with lust when she saw what I could become. She made a choking whimper-gasp of joy, scrabbled around and hunkered down on all fours; hoisted her estrus-smeared hindquarters aloft for entry. I watched a few thick drops of the stuff trickle down the insides of her matted thighs. She had already made a small puddle on the rug.

Now then.

I am sure some might have found Glenda Rogers-Gracey very attractive at that moment. But I did not.

I leaped at her, battered into her hip with my chest, bowled her onto her back, and clamped my jaws on her naked, pulsing throat. I let my fangs slip ever so slightly into her flesh. Her blood seeped over my tongue. It tasted rather good, and I was tempted to rip out her throat, kill her, and eat her.

No. At least, not yet.

"Bitch!" I snarled silently. "Now you will tell me everything. Open up! Open your mind and let me see it all!"

"Nooooo!" Glenda wailed.

I sensed her utter, pained despair, and I heard it too, because in her surprise and sorrow, Glenda had instantly shifted fully back into human form. Her despair was as black and deep as her soul. She tried to crawl away from me, not with her frail, pink, human body, because that was impossible. But with her mind.

"Please, Jimmy?" she thought. *Oh, please please please, Jimmy? Don't kill me. Just love me . . . I will give you anything you want. Really I will . . ."*

So much despair; so much emptiness.

I pitied Glenda for a moment, because I knew how horrible emptiness could be. So much pain. Suffering. Loneliness. I took my jaws from her throat.

And then in an instant, I thought about loneliness very, very clearly. I saw all of my best friends gone. Blasted. Dead in Spanish earth. Worse. Much worse: I saw the children. And the old men. And the women. Dead dead dead. Starved. Murdered. Raped. All torn to pieces by the dirty fascist bastards and the rich, filthy swine who . . .

I looked down at Glenda and saw she was smiling hopefully up at me. And I saw that I'd become a man again, a naked man leaning over her on my hands and knees.

I flashed back into a wolf. I stepped my huge paw onto her chest. I would not kill her, even though she was as bad as the worst of them, nor would I torment her with any lies of affection. But I would have what I wanted from her. An easy task, really. I reached into her mind, and I paused only a moment to listen to her voiced screams of rage.

"You bastard! You shit! You Jew-loving, Commie-loving, nigger-loving, fuck! Think you're so goddamn superior, hah?

You with your nigger kike friends. Your fucking syphed-up Commie whore. Wait till you see! Wait till you see what we have planned! Not just for you! For that bitch, too. We'll fix her wagon good . . . !''

A quick flash image of Clara and Gina.

I plunged in past Glenda's raving to see exactly what she meant. I reached in to take what she knew.

An image of . . . *Oh no!* Even worse than I'd thought. Much worse! I grasped her mind, ready to tear it apart for the details, for everything she knew about . . .

And suddenly I had to leap out of Glenda, leap and whirl with my wolf body to face the new attack coming at me, the hideous power that had just bashed in the door to Glenda's room, the door and the frame and enormous shattered pieces of the wall around it.

I dodged the wood and chunks of plaster crashing past me, and made ready to spring.

There in the swirling dust he stood, Entimemseph the Mummy himself, monstrous even to an enormous monster like me.

He stood framed in the wreckage for a moment, then snarled and strode in to get me. But why wait? I snarled back and launched myself directly at his throat.

Kill!

Or whatever you do to a mummy.

He was a huge, lumbering lummox, Entimemseph, but God, was he fast. I never saw the fist that smashed into my side.

Spin!

I whirled through the air, all tangled in pain, swept smashing clattering tearing through glass and wood and cloth. I scrabbled up from a pile of unrecognizably splintered furniture, shook my head, and looked for him.

At last I realized I couldn't see him, because, mountain-like, he was looming so close above me.

I coiled and sprang for his face at once, faster than sight.

But I wasn't nearly as fast as the stone-hard, boulder-big hand that flashed up to grasp my throat, the gigantic fingers that wrapped like steel around my neck.

Entimemseph held me aloft in one hand, and shook me like a snared rabbit. I snapped and snarled at him, striving like a mad thing to get my dagger fangs at his gray, leathery face with its enormous yellow teeth and its sunken, dolorous eyes.

"Oh yah?" he rumbled. "You want bite, big bad wolf? Here! Bite!"

He brought my muzzle up so close that I could smell the age-old must of his flesh, the desiccated rot of his breath. But in the very instant I would have clamped down to eat his face off, he tightened his impossible grip even further.

Paralyzing pain seared through my head and neck. My jaws creaked as if they were about to crumble away.

"Now you stop, goddamn fuck you. I rip you frigging head off and drink blood. Entimemseph crush you up, shit dog. You *change* goddamn you!"

He shook me again, rattled my entire being in a roaring crescendo of pain.

"Change change change! Go back human or I tear off you head. *Do! It! Now!!*"

I did as ordered. I became a small white human thing wriggling weakly in Entimemseph's vise.

I felt the release only faintly. Only faintly did I feel myself flying through space and battering the rough, rubble-strewn floor. For even as I flew and fell, a sweet, merciful darkness had gently wrapped its arms about me and was blessedly gathering me up into the very center of its soft and comforting heart.

First I heard: the quiet jingle of silverware, the chiming of wineglasses, laughter, and soft music—a Brahms quartet to be exact.

Then I smelled: the superb seasoning of the food, the perfect age of the wine, the polite muskiness of the perfume, the ancient wood of the cello.

Then I felt: a dull ache from my jaw when I moved it ever so slightly, a flame of pain from my bruised throat when I tried to swallow, and at last, beneath my fingertips,

the thick velvet of the plush armchair in which I'd been prop-
ped.

"Oh, open your damned eyes and stop playing possum,
Mr. Underhill," a voice drawled with extreme amusement.
"I know perfectly well you're back among . . . the living."

What a word for them.

I slitted my lids open and saw, seated across a damask-
covered dinner table, from left to right, Entimemseph the
mummy, Rachel Bukhovna, Glenda Rogers-Gracey, and yes,
you guessed it, none other than the Tibetan goblin himself.
He was all decked out in a black tuxedo. The tuxedo's formality made his green leather gloves ridiculously inappro-
priate; but still and all, he could not have looked more pleased
with himself.

Lo Fang.

In all these months, I had never been this close to him.
Nor did he improve upon careful scrutiny. But perhaps he
was being less careful now, less concerned with maintaining
. . . certain pretenses.

Lo Fang's skin was not yellow, but of an eerie golden hue,
strangely smooth, and not the color of any racial strain I'd
ever known.

His eyes were green.

I mean *all* green. The whites were milky green, the irises
the green of emeralds.

His ears . . . certainly their lobes were extremely long and
floppy; certainly their upper tips were pointed. But were his
ears longer on the bottom, pointier on the top, than a human's
ears could reasonably be expected to be? Call me unfair, but
I decided not to give them the benefit of the doubt.

And then there were those gloves of his.

Green leather gloves, in my experience, do not often come
fitted with longish, pointed fingernails of a blacker green.
Nor are they often covered by bright, chitinous scales, which
blend smoothly into the wearer's wrists. Yes. You've guessed
it. No gloves. There had never been any.

In fact Lo Fang, I finally realized, was not human at all.

Rather, he looked like a fairly close approximation of what a human being might possibly be expected to look like. Close but no cigar, if you catch my drift. Lo Fang looked like no human being I had ever seen. Like none you have ever seen either.

"That is true, Mr. Underhill," he said. "But only because you have never visited an Atlantean city. And now of course"—he made a moue of totally feigned unhappiness—"it is too late to do so. Oh, and by the way . . . not to change the subject, but have I complimented you on your attire? Allow me. You are looking very well, all things considered. Snazzy."

I glanced down and realized that someone had fitted me out in a black tuxedo. It actually looked rather good.

"Doesn't it?" he said. "Kristara chose it for you . . . dressed you, as well. By the way, she says you're hung like a horse."

Excuse me. I neither confirm nor deny Kristara's assertion. But Lo Fang really did speak those words.

"Kristara really did say that, too. And she's hard to impress. Oops!" Lo Fang chuckled. "Silly me. Now I've gone and made our Glenda jealous. She was all for humping you while you were unconscious, you know. Wants to breed with you. Don't worry, darling. The serving wench didn't beat you out. Remember? Already has a bun in the oven."

"You did promise me, Master," Glenda purred demurely.

"When the time is right, m'dear. Only when the time is right."

"But . . ." she began.

"Ah, ah, ah. *What* happens when you say 'but' to me?" he chided.

Although he'd spoken good-naturedly enough, Glenda's eyes widened with fear. She caught herself, huffed, tossed down her napkin, and looked away haughtily.

But she said nothing.

"This kid"—Lo Fang pointed an ear at her—"she's lucky I'm in a good mood."

He reached into the ice bucket beside his chair, extracted a dripping wine bottle, tipped it to his mouth, and sucked. The bottle had been almost full when he lifted it. He drained it all, smacked his lips, burped quietly, and frowned.

"I know, I know. You're not supposed to chill red wine," he said. "But I like my burgundy *cold*. Don't you, Mr. Underhill? Now where was I . . . ?" His face brightened. "Ah yes. Atlantis. All gone! Lost beneath the waves! Kaput! Finished! So solly! Better luck next time!"

He giggled impishly, leaned toward me conspiratorially.

"Mr. Underhill, it was all my fault, you know. Atlantis sinking I mean. Experiment gone haywire. Slip of the wrist. Back to the old drawing boards. Listen. Am I afraid to admit a blunder? Not on your life. When I make a mistake I'm the first to own up." He grinned. "Especially since I don't exactly hear any complaints from the Atlantean citizenry. Do you, Mr. Underhill?" His tone darkened. "Well, *do* you?"

Entimemseph tipped forward slightly. He was wearing a tuxedo, too. It made him look almost human.

"Answer him, fuck head," he growled.

Rachel, I noticed, was just studying her empty plate, her face as still as stone.

I had an answer for him all right.

Faster than the sound of my snarl, so fast that only I could see my flight, I bolted out of my chair and lashed my arm toward Lo Fang's throat.

My change was so swift that before I was near him, the fingers of my halfling hands were tipped with enormous razor sharp sickle claws. I would slash his filthy throat out, hack off his vile head and hold it in my hands.

Or at least I would have, if Entimemseph hadn't snared my arm in mid-flight, held it, and then, with a mirthless sneer on his gray, leathery face, slowly started to crush my wrist like an empty cigarette package.

"You no change," he sneered. "Not yet. You change before we say, you die. I mash you all up slow. Like this."

Pain sizzled through my arm; the slightest addition of pressure would turn it to pulp.

"No no no!" Lo Fang whined and fluttered his hands. "Stop at once!"

Entimemseph frowned at his colleague. But the vise slid open; he discarded me back into my chair.

Rachel. Most interesting. She winced at my pain, turned her head away to her left, recoiled because Glenda and Lo Fang were there. To her right. Recoiled from Entimemseph. But she would not look at me. She glared down into her lap. I saw one drop of crimson well up in the corner of her eye. Up and over. It started to trickle down her cheek. She brushed it away in a flash.

Lo Fang seemed not to notice or care. He was too busy lecturing the mummy.

"How is he ever going to learn if you don't let him try?" Lo Fang chided. "And besides, don't you realize how gauche it is to use these mere physical chastisements? Why can't you be more refined? Show your higher nature?"

"You mean like *this*?"

Suddenly Entimemseph's eyes glowed red, not the red of blood, but the red of flames. He grinned, and his mouth was filled with the fires of hell. My flesh tingled weirdly, a wave of nausea took me, and my whole body was suddenly lifted, *drawn* straight upward. I hovered in space, paralyzed, floating five feet above my chair. Then I slammed down into it.

"Like *this*?"

Stretched up, slammed down.

"And *this*? And *this*?"

Slammed and slammed and slammed . . .

"Stop!" Lo Fang shouted. "That's quite enough!"

Entimemseph growled. But the flames subsided, and I stayed crumpled in my chair.

"Excuse my friend, Mr. Underhill," Lo Fang said. "Or may I call you James? Or Jimmy? The High Priest Entimemseph here gets terribly upset when he thinks I have been threatened. He is sometimes overly zealous concerning my welfare. Totally devoted. He's so grateful to me for having reawakened him, don't you know. Isn't that right, Your Excellency?''

"You go to hell, too," Entimemseph rumbled.

"See?" Lo Fang chuckled. "My biggest fan . . . no pun intended. But in any case, you are more than welcome to try slashing my throat. Or breaking my neck. Or hacking off my head. Or anything you choose. No? Thought better of it, have you? Well, good, James. Very good. I will take that as a sign of your growing maturity. Your understanding. Whether it is so or not.''

It was and it wasn't.

But there being nothing to do about Lo Fang or the other members of my dinner party at the moment, I took the time to look around the room.

I realized where I was almost at once.

As I mentioned a long while back, I had never actually been to the place myself. But one could hardly read a society column without knowing secondhand what the joint looked like. And yes, I saw that all the walls were covered with autographed photos and caricatures . . . I smelled the elegantly prepared French food . . . and I noted that while fewer than half of the dozens of tables and booths were occupied . . . those that were, were populated by some of the society columns' most famous New Yorkers . . . and by personages entirely too wealthy to ever find themselves in the society columns at all, persons too powerful to be famous.

Some of the assembled guests were yammering into telephones, because every table seemed to have phone plugs available.

And then I saw the final proof of the pudding.

Off at the entrance, surveying his domain imperiously and nervously, watching every gesture of every serving person . . . yes indeed, there was the saloon keeper. Mr. Maurice Chen.

At least Lo Fang knew how to entertain his guests. He'd taken me to the poshest night spot in Manhattan: Chen's fancy French restaurant, Le Bistro d'Or.

And speaking of Maurice, wasn't that . . . why, yes it was! Her eyes were down, her shoulders hunched as Chen berated her in tight-jawed whispers, his glassy snake eyes flashing. Kristara. Her long, silky hair was up in a bun, her voluptuous body hidden beneath a red and black waiter's uniform.

Lucky Maurice.

Sexual servicing and table service, too. His slave might not be a satisfactory baby breeder to his way of thinking, and she was no bargain in the mental health department. But in the balance, Chen was getting his money's worth out of the poor kid.

And now, I noted a number of other curiosities, there in Le Bistro d'Or.

Firstly, New Yorkers as a group are much too polite, or at the very least much too jaded, to stare. But that alone did not adequately explain how a seven-foot-tall mummy, a golden-skinned, green-eyed-and-handed dwarf, a redheaded Valkyrie, a maiden as pale as the snow, and an unconscious private detective could all sit down to dinner in a restaurant together, without exciting, if not concern, then at least more than passing interest from their fellow diners. Even if the mummy, the dwarf, and the dick were all decked out in beautifully tailored dinner jackets.

But no one was looking in our direction.

Even when I'd turned halfling, snarled and leaped for Lo Fang's throat, not a soul had paid us any mind, at least no one that I'd seen.

It was quite a puzzle. And the solution to the puzzle, which would be presented in a mere matter of moments, was going to be a real stomach turner.

"So you're impressed by all my friends here, huh, Mr. U. ?" Lo Fang gestured at the room all around. "Quite the high-tone collection I have, wouldn't you say? Just you wait. This crew has not even *started* to show you their stuff. Wait till you see. Moxie plus.

"Uh, not to change the subject . . . but answer me this. You are a gambler, am I right? A game player; yes or no?

Now *there* is a trait I admire. Frivolous on the surface of course, but underneath . . . I have always believed that a love of gambling betrays a deep fascination with the inner workings of existence, with the structure of the universe. Don't you agree? I thought you would. Observing the mechanisms of chance occurrence, *participating* in the operation of those mechanisms. What a joy! Don't you think so? Why, the most simpleminded darky, shooting craps down on his knees in an alleyway, is light years closer to the essence of existence than that Jew distorter, that mockie raver, that . . . that . . . *Einstein*. Don't get me started on Einstein with all his relativity horseshit.

"True, no? But in any case, what I mean to tell you is this . . . Since you are a gambler, you know the joy . . . you know what it can be like in those moments, those divine nexuses of time-space when you can do no wrong . . . when your every choice, your every gesture brings you more and more . . . when you can do nothing but win!

"Why do I mention this, Mr. Underhill? Glad you asked. Because these are just such times for me and mine. Do you understand? Mmmm! The ecstasy of conquest . . . the sweet taste of victory . . . the loftiest pinnacles of power . . . I'm on a roll, buddy! Nothing can stop me.

"You'll see, Underhill. You'll understand it all, soon, in the hours and days ahead. I can see quite clearly you know, and what I see is this . . . I am winning. The forces I ride, the glowing crest of the blood-dimmed tide . . . it's the future, Underhill. The new world. An age of gold . . . scrap that. An age of fire. Fire. Yeah, that's it. *Fire!*

"Why . . . a whole vast, dark universe is opening, James. Vast. Gorgeous. Triumphant. You have started to see it . . . you've gotten a glimpse of what it will be. This change we've worked in you . . . the enormous power you possess now . . . you *have* noticed how delicious it is, how utterly thrilling each time you use it.

"You need not say a word, dear boy, I know perfectly well what it's like for you. The joy you experience. Why, the first few times the change hit you . . . you shot in your shorts, didn't you? Oh don't worry, you can admit it. You're among friends here. Isn't he, Entimemseph? Isn't he, Rachel?''

And with that, he winked and grinned and reached past Glenda. He hefted Rachel's left breast in his hand, flapped it and waggled his tongue obscenely. His tongue, by the way, was an obscenity itself, long and thick, warty and purple.

Rachel stayed still as stone throughout his humiliating usage. But after a moment Entimemseph growled and slapped Lo Fang's hand away.

Lo Fang stopped grinning. His green, green eyes flared, a sickening hint of what lay just beneath the surface of his cheery psychotic rambling. My heart thumped in my chest.

''James, everyone at this table . . . we all know what it's like, the ecstasy of the dark power. A word of friendly advice? Surrender to it. Delight in it. I told you I can't seem to lose these days? That everything I do, every single gesture leads on to greater and greater victories? Well, it's the same with you!''

He grinned like a gargoyle again.

''Oh yes it is, Jimmy, old skate! You have only to allow your power to unfold more fully. Trust your instincts. Go with the flow . . . hmmm, I like the sound of that . . . must remember to use it again. You *will* be one of us. Guaranteed. You have only to step the one final step . . . cross one bridge more. Do you know what that bridge is, James? Do you know what you have yet to do with this power of yours? Now don't fib, dear boy. Yes, you do indeed know, young bucko, me lad! And now we're going to help you do it. Just sit back and relax . . . Hah!'' Suddenly his eyes lit up. ''Well well well! And what have we here? Our first course at last!''

So. Quite the long-winded speech, wasn't it?

I have faithfully reproduced every single word Lo Fang said to me up to that moment. Believe me, in light of all that occurred, his every word is etched deep in my memory. For better or for worse.

And now I shall tell you what else the Tibetan troll—

Tibetan or Atlantean or wherever in hell his true origins were—showed me.

What had stopped his panegyric was Kristara's arrival with a serving tray. She set plates before Lo Fang, then Glenda, then me. Entimemseph got a larger platter, and a quart-sized crystal chalice. Rachel, only a goblet.

Both vessels brimmed with crimson liquid.

I looked down at my plate. It held a large, thick cutlet, perfectly cooked, deliciously seasoned, artfully arranged. Hardly had I sniffed it, but I felt the juices filling my mouth. And my innards roiling. And a stirring in my groin.

My hands grew gnarled and twisted, my pelt shimmered forth. Glenda, the dwarf, and the mummy were all grinning at me. Glenda's face was already flattened and fully covered with fur.

"Dunno bout anyone elsh . . . but ah ammm grrehhhh . . ." Glenda slurred.

She grasped her cutlet in murderous paws and started ripping and chewing it.

Lo Fang sliced off a chunk of his meat and held it up on his silver fork.

"They say human flesh is closest in taste to pork. The South Sea Islanders even call it 'long pig.' Hee hee. Do you agree, James? . . . Ooops, you can't really say yet, can you? Mmmm, but you do know how delicious *it* is," he crooned. "So good, so sweet . . . Oh, not this silly piece of flesh, succulent though it be. Smell . . . taste . . . *feel* it, James! Feel the dark new world! Feel it coursing through you! Heat without light! Light without heat! Black . . . cleansing . . . fire. You do love it, don't you?"

And then, his green eyes searing through me, he crammed the slab of meat into his mouth and started chewing it with loud, wet, smacking chomps.

Beside him, Entimemseph looked down at Rachel Bukhovna . . . at Rachel, still as stone.

"Feed," the mummy said. "You feed. Now."

There was mad power in his eyes. But Rachel gazed up at him, unafraid.

"I say you *feed*," he rumbled. And then, very, very softly. "Please? Please, my darling? You must feed. I beseech thee. Thou must feed to . . . to live."

Rachel smiled bitterly at Entimemseph's unintentional joke. Without taking her defiant eyes from his, she lifted her goblet. And drained it to the dregs.

She placed it back on the table.

Rachel's lips were red. A sudden blush of pink suffused her pale cheeks.

At the corner of her eye, a single crimson tear.

Entimemseph saw it.

His impossibly huge hand lifted a napkin, and with the lightest of touches, he wiped the bloody drop away.

He turned frowning from Rachel, grasped his own enormous goblet, and tossed its entire contents down his gullet in one quick, angry gulp. Then he tore into the meat with his bare hands.

I put my paws on my lap, made my fur shimmer away, and sat watching them all feed. Long minutes passed. At last Lo Fang licked a final streak of gravy from his dish and squinted at me. He nodded to my full plate.

"You think you're smart, but you're not," he sneered. "In fact, you are a fool. You are doing nothing but putting off the inevitable. *Nothing!*" Then he sighed and smiled again. "Ah, well. No problem."

Kristara scurried up to our table.

"Finished?" she asked me softly.

I nodded, and she collected my plate, then started around for the others. Lo Fang had been staring at me, an angry grin frozen on his face. As Kristara stepped next to him, he suddenly lashed out and slapped her face. Her head snapped, the dishes on her tray rattled. But she didn't drop a one.

"*Bitch!*" Lo Fang snarled. "He's not finished till I say! Understand?"

"Y-yes, Excellency!" Kristara gasped in horror. "I . . . I'm so sorry, Excellency!"

Lo Fang's nails were long, and he had slashed her cheek.

Blood was welling from three parallel slices. He seemed satisfied.

"Fine." He smiled, his good nature restored. "Now you may continue clearing."

She hurried to do so, and scuttled off with a fully loaded tray, the blood streaming down her neck. But as she rushed past the table nearest ours, one of the diners seated there extended his foot and tripped her.

I happened to recognize the tripper, a distinguished-looking older gentleman who held a very influential position in Tammany Hall. He had spent a term as mayor some few years back. He was known for his flamboyant manner and his sticky fingers. He was not known for his sense of humor.

But his practical joke brought the house down. Kristara's tray went flying as she spun in a circle and fell, grasping ludicrously at the cascade of silverware and crockery that tumbled with her.

I suppose it was really quite funny. Every face turned to her with an eagerness quite the opposite of the earlier inattentiveness to our party. The diners laughed uproariously as her dishes clattered and smashed.

Now Kristara seemed to have her first good luck of the evening. She didn't fall to the floor. Instead, she landed in the lap of another of the diners—a dashing, mustached actor famous for his swashbuckling roles on stage and screen. He caught her in his arms and grinned down at her like a jolly pirate at a captured maiden.

She gazed back up at him as the audience chuckled, and for a moment the two of them looked like stars in a musical comedy. Despite her bloody face.

Then the actor grasped the front of her blouse and *ripped* it open, tore it off of her breasts and away from her shoulders, yanked it halfway down her arms, trapping her elbows.

The crowd loved it.

But worse was on the way. As the jolly swashbuckler stripped Kristara bare to the waist, he was also ripping at her flesh, clawing deep cuts into her shoulders and her full, milky breasts. His nails had grown very long and sharp.

Kristara squealed in pain, the diners roared, the actor bared his fangs in a snarl of thanks. He lifted the girl by her arms and held her aloft. She wriggled and bicycled her legs, but too many others were up and at her already. Razor claws slashed her trousers and undergarments away; hunched halfling hands clutched at her ankles and wrists.

Her clothes were gone, save for a few tatters, but Kristara was clothed in red. They mobbed her and held her aloft, face up; a dozen paws dug their daggers into her legs and buttocks and arms and neck.

Naked, stretched out and up like that, Kristara's gravid belly was quite prominent indeed.

She wailed loudly, which didn't fail to amuse the thronging sophisticates. But none of them could laugh anymore. The mobbing men and women . . . males and females, rather . . . could only snarl their delight.

They were halflings, each and every one. Their eyes glowed and their mangy pelts shimmered; their tortured bodies twisted and shifted. Kristara's blood scent had dredged out the beast in all of them.

Some of the distinguished diners were as completely changed as Glenda, or as the dacoits who had attacked me, lo, those may days ago. That is to say, they were changed quite completely, and quite poorly.

Others were barely changed at all; glowing eyes, thickened features, elongated teeth, and ragged patches of fur were seemingly the extent of their ability to shape-shift. But they were all Lo Fang's creatures; each and every one of the upper-crust cruds.

Lo Fang reached inside his jacket and withdrew . . . the ancient tablet of clay, the Key of Entimemseph. It was fully mended, just as Bukhovna had predicted, the pieces patched together good as new. The tablet was already glowing and pulsing cheerily.

So were Lo Fang's eyes, brightly, golden green.

So was Entimemseph. In his eyes, and behind the enormous, clenched teeth in his wide-grinning mouth, the fires of hell raged in rhythm.

So were the assembled werebeasts. They snarled and howled to the beat, the vile puppets, as they marched toward us with their moaning, bloodied prey. They slammed her down onto our table and held her wriggling in place before us.

The main course. Her blood smeared the damask.

"Righty-oh, James," Lo Fang burbled. "And won't you join us? Won't you have a bite?"

I freely admit it: the smell of Kristara's fear and blood was maddening. Very, very delicious.

I glared down at her tender, tormented flesh. My body shifted and changed smoothly, gracefully. The ill-fitting evening clothes were now a snare around me, but my change was too strong for them, and they burst and fell away as I became the wolf. Slowly, inexorably.

I saw that all eyes were on me. The werecreatures stared with awe, Lo Fang and Entimemseph with amused pleasure. Even Kristara was looking up at me, with the dumb, glazed relief of a victim who knows its hopeless struggling will soon end.

I glanced at Rachel. Only she had not changed. Only she had managed to stay . . . exactly as she was. She looked back into my baleful eyes, looked at me without judgment, without contempt. Nothing. But I do believe it was her very coldness that gave me the strength I needed.

Lo Fang grasped Kristara's hair and yanked her head aside, baring her neck. For me.

"Well, Mr. Underhill?" he said quietly. "*Do* have some."

The tablet of clay mimicked his command in light. Entimemseph's raging eyes pierced my chest.

I was almost entirely the wolf. I reached my muzzle to the girl's poor, ravaged cheek. Then I became a man again. There was really nothing I could do for her, of course. So I just kissed her cheek gently, a pale caress of comfort and farewell. Then I pushed back from the table and stood.

I was buck naked, but with what few shreds of dignity I could muster, I picked up my shoes, draped my torn pants over my arm, and walked slowly toward the door.

I half expected . . . oh, I don't know, a lightning bolt from Lo Fang's Key, a crushing death blow from the mummy, a knife in the back from Glenda. All I got was Lo Fang's cackling laughter. He seemed genuinely amused.

"You're a *scream*, Underhill! A scream! You think you're above all this. Ha ha ha! Just watch! You'll come around. You really believe those fools? You really think you're a superior being? Too high up the ladder for a nibble, eh? Mr. Evolution. Hah! Superior, my purple ass! You watch. Watch what happens when the change *really* fills you."

Suddenly, he burst into song, and the Key pulsed brightly in time to the music.

"*New York, New Yorrrk . . . la lalala laaah!* It's mine now, Jimmy boy, all mine! *You're* mine, Underhill. Go! Go find out how much mine you really are! Go find out who made you. Oh, and send my regards to your friends. Tell them I hope they have a nice night. Ha ha ha! See you later. Just wait! You'll see!"

Maybe I would see, maybe I wouldn't.

Maybe I knew something Lo Fang didn't know I knew.

Maybe.

But I definitely knew something Maurice Chen didn't know. *He* thought being such a faithful servant of Lo Fang and Entimemseph made him safe. So safe that when I passed him at the edge of the dining room, where he stood ready to attend his guests' every wish, he thought it was perfectly appropriate to favor me with a contemptuous sneer. Perfectly appropriate and perfectly safe.

Behind me, the assembled guests had begun their snarling feast on Maurice Chen's slave girl, just one more piece of livestock to him. I decided to play a joke.

As I passed Maurice, I shifted for an invisible instant, and in the same instant I reached out my paw to him.

Then I was human again, and strolling past. He flinched, clutched his neck, and gasped.

"Touch of laryngitis, Maurice?" I asked solicitously.

He didn't answer. His glassy eyes stared, his hand dropped away. An open hydrant of red geysered up over Maurice

Chen's starched white collar and doused the empty tables like a loose fire hose, as he pitched forward.

Talk about slapstick. Maurice landed quite loudly, flat on his face, his life pumping out of his throat.

His legs continued to kick for a while, his wing tips clucking softly against the polished oak floor. Then he was finished.

I put on my torn tuxedo pants and my shoes, then expropriated an overcoat from the unattended cloakroom. I selected a nice one while I was at it; a soft, heavy, camel hair, all the rage with the young fellows that year.

The owner's label said "E. Koch." I prayed I wouldn't be run over by a truck on the way home, or the authorities would be frightening E. Koch's next of kin. On second thought, to hell with them. Serve them right for being related to a werecreature.

I hit the street and hailed a taxicab. Speaking of home, I had decided that was my first stop. Time was short. In fact, there was no time: I was probably already too late. But my apartment was pretty much on the way to my final destination, and I had to admit I needed reinforcements, and clothes. A pistol might be nice too. And money for the cabby . . .

When the taxi screeched up to my awning, I was out barking orders before Ernst could touch the door handle.

"Call Gina! Tell Joe and Eli the attack is coming! The werewolf . . ."

Then I saw Ernst was not wearing his doorman's uniform. He had on his leather commissar's jacket and his black beret. Five of his comrades, also in black berets, were lounging near the entrance, smoking, talking quietly.

"Joe Jefferson asked us to wait here, on the off chance that you might return," he said grimly. "Bukhovna is at the mansion, trying to help Eli. There was no need for us . . ."

"Eli. What happened to him?"

"Wounded. By the wolf."

"How badly?"

"Quite badly. Bukhovna is assessing that now. Jefferson was injured, too, but he's up and about."

"And the women?"

"Gone. Both gone, of course."

Of course.

"What time was the attack?"

"About two hours ago."

Just after they'd caught me at Glenda's. Just before dinner. Quite the busy evening for Lo Fang and friends.

"Ernst?"

"Yes, Mein Käpitan?" There was just a hint of irony in his tone.

I opened my overcoat to display the rest of my evening wear.

"Would you pay the taxi driver, please? I seem to have left my money in my shirt."

"I see. And where did you leave the shirt?"

"Remind me to tell you all about it on the way to our next stop."

It was time to play private eye and actually go examine the scene of a crime; one of the scenes, of one of the crimes.

The mansion's tall, elegantly carved entrance doorway was lying flat in the lobby, torn neatly and completely off its hinges, as if someone rather large had simply forgotten to open it before walking through.

The place reeked of fresh blood.

Aristotle was the first person I saw. He was sitting in the entrance hall, tux collar open, head in hands. Assistants were hovering around him.

They hadn't seen their way clear to disposing of the bodies yet. There were five corpses behind them, strewn up and down the wide, marble staircase. Black men; recruited by Joe and Velma, no doubt. They all looked very tough. But not tough enough. Tough and dead.

Aristotle lifted his head and peered at me. His face went hard.

"You!" he snarled. He jumped up and grabbed me by the lapels.

"I tell you to fix, goddamn it and what you do? Hah? You bring these *mavros* into my house. And now my Gina gone. Clara too. *Gone* goddamn you! I break you neck. You and these goddamn *mavros*, these . . . these . . . *skilarapes*!"

I would have let him go on, because as I believe I've mentioned, I knew he loved Gina very much, in his shabby, rich man's way. And I knew, too, that it is the businessman's instinct to blame somebody, anybody, when things go badly. The raging boss requires a goat. And nobody ever said the goat had to be guilty of anything except being a goat.

But I was no goat.

And more important, "skilarapis" is a derogatory Greek term for Negroes. Several of the skilarapes Ari was referring to were lying dead on his stair. They had died trying to defend his beloved wife from harm, while he was out somewhere, busy being Ari.

So, in honor of the dead, I brushed Ari's hands away from my jacket, and I picked him up a few inches off the ground, by *his* lapels, and some of his flesh. I held his face very close to mine and I growled quietly to him.

"You have just outlived your welcome in your own house, Ari. I am going to go and talk to my friends now. Perhaps I will also look around for clues. But I don't want to see you again tonight. So when I put you down . . ."

His toadies had been stunned for a moment, but just then, one of them tried to interrupt us.

I shifted Ari and held him up in one hand while, with the other, I broke the toady's jaw.

Another drew on me.

It was very tiresome. But since he was only doing his job, it wouldn't have been fair to kill him. So I punched him in the solar plexus and kicked him in the nuts, in both cases only hard enough to make sure he would spend the next little while focusing all his concentration on breathing and on worrying about his future as a progenitor.

The others caucused and decided it would be the better

part of valor not to risk disturbing us again, so I returned my attention to Aristotle.

"When I put you down," I continued, "I would like you and your friends to go away. Hide. And make sure you don't come out until I leave. Yes?"

"Yes," he hissed.

When I did put him down he was good as his word. He and his whole entourage shuffled off, carrying some of its members.

"Jimmy!" Joe shouted from the top of the stairs. "Cut the bullshit and get up here!"

I ran up to the landing, trying my best to ignore the freshly killed corpses. Joe sported a deep gash on his left temple. It had been bandaged, but only lightly, and I could see the cut very well. It was sure to scar up nicely. Joe's nice new scar would provide fine aesthetic balance to the older one on his right cheek.

What a comfort. At least one person would be taking something positive away from the evening's debacle.

"Eli?" I asked Joe.

"Bukhovna's working on him now."

"So what happened?"

"So they hit us hard." He shrugged. "Where were you, by the way?"

"Otherwise detained. Who . . ."

"Hey. That shit don't wash anymore, Jimmy," he snapped. "Where were you?"

He was actually right for a change.

"I went over to Glenda's to question her. As planned. But right in the middle of our talk Entimemseph walked in." I cocked my head to the entrance door. "Just like he did here."

"Somebody should teach that boy about doorknobs," Joe muttered.

"I don't think he's trainable. Anyway, I didn't get a chance to ask Glenda many questions. But I got some interesting answers. More than I bargained for."

"How'd you escape?"

"I didn't. I walked away."

"From Entimemseph?"

"No. From Lo Fang. Walked out on him in a crowded restaurant. But that *is* a long story. Oh, and by the way, Glenda Rogers-Gracey's one of them."

"No kidding."

"Uh-uh. I mean she's a werewolf."

"What? Is she . . . *the* werewolf?"

"No way. There's werewolves and there's were*wolves*. She isn't nearly as gifted at the change as the wolf who's been hanging around here. All she can do is a sort of bearded lady number."

"Sounds appetizing."

"If you like that sort of thing. Now it's your turn, Joe. Show and tell."

"You can probably figure the sequence of events. Eli and I were upstairs with the ladies. In Clara's room. Eli had just started in with some kind of hoodoo number . . . 'draw a circle round them thrice' or something. He said it was to protect them from the worst of Lo Fang's influence. Might have worked, too, but before he really got started, Entimemseph blew the door down.

"Then I heard the sound of our guys opening up. Don't know if you noticed, but they came equipped with some pretty heavy ordnance—Thompsons, sawed-off shotguns. One guy even had a Finnish antitank gun." Joe chuckled. "Wonder where in Harlem he found *that*. Anyway, they were really earning their keep, blasting away out there. Then it all stopped. Real sudden.

"Right after that I heard the sound of bones breaking. Our guys' bones. Eli and I hit the hallway. Lo Fang was standing at the bottom of the stairs with his hands raised. He was wearing those green gloves . . . and he was holding up that clay tablet . . . the Key. At least he was sort of holding it. Actually he had his hands up and out and the Key was floating in the air in front of him. There was a . . . a *glow* coming out of it. I don't know what the hell it was, but every machine gun in the mansion was jammed all of a sudden. My heater, too. Believe me, I tried it. And there's Entimemseph the Mummy, ripping our guys apart.

"So then Eli pushes past me and he stands right at the top of the stairs with his arms out and he shouts, *'You! Cease!'* Real loud. Like, louder than a person should be able to shout. The thing is, he's not talking to the mummy. He's talking to Lo Fang. And for a second, the glow from the tablet sort of withers away. Then our guy on the antitank gun opens up. Puts a round right in the mummy's gut. It throws him back against the wall and explodes.

"That slowed the mummy down. For roughly three seconds. While our guy's loading in another round, the mummy steps right up to him, picks up the antitank gun over his head by the barrel, and whacks our guy with it. Crushes him like a bug. The sound . . . it was quiet by then because the rest of our guys were already dead. So I could hear the sound of that gun coming down real good. . . .

"Meanwhile Lo Fang aims the Key right at Eli. And Eli gives him the Eye. So weird. Not a sound now. But it's like they're having kind of a long-distance wrestling match . . . this fire arcing between them. I don't know who would have won. But there was a crash, and screaming from Clara's room. That sort of broke Eli's concentration, and Lo Fang started bearing down on him.

"I made for Clara's door. But before I got there, it kicks open and three, four wolfmen come barreling out. They were *fast*, Jimmy. My gun worked fine, away from Lo Fang. I blasted one of them. Knocked him apart and threw fur all over the wall. Hmmm . . . right *there* in fact."

He wasn't kidding. Regulations require New York City police officers to carry .38 caliber revolvers with solid slug ammo. But the spray of blood and Spam that Joe pointed to on the hallway wall, had the look of a .45 dumdum splatter to me. Very unsporting of him.

"Then they took me down. Only reason they didn't bother to kill me was they were too busy going after Eli. They mobbed him."

Joe tapped his bandaged head.

"I was kind of dazed. But I wasn't asleep. And I saw what came out of Clara's room next. It was the she-wolf, Jimmy. She came walking out real slow, like the queen of the ball. And her eyes were on fire.

"Eli was actually holding his own pretty damn well . . . fighting off Lo Fang *and* landing some good ones on the wolfmen. But then the she-wolf growls, and her pets back off. She jumps right at old Eli and smashes him. Knocks him ass over teakettle, right down that whole flight of marble steps.

"I heard screams. The girls, I think. Then I blacked out. When I came to, our guys were dead. The girls were gone. And Eli was . . . see for yourself."

We were at Clara's door. And guarding the door was none other than Ruvon, Dr. Bukhovna's Hasidic gorilla.

"How's business, Ruvon?" I asked politely. And held out my hand.

"Could be better, Underhill," he grumbled.

Ruvon stepped completely in front of Clara's door. He started to give me the Hasidic handshake; the one reserved for non-Hasids. That involves holding the non-Hasidic greeter's hand with just the fingertips.

The point of such a handshake, I have always assumed, is for the Hassid to have as little contact as possible with the unclean flesh of the goyim. Very complimentary.

I'm a regular mind reader, and I knew Ruvon was about to tell me that Bukhovna was not to be disturbed. But the last thing I was in the mood for was trouble from Ruvon. So I shifted my grip and grasped hold of Ruvon's whole hand. And I squeezed. Hard. Hard enough to show him just how strong I was.

Uncleanly strong.

I smiled pleasantly and said, "Won't be but a moment," and used his hand as a sort of leash to steer him aside.

Out of my way.

* * *

Eli was stretched on Clara's bed, and Bukhovna was seated beside him, bent toward his bandaged brow.

"Hello, James," Bukhovna murmured, without looking up. "I wish you'd gotten here a few hours earlier. Wish I had, too."

He pushed himself up and scowled at me over his shoulder.

"Actually, I don't know if we would have done any good. Maybe we would both have ended up like Eli here." He shook his head. "He's strong, James. But Lo Fang has grown even stronger."

"Is Eli dying?"

"That does seem to be his plan."

"Excuse me?"

"The physical wounds are not mortal." He shrugged. "Some scrapes and bangs, a fairly mild concussion. Not near enough to make him feel like this."

He lifted Eli's big limp paw with its enormous, brown sausage fingers; then he took hold of my wrist and made me touch it.

Clay. Damp clay. Cold and dead.

"Are you sure he's not . . . ?"

"No. Not dead yet. But he's been like this since I arrived. His soul, his spirit, I have discovered, has fled into a distant province of his mind. Very far away. At first I thought it had left his mortal flesh entirely. When I found Eli's soul, it was . . . you could say it was curled up in a ball, cowering in a corner. It scurried away from me, from me, one of his oldest friends. All I could discover is that his soul wishes to flee his body, but has been so deeply frightened, that it can't seem to do so.

"You've seen similiar cases in war, James. Perhaps without even knowing it, you saw this in Spain. Horribly wounded men who cling miraculously to life. Often what you're really seeing there is a soul too terrorized to leave its ruined house. I think that is Eli's paradox. Lo Fang and the she-wolf have been overly zealous. They've managed to wound Eli's soul so deeply, he can't even die!"

Poor old Elijah P. Woolwock. Maybe there was something . . . but first things first.

"Hope you won't think I'm callous for changing the subject, Dr. Bukhovna. But do you have any idea at all about where they've taken Clara and Gina?"

"If I had any idea where they are, I wouldn't be wasting my time nursing a cantankerous old fool who doesn't have the sense to keep his guard up." He frowned. "We'd be up and after them. But I haven't the foggiest. Yet."

"And his plans in regards to them?"

"Also unclear."

I studied Bukhovna for a moment and judged he was telling the truth about that last bit. Good. There was some information I was pleased to reserve for myself. One part of what would need to be done, I wanted to do alone. I decided to push a little more though. Just to be sure.

"A long time ago I accused you of being afraid to fight Lo Fang," I continued. "I was wrong, of course. You've been fighting him for years."

"You'd be alarmed if I told you just how many years," he replied.

"And yet, you can't predict him? No idea about where he's gone?"

"You don't understand how unpredictable Lo Fang is. Or why. This world of ours is very much like . . . like a dream to him. The earthly plane is not his home, and when he is here, he sleepwalks . . . he is sleeping much of the time, even when he appears to be wide awake. Sometimes his dreams are playful, and at such times he can seem quite ridiculous. Almost harmless. But that is not his true face. Lo Fang's deepest dreams are nightmares. Nightmares for others. And when he is fully awake . . ." he shook his head. "Trust me, Lo Fang's evil begins and ends far beyond the bounds of reason. Battling him is like fighting in a surrealist's landscape. It is an understatement to say he is unpredictable."

"Who is he, really?"

"In a sense Lo Fang is just what he claims to be. A Tibetan

holy man. A German archaeological expedition into the Himalayas found him several years back. The Nazis have been sending research teams into the East for years, you know. Looking for the origins of the Aryan race, supposedly. They discovered Lo Fang, and eventually invited him to Berlin, to set up an ashram. He was more than happy to oblige. His world vision coincides quite nicely with Mr. Hitler's.''

"I saw Lo Fang tonight," I said.

"So I gathered."

"Entimemseph and . . . and Rachel, too."

"Yes yes, go on." He waved his hand with annoyance.

"He threw a dinner party for about three dozen of his American friends. Werewolf friends."

"Truly that many?" He frowned. "I knew about Glenda of course, and we suspected a few others."

"At least three dozen. Rich ones, too."

"Not good."

"No kidding."

"I mean that he has been able to gather that much evil unto himself. It's the Key, of course. He's learning to use the Key. Entimemseph is quite a good teacher."

"You wouldn't know it. That mummy sounds like a big doofuss. And the two of them are always bickering."

"As soul mates so often do. Be careful not to overestimate their differences, James. And be careful not to underestimate Entimemseph. It's the same with both of them. They can seem exactly as they want to seem. They are kindred spirits. Very powerful indeed. And all of their powers flow from the same source."

"The Key?"

"No. The Key is just a reservoir."

"Pretty big reservoir."

"Yes. Bigger even than Entimemseph knows."

"Huh? How could that be? It's his Key."

"Only in the sense that he held it for many years, and explored its potency more deeply than most men. Actually, the Key is much older than Entimemseph. Older in fact than Egyptian civilization."

"That reminds me. Something Lo Fang said. He implied that he came from the island of Atlantis. And he told me he destroyed it."

Bukhovna raised his eyebrows.

"Did he really tell you that? It's true, as far as it goes. Actually, Lo Fang lived on an island off the coast of Atlantis. Thule, it was called; world-renowned for the blackness of its magic. Still, it was surprisingly arrogant of him to reveal so much about his origins."

"So much? You mean there's more?"

"Yes."

"I'll bite. Who else is Lo Fang? Where else is he from?"

"Why, he's a demon of course. Come straight from hell."

"I couldn't agree with you more."

"I'm speaking literally, I'm afraid. Lo Fang's name in the satanic regions is Azazriel." He paused to spit through his fingers over his left shoulder. "According to the Kabbalah, he was one of the most exalted of the fallen angels. He arrived on earth 9,723 years ago, and he has been striving toward this culminating moment, or at least these moments, for all the intervening years."

"You are serious."

"Of course." He studied me. "And now you are concerned. You are thinking this means Lo Fang is even more formidable than you imagined. Well, it's true. He is. But he is also less so. Remember . . . it is dangerous to underestimate the power of evil, but it is just as dangerous to overestimate it. To do so only helps evil's conquest. Lo Fang is a demon, and that means he has considerable power. It also means his powers are severely limited. The dark ones who come among us . . . when demons walk up and down in the world, and to and fro in it . . . the rules of conduct they must follow are quite harsh. Ironclad, in fact."

"Azazriel, eh?"

"Yes, yes, but . . . best not to speak the name aloud. It enhances his power, in a way. Besides, I'm sure he doesn't want the world to know *that* much about him yet."

"Why? Is he afraid the news will get back to Mr. Hitler?"

"Mr. Hitler has long been perfectly aware of Lo Fang's origins," he said flatly.

"You were surprised at how much he told me about himself. Why is that important?"

"Simple. His willingness to reveal himself . . . his arrogance, tells me how complete his plans are."

"How complete?"

"Very. Something will happen tonight. Something quite decisive in terms of his ambitions in this part of the world."

"I see. And what do you suggest we do about it?"

"Why . . . I will stay here with our dear friend, of course. He has been hurt, James. I will stay with him, and see if he can be saved. As for what we will do directly against Lo Fang . . ." He shrugged. "Just at the moment, one thing is as good as the other. I'll wait. Be ready. Something will happen very soon. I can feel it in my bones. You, on the other hand, are a werewolf and a detective." He grinned. "Why not sniff around for clues? You never can tell."

"Just what I had in mind. But I'd like to try something first."

"Namely?"

"Rather not say. I'll just embarrass myself if it doesn't work. Pardon me, please . . ."

I stripped my clothes off quickly, and just as quickly changed wholly into the wolf.

I padded up to Eli and glared down at his poor, cold, human flesh. Then I stepped inside his mind.

How to say this . . . Empty. The rooms and hallways were empty. Deserted. Nothing lived there anymore. It was cold in the dead silence of Eli's mind, as chilling to the mental touch as his flesh had been to my hand.

I went deeper. And I began to see, to feel the signs of what had happened. Imagine, if you will, the worst surge of sudden terror you have ever felt: your blood roars and your heart knots and your soul screams out a plea for impossible flight.

Now imagine that fear surge suddenly frozen, a petrified instant, doomed to go on forever and ever. A crystal of terror.

Elijah P. Woolcock's mind had become such a crystal. I was walking through the corridors of an ice palace.

Bukhovna said it had taken him a long time to find Eli. But unlike Bukhovna, a being of infinitely greater skill and understanding than I in such matters, I was merely a wolf.

A hunter.

I began to lope, then to gallop. Straight to him. Straight to the place where Eli . . . his soul or his spirit or his consciousness . . . was still very much alive. I raced to him swiftly.

"No no no! Leave me! Away! Be gone be gone be gone . . . !"

He tried to wriggle away from me, another invader, but I would not let him. I wouldn't hurt him; but I would not let him fail to regard me, either.

"Eli! Stop running, damn it. Talk to me."

He did stop running. He stopped cringing, too. And he looked at me.

"James. Whispering Jesus, man! You should've seen what they did. Lo Fang. And the Mummy. The she-wolf. And the Key . . . the Key has given them all such hideous strength . . ."

He started to show me what they did to him.

A universe of pain. Suffering. A blind idiot god; a skull with a clacking, screaming mouth; horror forever past, forever present, forever future. The crawling terror of being. And of not being. Fear. Utter terror . . . I was drowning in it, engulfed, smothered, crushed, squashed flat . . .

"Enough!" I'm afraid I raised my voice. *"I don't want to see any more of that crap, Eli. Really I don't. It's over. Finished. Now come back out with me."*

"Leave me alone, James. Just let me stay here. I want to rest. And die. Please?"

"Sorry, friend. Die on your own time. We need you now."

"Can't."

"You must."

"Yeah? What if I won't?"

"What if? It's not even worth talking about. Now get it in gear."

"Goddamn it. Underhill! Get the hell out of my mind! Who goddamn invited you in here anyway? Beat it! Shoo! Scat!"

He aimed a mental boot at my hindquarters that sent me skittering back down the corridors.

And out.

Elijah P. Woolcock had bolted up in the bed, his eyes wide and unfocused. But I could feel the returning warmth of his skin against my muzzle. I waved my tail happily; he shook his head and finally focused on Bukhovna, who was busy gaping at us both.

"Avrom!" Eli croaked. "Something to drink."

"A nice glass of tea?"

"Are you kidding?"

As usual in my experience, an inspection of the scene of the crime unearthed no profoundly revelatory clues: no hastily scribbled note betraying the final destination of the abducted, no faint line of breadcrumbs trailing off into the night.

Nor were my wolf abilities any big help.

I knew the antique scent of Entimemseph only too well, likewise the utterly foreign scent of Lo Fang. I knew Clara's delicious smells, too. And Gina's. And yes, I smelled the she-wolf. The mansion held all these essences in confusing abundance. It was actually a relief to follow them out of the wide front door.

The intertwining essences ended at the curb.

No doubt that indicated the victorious raiding party had made off by car, and I discovered I could distinguish the scent of the specific car, or at least of one that had stood at the mansion curbside recently. But have you ever tried tracking the scent of a single auto through Manhattan streets? Good luck. The scent blended in with dozens of others after just a few feet, with hundreds of others by the time it reached the corner. I, at least, found it impossible to follow.

And yet . . . something called to me.

Ernst and I conferred. We decided he would station three men at the mansion, take two with him, and head back to guard our building. It was a classic and compounded example of closing the barn door after the horses escaped. But what the hell. It was something semiconstructive to do, and it left me where I wanted to be.

Alone.

I found myself walking west. It was the middle of the night, and there was a bitter chill; I had the streets almost entirely to myself. But I craved even more solitude, and when the dark wall of trees loomed up, I knew I must enter.

Central Park on a winter's midnight: a perfectly congenial place for the likes of me.

I entered at 86th Street and walked in a few hundred feet, ignoring the auto paths and walkways. It was hardly a wilderness; the whole park was too brightly lit for a werewolf's tastes, by the widely placed streetlamps, the milky purple reflection of the city from the cold clouds above, the pale lambency of the grimy city snow-patched about on lawns and rocks.

South, through a black web-work of trees, I saw the north wall of the Metropolitan Museum of Art. I recalled that my first knowledge of Entimemseph . . . mine along with most people's . . . derived from there, from the Egyptian installation Glenda had donated.

Entimemseph's Tomb . . . a hoax according to Bukhovna: real stones and paintings and carvings and artifacts, but false at its core, since it held only a forgery of Entimemseph's mummy.

Hmm. On the other hand . . .

Couldn't hurt to check. Besides, I always preferred visiting the Metropolitan when it was least crowded.

But in the next instant, I saw something that laid an undeniably greater claim to my interest.

I'd been crossing a rise, a basaltic outcrop that dropped down beside a footpath. Standing on its crest, I actually caught a glimpse of the top quarter of my apartment building, more than a mile away, far across the park and south.

Most people would not have seen what I was able to see, in the moment I glanced off at that familiar, distant sight. I would not have seen it either, were it not for one more peculiar aspect of my new wolf nature; namely, the ability to distinguish very small movements, very far away.

No, not just the ability. The inclination. My eyes sought out such sights. When long vistas presented themselves, I found myself staring into them. I examined them in impossibly minute detail, with a hunter's cold, hungry, heartless gaze.

Now, I saw something inching up the side of my building. Slowly, slowly. Already just a few floors below my penthouse apartment. It was a human figure. From the distance . . . my eyes were inhumanly good, but not all-seeing . . . it seemed to be wearing a long gray cape.

I shifted. Not enough to trip over my clothes, just enough to give myself tireless speed in the race for home. A mad race it was, over snow and frozen mud, across ice-smooth rocks and rock-hard ice. I halted at the park side of the wall on Central Park West, peered up through brittle branches and the mist of my breath, at the building's face.

She was very near the top by then, walking slowly, steadily, as if in a trance. No doubt it took a great deal of concentration to do what she was doing, because she was walking straight up the face of my building, feet against the brick, her body extended perfectly perpendicular to the wall.

The gray cape she wore was unaffected by her trance, and thus was still a slave to the tediously predictable law of gravity. It hung down behind her, billowed softly, gracefully, in a sudden puff of chilly breeze.

I'd have to hurry if I wanted to spoil the surprise.

I ran toward the servants' entrance in fully human form, since I knew I would regret overly alarming the guard Ernst had posted there. I signaled to him, ran past, shifted to halfling for the race up the fire stairs.

I'd have made it up the stairs faster as the wolf, but I calculated I would still have enough time as a halfling. And that way I could also preserve the old-fashioned formality of being fully clothed when I greeted Rachel Bukhovna on my penthouse terrace.

I stood in the living room and watched her reach the outer lip of the terrace railing. Her body stayed perfectly rigid; she rolled up over the edge and stood erect on the rail, smooth and stiff as a moving target in a shooting gallery.

Her eyes were shut, her face was very still and beautiful.

She hopped down from the railing; actually she floated down. Her head turned slowly in my direction. When her eyes opened she was looking at me so fixedly that it seemed she'd already been seeing me before her lids went up. Her body loosened.

"Hello, Rachel," I said.

"Hello, James. It's been a long time since we've been together."

"Not if you count dinner tonight. Or that evening in Chinatown. Or . . ."

"I don't count any of those things," she interrupted quickly. "Neither should you. I hope you won't."

"Why, Rachel? Why shouldn't I count all you've done for Lo Fang and Entimemseph? And for me?"

"Because what has happened . . . all of it . . . is simply the way things have to be. I could imagine it being worse, you know."

"One always can, if one has a good enough imagination," I said unpleasantly. "Oh, and by the way, is the mummy your new beau now?"

"Entimemseph claims . . . he claims to love me." She shrugged. "I'm sorry, James. There is hardly anything I can do about that. I think you saw I do not give him any encouragement. He . . . he was responsible for my reawakening. And now he is very possessive about me."

Her words finally reminded me of who, in the balance, had the most right to be angry with whom.

"Sorry, Rachel." I frowned. "It was my fault you were . . ."

"I do not blame you in the slightest," she said gently.

"There was no reason you should have known how it was necessary to . . . dispose of me. It was my fault in my haste, for not telling you the rules. But Entimemseph . . . I was talking about Entimemseph. I . . . I seem to fit in his plan in some way. And his love . . . it's a very strange thing, James. He can be so *gentle*. I know what a profound enemy he has been to my people . . . what a destructive force he still is. And yet, there is something very . . . loving about the way he treats me."

"Does he have sex with you, Rachel?"

I don't know why I asked that.

"Do you really want me to tell you, James?"

"Yes. I want to know."

"Well . . . I suppose you could call it that, what he does to . . . what we do together."

"Like what we did together that night?"

Sorry, I know I was getting a little weird there. Jealous of a mummy. Really. Next step was to ask her that classic cuckold's question: Who was bigger, him or me? I might have, too, if I hadn't been afraid I already knew the answer.

"No, James. It is very different. But if you don't mind . . . I didn't come here to discuss him with you. He is part of my doom, and there is nothing you can do to change it. Nothing I want you to do."

"Then why did you come here, Rachel? To do a some checking on my conversion to lycanthropy? Don't worry, I'm a very good werewolf. The work was top-notch . . ."

"Do you really believe that, James?" She actually looked puzzled. "I came here because I was able to slip away."

"First time in all these months?"

"I didn't say that. I have had few enough opportunities, because they watch me very carefully. But this was the first time I had the time *and* the reason. And now, James"—her eyes flashed, and suddenly her voice was hard, and strong— "you must stop your childishness, and you must listen to me. I don't know what you will do with what I'll tell you . . . but you must have the information."

"Why, Rachel? Why should I trust anything you say?"

"I don't care if you trust or not!" she snapped. "Just listen. Then do what you want. The change . . . the change that was made in you? I believe you know it got out of hand, as far as Lo Fang was concerned. He really believed he could enslave you by having you made into a werewolf. He was looking forward to it. He is very disappointed with what you have become."

"What about you, Rachel? Are you disappointed?"

"Not at all, James. I think you are very beautiful now." She grinned wickedly. "But I never knew you to fish for compliments. Let me go on. It's very horrible, what he has planned."

"And I, no doubt, am expected to do something about it."

She took my hand, and she looked into my eyes. Her fingers were cold; her eyes were beautiful.

"James, my sweet, sweet darling," she said softly. "All I can do is tell you what Lo Fang has planned, and where he is planning it, and how you can get in to see him secretly, without him knowing. Oh. And one thing more. You saw . . . in Chen's restaurant you saw his new circle of friends. They should give you some idea of how far his influence already has reached in this country. But I can tell you that, if he succeeds tonight, he will, for all intents and purposes, control America. He will be unstoppable here.

"So. Those are the boundaries of what I can tell you. But I cannot tell you what to do about it. Or whether you should do anything. I don't even want to know your plans. Because *you* know I must . . . I must go back to him. To them. And if you tell me what you are doing, they will most assuredly force that knowledge from me." She frowned. "As Lo Fang has forced me so many times before."

"Tell me, Rachel," I said grimly. "Let's hear it all."

She told me everything. Then she left me.

And now, before I relate a single detail, answer me this: Does it sound like it could possibly have been anything but a trap?

Of course it was a trap, whether Lo Fang had ordered Rachel to come to me, or was simply allowing her to do so, or even if he was totally unaware of her betrayal. Because one way or another, any move I made was bound to go badly.

But so what? The time for killing and dying had finally arrived. Time to go.

Out again, into the night.

I walked in human form, and Ernst walked beside me. We entered Central Park and pressed along quickly. Perhaps we could have used an entire army, considering all that would have to be done. And perhaps, considering the same task in another way, not even an entire army would have been of any use.

We didn't even take Ernst's men. They were good. But everyone has a limit. Very few sane people could reasonably be asked to witness what I knew Ernst and I were going to witness.

We would go out alone, and do whatever could be done, and then we would die. Most likely we would die.

Cleopatra's Needle stands in the park near the Metropolitan. Very amusing name it has, since it's not a needle and it's not Cleopatra's.

Very amusing.

Cleopatra's Needle is a seventy-one-foot tall, 488,000-pound votive obelisk, and it was first installed at the Sun Temple in Heliopolis by King Thotmes, some 3500 years ago. But rumor has it that the obelisk was already old at the time of that ancient installation.

The same rumor says it was originally dedicated to something considerably less bright and cheery than a sun god.

The obelisk was donated to the City of New York by the khedive of Egypt in 1877; and in 1881 it was installed in the park for kiddies to dance around. I recalled that over the years I had occasionally wondered to myself, in an idle sort of way, what in hell had ever possessed our City Fathers to erect a monument to Egyptian black magic in Central Park, and to see that it was named, for no damned reason, after an

Egyptian princess and sorceress, the "witch whore of the Nile," as Pliny the Elder called Cleo.

Now I knew exactly what in hell had possessed them; and I was soon to learn their damned reason for naming it.

I left Ernst far from the Needle, shifted, and moved forward. I reconnoitered the entire area and verified that Lo Fang had posted neither human nor inhuman sentries there. No doubt he saw no need. There were other, more vulnerable entrances to his underworld; and this one was guarded by words of the highest power.

I went back for Ernst, and in a moment we were standing together at the Needle's base, staring up at it. The sky had cleared. In the blue-black, star-spattered darkness above, a few icy clouds scutted by, their plumed fringes lit by the cold, hard, midwinter moon. A gibbous moon it was, bright but far from full; as bright as on the night when Lo Fang had roused Entimemseph from his unquiet sleep.

Ernst studied the challenge for a moment. Then he gave the limestone a rough, affectionate pat, as if it were the flank of an untamed beast he was about to break.

He took out his equipment; nothing much, really. Just a length of rope with straps and steel links at either end, and his climbing gloves.

He vaulted up onto the base while I looped the rope around the Needle. Then he strapped an end to either wrist and began shinnying up the obelisk. There was quite a bit of light, and I watched him go all the way to the top.

When he reached the Needle's tip, he pressed the inset stone just where I had told him to, said the words of power I had taught him, the words Rachel had just taught me, the words she had learned from her doting, ancient lover, the words of entry Entimemseph had known could only be used by Rachel . . . or by a creature capable, like her, of climbing to the very top of the Needle and speaking them while pressing the inset stone.

A seamless panel in the Needle's base began to rumble open. By the time Ernst stood beside me again, an entrance-way was gaping wide, with stone steps leading far down into blackness. I did not need the stabbing light of Ernst's electric torch to see the hieroglyphs carved along the walls, but the extra light made them much more legible.

Their content was quite different from those on the face of the Needle. In fact, they were an incantation, a charming ditty with which I happened to be familiar.

They began: "I, Cleopatra, sorceress, divine priestess of the eternal Slut-Mother Nile, do thus invoke the dark powers of Yog-Sothoth, Nyarlathotep, Cthulhu. Defile her, oh ye Elder Gods. Her mud-slickened thighs are spread for thee, hot waters lap her waiting delta. Plunge your stiff avenging spears, your blood-drenched horns, your ravaging tusks, into her pulsing flesh. Rend her moist, hungry . . ."

And so on and so forth.

Trust me, the incantation did not wax any less luridly obscene. It is credited to Cleopatra, is entitled "Cleopatra, Her Song of Songs," in fact. But it can be found on the pages of the *Necronomicon*, a vile grimoire of black magic, compiled by a charming ninth-century character known as the Mad Arab, Abdul al Hazhred.

It is considered *the* invocation for the Nether Gods. Not exactly something I'd have inscribed on my welcome mat, but quite appropriate, considering what I knew awaited us at the end of the labyrinth.

Ernst nodded to me, hauled on his rucksack. I lifted my own equipment bag onto my shoulders.

Reading those pearls on the wall had given me second thoughts. For Ernst, not for myself. As Ernst started down the stairs, I put my hand on his arm to stop him.

"Wait, comrade," I whispered in Spanish. "You have already done what was needed. Go home now."

"No," he whispered back. "And stop wasting time."

It should come as no surprise to anyone that an entire labyrinthine world exists under the streets of Manhattan.

The average person no more glimpses the innards and vitals of the city than he does the innards and vitals of his own body. In both cases, we leave the inspection, care, and maintenance of the plumbing to the experts. But every building has its necessary lower levels; the bigger the building, the more sub– and sub–sub–basements it requires and gets. Every city has its essential underworld, too . . . of sewers and water lines and gas mains and telephone cables and electrical conduits. New York adds a web-work of subway tunnels. And more. Much more and much worse.

We headed down into the world below Manhattan. Our trail was a tortuous one, and miles long, counting all its ups and downs and twistings. In part we went as Rachel had told me we must go. In part I was led by, oh, a number of my senses, because I could smell, and hear, and . . . feel the correct path.

The grim elegance of the steps below the Needle soon faded, and we found ourselves in a dark, stone-vaulted corridor that seemed to go on and down forever. The path under our feet was stone too, at first. But stone gave way to dirt, and dirt to mud.

The sound of rushing water grew, until at last we found ourselves at the steeply sloping bank of a cold, black stream. Its water smelled fresh, and I knew we were not beside a sewer; an underground river, more likely, one of the dozens that rush beneath Manhattan's streets. It was wide, perhaps twenty feet across, and swiftly flowing.

I was then in halfling form, and because I was the stronger, I stepped into the torrent first, holding to one end of Ernst's climbing rope. The water was fast, and cold. Soon it reached my chest, and I needed all my strength to plow straight across.

When I had reached midstream, two, then three pairs of eyes flashed open on the opposite shore. Four. And then five. They were palely luminous and far bigger than the eyes of rats. The faces behind them were roughly man-shaped, and yet far less than human. They stared, and they waited, because the torrent was very fast, and I believe they felt their bellies had an interest in the outcome of my attempted crossing.

I strode the rest of the way to the far bank and clambered up. As I did, I snarled hungrily at the creatures. You can tell much about an unknown being by causing it to experience fear. I heard squeals of terror; and the tunnel things ran off with swift, heavy paces. They ran on two feet. And their fear scent was not the smell of any beast I recognized.

Ernst stepped into the black torrent. After no more than three or four paces, he lost his footing, slipped, and was carried away in the icy race. I dug my heels into the muddy bank. The swift current rushed him downstream to the end of the rope; it twanged stiff; his wrist still held in the strap. I hauled him to me hand over hand and at last reeled him out of the river, shivering but quite alive.

The instant he was up on the bank, he checked quickly to verify that the oilskin equipment bag was still in place on his back.

He had never lost his grip on the electric torch. He wiped it, shook it a few times, and switched it on. It flickered for a moment, then shone brightly.

Ernst's tight-knit, oiled wool sweater had already shed much of its moisture. His pants were soaked, but his climbing boots were dry enough. I signaled him on. He was chilled to the bone, but that only made a greater inducement to quicken our pace.

The tunnel turned to the left and down after another few dozen yards, and we stepped out onto a narrow concrete ledge. An iron railing ran along its lip, and down below tarnished railway tracks trailed off in either direction.

I estimated that we were now near five hundred feet below the street. These were not the tracks of any train line I'd ever heard of; perhaps a forgotten service spur, or an abandoned storage area, not used for years, from the look of the steel.

I saw movement on the tracks below, some thirty yards off to the left. A figure stepped fully into view.

A human figure, this time—in fact, a man. He wore the clothes of a worker, old clothes; that is, working clothes not quite of our age. His eyes were sad, his expression wistful.

He seemed somehow . . . hungry. He waved to us. Beckoned us to follow him with a wide, slow gesture.

A warmish, dank breeze was puffing down the track from the man's direction. And as it reached us, I smelled . . . nothing. Nothing at all.

He had no scent.

He turned away, waved us on again, and took a few steps, still peering sadly back at us, as if fully expecting us to follow him.

He was looking at us so intently, he did not see the girder he was walking toward. And so he walked right into it. Literally. His body passed through the filthy steel smoothly as if it wasn't there, reappeared behind it, partially hidden from view.

He turned fully and peered around the girder at us. Anxiously, hungrily. Behind him, a black forest of steel loomed. And now, in the endless night between the steel trees, I saw other figures poking their heads: working men like him, and working children, dressed in shabby clothes, their feet wrapped in rags. There were animals among them too: mangy, beaten dogs, a few stray cats.

They all peered out at us as they shuffled forward shyly.

Beside me, Ernst was trembling, his mouth agape, his eyes wide. I grasped his arm and shook him.

And led him away. There were lots of them in that lost tunnel. But their story was for some other night. Some other eyes and ears.

I dragged Ernst along. Down to the right, there was a long bank of doors in the walkway wall. Rachel had told me to take the seventh, but when I tried, it was locked.

Runes had been painted on the door, with a reddish material I knew was not paint. Although the runes were none I understood, it was surely safe to assume they said something in the spirit of "trespassers will be prosecuted" or "beware of dog." But far worse.

The door was made of sheet iron riveted to a wooden frame. I could have punched through, or just ripped it off of its hinges, but we were getting very near. So I resorted to the tool kit instead, and had us through in quiet minutes rather than noisy seconds.

The door had been sealed quite tightly. When I cracked it open, a smell billowed out. It reached our admirers in the tunnel almost at once, and it made them press toward us quickly.

Hungrily.

So we slipped through the door, Ernst and I, sealed it again just as quickly as we could, and prayed the blood runes on its outer face would be harder for them to pass through than mere steel apparently was.

Actually, the runes must have had great power, or the lost tunnel spirits would have slipped through long ago. Because the smell from beyond the door was very strong and very tempting . . . especially tempting if, as fleshless beings so often do, you have a liking for the smell of roasting human meat.

Our trail led downward again. From blackened corridor to dark and stony caverns we raced, quickly now, because I needed nothing but my sense of scent to guide me, a short distance really. And at last we found ourselves in a hallway which, oddly enough, looked quite familiar.

I actually knew where I was. Where in Manhattan, I mean. Our trail had twisted and turned, pitched and rolled. But at present, I would have said we were standing some three hundred feet below street level; specifically, below Broadway and 96th Street. Give or take a few blocks.

Back to the hallway: It had given me a clue, because it was decorated in a style I knew. You know the style too, if you have ever ridden on the Broadway–Seventh Avenue subway line, and observed the stations on the line whose walls are decorated in well-crafted mosaic tiles.

These walls were likewise decorated, with tiles of brilliant reds and blues. The scenes you may have seen depicted closer to ground level are of locomotives, and simply drawn pastoral scenes. These however, were elaborate, finely detailed mosaic depictions of the most horrific nightmares of sleeping demons.

I will not trouble your sleep by describing them here at length. But I will tell you I saw scenes I'd previously only read about . . . and wished I hadn't . . . on the defiled pages of the *Necronomicon*.

The birth of Cthulhu was here portrayed; his murder-rape of Seg, too . . . both events in all their painful, pornographic detail. Yog-Sothoth was prominently featured . . . every hideous step in his treatment of the virgin offerings, from the moment they were cast into his temple until he finally tired of them and answered their pleas for death.

And all, I mean all, Nyarlathotep did to Dyaphna, Beel's sister-mother, after he captured her in . . .

But let's move on to less pleasant matters.

Ernst and I crept to the end of the corridor, where we discovered a door. Behind it, antic music wailed, mad reeds and percussives, wild enough so that none could hear us as we convinced the door to open, and slipped through, and at last found ourselves high upon a balcony, gazing down into a cavernous, torchlit chamber.

Now.

Much of what Ernst and I had seen and done to this point had many of the earmarks of a rollercoaster ride to hell.

So believe me when I tell you, the ride was over. *This* was hell.

Start with the torches.

They blazed and flashed and guttered at each of the chamber's many columns, bound in bands of iron that tipped them out from the column faces, so the hot, rendered oils dripping from them pooled and flamed in the wide pans at their feet. The torches were flaming human bodies, tightly bound in chains, naked from their feet to their breasts, their heads and shoulders wrapped in fiery rags!

And now the altar.

It squatted in the center of the chamber; six feet high and twelve across; round and flat and carved of glistening black obsidian. In the middle of the face, a five-foot-wide bulging dome thrust up like the yolk of a fried egg. The dome was carved in the shape of a rounded swastika, lying flat. Gold rings rimmed the altar's edge; the darkly stained blood gutters that led out from the center of the swastika were gold, too. The blood troughs into which those gutters emptied were also wrought of gold.

And brimming full of red.

Now the corpses. Were there five, or six, or seven, scattered on and about the altar? Hard to say for sure, because they were all in pieces.

Now the assembled orgiasts.

Fifty or more there were: faces I recognized from earlier in the evening at Le Bistro d'Or, and others, too.

Some had stayed human; others had shifted as far into halflings as they could. Some were naked as jaybirds, others wore cowls, or boots or leather harnesses, designed to accentuate rather than hide their nakedness.

A few were completely shrouded in hooded cassocks.

Many of the women were beautiful; many of the men handsome. But they were all repulsive, each and every one. For they writhed and rutted and clipped in rough tempo to the asylum wailing—one hot, joining, rejoining, shifting mass. They glistened in red, drank and splashed and dabbed themselves from the trough, entwined and lashed and bound themselves with the gleaming vitals of their victims!

How fortunate. We had arrived just in time. For now the wailing pipes shrieked their way to a crescendo, the drums tattooed and rumbled till the walls throbbed, the orgiasts wriggled and humped and bucked and squirmed and lashed. In the space of moments, I saw dozens of climactic splashes and pulsing fits. A wall of crazed sound, a cauldron of quivering flesh; and then . . . *stop*!

No noise but the sputtering of the torches, no movement but a few quick scrabbles, as the last of the maniacs hunched down in huddled obeisance, foreheads to floor, knees to chest.

From the darkness behind the altar, two lines of guards marched in; shape-shifter dacoits, twelve of them. They led a file of naked initiates . . . paunchy, shuffling old men and clean-limbed, striding young ones; ancient women with teats flapping against their bellies, and tight-flanked, high-breasted young virgins prancing out to meet their grotesque deflowering. The file began in the shadows behind the altar, snaked around in front of the swastika, circled it, furrowed back into the darkness, and emerged again, still without ending.

Only when the line had ringed the twisted cross three times did it stop, with all the supplicants at last arrayed in place. There were fully two hundred of them.

I saw them all; what's more, I recognized them. There in the horrid glow of the guttering human torches, I beheld Lo Fang's plans for these United States; displayed, revealed, laid bare in all its vile pride.

I've already said that the werecreatures I'd seen in Chen's restaurant were each and all the crème de la crème . . . a solid cross section of American upper-class crud. I've even hinted at the identities of a few, at risk of hearing from their attorneys. It was now clear that every single one of Lo Fang's new-made slaves had brought a friend along to this gathering, several friends, and all from the very best families, the very highest social strata . . . real nosebleed territory.

And now, by way of welcoming inquiries from a whole flock of lawyers, let me say this:

I saw the obese old heiress to an oil and harvester fortune whose hyphenated last names begin with B and H, and the sweet young heiress to a coal fortune, all pink nipples and eagerness, who has a strawberry birthmark at three o'clock on her right buttock. I saw the bull-jawed military man with a Scottish last name whose paternal grandpappy was Robert E. Lee's first chief of staff, and the self-made automotive millionaire as skinny as a pencil, whose self-induced erection had the girth of an exhaust pipe . . .

And so on and so forth.

The point, dear reader, is that if all those assembled supplicants had been diced finely, tossed into an alembic, and boiled briskly enough to distill off every drop of their collective net (perish the word) worth, said net worth would have been a very sizable wedge of the American pie.

Hmm. And what could they possibly all have had in mind, standing there buck naked in the middle of Lo Fang's Friday Night Dance Party? I already knew; you are soon to find out. In fact you are about to see it demonstrated, on and by the two supplicants who stood waiting at the very head of the file, first in line for the altar—two naked women.

Yes, Gina was one of the two.

She struggled in the clutches of a pair of dacoits, but slowly, helplessly, as though she'd been drugged. Her guards mounted the stairs at the back of the altar, hauling her up between them. They tossed her down beside the black domed swastika that lay in the center of the stone face, and she stayed where they'd thrown her.

Quickly, quickly, the guards adjusted golden chains through the rings of the altar's edge. Just as quickly, they lashed Gina in place face up, stretched her out across the bulging swastika, her arms pulled wide, her legs spread open and akimbo at the knees, so her back was arched, her breasts and belly and mound thrust up, her head with her loosened, golden hair hanging down.

Then came Clara Steiner.

She walked up the steps gracefully, almost regally, and the guards at her side seemed afraid to touch her. They escorted her to the spot of honor, left her standing between Gina's thighs.

Clara gazed at Gina dreamily.

From somewhere a lone pipe wailed, and to its sound, Lo Fang himself strode out onto the altar and stood at Gina's head, facing Clara Steiner over Gina's vanquished body. A saffron robe was draped over his shoulders. It hung unfastened, and revealed that beneath, he wore only a green loincloth. He held a thick, oily black whip in his scaly green fist.

Entimemseph lumbered in and stood beside the altar—loomed over it, actually. Rachel stood behind him. The mummy was dressed much as he had been on the night of his awakening, swathed from neck to feet in broad bands of linen. But now the linen was fresh, and rich, and new.

He looked down at Gina; he looked up at Clara. Then he grinned at Lo Fang.

"Good," he rumbled. "All is good. Now is right time. Perfect!"

Lo Fang reached into his saffron robe and withdrew the Key. He held it aloft. Entimemseph stretched his arm out languidly. Lo Fang released his grip, but instead of shattering on the stones, the tablet stood suspended in air. It shimmered, then floated slowly up to a spot between the dwarf and the mummy.

Hellfires flared in the mummy's eyes. Lo Fang's eyes glowed green. Entimemseph grinned wide and puffed out a long, serpentine lick of phantom flame towards the suspended Key.

Lo Fang blew it a kiss.

The tablet itself began to glow, first red, then blue, and then corpse white. Flame without warmth, it bathed the cavernous room with its graveyard luminance.

"It can begin!" Entimemseph groaned.

Lo Fang sneered his agreement. Suddenly, the whip lashed out, cracked viciously against Clara's bottom. Her buttock quivered like a horse's flank, but she did not seem otherwise pained by the blow.

"Now!" Lo Fang snarled. "Prepare the sow at once!"

Drums pounded, the pipes reeled up, and Clara Steiner dropped to her knees, crawled and stretched out over Gina's pinioned body, began kissing and nibbling her with wild abandon. Lo Fang cursed and kicked and batted them both with the whip.

"Hurry! Yes! Yes! Yes! The Staff of Agarthi! Lick it, you creature! Make the sow lick it too!"

And so they did. Quite eagerly, in fact. At least Clara was eager about it. Gina was too drugged to be eager about anything.

Now as to this Staff of Agarthi . . . It is difficult to describe the Staff of Agarthi politely, while still providing any real detail about it. Suffice to say that what I had taken for a loincloth was not one at all, but rather the Staff coiled around

Lo Fang's middle in its quiescent state. It couldn't possibly have stayed quiet for long, considering the attentions Clara, and to a lesser degree, Gina, now gave it.

And it didn't. Soon it was, to paraphrase the old song, taller by half than Lo Fang himself. Of course, Lo Fang wasn't very tall. Still, it was easy to see where all *his* adolescent growth spurts had gone. And yes, the Staff was just as green and scaly as his hands.

"Ahh, good!" he crooned, seemingly more to Clara than Gina. "Now your reward, my darling!"

He scooted around behind Clara where she lay, still spread out over Gina. When he was in position, Clara arched her bottom up for him.

Lo Fang poised himself for a moment and then *plunged*. He thrust his way up into her in one long, vicious jab. What he was doing would have ruined an ordinary woman.

But Clara Steiner, my beloved, my own, the love of my life and the light of my days, was no ordinary woman. Clara pushed herself up and lifted her head back and she *howled* her horrifying delight! In the next instant, so swiftly that I could hardly see it happen, much more swiftly than even I could have managed, Clara Steiner transformed into exactly what she was: an enormous, silver-pelted wolf.

No. Not a wolf. *The* wolf. The giant, fire-eyed, dire wolf who first had slashed and infected me!

Clara Steiner, traitorous, rebellious daughter of Rolf Steiner; Clara Steiner, lover, consort, slave of Lo Fang and all his satanic minions. Oh damn it, I'd known what she was, or at least suspected much of it, almost from the beginning.

But I wasn't just being coy for all these pages . . . at least not as coy as Clara was being with me. I was praying I was wrong. I was praying the woman I loved was not utterly, unredeemably corrupt. Compromised, perhaps. So are we all. Seduced by evil, perhaps. Not totally lost to it. I had hoped it would not be too bad. I had hoped she would prove to be just a simple slave, an ordinary fifth columnist.

Salvageable.

I'd only discovered the whole truth fairly recently. It wasn't until I plundered Glenda's mind that I confirmed what I'd only suspected. Clara was *the* werewolf.

Lo Fang was bellowing.

"Now! Now is the time! The Power is in me . . . the Staff is in you! Slash the sow's throat! Drink deep, my darling. Drink and make her mine! All mine! A child of the night! Hah! She and all she possesses will serve the Dark Master. *Now bite!* First her . . . then all of them. *All!*"

Like hell she would.

I signaled to Ernst. We both brought up our revolvers. We both had perfect shots. And yes, we'd milled the bullets ourselves. Melted quite a few dimes down for them, too. Silver bullets, of course.

I was aiming for her head, Ernst for her heart. We fired in such unison that there was only one blast.

Lo Fang's hands snaked out.

In the next moment, he was holding up both our slugs, between thumb and forefinger of each hand. He grinned up to us on the balcony.

"Close, but no cigar, Mr. Underhill," he chuckled, and rolled his eyes toward the Key. "We're all of us immortal here in the blessed light of Darkness. Hah!"

He made a complex gesture with his hands. Our guns would no longer fire.

He turned back to Clara.

"Now bite the slut," he snarled, and twitched his hips. "Hurry! We have hundreds more beasts to create this night!"

But Clara shook him off and wriggled away. Suddenly, she was a woman again, a beautiful woman, crouching on the altar, looking up at me. There was shock and hurt on her face. And fear.

"You . . . you didn't tell me he knew!" she hissed to Lo Fang. "You didn't say he would be here!"

"I wanted it to be a surprise," he chortled. "Don't worry, Clara, he is one of us. Has been for ages. His destiny. Just a matter of helping him realize it. Right, Mr. Underhill?" He cocked his head at the Key again. "I just thought that seeing you, his dearly beloved, for what you are . . . seeing his other friend here for what she is going to become . . . to say nothing of this whole distinguished herd of werebeasts-to-be . . . pillars of the community . . . society's darlings . . . I thought all this would be very instructive. And I'm right, aren't I, James? The truth is beginning to dawn on you, isn't it? Wave of the future? Hmmm?'' He burst forth in song, and the Key above him, emblem and fountainhead of his power, pulsed along in rhythm. *''Ah-MURR-ica, Ah-MURR-ica, doo dee doo dee doo DEEE!''*

And he waggled that tongue of his, and rolled his eyes. Then he clapped his hands.

''Now then! On with the show. Ready for this, Jimmy boy?''

As an answer, poor though it might be, I flipped my pistol around, held it by its barrel and flung it right at his vile head. I did it with wolf strength, so swiftly that it split the air with a roar as it tore toward him.

And vaporized in a flash, long before it reached his face. Lo Fang just frowned.

''Now you are being annoying,'' he growled. ''Fine. In that case, I will *make* you watch. You will watch me defile your beloved. I'll pork her good. And you will watch *her* defile our newest sow. And *then* . . .'' he was chirping along now, as revoltingly cheerful as a tour guide, ''you will watch the rest too. All these willing converts of mine . . .'' he gestured to the flock of supplicants, werewolves in the making. ''What fun. Right, Entimemseph?''

The mummy was still standing beside the altar, looming over it, rather.

''Just begin,'' he rumbled. ''Quick! Is not much time. We do it now.''

''Yes, yes. Certainly. Good idea.''

He leered at me again, his green eyes flashing. I would have done . . . I don't know; something. But I could not. Suddenly, I was utterly paralyzed. Frozen. Even the slightest attempt at movement caused thrills of excruciating pain to ripple through my body.

"Hurt, does it?" He chuckled. "Good. Now stop annoy-ing me or I'll get sick of you and make you die. Ahem . . . where was I? Ah yes. You, my dearest bitch! Get your haunches back here! I was just warming up!"

And he patted the Staff of Agarthi as close to the far end as he could reach.

Clara looked up at me, and I know she could feel the contempt with which I returned her gaze. I saw love, and then hurt, and finally hate on her face.

She shifted again. Clara Steiner could shift so quickly that she went from one beautiful creature to another, without any of the ungainly homeliness of transition.

A great dire wolf stood on the altar.

"Heel!" Lo Fang snarled lubriciously.

She did as she was told. The noble she-beast slunk toward Lo Fang like a whipped cur. She hunkered down between Gina's splayed thighs, nuzzled Gina's pillowy breast, and raised her own hindquarters for penetration. The Key flut-tered above, the Staff of Agarthi snaked out, poised to drive home.

But it never even reached the driveway.

Because just then two of the orgiasts, two fully cowled and shrouded hierophants at either edge of the flock, stood up, jerked sawed-off shotguns from beneath their cassocks, and tore off two earsplitting blasts. Solid slugs they fired, with clinical accuracy.

The first round caught Entimemseph square in the chest and bowled him over backward. The second hit the Staff of Agarthi, about six inches from Lo Fang's belly . . . and lopped it clean off!

The Key *skree*ed like a startled raptor, then skittered through the air and hid itself behind the altar.

Entimemseph lay on his back snarling and gurgling. He flailed his arms and legs as he tried to right himself. The hole in his chest was as big as a softball, and when he finally managed to flop over I saw that a good third of his back had been torn away. Some of his innards sloughed over the rim of the exit wound. The mummy was not a creature of straw exactly, but most of what was inside him was grayish and dried and twisted.

Long-rotted meat. Reddish brown sludge seeped from the edges of his wounds.

Lo Fang was by far the more interesting case, however.

He just stood there for what seemed an eternity, clutching the severed Staff in both hands, staring at it with his mouth agape.

Then, at last, he gasped in a breath and *shrieked*. An ear-splitting wail. At first I thought the obvious: I thought Lo Fang was wailing for the same reason that I, and you, too, most likely, would wail under similar circumstances. That is, I thought he was wailing in pain and horror, maddened by the hideous, irreparable damage just visited upon him.

But no such luck. Lo Fang's shriek ended in a peal of insane laughter. He held the Staff aloft and shook it victoriously.

"At last!" he snarled to the shorter of the cowled figures. "I finally have you, Bukhovna! I've finally caught you, you dirty old Jew! Get down on your bony knees! *Do it*, kike! Get down and pray. You dare come to steal *my* Key back? Hah! I have you now. I'll drain you . . . squeeze everything you know about it out of you. I'll bleed your filthy mind dry. And then . . . only when you've given me everything I want . . . then maybe I'll let you die. When you beg me for death. Ha! . . . Whoops!"

In reply to the ranting, Avrom Bukhovna had calmly raised the shotgun to his shoulder. Now he fired again. Lo Fang ducked, but the slug managed to graze him, ripped away his left ear, a chunk of his temple, and most of his eye socket.

The bright green eyeball rolled out of the split socket like an egg cracked from its shell, hung by a strand for a moment, and then dropped away.

Lo Fang shook his head, frowned, and dabbed at the monstrous wound as if it were a mosquito bite. Bukhovna broke the shotgun and calmly began reloading.

Entimemseph, meanwhile, had managed to lumber erect. But to no avail. The taller assassin shook back his cowl to reveal his wooly head. Elijah P. Woolcock, I am pleased to report.

He fired from the hip again.

This time the slug caught the mummy in his belly, just off center enough to send him spinning away like a top. His soiled linen wrappings blasted apart and unraveled. He smashed into one of the sputtering human torches, and then his own wrappings flared up in bright red and yellow licks of flame. He growled and batted angrily at the flames, but he was soaked in grease, and the fire refused to die.

Things were not going well for Lo Fang. I wish I could say he looked perturbed. But he just grinned at me.

"See, Underhill? What have I been telling you? I'm on a roll. *Everything* is coming out my way. I wanted you with me . . . and here you are. I wanted this old dog . . . and here he is! Would he have ever come if *I* invited him? No! So I get you to do it for me. Ha! I wanted to be rid of this annoying jigaboo over here, and what do you know, here he . . . *stop with the shooting already!*"

Eli had reloaded faster than Bukhovna, and was aiming at Lo Fang. But the goblin raised a green paw, and suddenly the glowing Key rocketed up from behind the altar. It jerked to a stop twelve feet aloft. A sudden flare of sickly light arched from it. It hit the shotgun muzzle, engulfed it, and sizzled down over the gun and Eli's arm and face and chest.

Elijah P. Woolcock screamed in agony. The shotgun exploded with a roar and flung his shattered body back into the shadows. Bits and pieces of my old friend showered onto the already sullied backs of the cringing satanists, all of them still cowering on the floor, frozen in their fear.

"Damn it!" Lo Fang said. "And I wanted to kill the coot slowly! Entimemseph! Go see if there's any life in him. Maybe we can nurse him back to health," he simpered sarcastically. "Then we can really have some fun with him."

Entimemseph had managed to bat out the fires. He seemed regrettably little the worse for wear, despite all the charring and holes in his carcass. He stepped forward.

"Enough!" Bukhovna bellowed in rage, and stopped him in his tracks.

He raised his hands. For a moment . . . nothing. Then, slowly, a ghostly shape began to form and coalesce: an ancient tablet of clay, a small and fragile-looking thing, really. As he raised it aloft, it began to glow, to pulse. I heard a humming, and a clean, sharp electrical smell crackled in the air.

"You're a fool, Bukhovna," Lo Fang sneered. "Think you'll do anything with your cheap forgery?"

"Forgery? This is no forgery," Bukhovna said grimly. His words were spoken softly. But they filled the entire cavernous space. "*This* is the Key. Do not trouble yourself pondering that truth, Azazriel. Just gaze upon it. And *be gone!*"

The phantom tablet flared brightly in the old man's hand, more brightly than the real tablet hovering above Lo Fang. A hot tongue of golden flame lashed out toward Lo Fang. He raised his reptilian hands to ward it off . . . and the flames roared back toward their sender with doubled strength.

Avrom Bukhovna screamed; his whole body was engulfed in golden fire. He writhed and danced in place, shivering in paroxisms of agony. His tablet faded away.

"No . . . no . . . noooo!" he wailed as he danced.

"See? *See*?!" Lo Fang screamed. "And you thought you were so goddamned strong, didn't you, you old bastard! I have you now! I tricked you! Ha ha ha! *You're mine to have fun with!*"

"Yah! Mine too!" Entimemseph wheezed. He lurched toward the tortured old man.

She came flying across the room at him, as swift as her snarl of fury. Her black hair was streaming; her eyes flashed red; her gaping mouth bristled with fangs; and she wrapped herself about her lover's shoulders with a daughter's unstoppable rage, a vampire's lust for vengeance, a slave's thirst for freedom.

Rachel was all those things: daughter, vampire, slave. And now she was going to be free. Entimemseph bellowed, and his tormented eyes glared with the bottomless disappointment of his ancient love. And then they held nothing at all: Rachel Bukhovna with her murderous claws tore them right out of his head.

He roared and pitched and moaned and punched at her, but she rode him and slashed and screamed and bit.

Her father stretched his arms wide, and all the golden fire Lo Fang had bestowed upon him, all the flames that had seemed to consume him, now danced across his tiny frame like a mantle of ancient might.

He *was* the Key of power; that was exactly what he was. And always had been.

Bukhovna brought his arms stiffly out and forward. The fire danced down and flew at Lo Fang, splashed against him, sizzled out over his evil form.

The tablet of clay dashed to the altar, shattered again in a spray of jagged shards. The Staff of Agarthi shriveled in Lo Fang's hand. His skin peeled away. He was a demon, dancing on a spit in the fires of hell. Right back where he belonged.

"You dirty mother fucker!" he wailed indignantly. "I'll get you for this! You and all the rest of you stinking Christ-killers! Just you wait! I'll be back for you! I swear to Jehovah I will!"

And he disappeared in a thick puff of greasy, sulphurous smoke.

An excessively theatrical exit to my way of thinking, but it got the job done.

At least for him it did. Rachel was still tearing Entimem-seph to bits.

"Rachel! Enough!" her father shouted.

His voice was stern and disapproving. But his arms were open for her.

She looked up from her work, this ravening vampire thing. And suddenly, Rachel Bukhovna was back, Rachel, with her gentle eyes, her fragile mouth, her soft, ebony hair.

She sobbed and raced to her father. Then they were clutching each other and crying together happily. I don't believe it mattered to Bukhovna at that moment that his daughter's tears were red.

Entimemseph leaped blindly to his feet. His whole upper body was in tatters now; the ruins on his shoulder could hardly be called a face. He reached out his arms silently, because he had nothing left with which to make sounds.

The sulphur cloud had nearly dispersed. Then, as if in some weird reversal of time, a solid demonstration of the relativity theory for which Lo Fang had voiced such contempt, the cloud reformed and coalesced.

Lo Fang poked his head through and scowled.

His head now was gigantic, six feet at least from brow to chin, but still grievously wounded. He peered out with one enormous emerald eye.

"Idiot," he said, in a voice as big as the hall. "Don't you know when it's time to quit? Come here."

A gargantuan hand, perfectly in scale with the head, reached out, grabbed Entimemseph like a wriggling fish, and yanked him into the cloud. Almost as an afterthought, Lo Fang cast his baleful orb at the Key on the bloody altar, the shards of his shattered pride. The hand shot out again, scooped up the pieces, and snapped back into the nimbus. The cloud sucked in upon itself again. And then they were gone.

But the fun was just beginning for the rest of his crew—the satanists, that is.

Their master had vanished, and now their fear was unleashed in one mad flash. A hundred voices squealed their terror; their gore-soaked bodies wriggled; they crawled all over one another in their lust for flight. A few of the shape-shifter dacoits crouched among the cowards, snarling, hunched against the tide, looking for someone to kill.

The deafening stitch of a machine-gun blast froze them all in place.

"Stop!" Joe Jefferson bellowed. "Move and you're dead!"

Joe strode out from the temple shadows. A grim array of hard-faced men fanned out around him. Most were Negro; but Ernst's comrades were there, too. A few of the dacoits leaped forward. And then, just as Joe predicted, they were dead.

But that wasn't my business.

My business had been squatting on the altar, watching everything that occurred just as eagerly as I, though praying, I knew, for a somewhat different outcome.

I glanced at Ernst. His face was white as cheese; his hand trembled as he handed me the pistol. I took it quickly, and just as quickly raised it. Clara Steiner looked up at me, a woman.

Suddenly, she was the wolf. And I knew I wasn't going to kill her. Not with a pistol, I wasn't. Too quick.

She knew it, too. In the next instant, she was gone. Oh, not disappeared in a cloud of smoke, but vanished just as completely.

I leaped down from the balcony, hit the floor, and stumbled toward the shadows behind the altar, ripping at my clothes. I nodded at the cowering prisoners as I loped up to Jefferson.

"Think you can take care of this?" I snarled.

"Don't tempt me." He grinned coldly. "We could really, uh, alter the fabric of society here." He hefted his machine gun. "Don't tempt me."

I looked at him.

"Why not?"

Bukhovna shuffled toward us, leaning on his daughter. "We will destroy only those lost beyond all hope. We will save those who can be saved," he intoned. "And we will free all who are untouched by the wolf. Sorry. Perhaps they will be . . . instructed by what they have seen tonight. Probably they won't. But those are the rules."

There was no time; I needed to be gone. But I needed to know the truth about a certain something even more.

"The Key," I said. "You *let* Lo Fang steal the Key from you."

"Guilty," Bukhovna said. "It was touch and go. Very risky. But I had to draw him out . . . make him extend his neck so I could chop it off. Or at least try . . ."

"But there's more. The Key you let him steal was a fake."

"No. The tablet really is a priceless relic . . . and one of very great power. Lo Fang . . . Entimemseph . . . they'd hardly be fooled by anything less. It is a Key . . . simply not *the* Key. The true Key could hardly be a thing of clay. It is of the spirit. Very pure. Fortunately, an evil mind cannot make sense of such a concept."

"You are the Key," I said quietly.

"Get the hell out of here, Underhill. You have an appointment to keep."

Manhattan huddled beneath wintry covers, holding tightly to its last few hours of rest. Dawn was far away, the city streets were cold and bare. I ran as the wolf, and I didn't care what fear or confusion the sight of me might cause. Few people were about then, and, more to the point, I ran with such speed that none who saw me would truly know what he saw.

I might be the last trailing tatters of a troubled dream. Or a shapeless city wraith. Or nothing at all.

At first I had neither sight nor sound of her; I plunged forward driven only by faint wisps of scent, and by the nameless inner knowledge that she was there, up ahead, fading swiftly. But not swiftly enough.

Nothing would stop me. I would have her, and she would die.

I pounded west until I saw the hard, black Hudson, wheeled north, and raced along the river's edge. I was tireless.

It was far north of Harlem, as I loped along a suspension section of the West Side Highway, that I first heard her. The drumming of her paws on the steel and concrete ahead vibrated back, and with it, the fiery roar of her breath. Then her thoughts came hurtling to me, thoughts of hate and rage.

"Stop! Stop stop stop you stinking bastard! You've done enough already . . . torn apart all we've built . . . spit my love back in my face! I hate you! Get away! Come for me and I'll kill you! I'll . . . I'll . . . !"

I wouldn't give her the satisfaction of words, but she did deserve a reply, a small taste of what was in store for her. And so I sent her a bolt . . . a thought-flash of pain and rending and final obliteration.

I heard her yelp in terror, and I knew I'd grown strong enough to destroy her then and there, strong enough to hold her with my mind from the long and sightless distance, strong enough to twist the murdering bitch until she died.

She knew it too, and her mind struggled, panic-stricken, to break free of mine. I let her go. Because that was not the way for her.

I wanted to see her before she died.

We were in Fort Tryon Park when I first caught sight of her. I had just loped in through the southern gate, and far across the bare midwinter expanse of frozen promenades and flower beds, I saw her galloping for the trees ringing the Cloisters' heights. The moon setting low in the south flashed its silver on her long, beautiful pelt.

She was gone.

But not before I felt her fear. She had seen me, too. She was still strong, far from even a thought of tiring. But she had sensed my power and she knew that a long time and far from now, her strength would leave her first. And so she knew that I was a horrid dream come to take her, a dream from which she could only awake in death.

She galloped on and I followed after.

Over Spuyten Duyvel, up through the wooded western Bronx and on into the dark, deep countryside; I closed the gap between us slowly, relentlessly.

By now I was driving her on the hopeless course she ran, spurring her black, panic-stricken heart with goads of fear. Because I had decided that the place of our final meeting, our first real meeting, the very first time Clara Steiner and I would see each other with all the veils torn away . . . I had decided that the setting for our final meeting was most important.

I wanted everything to be perfect.

A wooded grove north of New York, a stand of white birches high on a cliff, looking down on the wide Hudson.

Far below, mist sprites danced on the cold, blank face of the water. The moon was set, but the starry sky gave some light; and off to the east, the weak glow of a false dawn added more.

A night bird cooed, tricked by the lying light, then ruffled its feathers and was still.

I peered into the grove's ghostly center. I heard the roar of her blood, her tortured breath. I smelled her musk and the heat of her exhaustion. She waited for me as the wolf. Strange, how Clara the wolf smelled nothing at all like Clara Steiner the woman. I caught the flash of glowing eyes in the grove's darkest core.

They flickered, then vanished away.

The birch grove was rimmed with brambles. Even within, it was a forbidding tangle of rock and ice and twisted, barbed branches. But I pushed through as the wolf; slowly only because I wanted to go slowly.

A few dozen yards and I burst into a round, empty space, a knoll carpeted with a thatch of dried grass and the crumpled husks of last year's wildflowers.

She was fully human now, save for her glowing eyes. She was nude of course, but she seemed not to feel the chill in the slightest, a dark wood nymph, perilous and beautiful, death to the lost traveler.

Clara was smiling.

"Just out of curiosity," she said aloud. "When did you first find out about me?"

I shifted too; no reason not to, for the moment. I wanted her to know in any case. We would speak before she died.

"Find out what?" I asked. "That you were a servant of Lo Fang? The very first time we spoke. 'An Agarthi adept,' you called yourself. A 'student of white magic.' I don't know much, Clara, but I know Agarthi has nothing to do with white magic. Agarthi is the spirit of the world's evil; the left-handed way. When I thought about it afterward . . . I was actually angry at you for that. Your arrogance. I was angry that you were so damned sure of yourself, you had no fear of being playful.''

"Perhaps you misunderstood my motives, James,'' she said softly. ''Perhaps I wanted you to know what . . . what I am. Perhaps I wanted you to stop me.''

"Not likely,'' I said bitterly.

"Don't *you* be arrogant,'' she said. ''It may be that you don't know everything.''

"Never claimed to,'' I said. ''In any case, that first evening I knew you were more than you seemed to be . . . or less. But Ernst was the one who gave me the next piece of the picture.''

"Your doorman?'' she asked contemptuously.

"Among other things.'' I shrugged. ''He was also a friend of your father's. On the night you showed up at my place, Ernst told me all he knew about you. Which was why I knew your story about seeing the vision of the evil dead coming to get you was just so much garbage. You were making a play for my sympathy. In fact that story just deepened my suspicions.

"But Ernst . . . he told me about the arguments you and Rolf Steiner had. How set Rolf was against you continuing your . . . studies. Too bad your father didn't realize exactly how far you'd gone . . . until it was too late.''

"He didn't even realize it then,'' she sneered. ''I'm very good at keeping my secrets . . . when I want to. I thought I recognized that doorman of yours, from the Center in Switzerland. I suppose I should have killed him.''

"The way you killed your father?''

"I didn't kill my father. I merely facilitated his departure,'' she said. And she didn't even bat an eye. ''But I do regret not killing Ernst. A job left undone . . .''

"I don't know about that,'' I said. ''Wiping out all of one's problem people . . . it gets to be a full-time chore. Till someone finally decides that you're *their* problem. Then it's your turn to be wiped out. . . .''

"As you have with me?'' she snapped. ''Give it a rest, James. We both kill our enemies, you and I. If there's a difference, it's just that I'm more honest about what I do. I take pleasure in it, and I admit I take pleasure. Which makes my pleasure all the greater . . . And sometimes . . .'' Her wolf eyes flashed defiantly. ''I eat the people I kill. So much less wasteful.

''You have yet to try it, James. Lo Fang is right about you, you know. You think it makes you superior, that you have yet to devour any of the many humans you have killed. To my way of thinking it simply means you have yet to carry the essence of who and what you are to its logical conclusion. You have yet to let yourself fully be what you undeniably are. And *that* means you are the worst kind of coward. Truly contemptible.''

''I'm sure you are absolutely right, Clara.'' I smiled. ''Only problem is, I like it that way. I've seen the damage people with the courage of their convictions can do. All those heroes . . . piling up the corpses. They can go to hell, Clara. So can you and yours.''

''Me and mine? I don't have anybody, James.''

''What about Lo Fang? Or all your friends in the reich?''

''Useful tools. Nothing more. I'm afraid I have become . . . unique. There is no one even remotely close to me. Except you, James. You and I . . . you *do* know there is no one else like us in the whole world, don't you? We're absolutely the only ones. Adam and Eve.''

She giggled. She actually giggled.

''Which reminds me. That night in my bedroom. What would you have done if I'd obeyed you . . . gone into the bathroom to kill you?''

''You mean, when you found the bathroom empty? Why, I would have revealed myself to you. Shown you who I really am. Hasn't it dawned on you yet, James? I left Clara Steiner behind quite some time ago. I *am* the wolf. And if you had gone in to kill Clara . . . the merely human self I killed long ago . . . you would have proven your readiness.''

''For what?''

''For me, of course. For what *we* truly are.''

''You do me too much honor, Clara. I could never be like you.''

"You'll never know until you try," she sneered. "But then again, you're probably right. So this whole conversation is pointless. I'll be going now . . ."

She turned away, started walking off toward the edge of the encircling woods. I let her go for a few paces, just staring after her, because she was so beautiful, so damned beautiful. But then I rushed up to her and grabbed her and spun her around and squeezed her arms in my paws. Hard.

"No, Clara," I thought, because the time for words was past. *"You're going nowhere. You're going to die now."*

She looked up at me without fear. There was sadness, and self-loathing, and emptiness. But no fear.

"Then do it, James," she said. *"Do it. Only . . . love me first. Please . . ."*

"No!" I snarled.

But her body was pressed against mine. And when she reached up and pulled my head down and crushed her lips over my mouth, I let her. More than let her.

"Clara Clara I love you . . ."

"I love you too James . . ."

And there in the middle of the frozen winter grove, at the very end of the darkness, I made love with Clara.

It was even better than the first time, the love we made then, which is saying quite a lot, since our first night together had been so much better than anything I had ever felt in my life. This was better still, because our lovemaking was, of course, thoroughly seasoned with the sweet pain of finality, the sorrow of knowing that when we were through, we would be leaving each other forever and ever and ever, parted by the grave. Her grave.

We made love as humans, there on the dead, frozen grass. And as halflings. And then I turned into the wolf. But when she tried to join me, I would not let her; I plunged deep into her mind and forced her to become a woman again.

"The taste I've never tasted," I told her. *"There is a first time for everything."*

And I dipped my fangs toward her waiting throat.

In the last second, the very last instant, I saw her eyes.

And her lips. They were laughing. Laughing at me. Laughing and waiting for my death bite.

The bite I would never take.

Did I ever say I wasn't a fool? I was. I am. I loved her too much. Clara Steiner was rotten to the core. In a field thick with contenders, she was deserving of death with a richness few could hope to equal. But her life was not mine to take. And that's just the way it was.

I drew my muzzle back from her throat and looked into her eyes again.

And then I saw contempt. And disappointment.

"You are a fool, James," she sneered. And she put her hands on my chest, and *threw* me off of her. I flew through the air, landed on my side ten feet away.

She was up and standing over me.

"Your second test and you've failed again. What a pity," she said. "You know, from the moment I saw you . . . when I did Lo Fang's bidding that night . . . I loved you, James. I knew you were meant to be mine. I never told Lo Fang of course, and he only vaguely suspected. But I recognized you for what you were. What you could become. You were beautiful. You *are* beautiful. Not enough though. Not enough for me. Not yet. And maybe never."

Her eyes flared, brighter than I had ever seen them before. "Look at me, James. Really *look* at me! Don't you see what I am? Don't you *see*? I have a heart like a diamond, James. That cold and hard and bright. You don't have it yet. And maybe you never will. No matter. Perhaps our child will."

"Our . . ."

She smiled.

"When?"

"Just now, actually."

I would make myself the wolf. I would spring up and tear her to bits.

"Like hell you will. Little man." Clara laughed.

Suddenly, Clara Steiner unfolded all the power she had so far kept hidden from me. Displayed it, fanned it out before me with the pride of a peacock. All the hideous strength, all the power to do evil in this world, all the power she would join with other, even greater, even more evil powers in the dark, dark years ahead.

I couldn't shift.

I couldn't do a thing.

"Good-bye, darling," she said. "You have greatly disappointed me, and I am leaving you now. Too bad. What a time you could have had with me. Love behind a mask is delightful. Deceit gives it such a bittersweet flavor. But love is so much better when the masks are torn away. It really is too bad. You still love me and now you have lost me. Lost us. Forever."

Clara Steiner snorted, and turned her back. She scuffed her feet at me, twitched her beautiful bottom in a final wag of contempt, and walked out of the grove.

Into the darkness.

Her last words . . . she was wrong. It wasn't really too bad. I didn't think so then; I don't think so now. I was glad I hadn't joined her, and I was glad I hadn't been able to kill her, not in my bedroom that night, not there in the birch grove of my dreams. Who in hell wants a diamond for a heart? There's hardness enough in this dirty, stinking world. A wolf is no better than a man, but he can feel the dirt and smell the stink in somewhat finer detail.

For all the goddamned good it does him.

But lest you think my feelings and thoughts at that moment were purer, stronger, more noble than they really were, let me hasten to tell you what I did when Clara Steiner strode out of my life and left me to face the first faint, heartbreaking trails of the rosy-fingered dawn alone.

All alone.

I shifted fully into the wolf—easy enough, now that she was gone. There was no moon left at which to howl, so I raised my head and I howled at the growing light. I howled long and loud, and every bit of the emptiness and loss my heart held was right there, echoing in my howl.

And my eyes were flashing and my fangs were out.

And the tears streaming down my silver fur shone like gold.

ABOUT THE AUTHOR

RICHARD JACCOMA was born in 1943, and raised in New York City. He currently lives with his wife and youngest daughter in Bucks County, Pennsylvania. Mr. Jaccoma is also the author of *"Yellow Peril" The Adventures of Sir John Weymouth-Smythe*.